New York Fried

a novel by
Robert J. Morrow

Robert J. Morrow

Other books by Robert J. Morrow:

Investing in Student Housing*
(Copyright 2016, Sunao International)
Sold Strategies *(US & Canada Edition)*
The Cheapest, Safest, and Smartest Ways to Sell Your Home!*
(Copyright 2016, Sunao International)
Buck Tradition
The Smartest Way to SELL YOUR HOME in Canada*
(Copyright 2014, Sunao International)
The Barre Chord Approach
Learn to Play Guitar in 30 Days!*
(Copyright 1993, Vandine Group)
25 Years of Magic
Corporate biography of Matsushita Electric of Canada Ltd (1967-1992)
(Copyright 1992, Panasonic Canada)

*available at www.amazon.ca and www.amazon.com
in paperback and Kindle version,
or at: www.robertjmorrow.com

This is a work of fiction. The events described are imaginary; the settings are based on real and imaginary places. The characters are fictitious and not intended to represent specific living persons.

ISBN-13:978-1540363237   ISBN-10:1540363236

Morrow, R.J. 1957-
First Edition January 2017 (trade paperback and e-book)

sunao

*To all my family and friends who have listened to me talk
about this for years and years. It's finally here.
The next one won't take as long…honest!*

Robert J. Morrow

Prologue

The scariest place in the world is also the quietest.

At least that's what Lieutenant Jeon Byung-Soon thought. He had been wandering through the slowly lightening dawn for about twenty minutes, the rest of his small platoon following behind. Every few feet, one of his men would pull at the wire fencing and another would prod the barbed wire above with the tip of his M4 assault rifle.

Beyond the fence was the most beautiful scenery the twenty-one-year-old Lieutenant had witnessed. He stopped and watched as a slow, creamy white fog drifted across the lowlands, filtering the sun's emerging morning light as it traced across tall grass and low shrubbery, its lazy entrails whispering around small trees and other outcroppings. Few if any humans had walked this land for over sixty years, leaving it to nature, which included rare and endangered tigers, amur leopards and Asiatic black bears. Lieutenant Jeon liked to stare out into the wilderness at times like this, just as night became day. He would let his eyes rest, eventually letting them defocus. It was a trick his father had taught him as a small child chasing crickets in the back yard of his home. Soon his eyes rested, focusing on nothing in particular but rather taking in the entire panoramic view as a whole. It was then that he could discern small movements in his peripheral vision, like a rare red-crowned crane stepping tentatively between the grasses, or a goat grazing lazily on the edge of a hill. And, of course, any stray humans attempting to cross the deserted landscape, seeking refuge on his side of reality.

A Seoul native, Lieutenant Jeon was patrol leader for a Republic of Korea platoon delegated with ensuring the Demilitarized Zone was secure and without breaches. Twice a day, Lieutenant Jeon and his camouflaged group of South Korean soldiers would trek alongside the eight-foot high fencing that marked the edge of the DMZ on the South Korean side. Two and a half miles distant was similar fencing creating the official edge of the Democratic People's Republic of Korea, better known as North Korea. Running the width in the centre of the DMZ was the Military Demarcation Line (MDL), which was the actual political border running along the thirty-eighth parallel. According to the armistice established in 1953, troops from both sides were to retreat twenty-two hundred yards from the front line, thus creating this no-man's land in between.

There were a couple of villages within the border of the DMZ but not many people lived in either and those who did kept to the village proper for fear of being mistaken for the enemy by either side. Panmunjom, near the western coast, was home to the Joint Security Area (JSA) and was really the only place where humans actually congregated; mostly soldiers from both sides who spent hours staring at one another across a five-inch-   wide concrete slab, which represented the border. Of late, there had been an abundance of tourists, which to Lieutenant Jeon's dismay, seemed to lessen the importance of what was actually happening here. Over a million soldiers were posted on either side, making the DMZ one of the world's most heavily fortified frontiers. All it would take is for one brazen tourist to skip over the concrete slab and it wouldn't be absurd to have that become the catalyst for starting World War III.

All Lieutenant Jeon wanted was to finish out the week and take leave to see his girlfriend less than 65 miles away in the South Korean capital and get away from the maddening solitude. He was an avid soccer player and the cacophony of shouting voices, thudding feet, and spirited after-game celebrations were like a magnet for his senses which had been numbed by the constant silence.

"Sir, we are ready to move on, Sir," Sergeant Park said, his Korean clipped and insistent. Lieutenant Jeon's mind quickly returned to the task at hand.

He brought his eyes back into focus, grasped his rifle tighter and, pointing the muzzle toward the ground, nodded his head for his men to move out.

Twenty minutes later, the terrain became steeper and Jeon knew they were approaching the last of three observation towers on their route.

"Sergeant, take Corporal Sung and go ahead to the tower," Jeon said, nodding toward the turn in the trail that he knew would lead them up the twenty steps built into the hill, ending at the tower that marked the turning point in their patrol. The Sergeant nodded and, together with the Corporal, disappeared around the corner.

Moments later, Lieutenant Jeon and the remainder of the platoon rounded the corner and saw the tower just ahead. Situated on a rise at the edge of a sloping cliff, it overlooked a lush green valley, dotted with small, ponds and mini-lakes. They purposefully climbed the steps and were almost at the observation level when Sergeant Park gestured at him animatedly, his arms swinging quickly, his eyes questioning.

"Lieutenant, Bob is not there," he said, his arms gesturing across the valley.

"What do you mean Sergeant?" Jeon said.

"I mean Bob has not emerged from the tower since we arrived Sir," Park replied. "And I see no others from the platoon in the immediate vicinity either."

"Let me see," Jeon said, impatiently jumping up the final steps and grabbing the younger man's binoculars.

He focused the lenses and gazed at the tower located approximately 1800 yards away, a little lower down the valley aside a clearing. He waited. And waited.

"You see, Sir?" Park said, his voice shrill.

"Perhaps he is taking a leak Sergeant," Jeon said, smiling. The platoon saw the same North Korean soldier every day, his binoculars raised in a similar fashion, aimed directly at them. Since they didn't know his name, they called him Bob.

"The others are not there either, Sir," Park continued.

Jeon surveyed the opposing tower, moving his focus up and down the tower's steps, then side to side, taking in the landscape to each side of the tower. There was no movement whatsoever. He thought for a moment.

"Sergeant Park, take three men and follow the trail to the rise," Jeon pointed in the direction of a hill that was the highest in the vicinity. The patrol didn't normally go that far as that part of the trail was designated to another patrol, but it was the highest peak for several miles. "Take your binoculars and see if you can locate the platoon."

Park nodded and turned, then quickly turned back, remembering to salute. Then motioning three others, he bounded down the steps and raced along the fence toward the hill.

Lieutenant Jeon continued to scan the lush area surrounding the tower, resting on the small pond to its left, and the clearing where the North Korean troops usually sat smoking cigarettes and cleaning their rifles. Bob was usually the only one at the tower and he never left unless relieved. It had been his habit for the months of observation Jeon and his platoon had been witness to. Jeon didn't really think Bob had disappeared behind a tree to take a leak; he had never done that before. If a North Korean soldier abandoned his post during a patrol, Jeon knew the others in his platoon would report his actions and the man would be immediately disciplined.

So where the hell was he?

"Sir!" Park jumped up the steps to the tower, his breathing fast and heavy. "I scoured the entire area, Sir. There is no sign of any platoon. Not only that but we didn't see smoke from the Dyang frontier either."

Jeon stared at him. The Dyang frontier was a nickname the troops had given to a camp post just beyond the fencing on the Northern side. It was known to be a place where several platoons met daily and, over raging barrel fires, smoked, talked and generally wasted time before heading back to or from their barren barracks deeper in territory. There was always a fire going, day and night, and as a result there was always a trail of smoke in the sky directly above its location.

"You are sure Sergeant Park?" the Lieutenant asked, knowing full well the Sergeant would not be mistaken.

"Yes Sir!" he confirmed. The other men were all looking at one another, blank expressions on their faces. Obviously they had no idea what to make of the mystery.

Neither did Lieutenant Jeon. In his two years patrolling the DMZ, this had never occurred before. He pulled at his lapel, searching for the communications switch that would connect him to his commanding officer in Panmunjeom.

Before he spoke into his tiny microphone, he stared one last time out into the wilderness, the green grasses glistening as the fog dissipated and the dawning sunlight filled in shadows throughout the lonesome scene. Silence pervaded, with only a light wind causing the low tree limbs to bristle.

Where the hell were all the Koreans?

Robert J. Morrow

Chapter One

The quiet was absolute. Outside the circle of light caused by the three-foot flames of the campfire, there was nothing but darkness. The high-canopied trees acted like insulation against the outside world and all they could see and hear were the orange and yellow flames and the crackling of the dried pine logs.

"If I threw a grenade in the middle of the fire, what would you do... dive for cover, or jump on top of the grenade?"

Frank Daro and Arthur Hart had been camping with their kids in upstate New York for nearly ten years. Pretty soon, the kids would be teens and have no desire to camp with them anymore. Then they'd need a fresh excuse to do what they were doing now: sitting around a roaring fire drinking beer, smoking expensive Cuban cigars, and discussing idiotic scenarios.

"I'm serious," Frank continued. "Would you jump on the fire, killing yourself but saving the kids, or would you save yourself and yell for the kids to do the same?"

"I'd kill you," Hart said.

"But I have the grenade."

"No, you just threw it in the fire."

Frank laughed. "You saying you wouldn't act on instinct? You've thought it through, right, I mean, something like this?"

"Frank, I've been your friend for what, a decade?" Hart said. He took a long swig of semi-cold beer and stared into the flames. "Of course I've thought about situations like that."

Frank's smile faded. "Ah, come on. Nothing's ever happened."

Hart's twelve-year-old son, Jamie, came out of the tent and ambled over to the fire. He grabbed a long stick he had previously carved into a point, slumped into one of the cheap beach chairs we'd lugged around for years and looked around for the marshmallows.

Frank tossed him one from the bag in his lap. It flew across the fire and landed in Jamie's lap. Hart glanced at Frank. He grinned.

"You moron," Hart said.

Jamie snickered and stuck the marshmallow on the end of his stick.

An hour later, the three kids were in the tents playing a game of Pictionary, an old standby that always occupied them well once they realized there was no TV, no computer, no video games, and definitely no smartphones. Both fathers agreed there would be no electronic gadgets after 11pm. If they had their way, they wouldn't bring them at all. But then, neither Frank or Hart could live more than an hour without their Androids, and hypocrites they weren't.

Frank could keep a fire going for hours, not huge but steady; the kind of fire you could roast weenies and marshmallows on, and then when it got a bit chilly, could be turned into a raging inferno with the twist of a stick. That was Frank's job, keeping the flame going while they finished off the twelve-pack.

Hart's job was setting up camp, unpacking groceries, cooking, washing up, and putting kids to bed. For almost a decade nothing much had changed and--despite Hart's ex-wife insisting that it was a ridiculous relationship (there was irony in that somewhere)-- neither Frank nor he felt it should. Recently, the kids had taken over some of the chores but then he felt useless and usually told them to go take a hike...literally. Frank would just laugh and pass him another beer.

They weren't really drunk all the time; that wouldn't be good parenting. But from Friday night to Sunday night they were never completely sober. A dull, summertime haze is what they called it. The kids didn't mind, or at least wouldn't mention it until they were in their thirties and in therapy. And they hadn't started drinking themselves yet so they weren't feeling appropriately guilty, again, according to Hart's ex. He figured within a decade, they'd be bringing a twenty-four pack to accommodate the whole crew.

"You talk to General Wade lately?" Frank asked.

"Not since your last get together," Hart answered.

"He wants to hold a gathering," Frank said. "I suggested your place."

"Of course you did," Hart said.

"You'll find this one particularly interesting," Frank continued. "And personally gratifying."

Hart tried to make out Frank's eyes across the fire but the flames were too intense. His face was a mask of smoke and flickering light.

"Don't bullshit me," Hart said. "You're spying on someone, and just need a place to do it."

"You're spoiling the surprise," Frank muttered.

Hart groaned. After a few moments of silence he said, "I'll set it up with Al. He'll know what to do."

"Yeah, Al's good.

They were silent for a while, both thinking about kids, parenting, and gatherings organized by high-ranking military acquaintances.

"Hey Frank?" Hart said. The other man looked up at him finally. He noticed Frank's eyes were a little glazed. "When they come for you, you'll let me know, right?"

Frank guffawed. Hart knew he hadn't taken him seriously.

"Oh, and by-the-way," he continued. "If anyone ever does throw a grenade into our campsite, I'll expect *you* to dive on it."

Robert J. Morrow

Chapter Two

The restaurant was called *The Artichoke Hart*, not because the specialty is artichokes but because of his name.

Since Art Hart was difficult to trill off the tongue he had grown up with monikers including *part fart* and, of course, *Art the Fart*. But sometime in his early teens a school friend had discovered the prickly fruit--her parents ran a grocery store--and he became *Artichoke*. Since he couldn't find anything disparaging other than the vegetable being mysterious and a little hard to swallow--which he thought was kinda cool anyway--it stuck.

Some twenty years later, his name was now associated, in subdued neon, with a barely viable, upscale casual dining establishment that arguably offered some of the best jazz in the Baltimore, Maryland area. He felt time had rounded him, physically and mentally, but knew he'd become even more prickly. Staying in shape was getting harder as he aged but he still exercised most days and kept his mass under two hundred pounds. He grinned recalling that some patrons told him he looked like Chef Gordon Ramsey without the hair. But since running a restaurant was not something he had ever aspired to do for a living, he was forced to hire Al Rocca.

Al was a former colleague of Frank's, but unlike the roguish, tough-guy persona Frank exemplified, Al was short, round and cuddly, in a brown bear kind of way. He would make some career-obsessed woman a tremendous wife someday, Hart thought. He was also the best chef Hart had ever met, despite having absolutely zero formal training. He was organized as hell too, which was good, because although Hart dabbled in cooking, he couldn't balance books if his life depended on it. Lately, that had become evident every two weeks when he sat down in his office and emptied his bank account via payroll checks and supplier invoice payments.

Things weren't all bad though. There was always the assurance that should someone have too much to drink, Al can easily double as the bouncer. Because Al used to be employed by the CIA.

"Frank called Friday," Al said, without looking at Hart as he strode into the restaurant early Monday morning. "Wants to do another one of his gatherings."

"He only told me yesterday," Hart said. "At the campfire."

Al smiled. He was wrapping cutlery in cloth napkins at the bar. He still didn't look up.

"He wishes to spare no expense," Al said.

"That's because the taxpayers will be footing the bill," Hart said, joining him at a barstool opposite. Hart knew Frank had already discussed his speakeasy with Al before laying it on him at the campsite. Telling him was a courtesy since Al did all the organizing and prepping. And besides, Frank knew Hart needed the income so why would he say no?

He grabbed a few recently washed cloth napkins and began folding them into triangles. "He's also expecting special guests, no doubt."

"No doubt," Al said. He finally looked up. "He wants us to record it."

"Of course he does."

"He didn't tell you anything?" Al asked.

"You know we never talk shop on campouts," Hart answered. Actually, Frank and Hart rarely talk shop at all. The less Hart knew about his best friend's life as Deputy Director of the CIA, the better.

"I've got a menu figured," Al said. "You want to have a look?"

Hart cocked his head sideways and smiled.

"Okay, just checking," he said, pulling away from the bar, leaving Hart to finish wrapping the cutlery. A moment later, he called from the kitchen.

"If you see Lazare, hold me back."

"Only if it gets me out of dishes detail," Hart yelled back. Al didn't answer but Hart heard pots clanking loudly as they were being racked. Daniel Richard Lazare was the current CIA Director -- Frank's boss. According to Al, Lazare stood for everything he eventually had come to hate about the Company.

Al Rocca looked like an Italian bricklayer, complete with the receding hairline and bulky forearms. He would be the owner of the *Hart* if he had the money and jokes that he would have called it *The Rock*, but since his ex got most of his money, it hadn't been an option. Hart had already solved his alimony problem by giving his ex the matrimonial home--Hart lived in a tiny apartment above the restaurant and strongly felt the kids shouldn't have to move-- so most of his savings had gone into the first and last month's rent and a lot of leasehold improvements for the restaurant.

Al likes to cook…a lot. And he had read a couple of books on running a restaurant which made him more informed than Hart, so Hart made him Manager. He paid him enough to be a partner, though they'd never considered formalizing the arrangement. Al wasn't worried. Neither was Hart. They probably should be, Hart thought, since they never seemed to make a profit at the end of the month. But Al created some amazing dishes and Hart hired some awesome bands. It was fun and the customers loved it. So far, their heads were above water. They were dog paddling but had yet to drown.

During the week Al and the staff handled supper easily most of the time which is why Hart played sommelier at his favorite spot at the bar whiling away the weekday evenings listening to CDs of new bands he was considering booking for the weekends. Occasionally, he'd get up and make the rounds, conversing genially at patron's tables. On Monday evenings, once a month, the doors closed at 3pm and he cooked for the staff and their spouses. It was costly, stressful for him, and they lost the evening dinner income, but it was his way of saying thanks for their running a four-star restaurant with very little help from the owner.

Prior to the *Artichoke Hart*, Al and Hart both had challenging careers and after a while they had both lost their jovial attitudes, their zest for life... and their wives. The *Hart* was therapy for both of them. For Hart, it was a chance to forget he was part of the reason Al had lost his spook job. For Al, it was forgetting how bad he knew the world really was.

Ten years after leaving their paying jobs and starting the restaurant, they'd got their lives back. Except for the jobs...oh, and the wives. In Al's case, he was still trying. In Hart's, he felt like she had never really left. Spending time with his two children meant he had to stay in touch with her. He couldn't wait till they turned sixteen.

A moment later, Al came out to the bar again. "So who's the party for?" he asked.

"I'm sure General Wade has a new pet project," Hart said.

"Oh? Anything earth shattering?"

"He's Military Intelligence's liaison to the CIA," Hart said flatly. "Everything he does is earth shattering."

"So we can anticipate some of the postulators?" Al said

"If I know Frank, he's going to take advantage of the occasion and do a little schmoozing."

"I'd better get out the boxed wine, eh?"

Hart laughed. Frank arranged for important intelligence community functions to be held at the *Artichoke Hart* as often as he could, and he always wanted the booze to flow. Once any official festivities were done with and the reporters had left, everyone took advantage of the rare chance for field agents, analysts, politicians and influential business magnates to mingle. They drank, smoked cigars, and talked about things they really shouldn't be talking about in public. Occasionally Frank would invite people he was investigating or researching. Thus the reason he often had them record the events.

"I'll help at the bar on this one," Hart said. Al's eyes narrowed. Hart grinned. "Don't worry, the tapes will be running, as they say. But you know what else they say: people tell bartenders things they wouldn't tell their therapists. Listening to drunken spooks is a great way to find out what's going on in the world."

Al returned to the kitchen.

Robert J. Morrow

Chapter Three

Although the *Artichoke Hart* prided itself on being upscale casual, this was Baltimore, not DC; people tended to be a touch more relaxed. At Company events, however, everyone was in their finery, and, depending upon their age, typically emulated Don Johnson's *Sonny Crocket* or his more recent television persona, *Hap Briggs*.

"Nice turnout," Hart said to Frank. He was dressed in a dark blue Armani pin stripe that Hart hadn't seen him in since the last event.

"Hmmm". They didn't make eye contact. Frank was distracted, or focused, depending upon your understanding of Frank's moods.

"Wine okay?"

He leered at Hart. "Just make sure there's one of the good bottles under the counter where I can reach it."

Hart smiled.

"Frank, I need you to introduce me to someone." Director Lazare had snuck up behind them, grasped Frank's elbow, and nudged him toward the center of the room where several strangers were gathered, talking animatedly. Lazare looked like an accountant, with receding hair, a paunch, and short, thick legs. He'd never been in the field and had ridden desk jobs in the quagmire of Washington legaldom before being appointed as top spook. He gave Hart a curt nod while leading Frank away. Lazare and Hart had a terse relationship, mostly because he didn't like that the *Hart* wasn't a CIA-owned facility.

Al came through the kitchen doors carrying fresh appetizers. When he saw Lazare standing with Frank and Hart, he quickly turned about and returned to the haven of the kitchen. The appetizers went back too.

Hart smiled again. Frank's events were so much fun.

Lazare had lead Frank into the center of one gathering and was introducing him to the very attractive Latina woman General Wade had introduced during his initial informal speech at the beginning of the gathering. Hart guessed her to be in her late twenties. About five feet, seven inches, she had classic long black hair, a noticeably narrow waist and long legs, hidden well at the moment in a very stylish business pantsuit but accented stylishly with four inch black heels. Her hair was tied back in a ponytail and for a moment Hart thought of other exotic young women he'd met over the years. If he hadn't heard General Wade call her one of America's brilliant young IT experts, he would have thought she was some Senator's aide.

Frank glanced at Hart who motioned with his head toward the table in the far corner, near the glass block wall that allowed a great deal of light into the room from DeQuincy Street. There were hidden microphones set in the centerpieces at every table but Hart could only engage one at a time. The recorders and ten monitors were in my office in the basement.

Frank could review the whole event from several angles afterwards, or he could sneak down to the office part way through and listen in on conversations he thought were important enough for eavesdropping.

Frank had paid for the entire system, including a security set-up that rivaled most banks. Bands often left their equipment overnight, so Hart liked the fact that the restaurant couldn't easily be broken into, though knowing Frank, the *Hart* could likely take a nuclear hit and come out of it intact.

"Who's the hottie?" Al said, returning with the appetizers and placing them on the table beside Hart.

"Lena Lopez Castillo," he said. "Wade says she's some kind of IT genius."

Al's one eyebrow rose questioningly. "In that outfit, she could be a Columbian drug runner and Wade would still be working the crowd with her.

"Wade can't be swayed by a good-looking woman," Hart said.

"Sure," said Al. "That's why his wife of thirty years left him and he has thousand-dollar call girls coming to his penthouse every weekend.

Hart laughed. According to the General, Ms. Lopez Castillo is about to unleash the next big thing," he said.

Al's head tilted sideways as he looked at Hart, then over at Ms. Lopez Castillo, then back to Hart. "I'm not even going there," he said.

Hart laughed again. Al could be the life of the party. Too bad he couldn't be let loose on the crowd.

"So why do Latinas always have two or three last names, anyway?" he asked.

"Maybe she kept her ex-husband's name and added it to hers," Hart offered.

"She's divorced?" Al said, his eyes roaming her body up and down.

"Doesn't look old enough to have passed puberty to me," Hart said.

"Geez, you're getting old. Or blind," Al said.

"I think she's with the greaseball," Hart said, nodding his head toward the skinny man standing just behind Ms. Lopez Castillo. He looked to be a similar age as her but with his shiny greased hair pulled back in a ponytail he looked a little like Leonardo DiCaprio in that Four Musketeers remake. The ponytail looked odd when he and Ms. Lopez Castillo were close together, making him seem a little effeminate somehow since they both adorned ponies and both wore pants. Hart did register, however, how easy it was to tell the male from the female, thanks to the young Ms. Lopez Castillo's curves.

"Jay Losano," Hart said. "Her security chief and partner."

"Mafia?" Al asked.

"He grew up in Vegas, has Italian ancestors, and likes poker," Hart said. "Of course he's mafia."

"Seems he's got Lazare eating out of his armpits," Al said. "Wonder if the old codger knows he's gay."

"Who's gay?"

"Your mafia dude," Al said. "Look at the way he stands."

Hart looked over and thought perhaps Losano's way of leaning on one foot, arm on opposite hip, and chin raised did look a little less than manly but even DiCaprio had questionable posing moments.

"What an idiot," Al said, shaking his head as he sidled back to the kitchen to retrieve more food. Hart wasn't sure if he meant Losano, Lazare, or both.

Hart watched Losano scribble something on the back of a calling card and hand it to Frank. He held the pen with the two middle fingers of his right hand and handed the card over with a little flip of his wrist. Hart still wasn't sure. He courted the prerequisite permanent five o'clock shadow, and he dressed very well, tailor made right down to the tapered white gino shirt with subdued frilly designs embossed on the chest. Okay, on second thought, maybe he was gay.

Frank looked down at the card, grinned, and lifted his gaze up to Hart. He gestured toward the kitchen door. Hart nodded and headed for the stairs that lead to his downstairs office.

Chapter Four

The basement ran the full length of the restaurant and boasted nine foot ceilings. Most of it was wide open and empty with floor to ceiling mirrors on one wall and an array of hand-held weights and other mandatory gym equipment along the opposite wall. Positioned around the open space were floor model punching bags, three treadmills, and in the centre of the room a makeshift, floor level sparring ring with roped sides and matted flooring.

When Frank offered to put in his elite security and monitoring system, he had thrown the training dojang in as a bonus. Hart knew why he'd done that and he didn't object; it saved him buying a membership at one of the mediocre local martial arts clubs. On a fairly regular basis, field agents who weren't really comfortable in the glass-walled corporate environment at Langley would come out and spend a day at the *Hart*. They'd work out, have lunch, chat a bit with Al and Hart, then head back to the compound later in the afternoon. Hart sent the lunch bills to Frank and he promptly had them paid. Hart didn't charge for the gym time; after all, Frank had paid for it.

At the far end of the basement, Frank's construction crew had built a twenty-by-twenty-foot office complete with two-way mirror and built in wall-to-wall desk. They had incorporated shelves to house monitors and recording devices in such a way that only the front facades of each unit popped through faux walls into the office interior, just above the desk. It made for a clean, very modern, very Matrix-ish security room.

Hart loved it.

On a busy Saturday night, he could sit down here and aim cameras at any table to see which menu items were being enjoyed, which were being nibbled at, and, occasionally, eavesdrop on interesting conversations.

None of the staff had any idea they were able to do that since Al kept the office locked at all times.

The stories Hart could tell about politicians and their plans for dealing with competitors, peers, and sexy staffers. They all came to Baltimore thinking they were escaping prying eyes in Washington, only to end up in one of the CIA's best equipped offsite meeting places.

Monitors and cameras allowed him to see the dining room from three different angles: the kitchen, the main entrance, the small corner stage, and the outside parking lot. The remote microphones allowed Hart to listen in on any table conversation, chit-chat at the reception desk, and, of course, the band on stage…in full surround.

Hart slipped into the leather chair which faced the main computer screens allowing him to control where the camera/microphone combos focused. Eight smaller screens above the two main ones showed other scenes available elsewhere in the restaurant. He could alternate from one to another with the flip of a switch.

It wasn't too difficult to find Frank as he was the only one staring at the center of a table. Hart pressed the X key on the keyboard that was connected to a small laser light in the centerpiece of the table. It flashed on and off quickly.
Frank nodded. He then placed the card Losano had given to him flat on the table top. He stepped back slightly and gestured with his head again.

Hart zoomed in on the card. The autofocus lagged slightly but when it caught up he was able to read the handwritten words: *We do not wish to be recorded.*

Hart leaned back in his chair. Lucky guess. There's no way Losano or the girl could know there were recording devices in the restaurant. He likely assumed there would be cameras somewhere with so many high-up Company people in attendance. Hart smiled. He couldn't possibly know how sophisticated the system really was.

Hart zoomed out to see Frank looking at the camera again. If he didn't cut that out, everyone would know where at least one of them was. He pressed the X key again. Frank smiled. He then turned and walked back toward the group surrounding Ms. Lena Lopez Castillo.

Hart panned the camera to the centre of the circle, increased the volume of the microphone and pressed record. From this angle, Castillo looked even taller. Her perch atop high heels allowed her to look straight into the eyes of the men conversing with her. She likely did that intentionally but the heels made her legs long which also attracted attention from every male in the room. Again, likely intentional. She was young and, Hart assumed, inexperienced, but she played this room as well as any other young attractive career-minded female would. He watched her talk for a moment, her hand gestures extravagant and obtrusive which took away from her elegance a little. Though clearly beautiful in a classic latin sense, her facial expression was strained, her eyes bearing an unmistakable aire of higher intelligence. It seemed to Hart she was being condescending to those around her, though unintentionally. She was a brave girl considering most of the people present were either politicians, journalists, CIA, or senior military. She answered questions politely but rubbed her hands together constantly, her eyelids flickering nervously. Hart didn't think she was used to crowds, but she wasn't intimidated, just overwhelmed.

"We will be up and running by the end of the summer at our test site. And we are inviting international delegates to visit and see what we have accomplished." Castillo said. Her voice was rhythmic and confident enough that other people in other circles were turning their heads to catch what she was saying. She was the main attraction, after all.

"You are inviting other countries to view your research before the Federal Energy Regulatory Commission has even given approval for you to continue," said a booming voice from the centre of the circle. Senator Andre Blais headed the United States

Senate Judiciary Sub-Committee on Anti-trust, Competition Policy and Consumer Rights. He was also known to have ties to various communications lobbyists in Washington.

Castillo nervously eyed the Senator, and reigning in her coquettish attitude slightly, continued. "Naturally your government's interpretation of what we are trying to achieve here is of concern to your group," she said. "I am just the contractor supplying the product to whoever is interested in progress."

Hart grinned. Ms. Lopez-Castillo wasn't as much an amateur as he had first thought.

"So you're confident that with one flip of a switch, the whole country's internet access will divert from cable or phone dial-up to electrical power lines?" Senator Blais said.

"If you have electricity, you will have internet," she stated, as if reading from a brochure. "Cable and phone line technologies will still exist. But they will slowly become redundant as the cost of BPL remains low."

Wade had explained during his introduction of Lopez-Castillo that BPL stood for Broadband over Power Lines, the ability to run data across existing hydro wires as though it were cable connecting one computer to another. He had noted that although not a new technology, all other attempts to utilize power lines had "*fizzled* out, pun intended". But Ms. Castillo had apparently solved the decades-old dilemma.

"Indeed, we have devised a method to armour data as it travels across power lines, protecting it from the incredible heat generated from electrical impulses of such high intensity." He turned to stare at Frank. "And unlike telephone and cable, electricity goes everywhere."

"We have, in effect, harnessed the intense energy passing through power lines and applied it to data transfer," Castillo said, pulling her arm out of Losano's and turning to face the Senator. "There are still some glitches that need to be rectified and that is why we cannot release the technology yet. But we are making great headway."

"So there is still some radio interference?" Senator Blais asked.

Castillo's smile faded and Hart could see the tips of her ears turn a light shade of red. "Signal interference for television and amateur radio has always been the nemesis of the technology," she said. "That's why the telephone or cable companies have never taken advantage of the infrastructure."

"But you've figured it out," the Senator said.

She continued to stare at him for a few moments, then her whole body relaxed as if in resignation. Hart thought she'd been trying to figure out how to diffuse the old statesman and not engaging him was the obvious solution.

"We believe we have, Senator," she said. "And by the end of the summer, I'll be able to prove it. Just as I promised you." She smiled then and most in the circle smiled with her. She had a contagious persona.

Senator Blais turned and left the group, walking out of the frame of the monitor. Hart watched Frank take a step forward to follow him.

"Mr. Daro!" Castillo called. Frank turned back. She moved away from her admirers, took his arm and led him further away. She leaned in close to Frank's ear and began to whisper. None of the microphones were situated close enough to catch what she said. Hart switched to one at a table now closer to them. He didn't hear what Castillo whispered but Frank leaned back and said clear enough for the microphones to pick up, "I thought you had that covered," he said, nodding toward Losano.

Castillo followed Frank's gaze, then sighed. "All is not as it seems Mr. Daro," she said, more clearly now. "I fear Jay's, ah... assets, may not be altruistically loyal, and they're certainly not as influential as yours. I would appreciate it if you contacted me, perhaps tomorrow. We can discuss it then. In the meantime, however, until we have a mutually-agreeable working relationship, I must insist that you do not make record any of our interactions with your government officials." She gestured toward Senator Blais. "I don't want the wrong information to get out while I am trying to negotiate with both the US and foreign countries. I prefer it all to remain low key until we know who will be involved long term."

She then turned curtly and walked back to the circle of admirers. Frank watched her, then shrugged and walked away.

"And you are suggesting," the Senator was spouting, "that we simply tell our major corporations, those who built the communications infrastructure of this country, that they must step aside and allow some young upstart to run things now? Is that what you are suggesting Ms. Lopez-Castillo?"

Hart watched Castillo sigh, her smile still intact. But she began rubbing her hands vigorously as she spoke.

"I had, of course, hoped the existing hierarchy would consider partnering with us, helping us…" she held up her finger in a *just one minute* gesture since it was clear the Senator was about to interrupt, "…helping the country actually. In partnership with our communications giants, we would be able to continue providing citizens with the quality programming and service they are accustomed to. Just via a new and better medium."

"And cheaper too," Losano added from behind. Castillo turned and shot him a stern glance and Losano's eyes twitched. Obviously, he wanted to continue but it seemed they had agreed this was Castillo's portion of the show, not his.

She turned back to Senator Blais, her face softening to look like a very sexy but extremely benevolent young high school teacher. "Our technology will, indeed, reduce the costs of mass communication dramatically."

"As long as we hand over the reins of the entire power grid to you," the Senator said.

Castillo appeared to be thinking for a moment.

"Not the reigns, Senator," she eventually said. "To expound upon your analogy, we merely want to ride in the power cart. The cable, telephone and other internet companies will be riding along with us. But the horses--the US government--will always be in control, the President at the reigns, so to speak."

That was too good, Hart thought. Had she really just made that up? She was either as smart as Frank and Wade thought she was, or a good actress.

Senator Blais continued to ramble on about the absurdity of having a private, maybe even a foreign company controlling such an important aspect of the American economy and infrastructure, but Castillo had taken the wind from his sail. She patiently reminded the Senator, and those around them, that the Japanese had run Hollywood, the Chinese owned most of the Pacific Northwest real estate and Germans owned the pharmaceutical industry, to name a few. The Senator huffed and puffed but it was evident to Hart that Castillo was winding down. Whatever she had hoped to accomplish here had clearly been achieved. Eventually she excused herself and headed to the bar, choosing a glass of red wine and sipping slowly as she took in the room. Losano ambled over and joined her, taking a beer bottle from a tray at the end of the bar.

They spoke in hushed tones, Losano seeming to berate her a little. Hart switched to the monitor that was always trained on the length of the bar but they were speaking too low for him to pick up anything.

"Arrogant little shit, isn't he?" Frank said, coming in through the office door. Hart hadn't seen him leave the upstairs gathering. He assumed he was talking about Losano, though admittedly, it could have been the Senator for that matter.

"Seems quite confident though," Hart replied, to be safe.

"Confident enough to piss off every politician he talks to," Frank said, pulling up a chair beside him and leaning in to look at the center screen where Castillo and Losano were talking in hushed tones while sipping wine. "Originally, Blais was on her side; was the first to hear about her discovery actually. But he wanted corporate America to take over and Castillo clearly had other plans."

"So what's the greaseball's story?" Hart asked.

"Son of some mid-level mobster out of Vegas, like I told you. Jay Losano was born here but his family is from Sicily. Italians don't consider Sicily part of their country so the old man's empire is small and influential, but not considered part of the big picture, so to speak."

"Hard to figure out who's the boss" Hart said, watching them talking at the bar still. "What's the mob's angle?"

"Maybe nothing," Frank said. "At this point, all we know is that Losano's family are ashamed of his... ah, persuasion. So, they sent him to USC where he met Castillo." He pulled up the other leather office chair and dropped into it.

"But someone's financing Castillo and my guess is that it's mobster daddy," he continued. "I can't think of any other reason why she would need the greasy little shit."

They watched Losano move away and begin working the room, speaking with various Senators and aides, lobbyists and their associates, all of whom were asking questions about various aspects of broadcasting internet signals across power lines.

"She doesn't seem too worried about getting senatorial support," Hart said.

"She doesn't really need it," Frank said. "If she gets FCC approval to do a test launch, and has foreign investment guaranteed, she'll be able to write her own ticket, at least initially. She's got the administration's support via General Wade so she doesn't really have to worry about the usual risks of a start-up. President Emerson's pretty much guaranteed her a government contract if she can prove its sustainability. She'll own BPL until a stronger player jumps in and either partners or buys her out. All Senator Blais can do is make things difficult. He can't stop it from happening."

"So why are you here?" Hart asked

"Because I can work outside the box," Frank said, grinning.

Hart knew that grin. Although Frank was second in command at Langley, he had recently been working connections to Homeland Security and, as such, seemed to have more influence than the Director himself in some areas. Communications was one of those areas, and Homeland was very interested in communications.

"You're going to sabotage the project?"

"Of course not," he said, patting my back. "I'm going to see that Ms. Lena Lopez-Castillo gets everything she needs to get this technology of hers to work, and I'm going to help her sell it to the world. Even Senator Blais can't stop it once it becomes an international commodity. "

"Is that why the Company's involved?" Hart asked. "Because of the potential for international rollout?"

"If various countries embrace the technology, we'll be able to tap into those countries' national communications. Think of the intelligence potential!" Franks eyes were wide, his arms gesturing with excitement. He was high on the potential power.

"And the FBI will monitor her actions here?" Hart said, grinning.

"Screw the FBI," Frank spouted. "They're too busy trying to figure out if she's breaking federal laws when she sends signals across state lines; petty stuff..."

Without warning, the lights suddenly went out. Then just as quickly they came back on again.

Hart's initial thought was a power surge but then he quickly recalled that there were no anticipated storms in the area and therefore no reason for a power shortage.

"What the fuck was that?" Frank demanded. He tapped the screens but they were black. Hart looked at the equipment. The power surge had shut them all off: no blue power lights, no orange standby LEDs, even the audio enhancer units were dark. Frank jumped up and ran out the door. Hart could hear him taking the stairs two at a time as he raced upwards.

Hart looked around the office. Lights were back on, ceiling fans were working, but all the recording units, equalizers, amplifiers and monitors were off. The surge had burned them. He took one last look at the dead equipment and followed Frank upstairs.

Robert J. Morrow

Chapter Five

"What the hell happened?" Frank forced out of pursed lips. We were standing just inside the entrance from the kitchen area to the main dining room of the *Artichoke Hart*. No one had been too perturbed about the lights flickering and the discussions had resumed without concern. Even General Wade had slapped Frank on the back thanking him for getting all the *right* people there.

"How can we have had a power shortage, it's not even raining," he continued.

"Frank, if I understood things like electrical currents, I wouldn't be running a restaurant," Hart said.

Frank's eyes narrowed. "What did you say?"

Hart frowned. He knew what he'd said. Hart waited for further insight. Frank appeared to be deep in thought. He waited some more.

"Castillo did it," Frank stated.

"Get serious."

Frank was looking out over the remaining, smaller crowd. As if feeling the gaze, Jay Losano turned and smiled thinly.

Al came up behind Hart and whispered in his ear. "All the small appliances are okay. One of the fridges is fried, but the stoves still work and I think the bar fridges are okay."

"Power surge," Hart said.

"No kidding," Al replied. "Generator didn't even have a chance to kick in, power was back on within seconds. I've never seen it restore that quickly before. Is there a storm outside?"

"It's sixty-eight degrees and sunny Al," Hart said.

"Maybe an accident knocked out a main power pole," he offered.

"It was no accident," Frank said, staring at the woman who was still conversing with her adoring group. "How the hell did she do that?" he added.

"You can't really believe she somehow caused a power surge," Hart said. "What purpose would it serve?"

"Ask General Wade to call me. I'll talk to you later," he said and quickly headed for the door.

"What do I do about the kitchen?" Hart called after him.

"It's your restaurant," he said. The hydraulic front door slammed shut as he raced outside.

Hart stared after him, thinking he'd pop back in with further insights or a reprieve. Then he thought better of it and turned to Al.

"Order whatever equipment you've secretly wanted over the past two years and that I have refused to pay for," he said. "I'll send him the bill."

"Works for me," Al said, the grin clearly discernible even as he turned back toward the kitchen.

Chapter Six

The white rental van didn't look out of place on De Quincy Boulevard since there were several businesses and eateries on either side of the road. Deliveries were a regular occurrence in the heart of Baltimore's Inner Harbor and although trucks often broke down deliveries couldn't be delayed. Thus, the sight of a rental van, the word "Ryder" emblazoned in bold red lettering on each side and the rear roll up door, was not an unusual sight for the neighborhood.

The fact no one had gotten out of the van to deliver anything for the past twenty minutes seemed to go unnoticed too. Had anyone attempted to open the rear lock and slide up the rear door, they would have found it to be welded shut. Both driver and passenger doors were locked barring entry, and the heavily tinted windows--a sure giveaway this was no ordinary rental van--ensured no one could see inside.

"This amazing!" the young Korean technician spurted, his excitement barely contained. He was seated inside behind an array of monitors and other high-tech gadgetry mounted to one side of the van's interior. LED lights flashed all over and a video feed on one monitor showed the interior of a restaurant with forty or so people milling about in huddled conversations. The lights had gone out in the restaurant just moments before but had come back on within a few seconds, so it had been little more than a distraction to most of the crowd.

"Speak English!" a taller, older Korean said, standing beside and just behind the younger man. "Even when we are alone, do you understand?"

The younger man's excitement evaporated and he bowed his head. He looked up at his older counterpart, noticing that he was rubbing his forehead with the back of his knuckles, his eyes partially closed, as if absorbing pain. The young man turned back to his monitor.

The older man leaned down, his large, muscular frame folding naturally. Without bending his knees, the man, in his mid-thirties, held the position while he watched the front door of the *Artichoke Hart*, a few buildings down on the left side of the street. No one had come out since he had ordered the code enabled which had caused the momentary blackout in five of the buildings along the left side of the road.

The young Asian was tapping a keyboard directly under the monitors and grinning again. The older Asian rubbed the side of his head. He could feel another headache coming on. He would need fresh air soon.

"We out of system now" the younger man said in halting English. He had never really learned the language properly and didn't use it much. His fist lightly tapped the desk. "No trace, no damage. We have done it!"

"You are sure it is back to normal?" The older man barked. The younger man nodded his head vigorously.

"It still needs work," the man muttered, his voice low and monotone. "It should have taken out the whole block."

"Yes, but what happen... It is good, yes?" the young man enthused. He looked up at his older counterpart, but the older Asian offered no enthusiasm. "We did good, yes? I mean, code work as planned?" he continued, obviously seeking reassurance.

The older Korean sighed. Despite this boy being a marvel with computers, his exuberance was unnecessary albeit inevitable. Young Koreans today were being used to monitor and occasionally integrate themselves in Western media. As a result, many of them had picked up the slang, the mannerisms, even the dress of their American and European counterparts. He knew that once this mission was completed, young Koreans such as this one would become even more immersed in Western culture and he was worried for them. The nonchalant, careless, free-wheeling attitude of the average American teenager was one of the things he stood against. Yet, these young Koreans emulated those teens as if they were Gods from another planet.

By the end of this summer, young Koreans like this one would have the chance to share their skills with the world. He just hoped they had the capacity to maintain their beliefs, their inner strength, and their devotion to a unified Korea. It would take diligence, it would take training, and it would take discipline. Because if these Koreans became any more American, the whole mission would be a failure. The whole thing depended upon the next generation bringing Korean ideals to the world, not the other way around.

He maintained his vigil watching the front door of the restaurant but nodded his head slightly so the boy would relax. It had been a test and it had succeeded. The *Artichoke Hart*. He knew it was named after the owner, a man the Asian had known a long time ago. He grinned at the memories. But it had no relevance to this operation and his attention was jarred back when the doors of the restaurant flew open. A well-dressed, dark haired man strode briskly out, punching a tiny key fob as he approached a black BMW parked across the street from the entrance.

Frank Daro. Of course it would be him, the older man thought. Former technical chief and now deputy director of the CIA, Frank Daro was the logical choice. He would make a good adversary, though predictable.

He watched as Daro drove away, tires squealing, and although he would have loved to go into the restaurant to confirm who else was there, he knew that would be too dangerous. It was too soon. He would be recognized and now was not the time for that. Soon, but not yet. He had seen all the people he had wanted to see as they had entered an hour or so ago. For now, that would suffice.

He turned to the younger man. "Shut it down. It is time to go."

He was able to access the driver's seat through a cut-out between the van's cab and rear box. It was a tight squeeze due to his size and hit the bulkhead once with his forehead which didn't physically hurt but did exacerbate his ever-constant dull headache. He made no sound as he maneuvered his tall frame in and behind the steering wheel. Moments later, the younger Korean did the same, squeezing himself into the passenger seat, a little more easily as he was not as big as the older man.

They drove off and headed toward Intestate 95 where the older man slowly brought the van up to speed and settled back for the four-hour drive north. He reminded himself he had one stop along the way and casually checked his watch to see how long the turnoff would be.

Two hours later, he exited onto a rural highway that seemed to lead nowhere in either direction.

"What is here?" the younger man asked. He didn't seem concerned, just curious. The older Korean looked at him. The boy was no doubt hoping for a pit stop so he could go to the bathroom, grab a coke and maybe a bag of American potato chips for the remaining drive. The boy and his associates had taken to these wonders of the western world and they were very, very addicting. He knew the boy wished he could send a package to his parents. But they would never appreciate the salty, flavorful taste. Their idea of luxury was meat in their soup. He frowned. No doubt the parents were getting plenty of meat in their soup, thanks to their clever son. Unfortunately, that would soon end.

The boy stared out at the lines of greenery that lead, in a straight line, as far as the eye could see. Planted earlier in the spring, their leafy sprouts were now forming, reaching upward to a glowing, warmer sun. He appeared puzzled that his associate had picked an exit where there had been no signs for fuel, lodging, or restaurants.

"I need to take care of something," was the only explanation the young Korean received.

A few minutes later, the older man pulled the truck over to the side of the road. The younger man looked around. There were fields on both sides of the road with small gulleys between the asphalt and the fencing running along the edge of the fields. No other vehicles were in sight and no structure other than a weather-worn concrete silo stood a few hundred yards away in the middle of one of the cultivated fields. He turned to the older man who was sitting still, staring out the front window, his eyes flickering between the road ahead and the side mirror.

After a few moments of silence, the young Korean's curiosity piqued. "Are we waiting for someone?"

The older man didn't turn his head but continued to stare out of the windshield, his eyes steadily flickering back and forth from front view to side mirror.

"Are we here for a reason?" the young man insisted. His eyes darted around the deserted fields. The older man, seemingly satisfied with what he had seen or hadn't seen in the mirror, turned his head and slowly nodded. He could see the miniscule motion sent chills up the younger man's spine. The boy's eyes widened as a flicker of recognition crossed his face. He opened his mouth, starting to form a word...

The older Korean's hand slashed out like a cobra, the fleshy part between his forefinger and thumb making contact with the younger man's throat and pushing his Adam's apple inward and upward, initially choking him and then smashing his larynx at the top of the Trachea so no air could pass from his lungs to his brain. The young man's head snapped backward, hit the back frame of the side window and bounced forward again. The older man's hand lashed out again, this time with a lightning fast strike to the side of the younger man's temple with his middle knuckle-- protruding from an otherwise tight fist--pounding the small davit below his temple splitting the fragile bone and sending tiny fragments into the lower brain. The young man slumped forward, his head bumping against the dash. He didn't move and his breathing was very shallow. If he hadn't been wearing a seatbelt, his body would have slumped to the floor. The older Asian sat back and listened for a few seconds until what sounded like air rushing out of a small hole in a balloon subsided. He reached over to the boy and felt for a pulse in his neck. After a few moments of silence, he checked the mirror one final time and stepped out of the van.

He strode around to the passenger door, opened it, and held onto the younger man's arm with one hand while unleashing the seatbelt with his other. He then grabbed the front of the dead boy's shirt and effortlessly pulled him out from the vehicle. With a quick glance in each direction to ensure he was still alone, he lifted the corpse up and as if passing a basketball to a partner in a thrusting manner, propelled it out into the air. The body flew forward momentarily before gravity took over and it dropped, slamming into the center of the gulley in an unnatural heap.

He then got back into the van, put it in gear and slowly drove forward a few yards and looked out the passenger side mirror. The body was at the bottom of the gulley partially hidden by wild grasses and couldn't be seen from the road.

He made a quick U-turn and accelerated slowly back the way he had come. Another glance in his own side mirror assured him that the body couldn't be seen from this side of the road either. It would likely not be found for a day or so since passers-by couldn't see it.

The young Korean had been extremely talented but, as the older man's partners had assured him, he was not the only one in their employ who could manipulate the code. Therefore, he was dispensable. The older Asian couldn't have risked the young boy telling his associates about the restaurant, or more importantly, the success of the test.

The boy had arrived in America three months ago on a direct flight from Singapore, the plane having been chartered by the older Korean's employer. Its express purpose had been to transport very talented young North Koreans to America illegally.

There had been five other eager, young Koreans on that same flight, all members of Bureau 121, the infamous cyber warriors who had taken credit for the Sony hack causing the delayed launch of the movie "The Interview" in 2014 which had satired the Supreme Leader. Four of them were still diligently working hard in upstate New York, helping to create the world's next communications breakthrough. Their families didn't know where they were but that was nothing new. This group of computer experts had been groomed since birth to serve their country in this manner. They regularly flew all over the world at the bidding of the Supreme Leader. They were an elite group of young hackers and their families lived in luxury in Pyong Yang thanks to their childrens' diligent and successful work.

Of course, one family would now be sent back into the countryside to eke out a living off the land, no longer deserving of the luxuries and status they had incurred. They would be told their son now no longer worked for the group. If they made an issue, the entire family would be sent to one of the camps where they would never be seen again.

The Korean reached the highway again, took the ramp heading north and, once he had the van back up to the speed limit, switched on the satellite radio, which was already tuned to his favorite station. He loved satellite radio. It wasn't available to the masses in North Korea. But he had every confidence that once his current mission was successfully concluded, satellite radio would be available for everyone around the globe. And it would be free.

For the first time that day, he smiled. And tapped his feet. Blake Shelton's voice had that effect on him every time.

Robert J. Morrow

Chapter Seven

"Hey Babe. How's my lovely wife this morning?"

"I'm not always sure what I am Arthur, but one thing I know I'm not anymore is your wife."

Hart casually threw the phone handset into his left hand and lifted it to his better ear. "A girlfriend maybe?"

"We tried that," she said, a little haughtily.

"Well you don't want to be known as my 'ex' do you?" he said, grinning, fully aware she would sense the grin across the line.

"I don't really want to be your anything," she said. Then she sighed. "But unfortunately, you're still our children's father. Listen, Arthur, this Saturday…. I, um… well…"

"You've got a date?" he asked, perhaps a little too happily.

"Arthur, it *has* been a while." She was flustered, her normally austere exterior crumbling just a little bit since she was forced to explain some kind of emotion.

"Are you sure you remember what to do Babe?" Hart asked, enjoying the moment immensely.

"Arthur!" she exclaimed. He waited.

"I was hoping the kids could stay with you Saturday night," she blurted.

"Wow, on to third base the first time out," he said. "I'm impressed."

"Arthur, just shut up and pay attention," she said, calmly. So much for emotion. She continued. "There's something else." She hesitated slightly.

"Don't worry, I won't bring them back till you've had a chance to cook him breakfast Babe," he said.

"Arthur, you are such an ass," she said. Then she inhaled quickly. "It's somebody you know."

That didn't really surprise him. They had been a close couple during the child-rearing years and most of the people they hung out with were mutual friends or family connections. The last two guys she'd dated had been former desk jockeys at The Company. Frank, her brother and Hart's best friend, had introduced them.

"It's Richard Hattis, Arthur," she said. "You remember him?"

Christ!

Hart took a moment to regroup.

"Yeah, he's been in here now and again. Eats primarily Italian, if I recall," he said slowly.

"Good God Arthur, do you relate everything to food now?" she said.

"It's what I do now," he said, wanting to avoid talking about boyfriends suddenly.

"What the hell does that mean?" she said, her voice raising slightly.

"There's something cosmically correct about a fully extracted Brule sauce over smoked salmon preceded by shrimp bisque dotted with freshly chopped basil."

"What the hell does that have to do with any...."

"I remember Richard," he interrupted. "Wasn't he one of Frank's underlings at some point; came to a couple of our house parties?"

Silence. Then quietly. "He did, yes."

There was nothing Hart could add really. Their marriage had broken up for lots of reasons but one of the minor ones had been his ongoing friendship with her brother, Frank. Cynthia loved her brother but thought it too dangerous to host family gatherings when some terrorist could drop in one Sunday afternoon and slaughter everyone on his patio while they were having a barbeque, according to her. It had been tough to reassure her when deep down he had to admit it was a plausible scenario.

"Is he still in the field?" he asked.

"No, that's just it. He moved over to the Secret Service a few months ago. Now he's posted at the White House. I'm not really sure what he does but he likes it and wants to put down roots, maybe buy a house--"

"Start a relationship," he finished for her. "That's a lot of personal info on someone you've just started dating."

"I…I've been seeing him for a while," she stuttered.

"It's your life Babe," he said, not really sure if it bothered him or not.

"I hate it when you say that."

"Why?"

"Because it means you don't care anymore," she said, a slight edge in her tone.

Hart thought about what to say at that point, wanting to be sure he wouldn't sound like a typical ex-husband and screw up a fairly amicable ex-relationship. After a few random thoughts passed through his frontal lobe, he gave up and chose to most logical male answer.

"Of course I care." Then realizing how callous that sounded, added "Are we still on for tonight?" She didn't respond. "What are we having?"

After what seemed like five minutes, she sighed and said "Steak and potatoes with creamed corn."

"Don't overdo it Babe," he snickered, thankful they weren't staying on the intimate track.

"Don't insult me, you cretin. I was cooking for you long before you decided it was your life's passion."

"True enough," he replied, thankful they were back to the insulting track. It was much safer. "And I seem healthy enough so the nourishment factor must have been appropriate."

She sighed again, probably knowing the serious talk was over for now.

"It'll be ready by eight," she said. "Don't be late. Jamie wants you to help him with his Geography. Richard tried to help him the other night but I don't think Jamie is completely comfortable with him yet"

That one hit somewhere just below the belly button.

"I've asked him to drop by later," she continued. "He thinks it would be good to say Hello and make sure no one thinks there are any secrets here."

"He's in the secrets business," Hart said.

"Arthur!"

"We're almost divorced Cynthia," he said. "You don't need my approval for anything."

"I think it would help if the kids saw us all getting along together," she said.

Hart stifled back what he really wanted to say. Him, his children, his wife—okay, ex-wife--and her boyfriend, all sitting around the dining room table playing Uno® like one big happy family.

"You might want to put a little oregano in the gravy Babe."

"Thank you Arthur," she said demurely. Oh, and Arthur?"

"Yes"

"Will you please stop calling me Babe."

Chapter Eight

Lena Lopez Castillo felt small and insignificant as she sat on one of two utilitarian but not uncomfortable chairs in the long, high ceilinged hallway. She stared up at the huge portrait hanging across the hall, the imposing glare of Abraham Lincoln reminding her of the magnitude of the occasion.

My Father would have been impossibly proud.

She had only been in Washington one other time, as a little girl. Her father had insisted they visit the Capital City where all decisions concerning the welfare, happiness, and liberty of Americans took place. Her Father had been proud of the fact he was the only one in his family who had legally brought his family from Mexico to the US. He felt it important that his children understand the value of following the rules, of being an official member of society, rather than a downtrodden, mistreated one, like his younger brother who had crossed the border illegally and was always hiding from the immigration officers.

Lena smiled as she remembered her Father. Self-taught and self-promoting, he had fenagled his way onto a building crew in the heyday of construction in their home village on the Yucatan Peninsula. Thanks to the influx of money from America and Europe, Juan Castillo had risen from labourer to supervisor, then site manager, and finally, into the role of project manager, representing the Mexican workers on behalf of the foreign hotel and resort developers and builders in what the promoters were beginning to call the *Mayan Riviera*.

As a young girl, Lena recalled chasing her younger brother in and out of huge half-finished concrete rooms destined to become cafeterias, ballrooms, and lobbies for large, international hotel chains. Her childhood was one long memory of playing soccer in the hollow, empty encasements of what would later become overheated swimming pools.

What had especially intrigued the young mind, however, were the masses of electronics built into the walls of the multi-room monstrosities. Her Father had explained the significance of catering to a modern tourist who was just beginning to demand larger screen televisions capable of receiving multiple stations from Mexico City, nearby Cancun, even as far away as Miami. And the wireless Japanese-made telephone handsets that connected by airwaves to base sets mounted on the walls with extra jacks on all the walls and even outside on balconies. These latter adaptations fascinated the young Lena when her Father explained that these connections allowed the rich tourists to connect with their businesses and families back home via miniature computers they carried with them. He had shown her the desktop computers that were being set up in the lobby which allowed the guests who had not yet purchased portable sets to communicate home via phone and cable lines that went everywhere in the world. He even allowed her and her brother to play around on them once installed. She had been fascinated with the capabilities of the square, nondescript boxes and with a child's unhindered wonder, understood the unbridled potential of such technology.

Eventually, her father had been asked to move to headquarters in San Francisco where he would act as liaison between the developers and the hoard of non-unionized Mexican work force. Lena had been eleven when they'd emigrated and she would be forever thankful to her father for making such a drastic change in her young life pre-adolescence. As an emerging teenager in a country full of opportunity and new-found opulence, Lena had flourished, both socially and academically. Her natural interest in emerging technologies formed during her childhood days in the hotel construction zones grew into a fervent desire to learn as much as she could about computer technology and find a place in the exploding IT industry somewhere. At nineteen, she left home to enrol in computer sciences at USC at a time when California was clearly becoming the epicentre of emerging breakthrough technologies.

"Miss Castillo?"

Lena jerked her head to see Peter Danfield motioning for her to follow him through the imposing wooden door into what looked like a sitting lounge beyond. She nodded nervously, stood, and followed him into a bright, naturally lit room, a stark contrast from the softly-lit corridor where she had been waiting for nearly twenty minutes.

Danfield was the Chief of Staff for President Daniel Emerson and the room Lena entered was the Oval Office, its custom tufted Sunbeam carpet complete with embroidered American Eagle dominating the centre of the room. Two plush couches faced one another in front of a fireplace and two colonial-style high back chairs were positioned directly in front of the mantel. At the opposite of the room stood the imposing Presidential desk which itself was situated in front of what is probably the most photographed bay window in the world.

Lena was awed by it all and stood, mouth agape. Danfield, smiling knowingly, touched the edge of her arm, motioning her to sit at one of the couches. As she did, a door on the opposite side of the room opened and three men strode in, talking with one another. Lena recognized two of the men, one in a rumpled suit, the other in full army dress. She made to stand but Danfield gently restrained her with his hand on her shoulder, shaking his head and smiling when she looked up at him.

She had met General Wade at the Press Conference the week before at the restaurant in Baltimore. He had been wearing the same full army dress uniform and his decorations sparkled in the filtered sunlight. He had been warm and friendly at that gathering but his staunch expression now made Lena think he was not in the mood for idle chit chat. Director Lazare had also been in attendance though Lena hadn't spoken to him directly. His rumpled brown suit and disarrayed hairdo made her feel he had just jumped off a helicopter and the blade wash had caused is unkempt look. She smiled inwardly. Considering the nature of the surreal situation she now found herself, that may well be the reason he looked the way he did. The men stopped speaking as they approached the opposite couch and sat, simply nodding at Lena as they made themselves comfortable. The third man was a stranger to Lena. He was a little older than the other two, early seventies maybe, and he wore a well- tailored grey suit with a fashionable blue tie. Though bald, his skin was clear of any blemishes common to most aging men.

A moment later, a waiter came in with a silver tray and tea service which he placed in the centre of the coffee table between Lena and the men. Danfield came around and poured what appeared to be tea into four cups, then offered one to Lena.

"Cream and sugar are just here," he whispered pointing at identical ornamental silver dishes on the tray.

Lena nodded, afraid to say anything lest her voice squeak. She knew she was here to meet the US President but she had never dreamed that meeting would take place in this room. She was virtually speechless. Thankfully, the others didn't seem to feel the need to engage her in conversation, so she simply revelled in the experience, sipping her tea quietly while the men across from her checked their smartphones and straightened their jackets. Danfield stood in front of the fireplace as if on point duty.

Just as the silence was becoming uncomfortable, the door opened again and President Daniel Emerson strode in. Tall, slightly overweight and with thinning grey hair, Emerson evoked a presence of power that Lena had witnessed via television whenever he took the podium at press conferences. In person, the aura of authority was almost palpable. She quickly stood, as did the other men. Emerson, all smiles, and ignoring the others, quickly strode toward Lena and took her hand in both of his, shaking it rigorously.

"Ms. Castillo, it is a pleasure to have you visit us," he said, his famously cultured and even voice washing over her. "Please, sit."

"It is my pleasure, Sir," she said, her voice quieter than she had hoped. She cleared her throat. "I am honoured you have taken time out of your busy schedule to meet with me, Sir," she said.

"Please, let's dispense with the Sir thing--" he motioned for her to sit again "--as it is always a pleasure to talk with our budding young American entrepreneurs, isn't it boys?" He looked over at the three men, the two suits quickly nodding in agreement. The General seemed pre-occupied with some papers he had taken from his inside pocket but the President didn't seem to mind.

"I must say I am excited about what you're doing," he said, sitting beside her in one of the high backs at the fireplace. He sat so that his body was facing her directly, at a ninety-degree angle to the others. Lena's nervousness abated slightly under the intense gaze of the top politician as he seemed genuinely focused on her. He placed his arms on either side of the chair, then leaned back and crossed his legs, his gaze never wavering from Lena's face.

"My understanding is that you will be spending much of the summer finalizing your project and that you are confident we will be able to present it to the nation sometime in August," he said.

Straight to it. She found her voice and began. "Mr. President, as you know, ArmourNet will revolutionize online communication in such a way that every American, regardless of financial position or geographical location, will be able to access the internet at an extremely low cost." The President nodded as Lena continued her memorized speech. "My team and I feel confident we will be ready to launch at least the first stage of the product by the end of the summer and I am honoured that you have chosen to join us for that celebration."

One of the men harrumphed but the President took no notice.

"I have been told by my advisors, Ms. Castillo, that your technology is truly remarkable and, of course, fits in ideally with President Barack's executive order from 2012. Its intent was to ensure that during a national emergency, this office would be capable of reaching the majority of citizens instantly, informing them of what actions they would need to take in order to preserve whatever liberties were in question during such crisis." He uncrossed his legs and leaned forward slightly. "My understanding, Ms. Castillo, is that your technology will allow me to do that without the need of manipulating private industry or other utilities such as the cable and telephone companies."

Lena nodded. "Wherever there are power lines going into a home, business, or institution, ArmourNet will allow data to be transferred quickly and without interference." She leaned forward, her excitement making her less conscious of where she was and whom she was speaking with. It was always like this when she began explaining how ArmourNet worked. "By simply switching the source to a pre-determined channel, you would have access to every end user instantly."

The President leaned forward too, his face less than a foot from Lena's. "And if someone else continued to try using the system?"

Lena cocked her head. She didn't understand the question. The President smiled. "What I mean Ms. Castillo, is that in a state of national emergency, we may not have time to notify all the, ah…. licensees, that the government is taking over the internet. What would happen to the signals being sent by, say the national networks, the cable or phone companies, for example. I mean what would happen to all the Google® searches that take place every second of every day?"

Lena's brows furrowed. She sat back, not sure how to answer. "Actually, Sir, once the channel is switched over to the pre-designated emergency status, then ArmourNet would cease to function from any other source. Once that switch is flipped Sir, then only one channel will be operational."

"And the data or information being sent by those other sources?" the President pressed. "I mean what would happen to regular online-sourced programming such as email or e-commerce sites like, say EBay? What would happen to those signals when that, ah… switch, as you call it, was pressed?"

Lena shook her head and pursed her lips. "The signals wouldn't reach their destination, Sir. The data would literally burn up within the lines, due to the intense heat generated by electrical pulses that traverse the lines every second of every day. Without the protection of ArmourNet, those signals wouldn't go any further than a mile or so from their source."

The President leaned back and turned his body slightly away from Lena. He turned his head to address the others.

"Gentlemen, your questions?" he stated.

Lena leaned back also and watched as the two men stared at her. The General was looking at his phone.

"Ms. Castillo, this is Benjamin Davies, Director of the FBI," the President said, motioning to the older, well-dressed suit sitting at the far end of the couch. Lena nodded. The man's lips curled slightly in acknowledgment of the introduction, but other than that, his body and face were still. I believe you have met Director Lazare. Both men nodded at Lena.

"Director Davies?" the President said. The FBI top man gaze at Lena momentarily. Then, his face opened into a huge, very fake smile.

Did that condescending attitude work for his staff?

"Ms. Castillo," he began, his voice low and gruff. "From what you just stated, you are assuming that everyone in the country-big business included--will willingly switch from cable, phone, fibre-optic, or wireless formats to that of the Broadcast over Power Lines model. Why are you so confident that will happen?"

"Mr. Davies, it will come down to simple economics, Sir," Lena said. "I am not a financial specialist; however, it seems to me that any good business is going to attempt to cut costs wherever it can, either to increase profits or--should it be so inclined--pass on savings to the consumer. "She smiled. None of the others did although the President seemed to be grinning slightly. Lena had answered this question many times before. "BPL will be so inexpensive, the incentive to join the network will be inherent in the immediate increase in profits. I don't foresee internet service companies reducing prices drastically once a switch is made; I mean, the consumer won't really notice a difference in service or quality. So, even though costs will be dramatically decreased, unless the government demands reduced prices, it will simply mean a higher profit margin. And since the goal is to create a national, government operated utility out of the technology, any anti-trust fears will be avoided."

Davies nodded. Lena figured he'd already known the answer but for whatever reason wanted to hear her state it verbally.

"It is my understanding that you have established a lab in Upstate New York, near the Fitzpatrick Nuclear Power Plant?"

Lena nodded and said, "Yes Sir."

"I have been informed that it is necessary for you to utilize the facilities there in order to access the Eastern Power Grid directly." He didn't wait for Lena to confirm. "And I have also been informed that you have financed the renovations of this laboratory out of funds you received from your partner, a Mr. Giovanni Losano, is that correct?"

Lena shifted slightly in her seat. "Jay, yes Sir. Jay's family has been generous in their continued investment in our venture, especially early on when the banks and other financial institutions didn't agree with our business plan."

"And you are aware, Ms. Castillo, that Giovanni--Jay as you call him--is part of a family that is allegedly connected with the Mafia."

Lena frowned. "Mr. Losano is very supportive of his son's activities, Mr. Davies," Lena said. Her gaze hardened. "I am aware that the Losano family has a reputation in Las Vegas for its dealings in Casino's, hotels, and other ventures, but to the best of my knowledge, he is not connected in any way with organized crime."

"It sounds like you've defended Mr. Losano before," Davies stated, his lips curling slightly.

Lena sat back. "Mr. Davies, my goal is to get ArmourNet ready to launch nationally so that every American can enjoy inexpensive and consistently strong internet service." She crossed her legs, wishing that for this occasion she had worn her pencil skirt instead of her usual dress slacks. Flirtation may have helped distract in this situation, she knew. "I will do whatever I have to do to get my technology to market. Mr. Losano has thus far been the only person with enough vision to see that our idea--mine and his son's--had merit and would eventually become a profitable endeavour. His funding of our efforts will no doubt reap great rewards, once our company goes public."

Davies pressed on. "And the father, Mr. Antonio Losano, has no involvement in day-to-day operations, Ms. Castillo?"

"All he did, Mr. Davies, was write a check eight months ago and gave it to his son. I then spent most of it on equipment, facilities, and renovations. The remainder is for salaries. I have not spoken with him since."

"I'm sure Jay has though Ms. Castillo, and I wonder--"

"Perhaps we can move on, Director Davies," the President interrupted. "The Justice Department is looking into the allegations and," he gave Lena a smile, "any alleged illegal activities Mr. Antonio Losano may or may not be involved in. That is not of any real concern for us today, now is it?"

Looking anything but chastised, Davies grunted and leaned back. He held up his hand, waving it in dismissive manner.

"Thank you Mr. Davies," the President said, his smile never wavering. Lena was pretty sure the President wasn't really smiling but it appeared so genuine, it was difficult to argue with its calming and controlling effect. If he had taken any offence to her comment or was concerned about Mafiosi influence, he didn't show it.

"Director Lazare, you had a question or two, I believe?" he said, addressing the smaller, more craggy-faced man. Lazare looked first at the President then back to Lena, his eyes steady, his face a mask of indifference. Or so it seemed.

"Ms. Castillo, you told us last week that you and Mr. Losano have invited delegates from several countries to visit your, ah, laboratory, to see your new technology in action."

It wasn't a question but Lena nodded anyway.

"You are aware, I'm sure Ms. Castillo, that the President… and all of us here," he said, waving his hands to include all of them, including the General who was now paying attention, "are concerned that foreign powers may be witness to activities which could someday become critical to the security of this nation. With the President's involvement, it is of vital importance that specific details concerning your technology not be distributed to any foreign power without our prior knowledge." He leaned forward and attempted a smile.

Christ, none of these guys were good at humility, except perhaps the President.

"Our plan," Lena replied, "as we outlined in the documents we provided to the President's staff clearly shows that it is our intention to license the technology to other countries. ArmourNet was not designed just for America, just as the telephone wasn't, or electricity. You can't hoard such important and life-altering discoveries such as this. Successful use of BPL will improve communication for all peoples, all over the globe," she said, her voice raising in excitement. She caught President Emerson's growing grin as she pushed on. Feeling encouraged she continued. "And President Emerson has assured me that despite our main focus being the ability to allow instant access to the system by this office, we will be free to pursue our unalienable rights and license the technology to any country wishing to take advantage of its benefits for their citizens also. Because of BPL, ArmourNet has the potential to improve communication not just across America but across the World."

Lazare nodded though it was clear from his scouring gaze that he really didn't agree with Lena's altruistic outlook. "Ms. Castillo, -
-"

"May I?" the General interrupted. His voice was more gentile, softer, yet with just two words, he held the attention of all the others.

"General Wade, please," President Emerson said. Director Lazare looked put out but he sighed and leaned back on the couch cushions.

"Thank you Mr. President," he said, his face, which up until now had been staunchly impassive, suddenly widened into a smile as genuine as the President's and one she had witnessed at the restaurant gathering.

"Ms. Castillo, my role as a liaison between the CIA--" he nodded to the man sitting at the other end of the couch--"and Military Intelligence allows me the opportunity to hear about such tremendous emerging endeavours such as your own early on, which is why I responded to your initial inquiry at approximately the same time as you were conferring with your state representative."

Lena pushed her lips out, her tongue licking the inside of her mouth. *Where was this going?*

"Since learning about your, ah... breakthrough, Ms. Castillo, I have had a research team attempting to address the BPL dilemma once again and, I am sad to say, they have not attained any of the successes you have in overcoming the problems of interference, data loss, or long-distance retardation of data."

Lena nodded. *Okay, so he knew more than he had ever let on. And the military had been trying to copy her. I wonder if they had begun their efforts before or after I approached Senator Blais' staff?*

"With this in mind, and of course, after listening to you last week, Ms. Castillo," the General continued, "I have asked the President if we may have access to your technology--as a licensee, of course--immediately after the launch at the end of the summer." The two suits shifted in their seats and stared at the old soldier. "Obviously, it's value to the military should be obvious but he has also assured me that our office, that is Military Intelligence, will be the arm of the government that will administrate the internet should a state of emergency be called."

"What!" Director Lazare gasped. President Emerson raised a hand to stop the man from continuing.

The General continued. "So I would like to offer the assistance of any of my staff should you require it, Ms. Castillo. As of this morning, I have cancelled the research into our own version of your armouring technology--at the President's request--" he nodded to Emerson. "--and my office stands ready to assist you in any way we can."

Lena thought about that for a moment. "Thank you General. Does this mean the US Army is prepared to take over funding for the project?" She lifted her eyebrows giving the General her best coy look. He matched her look, then puckered his lips. She turned to President Emerson.

"I'm afraid that will not be possible at this time Ms. Castillo," the President said. "Once you have launched a finished, working product, General Wade will provide a facility where you may shift your project over to practical use. We have begun to work towards creating a national utility, available to all, administered by appointed members of various government agencies, as well as yourself and any of your staff you wish to retain. We would assist in managing licensing activities and ensuring all international agencies adhere to strict guidelines of usage that we will all determine at a later date."

"Mr. President, I must object, Sir," Director Lazare intervened. Davies nodded in agreement. "We had not been informed of this decision and since it affects the Intelligence Community as a whole, I feel perhaps we should be making these decisions through the appropriate channels."

"I am well aware that you and others have not been in the loop on this, which of course, is partially why I invited you to this brief powwow. However, we are keeping a hands-off approach at the moment, allowing Ms. Castillo here to continue in anonymity, being financed by private sources, until such a time as our government can *legally* and effectively take over." The President emphasized the word *legally*.

"I must insist--" Lazare continued but Emerson interrupted.

"Gentlemen, perhaps we can discuss the intricacies of any decisions after this meeting." The President's glare was self-evident. He didn't want to discuss the matter any further at this meeting. "I believe lunch is being served. If you would excuse us for a moment, I would like a few moments alone with Ms. Castillo." He then abruptly stood which, of course, caused everyone else to stand. The two suits looked annoyed at being dismissed but the General seemed nonplussed and took the arm of Director Lazare, pushing him away from the couch and to the door where the President had entered. Lazare looked at him, his frown so exaggerated his face actually changed shape. Benjamin Davies merely nodded at both the President and Lena, then lead the way out of the room. Just prior to reaching the threshold, General Wade turned and Lena watched as the President gave him a quick and loose salute. The General grinned, nodded, and closed the door behind him.

Peter Danfield gathered the cups, picked up the tea service and headed to the door.

"I will be right outside Mr. President," he said. "A pleasure to meet you Ms. Castillo." And then he left through the same door.

President Emerson turned to Lena. "I apologize for the abrupt nature of my colleagues, Ms. Castillo," he said. "They mean well and are, in fact, genuinely excited about the possibilities your new technology presents for the country. But power struggles are actually as real as they are made out to be in the media and various popular novels. It is the curse of this office, I'm afraid."

"Thank you Mr. President," Lena responded, sitting back down when the President motioned her to do so.

"The main reason I brought you here Ms. Castillo was to assure you that your concerns are being taken seriously by this office." He leaned forward and Lena placed her hands in her lap. She waited anxiously.

"My esteemed colleagues seem to have forgotten that it was President Obama who initiated the idea of *neutral* internet back in 2014. He believed, as do I, that the FCC should reclassify consumer internet service under Title Two of the Telecommunications Act--while at the same time forbearing from rate regulation and other provisions less relevant to those services. In other words, it has long been a mandate of this office to provide uncompetitive yet high-quality internet services to the masses at the lowest costs possible. BPL has always been ideally suited to this goal. It just hasn't worked in the past.

Mr. Daro contacted me after your Press Conference and told me of your request. After conferring with General Wade, I agree." He lowered his voice conspiratorially. "Although the administration cannot be seen to be involved in your efforts, I have asked Mr. Daro to come up with something that will satisfy both yourself and the other two gentlemen who just left. I wanted to inform you personally."

Lena looked at the President quizzically. He smiled.

"I can't allow the FBI to provide security for you as that would require permission from Congress and various congressional committee's-including Senator Blais'."

Lena grinned. *So Blais had spoken to someone at the White House after all. She wished now she hadn't taken her idea to the Senator initially but he was an old colleague of her father's during the years when the hotel conglomerates had been lobbying for fewer tariffs on materials crossing the border. She had thought he would have been helpful, and inadvertently he had been. By whining to the President's advisors about her unwillingness to turn over her idea to the business world, it had been brought up during one of the President's briefings. And here she was.*

The President continued: "What I *can* do is allow Mr. Daro to provide some semblance of, ahhm… comfort shall we say for the duration. The CIA's mandate does not include domestic activities as you know but because you will be entertaining foreign delegates, it is within my power to request a certain level of input from them, despite it being on American soil."

"Mr. Lazare did not look like he agreed with your decision, Mr. President," Lena said.

The President frowned. "Director Lazare is busy with various international activities at the moment and his concerns about what you are doing stem mainly from the fact that foreign nationals will be on American soil and he won't have any eyes on the situation. However, I have assured him that Assistant Director Daro has suggested an acceptable approach to the dilemma. Once General Wade explains it to him, I assure you, he will be on board."

Lena thought about that for a moment. "General Wade was very successful in pulling together the press conference last week, ensuring a large number of influential people were in attendance, Mr. President. Am I to assume you had something to do with that?"

President Emerson smiled. "You are a perceptive and very forthcoming young lady, Ms. Castillo, as General Wade assured me you were. I find it refreshing these days. And yes, the General and see eye to eye of the future of this great country. We both feel you are quite capable of getting us to a point where your government can ensure the technology is integrated into daily American life, in the manner you and I have both perceived. It is for that reason that I invited you here, to impress upon you that even although I cannot show any public signs of my involvement, I do and will support you in every way I can."

"Then you are aware, Mr. President that I do actually have concerns about the long-term effects of financing from questionable sources," Lena said. "And that I am also worried about possible sabotage and other acts that would hinder the completion of the project in time for the press conference?"

"General Wade and Assistant Director Daro were here just yesterday morning Ms. Castillo. And we discussed those very concerns in depth." He didn't explain why it was the Assistant Director of the CIA instead of the Director himself who was in on the discussions but Lena didn't dwell on it. She preferred Daro anyway; Director Lazare didn't seem very supportive of the project's mandate.

"But I'm afraid that if the FBI or local police are visible when the delegates arrive, they may feel they are dealing with the government and not private enterprise. I'm afraid that may deter them from getting involved."

"I understand completely Ms. Castillo, and I assure you that was utmost on my mind also."

As if on que, Peter Danfield returned and waited by the open door. President Emerson motioned for Lena to head toward the door.

"Mr. Daro will be contacting you within the next twenty-four hours and I think you will be happy with the solution we have come up with." The President reached for Lena's hand. "Ms. Castillo, unfortunately, I do have to meet with the Directors to discuss other matters of national security. My chief will show you out. I apologize I cannot offer you lunch also but unfortunately, these days, working lunches are the norm.

"I understand Mr. President," Lena said, shaking his hand. "And I thank you for your personal attention."

"I look forward to seeing you again at the end of the summer," the President said, "and I want you to know I am very anxious to see the end results. I wish you every success." He then nodded to Danfield. "Till the conference, Ms. Castillo," he said. Then he turned and walked to the door where the other men had gone.

"Ms. Castillo?" Danfield said. Lena turned and followed the Chief out the way she had come. As she left the Oval Office, she briefly chastised herself for not asking the President for his autograph. Silly as it seemed, she knew Jay Losano would have been ecstatic. What she had received, however, she knew to be much more valuable.

Chapter Nine

Hart was busy cutting limes for the bar when the phone rang. After four or five rings, it was evident no one else was going to pick up.

"Yeah"

"What do you mean, yeah? Isn't this a restaurant? What if I had been looking to make a reservation?"

"Hello Frank." It had been ten days since General Wade's gathering and the so-called blackout. Hart had only taken delivery of a couple of new appliances just the day before. Frank couldn't have gotten the invoice yet.

"Have you been thinking about what our young friend the IT expert was discussing?"

"It was your meeting Frank," Hart said. "I haven't given it a second thought."

"I don't recall you having a rotisserie oven before Hart," he said.

"Ah..." The oven had been on Al's wish list. Frank had gotten the invoice after all.

"I need someone on the inside, and you're it," he said.

"Frank, I'm not one of your spies. Besides, she knows who I am, remember?"

"Precisely," said Frank. "That's why she's inviting you up to her facility."

"Ms. Lopez Castillo invited me to her house?"

"Actually, it's a converted shipping warehouse," said Frank. "And I need you to say yes and get your ass up there."

"What does she want to see me for Frank?" Hart asked.

"She wants advice on catering to a diverse group of people at a function later this summer."

Okay, Hart hadn't been expecting that. "Aren't there caterers wherever she is?"

Frank laughed. "Wait till you see this place. I think McDonalds is considered a three star."

"So why me Frank? How will my catering help you with your new buddy?" Hart asked warily. He and Al had thought about expanding the *Hart's* business by offering catering but since Al was kept busy running the restaurant, he knew he'd be the one running that side of the business. He wasn't sure he was up to it, both from an administrative and culinary viewpoint.

"She fried your security system last week, Hart," said Frank. "She's farther ahead than we thought."

"You don't *still* think she had something to do with a power outage do you?" Hart asked.

"Power surge Hart, and yes, I think she had everything to do with it," Frank said. "Or at least that insipid sidekick Losano did."

"So what exactly do you want me to do? I'm not a trained spy; never was, remember? I'm a restaurant owner and I'm trying to make a living."

"Don't worry, I'm sending someone with you," he said. "You handle catering. She'll look after the spying part."

"She?"

"Secret Service agent, name of JP Pierce. Just back from a stint in Columbia. Brought down a cartel boss single-handedly," Frank said, as if he was reading the morning paper. "You'll like her. She loves gourmet and I told her to bring along a couple of bottles of decent Malbec."

"Malbec is Argentinian, not Columbian," Hart said. "And since when does the CIA work with the Secret Service?"

"Since they've been put in charge of this end-of-summer soiree that Ms. Lopez Castillo is hosting," Frank said.

Hart waited. Frank had a penchant for drama.

"When a gathering is designated a National Special Security Event, the Secret Service is responsible for security."

"And what makes this little dinner she's having a National Special... whatever you said," Hart asked.

"Because President Emerson will be there," Frank said. "That's why Castillo needs your help. Who better to advise her on a menu than the man who feeds the President, what, two or three times a month?"

It was true that U.S. President Daniel Emerson, his wife Linda and his school-aged kids Jonathan and Ella dropped in, along with their entourage of beefy bodyguards, for an early evening dinner once a month or so. Hart had a special corner table near the back just in case they dropped by. The Secret Service usually gave them a couple of hours notice but Hart never informed Al till about thirty minutes before they were to arrive. He got too flustered if he had time to think about it too long.

Emerson was a decent guy; Hart had even voted for him. He was unpretentious when he was here, and the First Lady, Linda, was very charming. Hart wasn't sure why they brought the kids though, after all, the *Artichoke Hart* wasn't exactly fast food. Hart rarely brought his own kids here.

But Al had created a special menu just for them which included spaghetti, pizza, grilled cheese, etc. He tried to fancy them up a bit--more for his own sanity Hart thought--but if he went too far, the kids didn't eat it and Linda would be disappointed. Hart was sure there were better places to have a family dinner but didn't rock the boat. You couldn't buy the kind of publicity the President of the United States' presence generated, even if the media had been sworn to minimalize the visits.

Locals knew he came anyway, they just tried not to make a big fuss about it. The Executive Family usually spent the evening huddled together discussing family matters rather than subjects of state interest. Hart had never listened or recorded their conversations. Frank wasn't thrilled that the President could have meetings, even with his family, without him knowing the topic of conversation, but since he couldn't provide a good reason to eavesdrop, he had reluctantly conceded to Hart's decision. Besides, the Secret Service stationed a guard outside his office door for the duration of the Presidential dinners, being fully aware of the gadgets the CIA had installed.

The Secret Service wasn't officially part of the intelligence community but since so many heads of state had been brought to the *Hart* for various meals and meetings, Frank had felt obligated to inform them of his ability to listen in and record. He'd told Hart that if he had kept it secret, they would have wanted to install a similar setup anyway, so he saw no alternative but to bring them into the loop. It was a touch confusing.

Hart simply considered it an honour that the President and various other politicians considered the *Hart* their dining place of choice for special meetings. Of course, he knew Frank's influence had a lot to do with it but he still figured they wouldn't have come back if they hadn't liked the food and atmosphere.

The best part was that the administration paid their revolving account promptly and always added an 18% gratuity for the staff without being asked, so along with the free publicity, it was a pretty good deal financially too; in fact, Langley's support was a big part of why the *Artichoke Hart* was still afloat.

"So why me Frank?" Hart asked. "I'm not on the Company payroll anymore."

There was silence on the other end momentarily. "Spies can't cook, and right now that's the only in I have with Castillo over the FBI or Secret Service. You cook, you can look after yourself, and you're fairly intelligent. After all, you hang around with spooks"

"If you didn't keep bringing spooks here, I wouldn't hang around with them Frank," Hart said.

Frank ignored him and continued. "Castillo needs professional help with the venue and food. Pierce can do the spy stuff, like I said. Castillo and Losano made it clear about not wanting any police, FBI or other enforcement types hanging around. But the administration wants to keep an eye on them. They were willing to let you come and Pierce can act as your assistant."

Hart knew Frank didn't just want him to go up there and discuss catering. He had some other ulterior motive. Probably didn't want to rely on the Secret Service for his intelligence gathering, and he would want Hart to report to him about anything he saw while there.

"Castillo knows you have a connection to the Company," Frank continued. "She's curious, and is considering our involvement. I think she's worried about some of the visitors she has invited."

"The only connection I have to the Company is you Frank," Hart said. He also knew it wouldn't matter whether Lopez-Castillo was considering CIA involvement or not. Frank was already involved.

"So Frank, other than imparting our wisdom on how to feed the President, what are the Secret Service and I supposed to be looking for?"

Silence.

"Frank?" Hart urged.

After a moment Frank said, "It's complicated. We don't know whose side Castillo is on yet. If what she's doing actually works, it has global ramifications. The Feds want in but they want to swarm the place with agents, control the environment, and manipulate the project. Castillo doesn't want that. The President's got her to agree that the CIA is better-equipped to protect the project up to launch, because of our experience with foreign nationals. So he's instructed the FBI to back off for now. Since we have to include the Secret Service for the event itself anyway, the President suggested having a Secret Service agent act as your assistant. It's the perfect solution.

"The President suggested this huh?" Hart knew damn well the idea had been Frank's but it made sense that the President would see the logic. "And Ms. Castillo has met the President?" he asked.

"The Administration is very, very interested in the technology Castillo is developing," Frank said, ignoring the question. "When General Wade realized it's potential, he had her meet the President within the week. Emerson insisted she keep him up to date with her progress."

"And that's when you called Al," Hart said but didn't wait for an answer. "I thought the CIA wasn't allowed to operate on domestic soil."

"Precisely," Frank said. "Which is another reason why you're perfect for this. You don't work for me, remember?"

"You're manipulating again Frank," Hart said.

"We can't afford agency postulating over this," Frank continued. "The fibbies will most likely be hiding in the bushes but they won't be allowed onto the project without our knowledge, thanks to Castillo. They'd piss some dignitary off and cause an international incident. Military Intelligence will be lurking around too if we need them but General Wade is taking a back seat for the moment."

"Like you wouldn't cause an international incident?" Hart said.

"I will if she doesn't explain to us why she's building an empire that will eventually tap into every power grid around the globe."

"So can I tell my kids I'm a secret agent now?" Hart asked.

"No Hart. You're just the caterer. Pierce will do the spook stuff. I keep telling you that."

"Your spook better be good at mixing sauces," Hart said and hung up.

Chapter Ten

The old man gripped both his knees tightly with his fingers.

They were sitting in the back of a military issue, drab green, fully tinted Crown Vic, listening to the radio the driver had turned up to a blistering level.

"The crowd grows quiet as the two men face each other, perhaps for the last time today," the sportscaster was saying in a subdued, almost humble voice.

Garrison Bullard smiled at how engrossed the old man became in a simple game of baseball.

Any game.

Every game.

There was no use talking to him. Until this battle was over, his focus was somewhere other than inside the car.

Crack!

"Damn!" the old man exclaimed.

"I gather your team is about to lose, sir?" Bullard said.

"Turn it off Peter," the old man said to his driver, who immediately obeyed. "I don't need to hear the cleanup comments. How much did we have on that game anyway?"

"$40 to Colonel Donigan and $20 to Generals Hammerstein and Rolphson, sir," Peter replied.

The old man smacked his hands on his knees heavily and stared out the side window for a few moments. He would probably explode with expletives again but seemed reluctantly cognizant of someone else being in the car.

Bullard waited for the storm to subside.

Eventually, the old man released his knees and leaned back in his seat. "I have an assignment for you," he said in a clear, calm voice.

"Technically, I don't work for you, Sir, remember?" Bullard answered. Though a military man at heart, Bullard's experiences with various clandestine military intelligence operations had led to his leaving the official ranks and moving deeper into unchartered and unrecognizable status. And it was thanks to the old man sitting beside him. Bullard was not a team player and that had caused him much heartache and many nights cleaning toilets as a young cadet. The old man had seen something in him and taken him aside upon completing basic training. Bullard considered himself disciplined, he just didn't like feeling like he was a sheep being lead to slaughter. The old man had said he understood completely and started him off on a series of missions that required individual attention. It had started simply at first: A theft here, a beating there, disabling vehicles so diplomats couldn't reach timely destinations. But over the years the tasks had gotten more complicated and required less and less official reporting. Bullard knew he was *off the books*, a pawn of the old man's. But regardless, his paychecks always came from the Army, regularly, every month.

As Bullard had been reflecting, the old man had been staring, his eyes boring into the younger man' face. Neither broke the stare until, finally, the younger man grinned.

"I can certainly listen, sir," Bullard said, breaking the silence, his pent-up breath releasing slowly.

The old man frowned and continued to stare for a moment, then turned back to face the front.

"A young IT graduate from NYU has discovered a way to run internet data through electrical power lines," he said, and waited for the information to register. After a few seconds, he continued. "As I'm sure you can appreciate, if what she has created actually works, it will revolutionize communications across the country, if not the world."

"I thought that had been tried before, sir" Bullard said.

The old man raised an eyebrow, impressed, Bullard hoped. "It did work to some degree in certain parts of the country," he said. "An upstart company in New York successfully operated a service for almost a year in the mid-1990s. They then opened a second service in Virginia two years later and were about to launch to the rest of the country when two things happened."

Bullard said nothing. Having known the centenarian for nearly a decade now, he knew the old man liked to tell stories. Bullard's assignment, whatever it was, would be revealed somewhere near the end. He also knew there was no point asking impertinent questions prior to the old man finishing his diatribe.

"Firstly, a massive ice storm hit the Northeastern New York state, wiping out all the electrical power lines for miles. It was an unprecedented storm that brought commerce to a halt in the area for many months, including being able to provide internet service to all those who had paid for the service." As the car slowed to turn a corner, the General watched a young woman on the sidewalk lean down and pick up an envelope she had dropped. Bullard followed the old man's gaze and noticed the woman had extraordinarily long legs. He grinned, realizing that despite the old man's advancing years, he was still a young soldier at heart.

"The second thing that happened is that once several companies went in to try and salvage what the first one had developed, it came to light that the technology had a major flaw," the old man went on as they continued down another street. It was early in the morning but traffic was flowing nicely. Washington rush hour was over and the city's workers were nestled cozily at their desks for the next couple of hours until the midday rush began in earnest.

"It seems the electrical current also traveling along the power lines--in tandem with internet data--was so hot that it literally fried said data to a point of dissolution," the old man said. "The wiring running along the high-voltage lines, the ones you see in the middle of hydro-owned fields, are of such intensity that no form of data can survive the journey."

"But your young student has figured out a solution," Bullard said. He was aware of the technology's weaknesses and was intrigued by this new information. He was also mildly annoyed that he hadn't been aware of these recent successes.

"Indeed, she claims to have," the old man said, his eyes receding back into their sockets. "It was always possible to send data across low yield wires like those going from the main street to a building," he pointed abstractly to the building they were driving by. Bullard didn't see any wires and was pretty sure that within city limits they were mostly underground. "But she claims she has solved the problem of intense heat by surrounding the data with a digital shell that can withstand the intensity long enough to get data across the major lines."

"And we believe her?" Bullard asked.

The old man smiled. "We do. Unfortunately, so do a lot of other people, and not just Americans. She and her partners are looking to set up an international system that will essentially take over worldwide internet, giving new meaning to the term World Wide Web."

"So there is foreign interest, Sir?"

"Of course there is," the old man snarled. "And the young woman has actually invited delegates from various world powers to come and assess the technology's values for themselves."

"Sounds like what every technology start-up does, Sir," Bullard said.

"This is not just high-tech gadgetry, man," the old man growled, slamming his fist on his knee. "We're not talking about some social wizardry some college kid came up with to entertain the masses." He raised both hands upward in frustration. "What she's doing will change the very infrastructure of the web itself."

"That has upset a few people no doubt," Bullard said.

That's where you come in," he said, reaching over and tapping his knee.

Bullard grimaced at the contact. He didn't like being touched. But for the old man, he'd grin and bear it.

"A certain Senator who has considerable control over various communications conglomerates is making a lot of noise," he said. "Our fear is that his inane and blustering arguments will steer influential thinking in the wrong direction."

"You said *our* fear, Sir" Bullard said.

The old man smiled at the younger man's perception.

"The CIA suggested your involvement and I agree," the old man said, smiling.

Okay, that was interesting, Bullard thought. Although the old man was technically connected to the CIA, it was odd for him to consult with them prior to a mission. "And what exactly will I be doing?" he asked.

"The Senator is anticipating a meeting with a lobbyist charged with liaising with his Committee. This lobbyist's mandate will be to ensure this new technology doesn't threaten existing communications protocols put in place by the President in 2012; protocols the Senator is trying to take control of," the old man said.

Bullard cocked his head. *In other words, spy on the Senator and make sure he doesn't screw up the chance for the old man to control the internet.*

And just why do you and the CIA feel I am the best qualified liaison for this task, Sir?" he asked.

The old man's smile stretched from ear-to-ear. "Because you don't work for me, remember?"

Robert J. Morrow

Chapter Eleven

Hart hadn't really been expecting a Bond girl, though he did recall dreaming of a semi-naked Halle Barre waltzing around the *Hart's* kitchen while he shucked some oysters.

But when the door of the *Hart* opened at ten o'clock and a woman strode in, he realized maybe dreams can come true. Though no Ursula Andress, she would certainly give Maude Adams a run for her money: High cheekbones, a short but stylish bob of dark, thick hair, and large eyes that implied that she was likely of American Indian descent. Somewhere along the line though, her ancestors had definitely canoodled with an American or European because she also had long, muscular legs and several distinctly girl-next-door curves.

"Mr. Hart?" Her voice was perfectly matched to her all-business appearance: strong, a little raspy, but with sensual undertones. "I'm JP Pierce."

"Please, call me Art." She was about five-foot ten inches, but he'd caught the no-nonsense low heels as she'd sauntered over. Her hairstyle was not particularly chic, but it bounced a little as she walked which simply served to accent the fact that she was, indeed, a woman, and women bounced when they walked, whether they intended to or not. As she got closer, Hart noticed a tiny scar on her jawline, covered somewhat with make-up, but not entirely. He stood straight and gave her his best Bond pose.

"Art Hart," she said. "Your friends must have a lot of fun with that one." Her smile was wide, exposing white teeth and a slight flick of her tongue.

A lot of people had made fun of his name over the years but he sensed JP Pierce wasn't being critical. She was amused. It didn't bother him that she wasn't really impressed with his Bond pose. He considered himself more of a Vin Deisel type anyway. In his early-forties, bald, and since he had stopped seriously training for a living, about five pounds overweight. But on the positive side he felt he had a killer smile.

Pierce brushed away a strand of hair that had escaped her well-sprayed bob and had been invading her left eye. Simultaneously, she held out her other hand in a very macho, all business manner. it was much smaller than Hart's but her grip was firm. He felt a twinge in his groin as her fingernails scraped his palm.

"But surely your name isn't really Artichoke?" she said.

"Arthur actually," he said wondering what JP Pierce would look like in an evening dress and maybe a touch more makeup to accent those gorgeous cheekbones. Not that she wasn't subtly stunning in her dark blue business attire, which though very appropriate for daytime encounters, followed her curves very nicely. There was something very appealing about her altogetherness.

"The Artichoke thing is a long story. Can I offer you a glass of wine?" he asked, taking her arm and steering her to the bar. He could feel the sinewy muscle structure along her forearm. "You're not on duty are you?"

She smiled. "I may be Secret Service now Mr. Hart, but I used to be with the CIA and old habits die hard." Then she leaned in closer to my ear and whispered, "So I drink moderately all day long."

"Art, please," he said. "And in that case, I'll open up a good bottle."

"Frank told me you had special bottles hidden away for special people," she said. "I'll consider myself privileged."

"Frank isn't one of those special people. I serve him from a bottle I keep behind the bar which he thinks is a vintage but it's just for him. A non-descript French table wine, I think."

Pierce laughed. Her face was open and her smile genuine. She was the type of woman who was comfortable with her looks, even the scar, likely because in her line of work, appearance wasn't the most important characteristic. Hart liked that. He wondered if she knew she exuded a natural sexual persona.

"I understand you just came back from fun-filled Columbia," he said.

The smile faded slightly as Hart poured a glass of Konzelman Pinot Noir from Canada's Niagara Region.

"I was dating a Columbian businessman for a while," she said, her expression a sour, reflective one. Hart cocked his head slightly. "The idea had been to infiltrate the organization through a safe vantage point," she added.

"By being the bad guy's girlfriend?" Hart asked.

"It's an old standard, I know," she said, taking another sip. "His flunkies checked me out," She suddenly looked away. "But he was infatuated and didn't let them dig too deep."

She was tough to figure out. Though she didn't flaunt her femininity, it was hard to believe she was a determined undercover agent who was willing to go the distance to get her man. She noticed him staring at her and frowned.

"You're trying to figure out if I slept with the enemy?"

Hart's last sip of wine tried to choke him. "Not really," he stammered, lying. "Do they really ask you to do that?"

"Not officially," she said, putting her hands on her hips in a very un-sexy manner. "But the idea is implied."

Hart had a hard time swallowing that and it must have shown on his face because she continued.

"I am smart, dedicated and determined, Mr. Hart. But I also have an asset other agents--male agents--don't have, and to deny using it means I would miss some great opportunities. I can go places most male agents can't. It's that simple. I've built my career on it."

Hart didn't think she was bragging, just being blunt. He sensed she knew she was no runway model. But she had to be aware of her allure as a strong, determined, and very sexy female. So, maybe not all agents were Bond girls. Maybe they were more girl-next-door attractive women who compensated by being brazen because their government demanded things from them that were, in his mind, unreasonable.

"If I was in the corporate world I'd probably sleep myself to the top. At least this way, I'm helping the public good, not just my own," she said.

"You're kidding, right?"

She smiled and took another sip of wine. "I don't think I'd last very long at a reception desk."

Hart frowned and she snickered at what she probably assumed was embarrassment on his part.

"So Uncle Sam tells his girls to seduce the bad guys," he said, knowing he should change the subject but not really wanting to. He was intrigued.

Not always," she said, patting his knee. His groin reacted to her touch again and he hopefully wondered if the electric current went both ways. "Okay, usually he does. But the bad guys are often loaded and love to spend money on their women. As a result, I get to occasionally live a life of leisure and opulence that a girl can get used to."

Hart smiled. JP Pierce was a breath of fresh air. And she must have evening dresses after all if she hung around with rich drug dealers. She was a woman who knew men were attracted to her and took advantage of that to get the job done. He watched her sip her wine as she perused the restaurant. She didn't take herself too seriously, which of course, made her that much more appealing.

"In the past, my criminal boyfriends have had a problem with commitment," she continued, "and more often than not I'm forced to break the relationship."

Hart pondered that momentarily, then smiled. "Because you arrest them?"

"Yes."

"And if they don't believe you're a federal agent?"

"I shoot them."

"That would work." he said and took a large gulp of wine.

They were quiet for a while.

"Frank trusts you," she said finally.

"Does he?" Hart responded, not sure what that meant. Frank was his best friend but we rarely discussed his day job.

"He's sending you with me to see Lena Lopez Castillo."

"She said she wanted a restaurant expert," he said. "And Frank says you're going to protect me."

She grinned. "I understand you're pretty good at looking after yourself."

Hart ignored that. "So why send you then?"

She looked at Hart then gave him a really big, silly grin.

"Frank seems to think Ms. Castillo has the hots for you," she said, grinning. "I'm supposed to discourage her, so you can do your job and she can concentrate on hers."

"That's silly. I'm old enough to be her father."

"Some women go for older men," she said. "Remember what I said about the Columbian being enamoured with me and spending all his money frivolously?" Her lips curled up at one side and her eyes sparkled. Hart cocked his head sideways.

"It works the other way around too," she continued. "In order for Frank to get all the information he requires, he may just expect you to sleep with her."

Hart downed the remainder of his wine in one gulp.

Robert J. Morrow

Chapter Twelve

"How the hell did you get in here?"

The tall Asian simply stared back. His hands were loose at his sides but he made no effort to hide his continuous flexing of fingers in and out of tight fists.

"We can't be seen together," Senator Andre Blais said. He was not used to being in situations he didn't control. And having the indirect, but very real, threat of violence in his presence was disconcerting, to say the least.

The Senator spent most of his time arranging for others to feel anxious in his presence. It was unnerving to have that activity reciprocated by someone he considered hostile, though admittedly, they were working together for the time being.

This was his home, and despite having hired a very expensive security company to protect it at all times, somehow the Asian had simply walked in. It was more than unnerving. It was unacceptable. After the Asian left, the Senator would be changing security detail.

"Okay, so you're here. What can possibly be so important at this stage that warrants a personal visit?" Blais said. "You could have picked up a phone, you know."

The Asian tipped his head sideways and frowned.

"Okay, so phones aren't an option," the Senator conceded with a sigh "But coming to my home is even riskier, don't you think?"

"I have not been noticed," the Asian said. His voice was monotone but concise. There was a slight accent but it was almost undetectable. "And I thought a face-to-face meeting would impress upon you the importance of the message."

The Senator couldn't believe the man's impertinence. Did he not realize who he was speaking to? The man had come to America many times representing his Korean manufacturing company. He could easily pass as a landed immigrant, and to anyone who asked, was nothing more than a travelling businessman, selling his country's wares to U.S. conglomerates. But Senator Blais knew better. The Asian's official status was only a cover for his real purpose. And as it happened, that purpose suited the Senator very nicely. Sure, it had taken a while to be convinced that working with the Asian was in his best interests, but the man had been very convincing, as had the various associates he had met. One man, a very interesting Asian/American he'd met in California a couple of months ago, was particularly intriguing. He was a landed immigrant who was, in fact, of royal descent. Although the man lived a normal American lifestyle, as an architect with an American wife, he travelled overseas regularly to fulfill his mostly figurehead-style royal duties in Korea. Blais had been fascinated with the dichomatic lifestyle. The Asian had introduced them for a reason; however, he hadn't revealed what that reason was yet.

The Asian had never been particularly friendly or forthcoming about his needs but of late his underlying vehement nature was becoming more predominant with each contact.

"We need privacy," the Senator said and motioned for the Asian to follow him from the kitchen where he'd been confronted, down a wide, high-ceilinged hallway to his study at the far end his large, Georgetown home. He briefly wondered what the Asian had done to his men in order to gain access to the house but knew it would be redundant to ask. If he'd disabled them, there was nothing the Senator could do about it. If he had just eluded them, however, there was a chance his men would come by and check on him, as they routinely did. The study was the best place for them to be found. Although in retrospect, he realized he would have a hard time explaining who the Asian was and how he had gotten into the house unannounced and unnoticed. And more importantly, why the Senator hadn't raised the alarm; God knows there were enough secret triggers located everywhere in the sprawling mansion.

The Senator didn't feel his life was in danger although he sensed that familiar aura of violence just below the surface of the Asian's demeanor. The sudden sight of him was disconcerting, but after the initial shock, the Senator's fear had ratcheted down a few notches.

"I'm concerned about the CIA involvement," the Asian said, following the Senator into the study and standing by the large leather couch that, along with two side chairs, formed an informal seating area set just in front of the Senator's very large, very wooden, and very old desk.

"We knew someone would be involved," the Senator said. "I had hoped for Military Intelligence but as so often happens when the President gets involved, the military are kept at arm's length until there's a need for boots-on-the-ground, so to speak."

The Asian's eyebrows raised briefly at the military reference but he quickly resumed his blank expression. "Frank Daro is a persistent player," he said. "And I had assumed the CIA would have no jurisdiction on U.S. soil."

"Look, it's better than having the FBI muddling around the facility," the Senator said. "At least Daro's people will be low profile," he continued. "And his involvement was at the request of the President, not the woman. "

"The woman did not object," the Asian stated, accepting a small snifter of expensive brandy that the Senator had poured from a decanter sitting on the corner of the desk. He placed the revolver on its side, in the center of the large, round, glass coffee table, within reach of both men, almost like an enticement.

How the hell did he know Castillo and the President had even met, the Senator wondered. He felt for his small caliber hand piece which was mounted under the chair, loaded and cocked. In a pinch, he would go for it but he sensed that the Asian would be very quick and the odds of him being able to pull it free, aim and fire before the agile man was on him, would be slim. He really didn't think it was going to come to that anyway, at least not yet. He watched as the Asian took a very slight sip of the brandy.

"Frank Daro is vying for a move to Homeland and the President likes the idea of him being involved. He's given him leeway, but it's not official," the Senator said.

"We were comfortable with the Secret Service involvement," the Asian said. "They were focused on protecting the President which meant nominal presence. But with the CIA on site, we have to be very careful about exposure."

"You had to be careful about that regardless," the Senator said, sipping his own brandy. He enjoyed the delayed sensation of liquid heat dripping down his esophagus and anticipated the burn once it hit his stomach. One of the advantages of old age was the deterioration of one's inner organs. In his youth, he needed several shots to acquire the burn in his stomach. Now, thanks to years of indulgence, his stomach lining was thin and fragile and he felt the burn instantly. It encouraged him but did not provide any level of bravado. "Perhaps having someone on site constantly will ensure you and your..." he thought for a moment, seeking the right word. "...your people... will guard the software even closer. "

"It is an unnecessary risk," the Asian said.

"It was inevitable," the Senator stated. "And now, any argument is redundant. The President has dictated CIA involvement via Daro. There is nothing I can do, other than redirect, ah... inquiries, when necessary."

"It will be difficult to test our ability to manipulate the software with the CIA wandering around freely," the Asian said. "It would be better if they were limited to everything except the lab."

"Their job is to guarantee Castillo can work unhindered," the Senator said. "They won't be looking over the technicians' shoulders. Besides, my understanding is that Daro is sending only one man, a chef for God's sake."

"Yes, and that is my concern," the Asian said.

The Senator took another sip of his brandy, it's warmth providing inspiration. "Why should one man concern you? He's not even an active operative, so I'm told. More of an observer. He won't get in the way."

The Asian eyed the Senator carefully.

"If he does, he may need to be eliminated," the Korean said.

The Senator blinked quickly. "If you kill someone Daro sent in, all hell will break loose and the facility will be crawling with CIA, FBI, NSA, and agents from every other alphabet agency in the arsenal."

The Asian thought for a moment, his eyes not moving but staring at the Senator.

"You just said he was not an agent," the Asian finally said. "I cannot guarantee what will happen." He stood, placed the empty snifter gently on the desk and started for the door.

"Why does this chef bother you so much?" the Senator asked, emphasizing the word *chef*. "You've managed to elude everyone so far. No one knows about our plans except you, your people, and me. Things are going well."

"Hmm," was all the Asian said as he continued to the doorway.

"I assume you'll find your own way out?" the Senator asked knowing it was a redundant question.

"I was never here," the Asian said and stepped out into the corridor.

"Next time, I'll come to you," the Senator called after him.

The Asian's head popped back around the corner of the study door.

"No Senator," he said, his voice lower and menacing, "If you ever approach me, it will be a breach of our understanding and you would regret the action, I assure you." He stared at the Senator for a few seconds. "If we need to talk again, I'll find you." He turned and continued down the corridor.

The Senator poured another inch of brandy into his snifter and sat back in his chair. He listened as the Asian's footsteps receded down the hall, fading away as he left the house, presumably the same way he had come in.

The Asian was right. But the Senator was beginning to question the *means to an end* mentality he had embraced. He was a patriotic American--had served in two wars-- and was willing to do anything to preserve the freedoms he had fought for. Which was why he had entertained the Asian's initial contact. The whole thing was unorthodox; hell, it was insane. But it was the right thing to do for America. The country couldn't keep going the way it was: financial turmoil every few years; military involvement in several overseas conflicts simultaneously; the always present threat of ISIS and Al-Quida; and alarming increases in unemployment and growing health-care system deficiencies. America needed new management, an influx of money, and maybe a new approach to how it dealt with both national and international issues. The Asian's presentation had initially seemed ludicrous, the stuff of science fiction movies. His superiors were a cabal of men who believed they were invincible and pre-destined to solve the world's problems. But after several clandestine meetings and one or two covert phone conversations, the Senator had been convinced. It was an unorthodox solution to the problem but the end did, in fact, justify the means. At least he had convinced himself of that. The Asian and his associates had assured him that he would be part of that solution but it did represent the first time he had made a decision that wasn't one hundred percent altruistic, and it could certainly backfire, very badly.

If the Senator's participation continued as he hoped it would, however, the Asian would become the catalyst for him to put in place the safeguards necessary to ensure the USA was able to respond to outside terrorist attacks quickly and efficiently, without massive loss of lives, or mis-communication, both of which had become common occurrences in recent wartime engagements.

Of course, should the Asian's plan not succeed, Blais had already set up a back-up plan. If the new regime didn't occur as the Asian said it would, at least their efforts would serve to sever the government's control over the economy, the social environment, even the very infrastructure of the country. Then Senator Blais' could step in and bring the country back from the brink of annihilation. He, Andre Blais, would be hailed as its savior, a leader emerging in the right place, at the right time. He smiled inwardly. He sounded like the anti-Christ and if he had been even remotely religious, he'd be scared shitless of his own ambitions. He also knew he would use that analogy sometime in the future to garner the confidence of the thousands of Americans who took Biblical prophecy much too seriously.

Robert J. Morrow

Chapter Thirteen

Hart hadn't been looking forward to his ex-wife's attempt at mending family dynamics and he wasn't to be disappointed. Predictably, the kids were upstairs in their rooms doing God knows what and Cynthia was putting the final touches on her meat and potatoes extravaganza. Which left Richard Hattis and Hart sitting at the dining room table trying to turn an unlikely meeting into a civil conversation. With nothing else in common, they had reverted to the intelligence business, the only common subject they had to discuss, other than Hart's family.

"I have often been asked to brief the President on matters concerning his activities," Hattis was saying, his chin lifting and his chest puffing a little. "Director Lazare has often said that I have an ability to understand all possible scenarios and gauge relative outcomes based on specific movements the President might make.

God, was he serious?

"So when a position for lead agent for advanced planning scenarios arose, I put in a request for an agency transfer," Hattis continued.

"I'm sure Lazare was sorry to see you go," Hart said. He was attempting sarcasm but it was probably true. Homeland Security's charter had broken the ice after 9/11, enabling official agency interaction and transfers between alphabet agencies for years now. But agency jumping was still a myth for the most part, regardless of what President Bush had intended when he first created the mammoth security agency. The CIA, FBI, and NSA particularly, would rarely share vital info or staff. It wasn't about control of territories, more about funding. Agencies chartered to look after security matters stateside--FBI, NSA, DEA, Secret Service, etc.-- were funded directly from monies allocated by senate committees. Full public disclosure was part of the deal.

The CIA, Homeland, Military Intelligence, etc., were also allocated funding, but it represented only 60% of the money those agencies received. With slush funds, secret accounts and the like, the agencies chartered to protect US interests overseas had virtually unlimited access to funding. As a result, these agencies were able to acquire more timely intel quickly, without concern for justification, and without the need to keep it legal. At least on the surface. They could also trade personnel easier. All of this Hart had picked up from Frank's various rants during family BBQ's and weekend campouts.

"I was able to apply directly to the Presidential Protection Division without going through the usual channels," Hattis said. "Frank Daro expedited the paperwork on my behalf."

Hart's eyebrows rose. So Frank was involved. Interesting. Moving Richard Hattis from the CIA to the Secret Service was more about putting an asset that followed rules into a role where he was better suited. Hattis played by the rules. Which was why, he realized, he had a chip on his shoulder about the man. What Frank gained from it--other than getting brownie points with his sister--was unclear. Those who played by the rules could live relatively normal lives. They worked nine-to-five, went for lunch regularly, and had families they went home to every night. Unfortunately, Hattis was going home to his family some nights. It wasn't Hattis himself, Hart realized. The guy was harmless for the most part. It was what he represented: a safe, reliable, and trustworthy provider who could also be a family man. He wondered if that was Frank's only motivation for moving things along.

Hart had never been able to achieve that role; working nine-to-five, and coming home every night to play doting husband and father. He had taken his work too seriously, working many evenings and weekends, and had often spent extra disposable income on toys like cars, motorcycles and the like.

"I hope you don't have a problem with me being here Arthur," Hattis said. His head had bowed slightly as if he wasn't sure how Hart would react. It seemed redundant to Hart.

"I don't live here anymore Richard," Hart said.

"I know that but the kids, you know, I mean..." he stammered.

"Yeah, well, Cynthia is a wonderful woman," Hart said, "and it seems you guys enjoy one another's company." He sounded like Doctor Phil. "So if she wants you here, it's her decision."

Hattis leaned back, cocked his head, and looked at Hart warily.

"I've been helping Jamie with his math," he said quietly. "I used to love math."

"I know," Hart said. "That you're helping, I mean. I didn't know you were a mathematician," he said, fully realizing how lame he sounded.

"Well, it just comes easy to me," he suggested, "that's all. I mean, I don't mean to be doing something you, ah... you might want to do."

Hart thought about several things he wanted to say but bit his tongue and chose, "If you're able to help him Richard, I'm sure it's a good thing. I can't even balance the restaurant's books, so it's not like I have a lot to offer."

Wow, Freudian slip or what?

"Jamie seems to need extra help understanding the questions," Hattis said, enthusiastically. "Once he understands what they're really asking, he's able to work it out, you know, slow but he gets there eventually."

"That's great Richard," Hart said. Where were the kids anyway? He didn't really want to discuss their educational needs any further. He needed to see them, not talk about them. Not with Richard *mathematician* Hattis, that was for damn sure.

"You boys talking shop?" Cynthia asked, bringing in a plate of crackers and cheese. Hattis smiled. Hart attempted a grin.

"The kids know I'm here?" he asked.

"Yes, I told them to give you two a few minutes to talk, then come down for dinner."

"We've talked," he said. "They can come down now."

Cynthia frowned, Hattis' cheeks fluttered slightly, and Hart pushed his chair back, got up and headed to the bottom of the stairs.

"Jamie, Lucy, let's go," he yelled up the stairs and out of the corner of my eye, watched as Cynthia began laying the table with various dishes. One held a large mound of garlic mashed potatoes, another, roast beef, sliced evenly, surrounded by small, oven baked and store bought Yorkshire puddings.

Hart turned his attention to the stairs as the kids stomped down, Lucy stopping just beside his leg, Jamie adjusting something on his iPod, large white headphones perched on the top of his head, pushed up from his ears.

"How about Fraticelli's?" he asked them, brushing Lucy's hair behind her ear and giving her a quick peck on the cheek. "We haven't been there for ages and I'm in the mood for some homemade Fettucine Alfredo, what do you think?"

"Dinner is ready Arthur. I've had this planned all week," Cynthia said, her hands on her hips, her eyes glaring. "I had hoped we could have a nice family dinner, just like always."

Hart pushed Lucy toward the front door gently, then gave Jamie a quick glance and after watching him shrug, turned toward his ex-wife.

"Not as always," he said.

"I thought it would be a chance for us all to become, ah.... acquainted, I guess. Get to know one another," she said, her hands dropping to her sides. Her eyes were still blazing and her cheeks were turning red. Hattis leaned back, his face expressionless.

"We won't be spending that much time together babe," Hart said and smiled inwardly when Hattis' eyebrows went up at the word 'babe'. "I think you guys should enjoy the fruits of your labor alone, you know, a nice romantic evening." He stepped toward the door where the kids were putting on their coats, oblivious to their mother's consternation. "We'll get out of your hair, give you a night off from family obligations, eh?"

Cynthia started to move toward them but Hattis put his hand on her arm gently. She didn't look at him but stopped moving.

Hart smiled. "Good luck in your new position Richard. I'm sure the President will appreciate your dedication and, ah, various other skills."

Hattis nodded. He got it.

Cynthia looked like she was straining on a leash. The fact that Hattis was able to hold her back by just touching her arm amazed Hart, but he was thankful. He didn't want a fight in front of the kids and especially not in front of the new boyfriend, but he also didn't want to be here any longer. He and Cynthia rarely fought but when they did it was like years of pent up anger releasing in an instant. She'd get over it, he knew. And if Hattis was as smart as he said he was, he would handle her.

"I'll have them back by ten," he said, opening the front door.

"Bye mommy," Lucy yelled as she ran out the front door. Jamie followed her, saying nothing but pushing the earphones down over his ears. Obviously he didn't realize the amazing meal he was missing out on. But then, he was ten. Hart was pretty sure food wasn't the most important thing on his mind these days.

As he closed the door, he caught a glimpse of Cynthia looking over the table, set for five, shaking her head vigorously. Hattis hadn't moved or said anything.

Hopefully, he liked leftovers.

Robert J. Morrow

Chapter Fourteen

Hart drove his thirteen-year-old BMW Z4 to pick up JP the next morning at the Sheraton Inner Harbor Hotel, downtown. They were heading four hours north to a town called Oswego east of Rochester in upstate New York, on the coast of Lake Ontario. They were going to meet with Lena Lopez Castillo and supposedly discuss catering. JP was supposed to scout out the facility. That was the plan. Frank hadn't elaborated. He just wanted them to go up there and meet the players on their turf.

"I have to stop off to see my daughter, do you mind?"

JP smiled. "How old is she?"

"Eight, going on seventeen," Hart said. "Are you sure you don't mind? I could drop you off at a coffee shop for a bit if you prefer."

"Don't be silly. I'm sure she doesn't bite."

Lucy didn't bite but her bark could be brutal if she wasn't happy about something, Hart knew. Visiting her before going on an overnight on the same day they were supposed to go to the movies was good reason for a little barking.

"If you're sure," he said, secretly welcoming the moral support.

Lucy's school was just off the highway in the Charles Village neighborhood where Hart used to live. It now housed his ex-wife, his ten-year-old son Jamie, eight -year-old daughter Lucy, and apparently, Richard Hattis upon occasion. Hart still paid for it and it was home to the entire family, including the tabby Leonard. The entire family except him, of course.

It was just past ten-thirty in the morning and recess was almost over. They walked to the gate at the edge of the frost fencing that surrounded the school's soccer field. All the kids from Grades One to Six played here during recess and Lucy always watched for him on the days he was supposed to come and usually came sauntering over as if she had all the time in the world. She waved when she saw her father.

"Hey kid" he said, bending down and pecking her on the cheek.

"Daddy, will you stop doing that?" she said, hands on hips in the manner that always reminded him she was related to his ex. "If you have to come here in the daytime, you can't embarrass me like that." She turned her attention to JP. "Hi," she said.

"Hi yourself. I'm JP."

Lucy stepped through the gate and walked up to JP, stopping just in front of her. She looked her straight in the eye. "Are you my Daddy's girlfriend?"

"Honey…" Hart started. JP held up her hand stopping him from continuing. She bent her knees and sat on her haunches so that her and Lucy's eyes were at the same level.

"Actually, your father and I just met, Lucy," she said, in a very soft, maternal voice. "I'm hoping we'll become friends." She smiled and Lucy just stared at her. "Maybe you and I can be friends too," she stated in the same soft voice. Lucy cocked her head and stared straight into JPs eyes for a few seconds.

"Sure," she said, and smiled. "What does JP stand for?"

Hart didn't interrupt this time. He was curious too.

"I can't remember," JP said, feigning deep thought. "My Daddy always called me that, so it just stuck. Guess my real name is too long."

Lucy thought about this for a moment then turned to me. "I guess this means we're not going to see Rainbow Rising tonight then?" she said, her mother's mocking tone clear, though a younger version.

Hart was always caught off guard when his little girl showed her perceptiveness so innocently. "Sorry sweetheart. Uncle Frank asked Daddy to do something for him. I forgot to tell you last night," he said and could hear the pleading in his own voice.

The girl watched him for a few moments, her face expressionless. "It's okay Daddy, I'm sure we'll have other plans," she said.

A knot began to form in Hart's stomach. Then he thought of something. "JP is coming to make sure it doesn't take more than a couple of days. So we can go see the movie Sunday night instead. That okay?"

The edge of JP's mouth rose slightly and she looked at Lucy again. They both grinned and JP got up and came to stand beside him. "I'll make sure he's back in time Lucy," she said. "Bye for now." Then she turned and walked to the car, leaving Lucy and Hart alone.

"I think she doesn't like her real name," Lucy said. "Maybe it's embarrassing or something." She then leaned in and gave him a hug. "Have a good trip Daddy. I'll see you Sunday."

He stroked her hair as her head nuzzled his stomach. "We'll have pizza after, okay?"

"Oh that's okay Daddy, Richard is taking us all out to Boston Pizza tomorrow night. I haven't had ice cream for a while though."

Oh, the innocence of a child. With one line, the knot became excruciatingly tight. And it hadn't even started yet. Richard. At least it wasn't stepdaddy, or worse, Mommy's boyfriend. Just Richard. For now.

"That's great honey," he said, edging his smile wider just for effect. "You behave and keep close to Mommy okay?"

She looked at him quizzically, then turned back to the schoolyard. "Gotta go Daddy."

As she went through the gate she turned to wave. "I like your friend Daddy. She's pretty."

Hart nodded and waved back.

"You're very good with children," he said to JP when he got back into the car. She smiled.

"I was a girl once, you know," she said. "I think you may have disappointed her."

Hart gave her a cold stare, then after a moment, relented and it turned into a frown. "I tend to do that frequently," he said. "I'm trying to be better but it doesn't help when I keep introducing new, ah... people into her life."

"You mean other women," she stated.

"The last one looked down at her and called her 'sweety'," he said, smirking. "Lucy hates that. You used her name and got down to her level. That's very intuitive."

"Francis had two young girls," she said, her smile fading.

"Francis?"

"The guy I sent to prison," she said. "It taught me how to deal with disappointed little girls."

Chapter Fifteen

After an hour of driving, Hart decided it would be a long trip made in silence.

"So I gather you are good at what you do?" he asked.

"What I do?"

"Well, I assume that's why Frank has sent you along with me on this little escapade," he said. She was giving him a strange look, her head cocked sideways slightly, brows raised, eyes intense. "Well, it's not like I need an assistant or anything." She continued to stare. He stared back, not sure what to say next, if anything. Suddenly her raised eyebrows lowered and her mouth curled up slightly at one end. She started chuckling. So he chuckled too, thankful that the stare hadn't continued. It had been a bit menacing.

"You're wondering if I'm here to pick up Losano?" She said, still smiling.

"He's gay," Hart said.

She grinned.

"What you do is your business. It's none of mine, of course." he said. "Frank must have immense faith in your ability to do what you do." He stopped talking. Maybe silence would have been better after all. He looked over. She was still grinning.

"Well, I don't do women," she said. "Uncle Sam may demand that of some but I definitely draw the line there."

"I didn't mean to infer…"

"Maybe you don't like the idea that Frank sent a girl to keep you safe?" she said, on the edge of full out laughter. "So you figure

I must be here to either pick up the partner, or keep Castillo away from you?"

Hart decided silence was his best option at this point. She watched him for a moment but he just concentrated on the road.

"Maybe I'm here to seduce you, make sure you do what Frank wants," she said, watching him. He took a quick look but her stare revealed nothing and her grin was gone. Her eyes were a deep green and almost sparkling, very intense. But there didn't seem to be a whole lot of warmth there. He turned his eyes back to the road. Eventually she turned away and stared out the windshield instead, seeming to assess the various and endless shades and shapes of green whipping past us at sixty miles per hour.

"My job is to assess the location," she said finally. "The President will eventually be coming and I'm what you call the front man, I suppose. Check it out, make sure the facility is something we can secure with minimal exposure."

Hart looked over but she was still looking out the windows as if the shrubbery whizzing by was of great importance and needed her undivided attention. What she'd said was bullshit of course, Hart thought. If her specialty was taking down drug lords from the inside, it seemed a stretch to think the Secret Service would waste her talents on what was essentially scouting out a location. He thought maybe Richard Hattis might be better suited to that type of mundane task. Then he shook his head. He would definitely rather have JP than Richard in the passenger seat right now. Her real mission was probably closer to what she'd first said: To make sure he did Frank's bidding.

She put her hands in her lap and clasped them tightly, then rubbed them around as if trying to keep warm. It was about seventy-five degrees in the car though. She looked down, seemingly surprised at what she was doing and quickly moved her hands stiffly to her sides. Hart kept his eyes straight ahead, though he could see from his peripheral vision that she gave him a quick glimpse to see if he'd noticed. He played dumb. His ex often said he was good at that.

They were silent for the next few miles, then she shifted in her seat and looked at him.

"I asked for a different kind of assignment," she said, her voice adamant, as though she was trying to convince herself of something. "I needed a break from the... ah, regular routine, you know."

Hart just nodded. Didn't turn his head to look at her. He wasn't good at warm and fuzzy; something else his ex had told him.

"Frank says you're not a letch and he figures the girl will see you as a father figure--eventually," she said. He caught the twitch at the corner of her lip.

"A father figure, huh," he said quietly.

"You can keep an eye on her--unofficially, make sure she isn't trying to do something sinister, like take over all communications in the US, or something," she said. She straightened herself and looked out the side window. "I'll try to get close to Losano but like you said, he won't be enamoured with my charms."

"Stupid man," he said, hoping to lighten the mood. He didn't do introverted or serious well either.

She smiled though it didn't reach her eyes. "What's your deal with Frank anyway?" she asked. "I mean, he told me you weren't agency, so what's your connection?"

"I used to be. But it didn't work out. I wasn't a spy or anything, just, well--part of the support team, you know." He took in a deep breath. "But he's my ex-brother in law," he said. "So he keeps hanging around. Thinks he's looking out for me."

"By putting you in harms way?" she said, looking at him quizzically.

He thought about that for a minute. Initially, his main reason for going along with another of Frank's feeler missions was for points. Castillo wanted to ensure the experience at her compound would be a memorable one for all her visitors, especially the President. If Hart's minor involvement instilled confidence in her, then Frank would be happy. And when Frank is happy, he arranges more events at the *Hart*. Which meant more guaranteed income.

Running a restaurant wasn't the easiest way to get rich. Clientele were fickle, and constant menu changes to satisfy the transient tastes of the off-Washington crowd could get expensive.

Thankfully, Al Rocca was more of a partner than an employee. The hours he spent experimenting and organizing the menu changes, along with all the ingredient ordering and training of staff, was never accounted for financially: Al took the same pay home every two weeks, regardless of how much time he spent at the Hart. It was his second home, or more likely his first. Although he and Hart had never discussed it, they both know that when it came time to retire and sell the place, they would share whatever profit there was. Hart just hoped there was some profit. And catering--pun intended--to Frank's whimsical maneuverings was a sure way to keep the money flowing.

Lately, the books had been showing more red than black. And Frank probably knew that. Maybe he was throwing Hart a bone, maybe he really thought he could help. It didn't matter. The *Hart* needed Frank, so if Frank needed Hart, he'd show up.

Of course, Hart also knew Frank had other motives. Sending Hart up was a way to get eyes on the situation unofficially. And yes, he knew Hart could handle minor skirmishes if they popped up; that was what he had been trained to do. But when and if he felt he needed pro's up there, he'd pull Hart out and send them in. He hoped. His job would be to keep the peace with the *person of interest* and make Frank look good. JP would be getting all the official info Frank needs.

But Castillo had inadvertently offered Hart another opportunity too. He did love to cook, ever since he'd been forced to feed himself as a teenager once his Mother and Father had divorced. He loved the idea that he owned a restaurant. But he wasn't dense. He knew that without Al, the consistency and innovation the *Hart* was growing famous for would never continue. This was a chance for him to do some experimenting too, a chance for him to see what he'd learned, and whether he was capable of pulling something of this magnitude off... without Al's help.

He also planned on charging Frank an exorbitant fee.

Chapter Sixteen

For the rest of the trip, they talked about cooking, music and eventually how the internet worked on power lines. JP had been studying up on it over the past week and seemed sufficiently knowledgeable on the subject. Hart was surprised to learn that in 2012, President Obama's use of an executive order gave Homeland Security ultimate power to take over all internet communications in a state of national emergency.

"To give one agency, government or otherwise, the power to control all communications entirely, without debating it in Congress, had a lot of politicians wondering if Obama had an ulterior motive," she explained.

"Like what? Hart asked.

"Like turning communications into a government-run commodity," she said. "You know, like a utility company or something along those lines."

"That would likely make it cheaper," Hart offered.

"It would effectively put the big guns out of business," she said. "AT&T, Bell, Rogers, all the carriers would either have to continue under government contract, or cut back overhead dramatically in order to compete."

"But President Emerson can't invoke it without a national emergency, right?" he said.

She deadpanned a stare.

After a moment the light bulb went off. "You think he wanted to create one?"

JP shrugged. "The Office of the President can do a lot of things," she said. "And over time, regardless of whether it's a Republican or Democrat in the Oval Office, eventually an emergency will arise. And that's when the government will pounce, take over the internet, and control communication. Once the emergency passes, you think they'll just hand back the reigns?"

"So you don't think it was just Obama's idea?" Hart asked.

"No, I think the powermongers in Washington have been planning this ever since Google became a household word and Facebook started socializing the world," she answered. "They've just been waiting for two things: A President that agreed with them, and someone to invent a foolproof method to serve the whole country," she said. "Emerson is a power-hungry leader. And Castillo may have just come up with the rest of the equation."

They both thought about that in silence. Ten minutes later they passed a sign announcing the road heading north to the Town of Oswego. The Port of Oswego was the head of a canal system that ended up pouring into the Hudson River, thereby allowing small vessels to transport from The St. Lawrence Seaway and Lake Ontario, out into the Atlantic, via New York City. The town had a storied and exciting history, especially during the 1800s, but was now little more than a starting point for recreational water travel from ports in the Great Lakes to the Eastern US and even the Caribbean. It was, however, right next door to Scriba, a small suburb noted for housing both the James A. FitzPatrick and Nine Mile Point Nuclear Power Plants. Both were located on the Lake Ontario waterfront just a few miles east of the town proper.

Hart followed the sexy British girl's GPS voice along Highway 481 into town and past the Highway 104 exit leading to the power plants and continued along East 1st street toward the Lake. Lena Castillo's facility was on the lakeshore between downtown Oswego and the outskirts of Scriba, less than two miles from the power plants.

After driving through the small but lively downtown, Hart found East Cayuga and then East Seneca, and followed the road out of town which eventually became Lake Road. After ten minutes, he located the road that would lead down to the waterfront and after two or three minutes arrived at what looked like an abandoned warehouse from a previous age, overlooking the vast blue lake. Beside it was an electrical substation with hundreds of overhead cables running the two or three hundred yards farther into the forest and eventually, Hart knew, to the Nuclear Plant itself. The warehouse was much older than the substation or the plant and Hart figured it dated back to early 1900's or even late 1800's. Lake Ontario was, after all, part of the Great Lakes shipping lane, where goods still travelled from the Atlantic to southern Canada and the mid northwestern States, as far west as Chicago.

Three stories high, all brick, with windows boarded up on the side facing the street, Lena Lopez-Castillo's renovated facility looked like anything but the site of the next breakthrough development in communication infrastructure. Even the massive carriage-style garage adjoining it looked to be original, complete with rusting door levers.

The gravel parking lot held spaces for about twenty vehicles and half of them were full with vehicles that looked completely out of place in this out of the way wilderness. Most notable were a new Porsche Boxter and one of those sporty four door coupes that were allowing Cadillac to make a comeback via Generation Xers. Hart parked, got out and opened JP's door, leading her toward the only entrance on this side, adorned by two massive and ancient-looking wooden doors. As they approached, one of them opened and a short Oriental man beckoned them.

"Would you be Mr. Hart?" he asked with a slight European accent.

Hart nodded and followed JP over the threshold and into a large foyer with twenty-five foot ceilings and a grand, heavy, curved wooden staircase adorning the centre of the space.

"Right out of an Agatha Christie movie," JP muttered under her breath.

"And completely out of place," Hart added quietly.

The man lead them to the left where double French doors opened into a large reception room, complete with high-mantle fireplace and heavily cushioned, overstuffed four-person couches facing one another in the centre of the room. To the right, a huge picture window dominated the entire wall and beyond, a stunning view of Lake Ontario, it's gentle waves extending as far as the eye could see. Hart hadn't realized how vast the Great Lake was. He couldn't see the other side and felt as though he was looking out at a very calm ocean. He also couldn't hear the waves breaking along the nearby dockside but his stomach felt them.

"Please help yourself to cocktails." the man said, pointing to a large bar set against the far wall, three stools appropriately placed in front. "Ms. Lopez-Castillo will be with you momentarily." And with that he turned and left the room, closing the doors gently behind him.

Above the fireplace, a large painting of an older, round-faced, darker skinned gentleman hung. He was dressed in a pin-striped double-breasted suit and stood in front of what looked like a hotel lobby.

"I wonder if it came with the building?" Hart said.

"Hmmm," came from JPs mouth, though her lips never moved. She put her forefinger to her lips and seemed to be kissing the middle knuckle until Hart realized she was shushing him. He raised an eyebrow. She nodded and circled the room with her finger. Spy paranoia. Hart shrugged and walked behind the bar to see how well it was stocked. Finding a bottle of Famous Grouse, he pulled two glasses from an upper shelf and poured an inch of the fine scotch into each glass. He then searched around for an ice bucket or even a freezer of some sort but to no avail. So he gave up and walked back to JP, handing her a glass.

"Aren't butlers supposed to do that?" she asked

"Frank neglected to tell you I put myself through high school as a bartender."

JP gave him a quizzical look, her lip curling at one end. Then she looked at the scotch in her glass. "And this is the best you can do?" she said, smiling.

He stuck out his tongue which stunned her momentarily. Then she returned the gesture, her pink extrusion curling slightly at the tip.

Now that's sexy.

There were several framed pieces of artwork on each of the walls but oddly, they were all photographs, albeit artistically done. Most depicted scenes from a sunny, southern location.

"Caribbean," JP said.

"How do you know?"

"I suppose it could be Central America too," she admitted, her eyebrows lifting in question.

"It is often mistaken for Cuba." The voice came from the doorway as Lena Lopez-Castillo strode in closing the doors behind her. She wore a no-nonsense dark skirt, a peasant top, and flats. So much for the ultra-chic businesswoman look. Still, she was young, vibrant and wore a knock out smile.

She walked straight up to Hart and extended her hand. He shook it. Very soft, very feminine, though he noticed she had short nails, likely so she could manipulate computer keyboard keys without hindrance.

"My family built hotels in Mexico," she said, pointing at another picture below the one we had been looking at. It depicted a resort situated on the edge of a beach. Her voice was as Hart had remembered it: soft spoken but forceful and with only a slight Latino accent. "This is now an all-inclusive resort on the Mayan Peninsula. It was originally one of the first hotels my father helped build nearly fifty years ago."

She turned to JP, smiled, and shook her hand too. "I was told Mr. Hart would bring an associate. I didn't realize you would be, ah... I mean you would be a woman. I was expecting Mr. Rocca."

Hart tilted his head. "You have done your homework Ms. Lopez Castillo," Hart said. "But although I value Mr. Rocca's insights greatly, unfortunately, someone has to mind the store while I'm gone. This is JP Pierce and she specializes in arranging seating, decor and the like. An event planner, if you will." We had come up with that on the trip up. JP seemed more comfortable with staging than food-related topics. She was afraid Ms. Castillo or Jay Losano would know more about food than she did and her cover would be blown before it was ever established.

"Please, call me Lena. Ms. Lopez-Castillo is too much of a mouthful, even for me." She gestured for them to sit on one of the couches and then she moved to the other one and poured herself a glass of red wine from a carafe that had been on the large glass coffee table.

"We were never formally introduced at your restaurant last week Mr. Hart, but as I trust you are aware, I was thoroughly impressed with your establishment and your fare." Castillo's eyes exuded friendliness and sincerity, yet something in her voice sounded contrived.

"Which is why we're here," he said, smiling in return, trying not to sound contrived myself. "And please call me Art."

"Indeed," she said. "Short for Artichoke, I'm told," she said, her eyes sparkling. "Thankfully I had Jose put together a decent platter of appetizers we can enjoy in the rear dockside patio. I trust it meets with your approval. I can assure you Jose was concerned when I informed him the famous *Artichoke Hart* would be having cocktails with us. I think he rustled up a decent bottle of Zinfandel though and despite the fare not being what I would consider gourmet, I am assured he uses the freshest ingredients we can muster in this rather fertile part of the country.

"You are too kind," JP said in a voice inflected with a sultry sensuality Hart hadn't heard till now. Maybe she'd changed her mind about going after the woman in this arrangement.

Lena looked at her strangely and then, standing up, pointed toward another set of French doors which lead to a patio. "Shall we? Lake Ontario is hardly the Caribbean but on a warm summer day, it's easy to pretend, don't you agree?"

JP and Hart stood up and Lena came over and put her arm through his, leading him toward the doors. JP followed behind.

"Would you mind grabbing the bottle, Ms. Pierce?" she said over her shoulder and without waiting for an answer, steered Hart out to the patio.

Hart gave JP a quick mock smile, then allowed himself to be lead outside to an ornate wooden dining table situated in the centre of the patio. The woman was almost young enough to be his daughter but that didn't stop him from admiring the shape of Ms. Lena Castillo's behind when he pulled out a chair for her. He sat next to her, facing the lake, and JP pulled out a chair on the opposite side, placing the wine carafe in the centre of the table, her eyebrows furrowing slightly.

"I apologize for what must seem like a long excursion just to discuss catering a conference, Art," she said, placing her hand gently on Hart's thigh. The patio had been built on a deck protruding from the building itself. The water's edge was less than twenty feet away, marked by an ancient concrete dock which ran the full length of the building. A tiny sliver of grass beginning beneath the deck was all that separated the dock and the rough, rock-strewn waters edge. Hart recalled reading somewhere that although you thought you were looking at the curve of the earth when facing a vast waterscape like this, your eyes could only see approximately twelve miles at ground level. Hart didn't know how far the Canadian border was but figured it was a lot more than twelve miles from this location.

"This is a magnificent building," JP said

Castillo smiled. "It was originally a supply depot for local shipping companies built in 1888. Then it gained notoriety as a brewery during prohibition. In the late 1990s a developer purchased it for conversion but since it was listed on the national Register of Historic Places in 2010, he felt the restoration costs would be too exorbitant since his intention had been to convert them to, ah... I call them flats."

"Condo's" Hart suggested.

"Yes, condos," she agreed. "But my offer was more in line with what the seller had in mind."

Meaning she'd probably paid too much.

"And you've done all the renovations?" JP asked, her coquettish demeanor continuing to amaze Hart.

"I hired a local architectural company to handle the remodelling last year," she said, "once we had satisfied the Historic Committee and determined this was the ideal location for our project."

"You've made it very aristocratic, and maintained much of the original heavy timber post and beam structure," Hart said. "When you're ready to sell, I could turn it into a lovely restaurant."

Castillo laughed. "I may take you up on that, Art. It would be nice to recover the insane amount of money it has taken to convert the building to what you see today."

Hart wanted to ask where all that money had come from but figured now wasn't the time.

"If it is meant to impress, Ms. Castillo, it certainly does," JP said.

"Please, call me Lena," she said, her eyes never leaving Hart's despite addressing JP. "I designed it so it wouldn't seem like a laboratory. I spent a lot of time in a University lab in Los Angeles and always felt it was too clinical an environment. Since I also have to live here, I felt some creature comforts wouldn't hurt."

"Your equipment is in this building then?" he questioned.

"The first two floors are living and entertainment space, the third is the laboratory and test facilities, and the attic level is a mass of cables and wiring, I'm afraid. We left that floor in pretty much its original state. The kitchen is on this floor, between this room and the lounge, all of which face the lake also."

"Which is where I come in, I presume," Hart said.

"I assure you, it is of the utmost importance that my guests receive the absolute best hospitality I can offer," she said. "You see, I will be asking them for a great deal of money in exchange for licensing my software." She smiled. "I was told by your superiors that your fare is unsurpassable, which is why they utilize it every chance they can."

"I don't work for the government, Lena," he said, shifting his legs, forcing Castillo to remove her hand. He wasn't about to explain that Frank liked the *Artichoke Hart* because of the listening equipment he'd installed, not necessarily the food.

She offered a dismissive gesture with her freed hand.

"You come highly recommended was what I meant, of course, and I feel confident such experiences with people like your good friend, Mr. Daro make you ideally suited for the diverse natures and palettes of other world leaders, which does, by the way, comprise much of my guest list." She leaned back and turned toward JP, as if assuming this was enough to satisfy any concerns he may have had.

"And your role in all of this will be what, Ms. Pierce?" she asked, sipping her wine. Hart could tell JP didn't like the *Ms* thing coming from someone ten years her junior. She shook her head, enough that her hair bobbed momentarily. "I am here to assess what will be needed to turn your establishment into a suitable Presidential venue," she said, a little curtly Hart thought, especially with the emphasis of the word *suitable*.

"Sort of like a caterer then," Lena said, her smile as ingenuous as possible.

"How many are we to anticipate attending this, ah…conference?" Hart asked, hoping to diffuse any sudden animosity between the two females. Neither JP or Lena looked at him right away, but eventually JP sat back, sipped her scotch and turned slightly to look out over the water.

"I like to think of it as my own G20 summit," Castillo said, after turning toward Hart. "Most of the civilized and some of the not-so civilized world will have representatives in attendance. This is why I was meeting with General Wade and his associates last week when Assistant Director Daro kindly invited me to your little get-together."

Hart didn't think it necessary to tell her the whole get together had been for her benefit.

Lena sighed. "People of diverse interests are often brought together through the most unfortunate of circumstances, "she said, reaching over and squeezing his hand. "It was fortuitous that I attended your fine establishment Art, as I am now convinced your expertise in this area is perfect for my event."

"My expertise?" Hart asked.

"Why yes, Mr. Daro is apparently well acquainted with your skills in event management and did, in fact, suggest to President Emerson that you would be ideally suited to the task at hand."

Frank was pushing the limits a bit this time, Hart thought. He had told her that before talking to him about any of it. "How many people in total, Lena?" he asked.

"My business partner--I believe you met him at your restaurant--should be joining us momentarily. He has the current count at just under one hundred and fifty."

Hart gulped. Frank was definitely out of his mind. He ran a restaurant. Catering an event for a over a hundred and fifty people at once was the work of a full-fledged catering company, not a sixty-seat restaurant owner.

Castillo had missed Hart's sudden discomfort but JP certainly hadn't.

"Actually Lena" JP exaggerated the name, "I will be the liaison between the *Artichoke Hart* and your conference."

"In that case, I am even more confident that we have chosen perfectly," Castillo said, her spurious smile invading her face again.

"But what experience do you have in this area, Ms. Pierce?" The voice was high pitched and soft, almost a whisper, and carried from the man who had just emerged from behind one of the columns supporting the rear portico.

"Ah, my partner Jay Losano," said Castillo, not looking up but waving a hand in Losano's direction. "Aside from being less than punctual, my partner is also direct if not occasionally rude. May I present Ms. JP Pierce," she said, pointing across the table. "Mr. Hart you have already met, I believe."

If it had meant to be a reprimand Jay Losano didn't take it as such. Whatever the relationship between these two clearly Losano wore the pants some of the time. Regardless, sensing neither of them was going to explain further, JP addressed the newcomer as if in the middle of a job interview.

"I have spent a good deal of time cultivating contacts within various government agencies and ministries, making good use of the success we have had with Director Lazare and Assistant Director Daro," JP said. "Whenever there are, shall we say, *delicate* discussions to be accomplished during official visits, I am asked to prepare what I call a venue/menu package that allows the guests to speak freely in an environment that is up to the standards of world leaders."

Holy crap, that was good. Hart didn't think she'd just made it up though. Maybe Frank had come up with it.

Losano stood just in front of the table, his arms folded across his chest. Castillo leaned back in her chair. She had edged away from him a little, he'd noticed. In fact, he thought she was clearly distancing herself from this discussion.

"But Ms. Castillo, you don't show up on any payroll records for the *Artichoke Hart* nor do you seem to have been there very long."

JP stared at him. Castillo said nothing. Hart wondered how he could possibly know that. Clearly, this was Losano's interview now.

After a few moments of silence Hart leaned forward in his chair. "Miss Pierce doesn't actually work for me."

JP angled her head in wonder and gave him a glare that said "what the hell are you doing?" but both Losano and Castillo turned their attention to Hart.

"Let's cut to the chase folks," Hart said, standing up and reaching out his hand to Losano who, visibly confused with the gesture, shook it. Hart motioned for him to take a seat and sat down again himself. Castillo smiled. Losano slowly pulled out a chair and sat.

"The catering thing is an excuse," he said.

"I beg your pardon?" Losano said.

"We cater a lot of get-togethers for the CIA at the *Hart*. They often need a private, secure place to meet and discuss operations, projects, heavens knows what," he said. "Deputy Director Frank Daro and I have been friends a long time and he trusts me, so he doesn't have to do worry about me giving away state secrets."

"And Ms. Pierce here?" Losano asked, looking at me, his manicured eyebrows furrowing.

"JP works for the Secret Service," Hart said.

There was silence momentarily, then Losano laughed. "That's rich," he said.

Castillo turned to look at JP who was in turn, staring at Hart, her mouth agape.

"Obviously, your activities here are of the upmost importance to our nation and others," Hart continued. "So in his ultimate wisdom, Mr. Daro has sent along someone who understands how to deal with important political figures from various countries. That, I'm sure, is just as important to you as, ah… getting the menu down."

JP, unable to speak, stared at all of them one at a time, waiting for someone to either smile or pull out a gun, Hart supposed. The former action prevailed and after a moment, Losano's' snickering broke the tension.

"Interesting revelation, Mr. Hart," Castillo said, smiling broadly. "So I guess we don't have to worry about Ms. Pierce giving away any secrets either?"

Recovering somewhat, JP addressed Losano who was still smirking at Hart who just grinned.

"My function, Mr. Losano..." she turned and smiled widely, "...Ms. Castillo, is to ensure that our visiting dignitaries are in a safe environment. That is the Secret Services' mandate. Working with Arthur and his staff right from the beginning allows me to understand what is going on at all times during the main event. I'm sure you understand that the United States Government cannot allow any activity involving national security to take place without incorporating full security protocols at all times."

"Now you sound like Secret Service," Losano said, his chuckling barely held in check. He seemed to be enjoying JPs embarrassment.

"Not so secret now, unfortunately," JP said, almost under her breath, looking straight at Hart.

If looks could kill, he thought.

Losano laughed again. "It appears, Lena, that we can count on Mr. Hart to be candid and forthcoming."

"A trait we greatly admire," Castillo agreed. She leaned in and clasped Hart's hand yet again. He made no attempt to remove it.

JP had fully recovered now and Hart could see her eyes sparkling again. Was it from relief or annoyance?

"Arthur underestimates his role in this, gentlemen," she said. "His job is to create meals that will appeal to a dizzying array of tastes, incorporating myriad cultural restrictions and expectations. It is my experience that only when men of this calibre feel they have been treated as royalty, will they be open to discussing investment in a country other than their own."

"Astute, Ms. Pierce, very astute," Losano said. "Indeed, our goal is to loosen the purse strings of leaders who may or may not see the immediate benefit of doing so. The way to a man's heart is through his stomach, so they say."

"Perhaps a bomb would be in order then?" Hart asked. Both Castillo's and Losano's heads snapped to look at him. He offered his killer smile. "A torte folks. The famous Bomb torte is often served at dinners where heads of state are in attendance."

This time JP laughed. It wasn't as hearty as Losano's. Actually, it seemed a bit strained.

"You're a real piece of work, Mr. Hart," Losano said. "I hope your food is as good as your wit."

"I agree," said Castillo, letting go of Hart's hand and patting his knee. She pulled a small notebook from her pants pocket and opened it up. "So far we have eleven countries committed to coming. I wonder what you would suggest for a main course?"

Losano pushed back his chair and reached for JPs hand. "Since you're not really involved in the menu after all, perhaps I can give you a tour of the building. I would imagine our existing security systems would interest you more, no doubt?"

JP hesitated only momentarily, then turned her hundred-watt smile at Losano. "That would be very kind of you, yes."

"When you're done Jay, perhaps you'll bring Ms. Pierce to the lounge," said Castillo. "We'll all have a parting drink. Say half an hour?" Losano nodded and steered JP toward the doors leading inside.

Hart winked.

JP rolled her eyes.

Robert J. Morrow

Chapter Seventeen

An hour later they were back in the car, heading into town.

"Do you think Losano is dark and dangerous?" Hart asked.

She appeared to be thinking.

"He's definitely intriguing," she said finally, "and a little shady. But dangerous? Not physically. He has that rich kid vibe and that un-earned gangsta swagger that comes from being the son of a mobster, even a small time one."

"Frank thinks he's a master criminal," Hart said. "Says the technology already works and that they've tested it in a few places already--including my restaurant."

"I heard about that," she said. She was silent for a moment then added, "Frank's hunches are usually good I hear."

Hart was about to laugh but gave her a quick glance. Her mouth was tight, her gaze fixed on the space outside the car.

"You've worked with Frank before?" he asked, surprised that he had never mentioned JP Pierce to him before.

"Just the one time, in Columbia" she admitted, "but I spent a lot of time in small rooms with him going over all the intel. He has a knack for knowing what the bad guys are thinking." She shifted in the seat, stretching her legs out as far as she could in the confines of the car.

"Three years ago, the Corgena cartel were having a rare upper-echelon meeting and he got me invited as a... well, a guest. The youngest son and American liaison to the South American export business took a liking to me, as Frank had hoped. No one thought we had enough to do them any damage at that point, so he left me in place to see what I could get. He and others felt I would be able to get the missing information we needed to attack the organization in several places at once." She continued to gaze at nothing. "He was right," she said after a moment.

"That's the guy you shot?" Hart asked. Frank had told him she'd been undercover for the past eight months. She turned back to him and he noticed a couple lines etched deeply across her forehead.

"I got involved in his life," she said. "It got confusing. I needed to end it."

Being nosy is usually not a good thing, so Hart stopped talking. After a while, she continued.

"He was a generous, fun-loving man," she said, a small smile pulling her upper lip up. "He was exciting to be with, loved life and could afford to enjoy all that life can offer."

Hart said nothing but stared at the road ahead.

"But he came from a family of greedy, murderous cockroaches." Her tone was steely, the smile gone, her native heritage surfacing as she slurred the 'ch' in cockroaches. "He never stood a chance against them. He was their puppet on American soil. His job was to legitimize all they were doing in South America, and smooth the process of transporting goods into the US."

"You liked him."

She laughed. Not a happy laugh but one tinged with sadness.

"Yes, I liked him. The family business wasn't in his blood. But he was good to me. I think he may have loved me," she said, the frown deepening. "Right up until the moment I shot him."

"You killed him?"

Her head spun to face Hart.

"No, I shot him in the leg. To stop him from escaping," she said sternly. Her cheeks were flushed but the tautness slackened quickly and she turned to face the front again. "I hadn't aimed for his leg but it did the job. When I last saw him, he was being handcuffed and staring at me with disbelief."

"You were just doing your job." *What else could I say?*

"What I do goes way beyond doing a job," she said turning back to the outside view. "I destroy people... from the inside out." She breathed deeply, her chest rising high and settling just a little more upright than she had been. "And I'm good at it."

Hart had no idea what to say or where this had come from so he drove on in silence. He glanced over after a few moments and saw that JP was deep into reflection. He left her to her thoughts.

Robert J. Morrow

Chapter Eighteen

They had already decided it would be too much to drive to Oswego and back in one day, so Frank's staff had booked them in at the Beacon Hotel near the waterfront.

They arrived around suppertime, checked into separate rooms, and decided that since Frank was footing the bill they were going out for a decent meal. The rooms were adjoining and while Hart was emptying his bag and freshening up, he heard a tap on the connecting door.

He unlocked it and JP strode in. She was smiling and there was a bounce in her walk. Obviously, reflection time was over.

"What do you feel like?" she asked.

"I feel like trading the car in for a quick flight home and catching the band I booked for the weekend at the *Hart*", he said, "but I'll settle for some comfort food somewhere in town with a decent glass of wine."

"Gee, I hope I'm not intruding," she said.

"Not at all, though Frank must not have much faith in my seduction skills," he said, pointing at the adjoining door. JP smiled.

"I think he's hoping someone else will want to seduce you," she said, "but I never tire of having handsome men giving it their best shot. You never know."

Hart laughed. "Well that sounds promising. Let's pretend we don't know Frank for a few hours and see if we can't make this trip worthwhile."

"Frank who?" she said. "You want to try downstairs?"

"Heavens no!" Hart said. "Contrary to popular belief, hotels do not house the best restaurants."

"So says the independent restaurateur," she said.

"We'll ask the concierge," he said.

Ten minutes later, they were headed to La Parrilla Grill and Wine Bar downtown. The hotel clerk said it was the most popular spot for travelling businessmen. Hart wasn't sure if that was the kind of recommendation he was looking for but with no other choice other than to drive around a town they didn't know, they decided to check it out.

The La Parrilla turned out to be a charming, family-run establishment that cooked all entrees from scratch and had with a decent wine menu. After spending most of the day on the road, it sounded perfect to Hart.

"You'd think Castillo would have bought something a little closer to the power plant," Hart said, munching on a beef carpaccio appetizer and some ciabatta bread that he was using to dip into a nicely aged, smooth virgin olive oil.

"Apparently, property around Scriba is pretty dismal," JP said. "No one wants to spend their lives too close to the nuclear plants, and no developer in his right mind would try to sell a suburb that close to potential disaster these days. Except for a few small communities, including Scriba itself, there aren't many places with properties worth more than $50-100,000 dollars. A lot of them, along the Lake Ontario shoreline, are like cottages. Apparently, it's beautiful."

"You realize the plants are actually farther north than Fort Erie, the lowermost point of Canada?"

"Thanks for the geography lesson," she said, chewing the raw meat thoroughly before swallowing. "What's the significance?"

"It's cold," he said. "Right in the snow belt. With a choice of all the power plants in the country, why pick one of the most northernmost ones, where weather might hinder installation of hardware?"

"The Heritage plant is a standalone," JP said. "It's privately owned and they were the only company willing to allow access to

Castillo and her team to set up their equipment and test facilities. The James A. Fitzpatrick and Nine Mile Point Plants are run by Entergy: Too much red tape. Every level of government has input into what happens there."

"Too high profile as well then?"

"Yes, that too," she said. "Castillo needed an established grid that she could tap into but she didn't want to have a committee meeting every time she wanted to test something. The Heritage plant isn't nuclear, it's turbine, so there is no threat that Castillo and her team could do any damage with catastrophic results. It qualifies as an ample test size. Its proximity to the other plants is such that the technology could be transferred over to the larger grid base, when the time comes, without having to lay too much wire. Weather shouldn't be a factor, especially if she completes it during the summer."

"And she's in the middle of nowhere in upstate New York, so no one can see what she's doing all the time," he said. "But close enough to the big plants to ensure that when the time comes, she can access the whole Eastern Seaboard readily."

"She's done her research," JP agreed.

"So now what happens?" Hart asked.

"You go home and start putting together a meal fit for a king, or kings," she said. "And wait by the phone like a teenage girl in heat."

He gave her a sour look. She was grinning but he sensed she was partially serious. "I am not going to encourage the girl," Hart said. "And I emphasize *girl*."

JP shrugged.

For the rest of the meal, they held to lighter conversation, discussing dysfunctional families, hobbies they wished they had more time for, and of course, how much they were enjoying the wonderfully prepared food. JP had tried a soft-shell crab sandwich and Hart had settled for veal medallions in a homemade marsala sauce. The place looked homey enough; surely it would be decently executed. They giggled like kids as they tried bites of each other's fare. Hart explained that he couldn't just look at food, he had to try it to truly appreciate the presentation. She told him most men don't like to share unless they're in a relationship, or trying to create a relationship. He told her he had a very strong relationship with food.

For dessert, Hart had a shot of Grand Marnier with Cappuccino and JP ordered the apple crumble, recommended by Ray, the cordial owner. After a couple of bites, she put her fork down and looked up at him.

"So how did you and Frank hook up?" she asked. "I mean, I know he's your brother-in-law--"

"Ex brother-in-law."

"Right. But he told me you guys knew each other before his sister dropped into the picture."

"Did he now," Hart said, savouring his orange-flavoured liqueur. "You two got personal I see."

She shook her head. "No. He was just explaining to me why he trusted with this assignment even though you weren't with the Company anymore."

"Oh, and why does he trust me?" Hart asked.

She stared at him momentarily. "It's not just because you're related," she said. "At least, that's my feeling. He seems almost reverent when he talks about you. And I don't think it was because you divorced his sister."

"Separated actually."

"Whatever. You and Frank had a relationship before, right?"

"Why is this so important?" Hart asked, putting his drink down and placing his hands in his lap. "What does it matter to you if Frank and I are friends, high school buddies, Company compadres, or whatever? I'm a chef, and he says that's what he needs at the moment for this assignment to work for him. My understanding is that you're doing all the spook stuff. I'm just cooking."

She grinned, his sudden antipathy breezing right over her head. The edge of her upper lip pushed upward till her upper teeth were visible. "Don't get your back up. I just find it hard to believe Frank is sending you up there just because you can handle the catering, as you put it."

"Look, Frank and I used to work together at The Farm years ago," Hart said, sighing. "Because of that--and the fact that he's my ex brother-in-law and supposedly my best friend--he figures he can disrupt my personal life now and again and use me to help his cause."

JP leaned back in her chair and folded her arms. The smirk on her face told Hart she was pleased with herself for getting him to talk. Ironically, he wanted to get it off his chest now anyway so it wouldn't keep coming up during the assignment.

"I used to train field agents in close-quarter combat in my past life," Hart said. "And Frank was a not-so-sparkling student. We spent a lot of extra time together because he had a hard time picking up techniques. He's not the most coordinated guy on the planet." Hart shifted in his seat. Although he wanted to get this out of the way he really hated talking about the past. "Anyway, since he was a desk jockey bent on becoming Director someday, it wasn't that important that he become adept at close quarter combat anyway, so we just had fun with it, and became friends. I couldn't do that with the others because it was more potentially life and death for them. For Frank, it was just exercise, better than going to the gym, you know."

"So that's what you taught, hand-to-hand combat?" JP asked.

Hart frowned. He knew Frank had told her all about him. It would be the only way she would agree to go on an assignment with a civilian. "The Company called it close quarter combat. Hand-to-hand sounds too World War II. What I taught was self defence combined with aggressive close contact offensive techniques, designed for small group conflicts as well as one-on-one. It's what I used to do in a past life, sort of."

JP raised an eyebrow. Hart hoped she'd let that last part go. He didn't know why he'd thrown it in and he certainly didn't want to expound upon what he'd done before Frank. Before the CIA.

"Frank says you can handle yourself," she said.

Hart smiled. "I'm sure he said more than that but yeah, you can count onto watch your back if that's what you're concerned about."

"Not for a minute," she said, unfolding her arms and leaning forward, placing her hands on the table. "I can look after myself too." She flipped over the bill that the waiter had recently left on the table. "This one's on Frank," she said. "And if I need any help with the natives in Oswego, I'll be sure to ring the kitchen bell for, ah... back up."

It was Hart's turn to grin. "Aye, aye, boss," he said.

She snorted.

They walked back to the hotel, the conversation back to idle chit chat. As they passed the front desk, the night clerk flagged them down.

"A package came for you, Mr. Hart," he said and handed over a long, narrow, white cardboard box with a large red bow on top.

"Ominous," JP said, grinning.

"Especially since we didn't tell anyone where we were staying," he said, pulling off the lid gently.

The roses were a vibrant rich yellow and lush. The freshly cut aroma surrounded JP as she gently pulled one out and sniffed its bud. Hart didn't have to count to know there were half a dozen. A small card on the inside read *I look forward to working with you. LLC* in flowing feminine script.

"There are appropriate vases in your room, sir," the night clerk said, grinning from ear-to-ear.

JP put the roses back in the box. Hart thanked the clerk, handed her the box and headed to the elevator.

"And you didn't even have to wait by the phone," she said, holding the box loosely and unceremoniously under one arm.

Chapter Nineteen

"You are such an ass Arthur!" Cynthia seethed.

Nothing unusual, not lately. Hart's ex had once been a calm, soft spoken, preverbally happy woman who could make him smile with a simple toss of her hair. That woman was gone now, at least in his presence.

They were at the neighborhood swimming pool and it was over 90 degrees inside. Hart felt ridiculous fully clothed but that's what parents did at these things. Richard Hattis was there, sitting on the edge of a wooden bench seat, tumbling a towel between his hands as if it was a football. His agitation was evident in the action but he kept it contained.

How did you keep the amount of frustration he must be feeling pent up so successfully, Hart wondered? Cynthia was parading around, hands on her hips, elbows jutting out like spears seeking to find something or someone to impale. Her eyes were wide open and fiery, her ears red around the edges, and her voice high pitched and incredibly grating, at least to his ears.

Hart almost admired the guy.

Almost.

"I just want to spend time with my son," he said, trying to keep his voice low in an effort to influence the level of Cynthia's voice down to a more civilized level. It had been three days since JP and he had returned from Oswego and despite taking Lucy out to a movie and ice cream on Sunday, he hadn't seen Jamie or Cynthia since the failed family dinner event.

"You haven't been to one of his meets in two months!" she shrieked. "Richard and I have been driving him around the county, sitting in this ridiculous sauna heat, waiting--sometimes for an hour or more--to see Jamie swim for about three minutes." She was pacing back and forth, crossing the white safety line a foot from the edge of the pool every couple of seconds. Hart caught sight of the young lifeguard nervously sitting on the edge of his six-foot high perch, debating whether to reprimand the parent but intuitively knowing that this was not the time to try and play superior force to a ranting mother.

"He's still my son," Hart said, standing loosely, hands in his pockets, feeling just a little weird dressed in shirt and tie but no shoes and socks. He knew all the other fathers were forced to take their shoes off when entering the deck but it still felt unnatural to be in full business attire minus foot covering.

"Of course he's your son, Arthur," Cynthia continued. "But Richard and I have been dragging around to these things all season. You can't just expect to come in here, sweep him away at the end of a competition for some kind of male celebration ritual, and leave us with nothing but a wet towel!"

"You don't want me to congratulate Jamie for doing so well?" he asked.

Cynthia tossed back her head urgently, her blonde curls bouncing in every direction, her hands still firmly attached to her hips.

"Of course I do Arthur," she said. "But maybe you can just come with us, have some wings, a couple of drinks, hang out with the rest of the team and their parents. That's what they like to do. Then you can leave whenever you want."

Hart looked over at the small gathering of kids at the other end of the pool. Everyone was high-fiving, and parents were hugging their kids, shaking hands with other parents, and generally looking like an ad for Good Parenting magazine.

Jamie was in the thick of things, but he wasn't participating. He was standing stock still, hands at his side, his funny little swim cap off kilter a bit, pushing his left ear down in an awkward manner. He was staring at his parents. Tears weren't far away.

Hart looked over at Hattis. His head was bowed slightly but his eyes were riveted on Jamie. He was on the edge of his seat, watching the boy while twiddling the towel around in his hands. He was trying to blend into the surroundings, avoiding Cynthia and Hart completely. It was if he was waiting for someone to give him permission to take the towel over to Jamie.

Who obviously needed it.

Hart stepped around Cynthia, strode over to Hattis and without saying a word, ripped the towel out of his hands. He then walked as quickly as his bare feet on slippery tile would allow to his son.

Jamie watched him approach but didn't say anything and didn't move. Hart handed him the towel.

"You did great kid," he said, pulling the swim cap off with one hand and ruffling his hair with his other. "I'm really glad I got to see that."

Jamie dried his torso quickly and then looked up at his father. "Yeah, I did pretty good today," he said, the edge of his mouth rising into a grin.

Hart grinned too. "Yeah, you did kid. Where'd you learn to flip the turn like that, Coach? One of the guys?"

Jamie seemed to sink into himself a little, and his eyes diverted in the direction of his mother.
"Richard showed me a while ago," he said, not looking at his father. He leaned down to dry his legs. Some of the other kids came by and slapped him on the back, offering congratulations. The parents, Hart noticed, stayed back.

That's when he realized he didn't know any of these people; the kids, the parents, none of them. He turned and looked at Cynthia. She was still standing there, hands on hips, staring at him. Her hair was dishevelled, her stance rock steady. He couldn't recall her ever looking that domineering.

Hattis was now talking with another man who'd just walked over. The man had his arm around a young boy Jamie's age. They were smiling and conversing like old army buddies. Another parent.

Hart turned back, patted Jamie's back and pulled out a twenty-dollar bill from his pocket.

"I'm real proud of you kid," he said, handing the bill over. "Why don't you buy something special, maybe a new video game or something, you know, for doing so good."

Jamie looked up at him, his eyes squinty. Hart could see the goosebumps on his arms.

"You're cold dude," Hart said. "Go get changed. Looks like you and your buddies are going to go celebrate. You deserve it."

Jamie watched him, the towel hanging loosely from his one hand.

"I'll catch up with you on the weekend maybe, okay?" Hart said, then patted his head again. "You be good eh?" He nodded, turned and ran to join his friends heading into the change room.

Hart gave Cynthia a quick glance, took one last look at Hattis and the other father in deep conversation, and headed to the pool exit.

He was halfway out of the parking lot when it dawned on him that Jamie had never asked him to join them anyway.

Chapter Twenty

"You did what?" Frank Daro's face scrunched, his eyes narrowing and the creases lining his forehead deepened as he turned a deep ruby shade.

"Arthur told Castillo I worked for the Secret Service," JP repeated. Her arms were crossed but her eyes were glinting. Hart stood behind the bar, two glasses of *The Show*--a delightful Argentinian Malbec he'd recently added to the wine list--in his hands. He wasn't sure if he wanted to put Frank's glass down in front of him yet. He may need to wait till the Hurricane passed. It had been nearly a week since JP and Hart had returned from Oswego and he'd almost gotten back into his usual routine. Though that routine had changed slightly since JP had chosen to stop by every day for a quick drink with he and Al at the bar. She was staying at the Sheraton indefinitely it seemed, as if she had nothing else to do. Between assignments, Hart supposed.

"She seemed to take it in stride that the President wanted the Secret Service involved," JP continued, taking a sip from her own glass. Hart had allowed her to do the taste test prior to pouring out a glass each for Frank and himself. "I think it further proves her good intentions," she continued, "since it will be much harder for her or Losano to hide anything if I'm there watching while Arthur does his thing."

"They'll only let you see what they want you to see," Frank said, still fuming. "You shouldn't have put her in jeopardy like that Hart. It was a big risk."

Frank called him many things but when he used his last name, he knew he needed to tread carefully.

"You told me Castillo didn't want agency interference. I think she feels this is your idea of a compromise," Hart said. "If she'd found out later Frank, the repercussions would have been worse. She'd have thought you were meddling."

"I am meddling," Frank spurted, his nostrils flaring slightly.

"If you're going to pull this off Frank, we need to be upfront with her. Losano would have been dogging JP's every move. It would have become obvious pretty quickly that she's had no experience in a restaurant or a catering company, or whatever it was you told them. He would have sent her packing. This way, they know what JP is there for and can use her to their advantage."

"And have the US government watching their every move?" Frank asked, his outstretched arms forming a *why* gesture.

Hart reached below the counter and pulled out the flowers, now trimmed and sitting in the vase of water he'd stolen from the hotel. Frank looked at the flowers, then he twisted his head to JP, and finally to Hart, his head lolling sideways, eyes imploring.

"Don't look at me. Arthur's the one who seems to have a new suitor," JP said, sliding the vase toward her. She put her glass down and began pruning the leaves with her fingers. Frank shuffled his feet and glanced at each of them. His color was returning to normal.

"I don't like it," he said finally. "Castillo specifically said she wouldn't agree to having agents roaming around his facility. It would be too obvious and they'd just get in the way. You guys were actually going to handle the kitchen duties, or at least you were Art. JP would have had free rein to go anywhere in the building without arousing suspicion from any of the visitors."

We were back to Art. Hart finally handed him a glass of wine.

"What happens now?" Frank continued, addressing JP "She'll have her buddy Losano watching you like a hawk. You won't see anything they don't want you to see."

"On the contrary Frank," Hart said. "Lena suggested that JP would be good company for Losano, since she is simply too busy coding. I think she's warmed up to the idea of having spooks around, now that she's met us."

Frank threw his head back, exasperated. Hart continued. "JP will see and hear more than if she was hanging around with me. Losano seems to like showing off all his fancy, albeit amateur, gadgets. Besides, if it's Lena's idea, who's going to question it?"

He wasn't arguing, which was good. But he wasn't agreeing either.

"I don't think Losano has as much influence on Castillo as we thought he did," JP said. "He actually seemed intrigued that I would be there. He loved bragging about his security systems."

"I'm a father figure so her guard is down. And she seems to like the idea that Losano is enamoured with JP"

JP swung her head toward him and frowned.

"As someone to brag to, I mean," he said.

Frank didn't look like he was paying attention, even though Hart knew he was. He was watching JP continue to arrange the roses in the vase, his eyes flickering quickly, the creases on his forehead jittering nervously. This was when Frank was at his most dangerous; when he was thinking through another angle because his own hadn't worked.

"Jay asked me if I would escort him to some of the local establishments," JP said, still pruning. "Sort of a bodyguard, he said. Thinks he may be kidnapped or something, and wants me to watch out for him."

"My original idea was so much simpler," Frank said, shaking his head.

"Yes, but this plan is much more fun," JP said, pushing her half-empty glass toward Hart. He topped her up.

Frank sat back and stared at the ceiling for a while. Eventually he downed what remained of his wine and placed the empty glass on the counter.

"Ms. Castillo has suggested you handle all the food requirements," Frank said

"We went over a preliminary menu for the dinner," Hart said. "We'll finalize it over the next couple of weeks. Meanwhile JP will stay to watch, protect...babysit Losano."

"Ms. Castillo has requested you take over the kitchen for the summer," Frank said.

"What!" Hart's hand shook so he put down his wine glass slowly. Lena had asked him to set up the kitchen for the staff Losano had hired, a team that was capable of producing gourmet quality food for visiting delegates from other countries. Hart had visions of playing Robert Irvine from the Food Network's *Restaurant Impossible:* Train staff, set up menus, reno the kitchen to look cosmopolitan. Then leave and send an invoice--a big invoice. He'd estimated that to be a week, ten days tops. And then be on hand to run the big dinner at the end of August.

"That's not what we discussed Frank," he said, staring at him. "You said help her with a catering job. I have a restaurant to run. I can't take that kind of time away. Besides, am I supposed to do this just because you asked me to? Lena Lopez Castillo is an intelligent and lovely woman but she's young enough to be my daughter."

Hart looked at JP but she conveniently fussed with the flowers some more.

"Frank, I'm not one of your spies. *This* is how I make my living now." He swept the restaurant with his arms.

Frank smiled. It was a phony smile, full of teeth, stretching from one side of his face to the other. Hart was leery of that smile. It usually meant he was going to do something he didn't want to do. In the past it had caused big rifts between his ex-wife and himself. Although he didn't have to worry about that anymore, he still didn't like being manipulated by his so-called best friend and former brother-in-law.

JP didn't look like she was going to offer any assistance. Had she known this was coming? He sensed he was in trouble.

"Did Losano give you an envelope?" Frank asked.

"Oh yeah, sorry," JP said demurely, pulling a simple white number ten envelope out of her skirt pocket. "I forgot all about it." She placed it on the counter and then, with two brightly coloured fingernails, pushed it slowly toward Hart.

"It's for you Arthur," Frank said, the smile still beaming. "Open it. It's the first installment, to cover set-up costs, equipment, renovations, etc."

Hart looked at him, then at JP. She had known about this all along. She'd betrayed him. For Frank trickery was normal but he had somehow thought he and JP had made a connection of kindred spirits or something like that. Obviously, he'd been wrong.

Hart could tell Frank was having a hard time holding in a grin. He sighed and ripped open the envelope and looked at the number written in elegant but clear script. *Whoa!*

He put the check back in the envelope and placed it back on the counter top.

"How many installments does she intend to provide, Frank?" he asked.

"Three equal amounts. The next one should cover food costs, extra staffing, whatever," Frank said.

"And the final one?" Hart asked.

"Don't know. If you can't think of anything to spend it on, I guess it's profit."

Frank was still smiling that silly, mischievous smile. JP was watching Hart closely, likely wondering if they were still friends. He didn't really have to think about it for long. That number had a lot of digits which would solve a lot of pending as well as future problems. But could he run a kitchen, every day? He'd have to do a little studying, and maybe get Al to do some tutoring. After a few moments, he picked up his glass and motioned for a toast. The others picked up their glasses and clinked his. JPs tense expression relaxed a little. Hart thought about that notion he briefly had about starring on *Restaurant Impossible*. Then he pictured the number on the check again.

Al would be fine without him.

"To Ms. Lena Lopez Castillo," Hart said. "And an interesting and profitable summer."

Then he slid the envelope under the counter where he could look at it again later.

Robert J. Morrow

Chapter Twenty-One

The Asian sifted through his credit cards till he found the slim mobile SIM card holder and detached the tiny piece which he then placed into the disposable phone he'd just picked up at a corner store.

Within a couple of minutes he was making the overseas collect call that he knew would be accepted because he was the only person with the number.

"Report." The gruff, Korean voice of an older man came over the line.

"The launch date is August 13th," The Asian said. "I believe that is within our window, correct General Hwang?"

"The Supreme Leader is under the impression we are amassing the army for a march from Chunghwa to Pyongyang to celebrate Chuseok," the General said.

The Asian shook his head. Only the self-absorbed leader of a country whose citizens could barely afford to eat would contemplate a fifteen-mile-long thanksgiving parade with more than three quarters of his army participating.

The older man continued. "All Air Combat Command and Air Divisions will be transporting planes to designated roads and airstrips within fifty miles of the parade route in order for immediate demarcation. You will call this number again once you have cleared the airspace. Be sure we will not be seen for at least ten hours, Captain. Is that understood?"

The Asian never used his official rank in conversations but General Hwang Youn Chol liked to remind him of his lowly position in this grand scheme--and how disposable he would be should it go wrong. The Asian's ability to travel the world as a sales rep for Singun had been his salvation, allowing him to leave North Korea and experience life, love, and liberty all over the globe. But he knew it to be a tenuous freedom. The highly secretive *Silla Court*, of which General Hwang was the Chairman, owned him because his aging father still lived in the homeland. If the Asian ever did anything to disappoint the cabal his father would suffer the consequences. It was a tired manipulative tool that North Koreans had perfected, regardless of where the victim's loyalties lay. Hopefully, the new regime could finally retire the technique and move forward to a new world order that didn't hinge entirely upon physical leverage. The Asian Captain's role in this scheme was critically important but General Hwang would still treat him as a replaceable pawn. He knew better, however, having been trained for this task since his early youth. Of course, the Silla Court hadn't known what his task would be back then, only that it would involve technology and that it would be the catalyst not only for unifying Korea but for enabling that Unified Korea to become the supreme superpower of the world.

Named after the ancient Korean dynasty that unofficially united the three kingdoms of Korea in 668 and ruled the peninsula for over 1000 years, the Silla Court was made up of high-ranking officials from both North and South Korea, the latter having always being loyal to the idea of a unified Korea in which abundances of a westernized culture would be shared by all Koreans.

Formed in the early 1960's, the Silla Court's first and foremost mandate was a unified Korea. And with each succession of the Kim family regime, more power had been given to the Generals through the back-door maneuverings of Silla Court members. Supreme Leader Kim Jong Un was now the third Kim to become leader for life but he had nowhere near the power his grandfather Kim Il-sung, and for the time being, much less than his father, Kim Jong-Il had. There had been a growing mistrust in the competence of the Kim dynasty as it became diluted generation after generation. The Generals of the secretive Silla Court knew they needed to take over the country soon or lose their chance to dominate the world stage forever. Only recently had technology caught up with the group's bold intentions though, and with it a way to fulfill their destiny had been revealed.

"Yes Sir, the Air Force will be undetected throughout its mission, Sir," he replied.

"And the American defenses will be completely disengaged?" the General asked.

The old man had never really understood the extent to what the Asian's commitment to clearing the airspace actually meant. "Yes Sir."

General Hwang reported to the National Defense Commission's General O Kuk Ryo'l, Vice Chairman with the portfolio for foreign intelligence and special operations. And although the Asian reported to General Hwang, he knew that members of top military brass of the DPRK--the majority of whom were Silla Court members-- were being made aware of his every move and were secretly covering his actions. The Supreme Leader and those few Generals who remained loyal to him knew nothing of their bold plot, which for the next few weeks, hinged on the Asian's covert preparations in America.

Currently, Generals Hwang and O Kuk Ryo' had access to and effectively controlled the DRPK's military. And keeping the Supreme Leader in the dark was critical. Should Kim Il-sung ever discover the existence of the Silla Court, they would all be executed immediately. Thus, the need for diversion and deception. The act they had been planning for nearly five years would be the most dynamic act of warfare ever staged at any time in history. Secret talks between the Silla Court and a similar group of patriots in China had already begun and, together with the established Russian hierarchy, a new, modern communist regime would be ready to take over the world, first by forcing the UN to recognize its legitimacy, then by physically moving troops and government officials into place. With Korea, China and Russia united in the action, there were enough troops to occupy every nation on the planet within a few days.

But the Americans had to be dealt with first. And that was where the Asian came in. His job was to blind the world superpower so it couldn't see what was coming until it was too late.

It was a bold and aggressive plan but one that had been carefully planned out in remarkable secrecy, the Silla Court protecting their anonymity with determined fervor. Exposure meant instant death as well as eventual failure of a world communist movement. And that simply couldn't be contemplated.

The Asian wasn't sure if there were any other agents working on foreign soil performing other tasks relating to the grand plan but wouldn't have been surprised if there were. However, he viewed his role being akin to the assassination of Archduke Franz Ferdinand, the simple act that had started World War 1; such a small task, but one with revolutionary results.

"I have been informed that the CIA has become involved, Captain, and that worries us," the old man said. "Do you need recruitments to keep our young minds focused and safe?"

He was talking about the five--now four--young hackers, all members of Bureau121, who had been smuggled into the US during the Spring. The Asian had managed to get them installed at the compound in Oswego, New York, where the girl and Jay Losano were finalizing the tool that would allow the Asian to blind the American defenses.

"It is under control, General," he said. "There is no need for concern."

"So be it on your head, Captain," the General said.

The Asian cringed slightly. It was a known line from the General, one that had caused the death of a handful of other operatives in years gone by. It was the Korean version of zero tolerance: You fail your mission, you die as a consequence.

"I am confident General, that all will proceed as planned," he said finally.

"Very good, Captain," the General growled. "I will await your contact."

The Asian was about to say something else when he realized the line was dead, the rustling white noise reflecting the empty connection.

He looked around. There were people on the sidewalk and one or two talking at cars parked in the diagonal spots in front of the stores. But no one was paying any attention to him. He dropped the phone, crushed it with one swift downward kick of his heel. He then bent, picked up all the remnants and strode to a nearby trash can where he dropped in the now useless components.

Robert J. Morrow

Chapter Twenty-Two

Ten days after their first visit to Castillo's facility, and with the weatherman's assurance that most of New York state was in for a hot, dry spell, Hart jumped on his Harley Road King and hit the open road for Oswego. He'd packed light and had strapped a backpack, his computer carrying case, soft briefcase, and a pillow--to lean back on--to the backrest of the bike and headed out looking forward to the four hours of whistling wind and the unhindered varying sounds of nature as it whizzed by.

The Castillo complex, as he had come to think of it, looked much the same as it had a week ago, when he had first met Castillo and Losano. This time, however, there seemed to be more activity around the building; a couple of delivery trucks in the driveway unloading what looked like office furniture, a water truck with a hose leading around to the rear of the building, and a FED-EX guy getting a signature from someone Hart recognized at the massive front doors.

He parked the bike close to the building's facade, grabbed the briefcase, and nodded to the FED-EX guy as he came back down the pathway.

"When did you get here?" he asked JP.

"I sort of moved in yesterday," she said, grinning. "Nice bike."

"Thanks. You're taking deliveries now, I see. Are you on the payroll?"

JP motioned for Hart to follow her into the house. They walked through the grand foyer and down the hallway toward a den, similar to the room they had been in last week but smaller.

The view of the rear yard was much the same. "They've moved into Phase Two," JP said, pointing to the roof. "You wouldn't believe how quickly they can fill up a room with equipment."

"The third floor?" Hart asked.

"Castillo calls it the Presentation Level. She's set up in some kind of show arena. It's starting to look like a *Ripley's Believe it or Not* with displays everywhere and interactive consoles for visitors. I'm sure Jay or Lena will want to show you themselves."

"Jay?" Hart said, cocking his head.

JP smiled. "Yes, Jay. He's actually a nice guy. He seems to be comfortable with my involvement."

"You mean the Secret Service's involvement, "Hart said. "Is there a reason he shouldn't be comfortable?"

"In the next thirty days, delegates from all over the world are going to come here to see what he and Lena are doing," she said. "Yet he seems confident that everything will go smoothly each time."

Hart took a hard swallow. He was reminded once again of the task he had taken on. "You don't sound all that confident," Hart said.

"I've been reading up on BPL. It has failed everywhere it has been attempted. Many think it is now old technology and other systems will work better. I don't know why Jay is so confident that Lena's version will not only solve all the issues of the past but become the most cost-effective system ever invented."

"Maybe they know something they're not telling anyone, "Hart said

"I see you've been giving it some thought too," she said.

"I'm curious, that's all. I have checks from her that I can't cash for a couple of months. I need to be confident they'll still be cashable at the end of the summer."

"You're cynical," she said, then smiled. "But then, you're just here for the food so it doesn't really matter what you think."

"Ouch!"

"Actually I can't wait for you to settle in. I'm so sick of greasy down-home food I can't wait for you to bring a little class to this joint."

"I agree," Jay Losano said as he strode into the den.

JP spun around. "I didn't mean I haven't enjoyed your hospitality Jay, it's just that--"

Losano held up his hand to stop her and smiled. "I completely understand, believe me. I'm Italian. The slop they serve around here may be good for the cows but anyone with any kind of a palette would be appalled."

Hart shook his hand and motioned for them to sit. Hart found an armchair facing the window and all the activity in the back. Large cardboard boxes were strewn all over the patio and several white-coated men and women were carrying pieces of gray metal equipment into the building. JP and Losano sat together on the couch. Losano put his hand gently on JP's knee. She looked at Hart.

Was that a blush?

"I'm glad you're here Arthur," Losano said.

When did we get to be on a first name basis?

"As you can see, things are moving quickly now. Our first guests will be arriving this week, from Canada, I believe." He looked at JP as if for confirmation. She smiled at him and nodded. "Yes, Canada. After that, Russia and China if I'm not mistaken. It's imperative we have something decent for them to eat, Arthur."

Is JP his assistant now?

"That's why I'm here Jay," Hart said, not completely comfortable with the intimacy of using first names. And even less comfortable with the knowledge that my culinary skills would be put to the test very early on. "I'll settle in somewhere this afternoon and scout out some local suppliers. I should have the kitchen up and running by the end of the week."

"There is no need to find accommodation Arthur. Lena and I had planned to have you both stay here for the duration. There are several extra rooms and I'm sure you'll find it more comfortable than any of the motels I've seen nearby." He patted JP's knee again. "JP has already settled in."

"Thank you, that's very kind," Hart said, wondering if this had been at Frank's urging. Hart also briefly wondered who was billeted next to whom. "That would, of course, keep me close to the kitchen in case of emergencies."

"Emergencies?" Losano said, his eyebrows furrowing.

JP laughed, the sound tinged with a nervous edge.

"Jet lag has strange effects on people traveling long distances Jay," Hart said. "I wouldn't be surprised if some of your delegates get up in the middle of the night and consider raiding the fridge. If I'm close by I can rustle up a sandwich or something in a pinch."

"Hmmm," Jay said and thought for a moment. Then he smiled, patted JP's knee a couple of more times and stood up. JP and Hart stood with him. "I hadn't considered that, Arthur. I can see Lena made the right decision after all. It will be a comfort to have you are here to look after any such, ah, emergencies." He looked thoughtful again briefly, then gestured toward the hall.

"Come, let's see the kitchen. I hope it's to your liking. If we are missing anything, please let JP know and she'll arrange to have it delivered."

Hart looked at JP with eyebrows raised and she gave him a deadpanned *go fuck yourself look*. He smiled and followed Losano down the hallway to the front foyer staircase.

Chapter Twenty-Three

Upon first appearance, the kitchen looked like the type you would see in a high-end loft reno. Lots of open space, countertops, and minimal storage. But on closer inspection, Hart realized this was the look the designer was going for here but, in fact, the appliances were restaurant grade and the counter was treated butcher block, the kind that you could actually cut things on without your knife slipping out from under your fingers.

Though designed to appear like a normal family kitchen, albeit a high-end one, the proportions were ideal for a two-bum professional work area.

Losano watched as Hart pulled out drawers--they slid as if on well-oiled bearings, which they probably were--and inspected utensils, pots and other cooking paraphernalia.

"Do you think you can make it work," JP asked, hands on her hips. Hart figured it must look like he was questioning that possibility.

"I'll order in a couple of things I don't see," he said. "Just personal items like a custom chef's knife and some cast iron pans. Otherwise, I commend your designer. He or she knew what they were doing."

Losano beamed. "I had a colleague of mine from Vegas drop in and set it up. Originally, he was going to head up the kitchen but something came up and he was unable to."

Hart nodded and tried to keep his smile in place. So he was a second choice? Or had Frank been involved with the other guy's sudden inability to show up? Hart wouldn't put anything past

Frank. Not that it mattered. The more he looked around the kitchen, the more he realized this just could be fun. Al Rocca had the run of the *Artichoke Hart's* kitchen, but he would have the run of this one.

"How big are the delegations?"

"For most, three or four people will likely come," Losano said. "Though countries like China and Russia tend to send extra people for security reasons..."

"And the Arab countries always come with a huge entourage," JP piped in. Losano turned to her and smiled. Hart gulped.

"Yes, we've left them till last as they will likely be the most demanding of our guests," he said.

"Most delegations will arrive in the mornings," he explained. "And after they've had a chance to become acclimatized they'll get an initial tour of the presentation level. Then we'll have a quick lunch, a quick trip out to one of the substations, and then we'll come back for a lavish dinner." He opened his arms to take in the entire kitchen. "Which is where you come in, Arthur."

JP stepped closer to Losano and put her arm through his arm, clasping her hands together around his skinny bicep. Losano looked at her like a puppy in heat and sighed. "Jay feels that since I'm here anyway, I can help ensure things go smoothly for the delegations. That is when you don't need me in the kitchen, of course." She smiled demurely and bounced a little bit for emphasis.

"So two meals per visit," Hart said, ignoring JP. She was obviously in her element. It seemed to him she should be thankful he'd spilled the beans about her being Secret Service because, apparently, Losano figured he had been given a free gift: A pretty assistant who could also handle herself in a crisis, physical or otherwise. It didn't seem to matter that he was supposed to be gay. Or maybe that's why it worked. Looking at them now, they looked like two high school BFF's arranging the Prom.

"Most of them will be flying out at the end of the day," Losano said, interrupting his thoughts. "For those who come a greater distance, a night's sleep may be necessary, in which case we have a group of suites prepared on the second floor to accommodate them. In those instances, they will be leaving early the next morning and perhaps a light continental breakfast would be nice. We can have those prepared prior to their departure and they can help themselves, if that would be alright with you."

"I'm sure I can come up with something, Jay," Hart said, thinking that continental breakfasts may be common in parts of North America where Bed and Breakfast's abounded, and possibly the more sophisticated parts of Europe. But he doubted the Asian and Arab contingencies would approve. He would have to research their breakfast rituals. Man, this was getting complicated. And it hadn't even started yet.

"Well, as you can appreciate, I am rather busy at the moment so I'll let JP show you to your room. Lena is setting up the lab but I'm sure she'll drop by to welcome you both later." Losano patted JP's hand, then gave her a quick peck on the cheek, nodded to Hart, and left.

"Jay, huh?" Hart said, once Losano was out of ear shot.

She punched his arm. "My assignment was to find out as much as I can about Castillo's BPL system and then ensure that the delegations don't steal or take enough info to copy said technology," she said. "And being close to Losano is a great way to do that."

Hart raised his hands in mock self-defence. "Hey, none of my business. You're the spy, not me."

She sighed and rolled her eyes. "Which is exactly why he's put me in charge of the house staff," she pointed a finger at Hart. "Including you, Chef"

He looked at her quizzically.

"Losano feels that since Frank was kind enough to send me here to spy on the delegations, he might as well take advantage and let me organize all the visits."

"So you have the run of the place?"

"Essentially," she said. "I've classed it up a bit, you know, put that feminine touch where needed." She winked. "Lena was too busy and frankly, I don't think she thinks about the comfort of the delegations. She's too absorbed in her work."

"Your particular type of feminine touch includes putting bugs in all the rooms, I presume."

She reached to punch him again but Hart turned sideways and her fist grazed his arm.

"Castillo's giving me a hard time," she said. "Keeps telling Jay I should be a guest not a part of the production team."

"She's jealous?"

"She won't be now that you're here," she said coyly. "Actually, I think she's hiding something, or at least keeping something from Jay, though what I don't know what yet. He's not in the lab as much as she is but he does spend a few hours a day up there. Here in the house, I'm slowly taking over and I think Jay is relieved so he has more time in the lab."

Hart nodded. She motioned for him to follow her and walked down the hallway, past a small den, a library, a bathroom and an office and eventually into the lounge they'd been in on the first visit. With floor to ceiling windows facing the rear yard, the room was about 40 feet long and 30 feet deep. It took Hart a few seconds but then he noticed that the bar had been extended along the inner wall and several tall bar stools had been placed along the front edge.

JP followed his gaze and apparently read his mind. "The bar was refitted this week by a local carpenter. Nice eh?"

"Parties here will be fun," he said, going behind the expanded bar and inspecting the now well-stocked shelves.

"Don't know. They haven't had one yet," she said jumping onto a bar stool and leaning over toward me. "Some of the crew were in last night watching a football game," she pointed toward a huge flat screen TV mounted off center behind the bar, just above where Hart was inspecting. "They got a little rowdy and Losano kicked them out. They'll be reluctant to come in again."

"Too bad," Hart said.

"Losano says he doesn't want any of the crew talking to visiting delegates, especially if they've been drinking."

"Worried they'll give away secrets?" he said.

She shrugged.

"Would any of them know enough to be dangerous?" he asked. "Maybe we should be thinking about abductions."

"Losano says the project is compartmentalized. Most of what the technicians are doing is with existing technology. In fact, some of them are locals and were here when IBSM was operating. There does seem to be a handful that he has setting up a small lab in the corner of the room, and they're all Asians. They don't interact with the others and I hear them speaking in their native tongue to each other."

"Losano hired them from overseas?"

"That's what he says, but he never interacts with any of them. And as far as I can tell, he doesn't speak their language. He has them reporting directly to Castillo," she said.

"Any proprietary technology is probably done by that handful of techs, "Hart suggested. "So they're the ones we need to know more about."

"Yes sir!" she said, saluting me. "I'll get right on it. I thought you were just the cook?"

"And a bartender," Hart said. "Everyone talks to the bartender. We need to get those guys in here for drinks. Do you think you can talk Losano into letting them come in when there are no delegates around?"

"Under what pretense?"

"Tell him I need guinea pigs for some of the tapas," he said.

She smiled. "That could work."

"Oh, and you'll have to be here too," he added.

"What, you need help behind the bar?"

"That and I need someone to occupy Losano while I talk to the Asian tech's."

Robert J. Morrow

Chapter Twenty-Four

"How could you just make that important a decision without consulting me?" Lena fumed.

Jay Losano was perched atop a desk, his one leg dangling loosely over the edge, his arms crossed loosely across his lap. He wore a calm, almost mischievous expression. "Lena, we agreed that you were in charge of the technology but when it came to operations, you would let me run things," he said quietly.

"I was talking about here, the facility, not for later when it's an actual company," she said, her voice louder than his. They were in the presentation centre on the top floor, the bright sun fading into a developing sunset, a rich red extravaganza at the edge of the lake on the horizon. Neither was in the mood for beautiful views, however.

"I considered all the quotes and went with the company that I felt could manufacturer and deliver not only on time but on budget," Losano explained. "I didn't fell the need to consult you because we need to be ready and the choice seemed obvious. Singun Electronics is second only to Samsung but their price per unit is several cents lower."

"They are both South Korean companies," Lena said.

"Of course. And that's because, right now, Korea rules the manufacturing world--at least for consumer electronics" Losano botched off the desk and placed his hands gently on Lena's shoulders. He lowered his voice even more. "The Japanese were more expensive; the Chinese couldn't guarantee delivery; and the Americans-well, they didn't even think they could handle capacity.

But they also thought it was their God-given right to have the contract which made me think they wouldn't try very hard to be competitive, and if things got tough they'd make excuses rather than create solutions." He sighed and let go of her shoulders, sitting back on the desk edge. "Lena, when the South Korean delegation arrives, I'll introduce you to their rep. He's coming with them to show that Singun works closely with the government. He'll give you any assurances you need. It will work, I guarantee you."

"Guarantee?" Lena said, still annoyed but mollified to some degree. "How can you guarantee that? It's not your company. You don't know if they can fulfill the orders or not Jay. What if we license to several countries and have orders for thousands, even millions of units?"

Jay was taken aback slightly. "Those are hefty numbers Lena. I don't think it's going to take off that quickly."

"But what if it does?"

Lena's eyes sparkled as she spoke and Jay smiled in response. The anger was dissipating. Her optimism was indeed infectious, her overall confidence that everything was going to work out beyond even their dreams. She was so sure that BPL would be the next *big* thing, that she was betting her future--and Losano's too--that it would literally spread all over the world like a virus. He grinned at the analogy. That was the term the Singun rep had used when they'd finalized the contract back in May, long before he'd let on to Lena that he'd already done the deal. A service that would permeate every lonely corner of the earth and allow everyone access to communications worldwide. The Koreans saw the vision. And they had backed it up with the best deal. The Korean he'd been dealing with had bent over backwards to get the contract; almost as if he would have given him any price he wanted just to get it. He'd even gone to Vegas to meet Jay's father, though he wasn't sure why that had been necessary. It hadn't gone that well.

However; over the months, they had spent considerable time haggling over details: Designs, costs, delivery dates, etc. They had become friends of sorts though he hadn't seen the guy since leaving Vegas. Apparently, he had an office in the States but Jay hadn't been there yet. All the negotiations had taken place at the in bars and at Jay's Berkeley apartment. The Koreans were also interested in investing in the company once it was launched. He didn't want to throw that out to Lena jut yet; one surprise at a time. But a partnership like that would give them the financial impetus they needed to launch the company properly. And he would finally be able to get out from under his father's unrelenting and restricting influence. The elder Losano's persistence that the new company would be ideal as a Losano family legitimate front was unnerving. Jay knew that had been the motive for his father's initial investment, but he and Lena had never verbally agreed to that. He knew his father probably figured it was an undiscussed reality and he dreaded the day they would have to tell him he could take his profit and sell his shares but maybe the Koreans could help with that too. He'd worry about that later.

It was uncanny how much the Korean guy knew about BPL. It was as if he'd been waiting for the technology to catch up with his company's manufacturing abilities or something. And when the South Korean delegation had suggested the rep come along for the visit next month, that had clinched the deal. No other country seemed to be that connected to their manufacturers when it came to overseas contracting. For Jay, it meant the guy and the company were really invested in the success of BPL, at first here in America, and then very shortly thereafter, all over the globe. He wasn't looking forward to explaining all this to his father but he knew the Korean would help get the message across. The Korean could be a good partner for any future dealings with the Losano clan going forward. Jay had a good feeling about it.

"Okay Jay, I'll stay out of it," Lena conceded, bringing him back to the present. "If you've done your research and this is who you think we can count on, then I'll go along with it. But I still want to hear what other countries think about the whole idea; whether it should be a government-subsidized or business driven operation in each of their countries. That could be critical to our expansion."

"I agree but how do we bring that up?" Jay said. He was thankful he'd won that argument. It was too late to change the decision anyway but he wanted Lena on his side, not fighting the issue all through the initial stages of manufacturing.

"I don't think we'll get their true feelings if we make it part of our formal presentations," Lena said. "It has to be a more casual setting, after they've seen the presentation. They need to be relaxed, have their guard down, somewhere they'll be more apt to discuss any trepidations they might have."

"And how do you propose we do that?"

"We try to get them drunk, what else?" Lena said, smiling.

Chapter Twenty-Five

"He's just a cook," Losano stormed, moving away from the desk and pacing in front of the huge windows. The sunset was reflecting on the inner walls and the dark red hue seemed to match Losano's mood.

"I value his opinion of people and would like his input on their responses to what they've seen."

"You have the spy for that."

"She's a woman. The men will embellish whatever they say to her to impress. But they will speak to a bartender candidly, especially if they've had a couple of drinks."

Lena had bought his idea at least. Hart was just outside the Presentation Centre doorway and had caught the tail end of their somewhat heated conversation as he came off the elevator. Obviously they hadn't heard him so he'd stopped and eavesdropped.

"But why show him this?" Losano continued. "His job is to make sure they have a memorable experience." Hart leaned against the wall and crossed his arms.

"Jay, he needs to know what they're talking about," Lena said, clearly exasperated. "If we want him to find out what people are thinking. Otherwise, he won't be able to interact and he certainly won't entice them into sharing some of their reactions."

"*You* want him to find out their reactions," Losano said. "I don't give a shit what most of them think. And if there's anything to concern us, JP will handle it." Hart could hear him shuffling his feet. "If they license it, great. This is just publicity. If these tightwads don't want it, there are other ways to get the product into a country."

"Jay, you said your father was keeping hands off operations," Lena said, her voice faltering slightly.

"Jeez Lena, I didn't mean Pops," Losano blurted. "I meant business. I mean, we don't always have to deal with governments you know. This is a profitable enterprise we're offering these people. If the administrations don't want to help their citizens by providing cheap internet service, then I know business will--and at a profit."

"Which goes against everything we stand for," Lena snorted.

Hart grinned. She was feisty. Maybe he should save Losano.

He pushed off the wall and, after taking a couple of heavy, noisy steps, strode around the corner and into the Presentation Centre. "Hey, I'm here for my private tour." he gave them his best killer smile. Losano turned, his face dark showing he was clearly still engaged in his argument. Lena, on the other hand, instantly smiled and stepped away, extending her hand to take Hart's.

"Come, please," she said. "I've got it set up over here on the main screen." She pulled him away from Losano toward a large screen monitor mounted on the far wall which he noticed was reclaimed brick from floor to ceiling. On either side of the monitor, lit by narrow-focus spotlights were large placards touting the finer advantages of BPL over existing land, cable, and optic services. Several faux leather tub chairs had been situated in front of the screen in three rows and Lena led him to the front row and sat beside him, facing the screen. She pulled a remote from her blouse pocket and pressed a button. The lights dimmed and simultaneously the screen came to life.

"This is how we introduce everyone to the concept," she said, her hand patting his knee. She pulled her chair closer and settled back into it. Her hand was still on his knee as the screen came to life.

Hart hadn't notice Losano leave but when the short video ended and the lights came up again, they were alone in the room. Hart looked around. Whoever had designed the space--presumably Lena--had gone for the lofty creative ad agency feel.

160

All the windows along the wall facing the lake were unadorned and would let in an abundant amount of light during the daytime. There were three desks lined up along the window edge, each bare save for a computer keyboard and large monitor. Plush leather office chairs sat in front of each desk. At each end of the huge room were more placards and what looked like a couple of information kiosks, similar to the ones you would see in museums or tourist attractions. They were brightly colored and had several buttons along each side of embedded screens.

On the side of the room where they were sitting, a large map of the world was mounted against the outer wall. There were pins depicting countries which, upon closer scrutiny from a distance, would be sending delegates to the facility over the next few weeks. On the other side of the double French door entrance was a custom wet bar with two coffee machines and three baskets that looked to be adorned with various wrapped baked good.

"You know, I could make fresh muffins or cookies or something for your snack bar," he said.

Lena laughed. "After watching that very expensive video about how BPL is going to revolutionize communications around the world, the best you can come up with is that our snacks aren't fresh?"

"Hey, I'm the cook, remember?"

She continued to smile and patted his knee again. Hart didn't remember her removing it.

"I think you are much more valuable to the overall effort than just being the cook Arthur," she said, leaning in closer and…"

Did she just bat her eyes at me?

"…in fact, maybe one night before all the delegations start, we could go out for dinner somewhere and talk about the future. I'd love to hear what you think of everything I've done and what I should do next."

"Lena, in another life you could quite easily be my daughter."

"Don't be ridiculous," she said, grinning. "You're not that old, and besides, I like older men."

Hart grimaced.

She shot back quickly. "I don't mean your old, just that I find older men more intelligent, more experienced, more fun."

"Sounds like you've dated one or two before," he said.

Her grin faded. "No, actually I don't have time to date, never have. At least since I started University. But my father was my best friend back home. He was the one who taught me about life, especially once we'd left Mexico and came to California."

"That makes me a father figure Lena," Hart said, taking her hand and moving it over to her own knee. "I'm flattered Lena, really I am. But I have two children, an ex-wife who still thinks she runs my life, a restaurant that takes up much of my time. There is little time left for myself, never mind finding time for anyone else."

"But you're going to be here all summer," she protested mildly.

Her smile told him she was only half serious, thank God.

"And it is very lonely up here.," she continued. "There's absolutely nothing to do in this town."

It was Hart's turn to smile. "We can be friends Lena. And I would love to share a movie or something one night, but I can't do more than that." He watched her eyes cloud over slightly but pressed on. "You are young and vivacious. You have a great idea, and you're building a great business that's going to give you a lot of money in the near future. You should travel, pick up strange surfer dudes on beaches, and dance the night away at beach parties with jet-setting dot.com billionaire twenty-somethings. What you don't want to do is latch yourself to an anchor with two children, a debt-laden business, and an ex that phones me in a rage every time I give the kids candy."

She smiled weakly. "I wasn't looking to get married Arthur."

Hart laughed. "I didn't want to paint that bad a picture. Sorry. But I'm beyond the lifestyle that you should be leading. Once your seminal progress--" he swept his arms around the room. "--is complete and you make the cover of TIME magazine, you'll have the world at your feet. I've done my travelling, hung out with the protestors and demonstrators. Spending the next couple of months with you and your visitors is a catharsis for me. My goal when it's over is to languish in solitude and re-adjust my lifestyle so I can be a better father, a better businessman, and, maybe… someday, a better partner for someone who envisions living life the same way I do."

"You make it sound so complicated," she said, drawing back. Her frown was gone replaced by a look of concern. "I didn't realize you were at such a reflective time in your life."

Hart smiled. She had intuition, and like most smart women, was able to assess things beyond her years. She would do very well provided the snakes and politicians didn't wear her down.

"Your father did a fine job Lena," he said. "And he would be proud of your choices thus far. Don't screw it up by giving your heart to someone who's already determined that life has limitations. You have none right now. The sky's the limit; the world is your oyster…"

"Stop!" she laughed. "You'll kill me with clichés." She stood and reached for his hand.

Hart looked into her beautiful eyes, sighed, and took her hand as he stood.

"Okay, I get it," she said. "And thank you for being so candid. Would you accept that I might want to drop by the lounge every now and again and just talk--over a glass of wine or two?"

Hart started to say something but she placed her forefinger on his lips, her long nail scraping the end of his nose. "It's okay Arthur. You just keep that wine cool and keep all our visitors in good moods. Once in a while, I'll drop by and take advantage of your hospitality." She stepped back and straightened her skirt with her hands, looking down as she did so. Then she grabbed his hand and pulled him to one of the computer station. "I want to show you something," she continued.

Hart looked at her for a full minute, holding onto her hand. She was so young, yet so intelligent, and so perceptive. "You are an amazing young woman," he said. "And I would be honoured if you would be my new BFF, at least for the summer."

She laughed and pulled him over to one of the desks. "As long as you keep making me laugh," she said. "I find very little to amuse me around here these days. Even Jay is getting moronic over the little things as we get closer to launch." She pressed a few keys and pointed to the screen, stepping out of the way so Hart could see. "I haven't shown anyone this," she said. "Not even Jay."

Hart raised his eyebrows. On the screen were lines of what he recognized as code, but it meant nothing to him. "So why show me?"

"Because you have no idea what it is," she said, laughing. "I just wanted someone to know that there are a few things about ArmourNet that no one else knows but me... And now you."

"I'm flattered but I'm not sure what the point is."

"Sometime in the future, it may be important for someone to know that ArmourNet won't work without me." Her smile had disappeared and her stoic expression surprised Hart. Then the edges of her lips curled and the smile returned, albeit not as vivid. She pressed one button on the keyboard and the code disappeared, leaving a blank screen. She patted Hart's hand, turned and walked to the door. "You can leave the lights on but close the doors behind you," she said.

Hart watched as she sashayed out the double doors. He knew he'd missed something here and not just Lena's amorous offer. He felt played but didn't quite know how. Lena Castillo was young and perhaps a little socially inexperienced. But she was no dummy. Either Losano or he had just been manipulated. Or maybe both of them had been.

Chapter Twenty-Six

Hart's room was on the second floor--a suite actually, with separate bedroom and sitting room, a small kitchenette, and a tiny two-person balcony off the bedroom window which, unfortunately, faced the driveway. The guests would get the rooms with a view, he figured. He admired Castillo's taste in modern furnishings though. She'd probably hired someone for that too but at this point he was willing to give her the credit.

There was a light tap on the door but before he could answer, JP walked in.

"How'd you know I'd be decent?"

She flew onto the bed and bounced a couple of times, using her behind to propel her body up and off the mattress.

"I told you I have the place wired, remember?" she said grinning. I heard you pulling out drawers."

"You might want to reconsider bugging my room," he said.

"Oh and why is that?"

"I've been known to pick up strange women and engage in all kinds of lewd behavior while away from home," he said.

"Good luck with that," she said. "Slim pickin's in this town. Besides, you're supposed to be seducing Ms. Castillo." She moved to the edge of the bed and put her hands in her lap.

Hart gave her his best exasperated look. "She reminds me of my daughter a little bit, you know what she'll be like when she grows up."

"Well Christ, that'll kill any chance of romance," she said, laughing. "Frank will be disappointed."

"Frank can go screw himself," he said and turned to his suitcase and pulled out some clothes.

"Frank said you were separated a while ago."

"What the hell does that have to do with anything?" Hart asked, not looking at her.

"Have you had your rebound relationship yet?" she asked, grinning.

"Okay, you'll have to explain that."

"When people break up, they immediately jump into a relationship with someone they think is perfect, usually because they're the exact opposite of the person they were just with." She stood, studied herself in the mirror above the drawers and began brushing her hair with her fingers. Like a young girl who seems to have everything your ex doesn't. Someone like Ms. Lopez Castillo."

Hart frowned. JP grinned and continued. "It never works of course because what they really want is someone similar to who they had before...minus the parts they didn't like."

"You're quite the expert," he said.

"What's your ex-wife like?" she said, turning to look at him.

"Annoying...like you."

"See, even we have potential. I have characteristics your ex had but I'm better."

"You're spoken for."

"Jay's like the little brother I never had," she said, walking back to the door. "Which puts us both in the same predicament, though mines easy to fix: He doesn't like women. You might want to try a couple of locals while you're here. Poor Ms. Castillo will get the point eventually."

"You've got it all figured out, I see."

He heard her open the door. "Ms. Castillo is only looking for a short-term companion, nothing long term. And since Frank probably told her your whole life story, she figures you're ripe for the pickin's."

Hart followed her to the door and watched as she walked down the hallway. She stopped three doors down and turned back to look at him.

"What makes you think I'm looking for a long-term relationship?" he asked.

"Every man does. It's like you can't function without a woman showing you what to do."

"Luckily for me, I have you to run interference," he said.

She smiled.

"Jay and Lena are going to be tied up till late tonight," she said, her grin fading. "He said you and I should go out on the town and entertain ourselves."

"Sounds promising," he murmured.

"You can tell me all about your wife... just the good parts."

"That won't take long," he said.

"I'm not sure we'll find anything nearby that's up to your standards," she said.

"You're probably right. But when in Rome...?"

"Meaning?"

"I know a place about an hour from here. We'll take the bike."

"Give me a few minutes to change and I'll meet you out front," she said. "I'm guessing casual?"

"You'll need a coat," he said. "It's a little chilly at speed."

"I've never been on a bitch pad" she said. "I usually drive."

"You'll suit it perfectly I think," he said, stepping back into my room. He wasn't really surprised she was a biker. He heard her turn a key and popped his head back out into the hallway. "My ex looked great in jeans and a leather jacket," he said.

"Not as good as I do," she said and closed the door behind her.

Robert J. Morrow

168

Chapter Twenty-Seven

JP had her hair up in a ponytail and was wearing a black baseball cap with the word "Police" emblazoned on the front when she met Hart at the front curb.

"Nice bike," she said.

"Cute hat," he responded.

"Helps with redneck control."

"You've met a lot of rednecks this week?" he asked, grinning and handing her the extra helmet I always carried in the saddle bags. She turned the cap backwards and slipped the helmet on over it. Obviously she'd done this before.

"I think a couple of Lena's techies are locals," she said. "One of them hit on me a few days ago. Next time I saw him, I had this on and he gave me a wide berth."

"Maybe Losano talked to him," Hart offered, jumping on the bike and pressing the start button. The initial roar settled into a low rumble.

"Naw, he's too busy to notice," she said loudly, waving her hand to emphasize the dismissal of the idea. "But I think Losano told them I was with the authorities or something." She smiled. "The hat just reinforces the concept at a level they're sure to understand."

He laughed as she jumped on as if it was second nature. She put her arms around his waist and they took off, heading out of town in hopes of finding something other than local fare.

"You were right, by the way," he said, raising his voice to be heard over the noise of the air rushing around them. "You do look better than my ex in jeans."

She nodded, smiled and put her arms up in the air, her hands catching the rushing wind. "I'm more fun too." She pulled her arms back in and hooked her fingers into his pant belt loops.

*   *   *

Three hours later, riding home, JP wasn't quite as animated. Hart figured the *Sampler Fandango* they'd devoured at Dinosaur's BBQ in Syracuse was the cause. The platter had come with ribs, chicken wings, pulled pork, beef brisket and something called bronzed catfish. And they'd washed it all down with two jugs of Grasshopper beer. Heartburn had the better of her.

"When do the Canadians arrive?" Hart yelled over the wind noise, mostly to change the subject. The first delegation of visitors to see Lena's presentation were our neighbors to the north. He figured the plan was to have a soft start; thus the Canadians who he considered Americans without attitude.

"Friday," she yelled back. "They're driving down from Ottawa, crossing the border at Gananoque. It's about a twelve-hour drive so they'll be tired. We may have to open the bar but I don't think we'll need a meal."

"So I've got three days to get up and running?"

She nodded, accidentally tapping her helmet with his. A couple of minutes later he braked for a red light.

"Got a menu in mind?" she asked.

"Poutine," he said. "Quebec's entry into the world of disgusting fast food. Except the way I do it will blow them away."

"Can't wait," she said. "I know one of the girls who's coming. You'll love her. She's some kind of assistant to the Minister of Defence. Nothing funnier than stories about Canadian defence."

"I look forward to it," he said. "Is she cute?"

"Don't even go there," she said. "She'll be happier spending time with me than you, trust me."

"You have little confidence in my charms."

"She prefers female company, if you know what I mean," Lena said, tapping my shoulder. "Light's green."

Robert J. Morrow

Chapter Twenty-Eight

"You ever get fresh figs?" Hart asked.

The old man looked up from the wooden countertop that ran the full length of the store. He looked like he'd spent most of his time in the squinting into the sun and couldn't be a day under seventy. Huge crevasses crisscrossing his face would be kindly described as wrinkles, crags being more accurate. He was chewing something big--chewing tobacco, a gumball-- but when he started to talk, Hart realized he'd just been shifting his dentures.

"Not much call for figs 'round here," he said, his voice matching the crevasses: deep, low and gravelly.

Hart had noticed the small, independent grocery store when we'd driven through downtown Oswego the night before on their way back from dinner. He often had to seek out small locals, those die-hard grocers who believed in getting daily deliveries of only enough produce and meat to last them two or three days at most. The best ones bought straight from a nearby market, admonishing the big chains and their preservatives. To the untrained eye, a lot of the produce looked old, wilted, soiled and dirty. To Hart that meant fresh.

"I was kind of hoping you could save me a few trips into Huntsville," he said, toying with a glass jar full of rock candy. *Who chews rock candy anymore?*

"We have other chains in town ya' know," he said.

"My clients have a somewhat sophisticated palette," he said. "And they're picky."

He looked Hart up and down, then sat back on a high stool he had set just behind the counter. He put his hands on his knees and turned his head sideways.

"You'd be that high-falutin' chef they brought in at the new lofty place by the river, right?"

Hart had been called many things but high-falutin' was a new one. He smiled. Looking around, he saw wooden shelves running in four rows down the store, following the line of the counter. Behind the counter, open baskets on their sides displayed small groupings of fresh fruit, some vegetables and various bouquets of herbs. He stepped closer to the look at a bushel of tomatoes on a lower shelf. They were bright red and most had tiny mottling on the skin.

"You get regular deliveries?" Hart asked.

He chewed his denture a bit and watched Hart pick up a couple of tomatoes. "Most is fresh from local farms daily but I got a kid comes by every Wednesday with a load from the market. No preservatives... ever. But you'd know that being a chef and all." He grinned and reached below the countertop, pulling out a large brown paper grocery bag and handing it to me. "Don't buy too much at a time, it'll spoil. Just tell me what you need and I'll make sure we got it on hand fer ya."

"Except figs," Hart said.

The edges of his mouth crinkled slightly. "I'll see what I can do." He looked out the large front windows and watched an older couple walk by. As they passed the door, the man yelled in "Howdy young Opplefarmer!"

Opplefarmer Meat and Produce was the name of the store.

"Young Opplefarmer?" Hart asked.

"My old man started the store back in the forties," he said. "Bought the old Ledger farm just outside town when he got back from the war but couldn't farm worth shit, so he started selling everyone else's stuff. Caught on."

That would make Young Opplefarmer somewhere between sixty-five and eighty Hart figured.

"So you're the only game in town?"

"Lucky for you."

"Oh?"

"Mostly it's veggies and potato farms round here," he said, "but *I* know what a fig is."

"And some of the best crawfish, I hear."

He walked toward Hart and helped pick a few of the larger, darker tomatoes. "You know what to do with a crawfish do ya?"

Hart smiled.

"So what they need a fancy cook for anyway?" he asked, ambling back to his stool. "This ain't New York city but there's a coupla' decent restaurants in town."

"Oswego is about to be inundated with contingencies from the G6 nations, each of which bring their own dietary requirements and cultural preferences," Hart said.

"Hi-falutin'," young Opplefarmer grunted.

"Got any artichokes?" Hart asked.

Young Opplefarmer grinned. "Yeah, that'll teach them," he said, referring to the bristly nature and often unappetizing taste of Hart's namesake vegetable.

"But in the hands of a master," Hart said, bowing slightly.

"Hah," he barked. Then he grinned. "They're at the back. Only ones using them are the bridge club ladies, so I don't get much in. You going to need lots?"

"Kind of a signature dish," he said. "I'll put together a list of things I'll drop by for regularly. If you can do that for me, it'll save me trips into the city," he said.

"Got that truck come from Syracuse once a week with stuff I can't get locally. Make a list and we'll keep you stocked up nicely."

Hart nodded and began filling up his paper bag with various vegetables and fruits.

Young Opplefarmer followed him down the centre aisle, his shuffling feet sweeping the floor as he moved.

"They planning on reviving that internet business?" he asked.

"I guess that's why they're here," he said. "Saved them starting up from scratch."

"Maybe the ice will get 'em agin," he grunted, pulling down a particularly large avocado from a shelf.

"You don't want fast internet here?" Hart said. He knew that more than 100 locals had lost their jobs with the closing of IBEC, the first BPL company to actually incorporate. With it's demise, high-speed internet had all but disappeared from the area. Cable companies felt it too cost prohibitive to run lines to the rural areas and although phone line internet operated, it was exceptionally slow. Cell towers were far and few between so even mobile phone service was spotty. he knew Lena had been forced to set up a dedicated satellite link to the compound.

"What we don't like is the interference with our ham radios," young Opplefarmer said.

"Apparently, these boys have solved that problem," Hart said, remembering the speech Frank had given him early on.

"Hah!" Opplefarmer snorted. "They been doing their tests early in the mornings so's none of us are up and running," he said. "And the test signals die long before they reach the airports."

He stood up and straightened himself as best he could, a glint in his eye. "I headed up the committee to get them to stop the last time," he said. "Called ARRL and everything, got them to come down and run some tests on interference. Sure enough, it was disrupting everything. "

AARL was the National Association for Amateur Radio, the powerful lobbyist that filed a complaint with the FCC about IBEC and would have likely got injunctions against their continued operation in the area, had the natural disasters not saved them the trouble.

"We got a lot of Hammers here, ya know," he said proudly. "And some of the crop dusters were concerned about losing communication 'cause of the interference. They came to the meetings too."

"And they closed the doors in 2012, right?" Hart said.

"Damn straight," he said, his voice higher pitched and excited. He sat down after a moment as the exertion had clearly tired him out. "The storms did most of the work though, saved us all a lot of trouble."

From the expression on the old man's face, Hart thought he probably had enjoyed the notoriety of getting a committee together and the rare northern ice storm had cut the fun short. But they got the result they wanted, so he was happy, nonetheless.

"Well, I don't know much about this operation's technical aspects," he said, walking to the front counter to pay for the produce. "But a lot of countries are sending over scientists to see what it's all about."

"Well, me and the boys are taking shifts 'round the clock, keeping an eye on it," he said. "If it starts up again, we're goin' straight to the FCC this time." He clapped his hands together in finality. "Can't have planes goin' down and messin' up our communicatin'," he said.

Hart could have told him that high-speed internet through power lines would be cheaper and faster than even cable, but that's like telling a trucker to use his cell instead of his CB. Too much tradition, especially in rural Northern New York.

"They're sneaky though," he continued. "They only do short tests and they don't go too far, mostly here in town, or out to the Nuke station. So's it's hard to get any solid data to file a complaint."

"Well, they'll have to be running long enough to impress all the visiting dignitaries," Hart said. "So maybe you'll get lucky. He cocked his head. "You don't care if we try to stop 'em again?"

"Hey, I'm just the high-falutin' chef, remember?"

He gave Hart an odd look, then grinned and slapped him on the back.

"Maybe I'll hang out back of your place with the cats and grab some left-overs," he said, shuffling back to his stool.

"I'll do better than that," he said. "I'll have you over for some taste testing if you're up for it."

"I don't know nothin' 'bout gourmet food," he said.

"That's okay, most of them don't either," Hart said. He picked up his bag and waved as he went through the door. "See you later Young Opplefarmer!"

"You too high falutin!"

Hart realized he hadn't given him his name. Upon reflection, that would open up a whole new can of artichokes anyway, so 'high falutin' would work for now.

Robert J. Morrow

Chapter Twenty-Nine

"Arthur, it's Richard Hattis."

Hart had been in the middle of putting beer in the fridge when his cell had rung. He looked at the bottle he was about to place in the fridge and popped it open.

"Hello Hattis."

"Ah, Arthur--I hope it's okay to call you by your first name, I mean, due to the circumstances, I mean, well--"

"Hattis," Hart cut him off. "It's fine." He took a big gulp of the luke warm beer. It tasted good anyway at the moment. "This must be personal if you're throwing out the first name basis card," Hart said, taking another gulp. "What can I do for you? Has Cynthia kicked you out already?"

Hattis' breath caught in his throat and he coughed quickly. "No, Cynthia's fine. Actually, it's about Jamie."

Hart slowly placed the beer down on the counter and switched the phone to his better ear.

"What about Jamie, Hattis?"

"Well, ah… well, I know how important it is to you that Jamie begin taking martial arts as soon as he showed any interest," Hattis began, his voice faltering slightly." At least, that's what Cynthia told me, I mean, I don't mean to interfere--"

"But you are Hattis," Hart said. "Interfering that is."

"Yes, well--" he caught his throat again. "Oh shit, this is ridiculous." Suddenly his tone sharpened and his voice became more business-like, at least what Hart assumed to be his more business-like voice. "Jamie wants to follow in your footsteps and although Cynthia is a little reluctant, I happen to agree with you on this one and would like your, ah… approval, to take him to a class at a place in the mall."

Hart racked his brain. He didn't know of any TKD dojang in the mall. But then, he hadn't been there for any length of time for quite a few months. And, of course, there was more than one mall in Baltimore.

"Which club Hattis?" he asked.

"Well, that's just the thing," he said, his voice faltering just a bit again. "I know you want him to take Taekwondo but there just isn't a club nearby, and anyway, Jamie's friends at school are urging him to join their club. I think it would be good for him, and with the support of his peers, I think he'd stick to it."

It unnerved him that Hattis was inferring to the fact that Jamie had trouble sticking to things he started, like the baseball last summer. He'd lasted eight games and grown too bored to go, ever again. But that was intimate family info. People outside the family shouldn't know, or be concerned about, such things. Hart shook his head. Unfortunately, he was beginning to think he might have to accept that Richard *stuttering* Hattis was now part of his family's life.

Shit!

"It's a Karate club Arthur," Hattis said quietly. "Shotokan actually, so not so bad." He coughed again.

Hart didn't say anything.

"Arthur, his friends are encouraging him and I think he's anxious to be part of that group," he said. "I think it could be positive. I mean, you could always switch him over to Taekwondo later, I guess. But he's interested in this now and I think it would be good to get him in while he's excited, know what I mean?"

Unfortunately, Hart did know what he meant. Jamie had the attention span of a knat when it came to sports and it had been a source of frustration since he'd tried him out at just about everything: baseball, volleyball, badminton, and swimming. The latter had stuck for some reason--*somewhere in the back of my mind I knew Hattis had something to do with that*--so if he was excited about taking martial arts, then should he really get his back up about which one?

Shotokan karate was the style that Choi Hong-Hi had studied during Japan's occupation of Korea. Many of the young men brought to Japan in essential servitude during that period studied the arts. In Choi's case, those studies subliminally filtered into the original syllabus he created once he returned home and united the nine disjointed kwans to form one national kwan, entitled Taekwondo.

Of course, that didn't make it any easier for Hart to swallow. Regardless of the close association of Shotokan with TKD, it was still Karate. In his mind, the Japanese and Okinawan arts were pedantry and stifled in tradition and philosophical adherences. Alternatively, Taekwondo was modern, ever-changing, and more vibrant.

But he was, of course, prejudice.

"I don't know Hattis," he said finally. "I don't want him to develop any bad habits that I would have to correct."

"I understand Arthur," he said, "but since I have gained Cynthia's reluctant agreement, perhaps it would be good--if even only temporarily--to get him into some kind of self-defence regimen. Later, we… ah, you, can correct it."

Hart didn't answer right away. He was right, damn it. Once he was finished up here in Oswego, he would be back home for the winter, which is when his own training picked up. Maybe he could even start a Youth TKD class in the basement gym. Jamie could get his friends to switch over and they'd start a new family tradition.

He looked up and stared out the window of the lounge. The water was rough this morning. It was approaching a half moon and the tides were escalating, waves crashing against the shore with increasing force as the day wore on.

Who was he kidding? He wouldn't have the patience to do a kids' class. He could barely stand out-of-shape CIA agents when they sparred. And those guys could take criticism. Kids required kid gloves--no pun intended.

"I think it's a good idea Hattis," he said, taking another gulp of beer. *That was weird.*

"What? Ah sure. Okay, that's great Arthur," Hattis stammered. "I'm sure Jamie will be thrilled. I'll tell him you said it was okay--"

"Tell him I think it's a great idea Hattis, okay?" he spurted, immediately regretting his enthusiasm. "Just tell him--ah, tell him I'm proud of him and I'll be back in time to see him get his yellow belt."

Hart could hear Hattis let out a breath.

"Of course, Arthur," he said. "I'll do that. Good luck up there."

"Sure. Thanks Hattis."

After they'd hung up, and he'd finished the beer, Hart realized they hadn't discussed who was paying for this. Extra-curricular activities were considered above-and-beyond child support and he was used to negotiating with Cynthia about such things. He grinned. With Hattis grovelling for his approval, maybe he'd dodged a financial bullet. God knows with a government pay cheque, the man could cover it. Martial arts classes weren't cheap. And Hart was still paying the monthly swimming club fees.

He grinned, turned back to the bar and finished loading the fridge with beer. *I can be a real shit at times.*

Chapter Thirty

The Canadians arrived around ten o'clock. They'd driven down in a stretch limo which seemed strange to Hart. They could easily have flown from Ottawa to Syracuse and driven up--would have taken less time--but as Michel Lasseau explained to him over a scotch, neat, "We Canadians love our road trips, eh?"

Michel, a cabinet minister's aide, told him they had stopped in Gananoque the previous night and spent a lively evening at the local inn doing karaoke and munching on locally caught perch. Although tired from the journey they weren't ready to retire yet and Hart had suggested a nightcap, to which they had readily agreed. JP had been the official welcoming committee and had given him a wink, presumably for the brilliant idea. It was a great way to launch the new bar/lounge.

"We fly everywhere" added Sandra Bries, JP's friend from the Ministry of Defence, who was, indeed, cute and didn't look at all butchy. "It's a refreshing change to drive somewhere for a meeting."

They seemed to be in no hurry to turn in and were looking around the lounge for something to do. Hart made a mental note to have Lena or Losano see about ordering a pool table or foosball or something for future delegations. In the meantime, he googled a trivia game and, using his laptop, hooked it up to the big screen via wireless connect. They could play using their cell phones as player devices. Michel, Sandra, and two of the Canadians settled into some barrel chairs in the middle of the room. Sandra explained to the group that she and JP went way back, so she was forcibly coerced into joining. Within minutes they were all laughing and ordering more drinks.

The last Canadian in the group, Francis McLeod, sat at the bar and ordered a draft beer.

"What's the strongest you've got," he said. "I find American beer insipid."

Hart smiled and pulled a Labatt's Blue out of the bar fridge behind him. "All the comforts of home," he said.

"Ah, you're a life saver."

Actually, Hart didn't drink beer much but had sent a couple of cases of imported Blue up to the compound from the *Hart*, before he'd left. He'd discovered the heartier Canadian beer years back while visiting Toronto for a Blue Jays game where it and Coca-Cola(R) products are the only choices. Upon returning, he had Al order several cases a month, mostly for his own consumption. Some of their patrons had found out and Al now ordered ten or twelve cases for the restaurant, so Hart knew he wouldn't miss the couple he had brought with him.

"So tell me, ah…" he began

"Call me Art. I'm the cook and chief bottle washer around here."

"Well Art, looks like you're the bartender too," he said and lifted his glass to him.

"Everyone talks to bartenders Francis," Hart said, winking. "I think the powers that be figure everyone will tell me their secrets and motivations."

He looked at him sideways, then smiled. "Not a bad plan but you're kidding, of course."

"Of course," Hart said, thinking that nightcaps in the lounge should become part of each delegation's itinerary. He'd mention it to JP later. He looked over at the trivia crew. All were enjoying themselves and seemed to be proficient at the game. JP and Sandra were huddled together snickering. She must have felt his gaze because she glanced over and upon seeing him watching, raised her arm, index finger extended, and twirled it in the universal signal for 'another round bartender'. Hart stretched his arms out and mouthed "who was your slave last year?", which caused them to snicker girlishly.

He took the round of drinks over to the table and was formally introduced to Sandra.

"So you can cook too, I hear," she said, a coquettish smile illuminating her face.

"Don't believe everything she tells you," he said, nodding to JP

"If I did, you might be coming home with me," she said and laughed.

He left them to their merriment, stole a look at the clock and made a mental note to stop drinking himself around eleven, if he had any hope of being on tap at seven am to prepare breakfast.

"So, we're the first then?" Francis asked upon his return to the bar.

"The first?"

"To see this magnificent internet breakthrough," he said.

"You're the first of several international delegations, yes," Hart said. "But I can't tell you what to expect. I've only had a brief introduction myself."

"Well, I assure you, if it's half as successful as our Prime Minister anticipates, we may reluctantly become one of their first major customers."

"Reluctantly?" Hart asked.

"Canada ranks among the top three or four in the world for internet usage per capita; something like 92% last I heard," he said. "And the service is never fast enough for us. If running the thing over power lines works like they claim, it will be the answer to providing high speed internet to the far reaches of the Dominion."

"Why would that be a bad thing?" Hart asked.

"At the moment, our internet is mostly Ma Bell. The phone was invented in Canada, you know, so they own all the lines in the country."

Hart nodded. McLeod was a rambler. He remembered the first rule of bartending: Shut up, listen, and keep the booze flowing.

"You think BPL would be a natural fit in Canada?" Hart asked.

"Well, since our electricity developed essentially on a level with yours, our power line density is practically nationwide, like yours. If these guys can promise even reasonably high speeds to places like Saskatoon or Ninivet, the CRTC would invite them to take over without much argument."

Saskatoon was in central Canada, Hart was pretty sure. Ninevet he had no idea, but it sounded like a place where igloos may be the main source of accommodation. The CRTC, he knew, was the regulatory government agency for communications, be it radio, television and, he assumed, internet.

"But if the service is better, it would be a good thing, no?" he inquired.

"For the average citizen, yes," Francis agreed. "But it would put a dent in Bell's profits and they're two of the largest corporations in the country, employing thousands in virtually every media industry you can name, including sports franchises." He took a deep sip of his drink. "But our biggest fear--my biggest fear--is that it finally puts us at the complete mercy of America." He took a big gulp of beer and continued. "We've always been considered the fifty-first state by many Americans and we've gone along with that notion because it has benefited our trade industries. We share the longest border in the world and we all cross back and forth virtually unhindered. More Canadians fly out of border cities like Buffalo, Detroit, and Seattle than they do our own cities. It's cheaper and your airline service is usually superior to ours. All this is okay because if we had to, we could cut that any time we wished." He used a scissor motion to his neck for emphasis.

"Right after 9/11, we almost did, if you recall," he continued. "The US government felt we had been lax in allowing terrorists into the States via Canadian borders and the spitting war almost caused embargoes on everything from trucking to travel on both sides. Those of us in Defence have always known it would be difficult to break trade ties with the US of course, but simply knowing we had the power to do so made us more comfortable."

The trivia group was packing up it seemed and were getting ready to leave. Obviously fatigue and liquor intake was taking its toll. Francis noticed and downed the last few sips of his beer.

Sandra came over and grabbed Francis' arm, pulling him away from the bar to leave with the others.

"Has he been boring you with his doomsday conspiracies?" she asked. "Naughty boy Francis." She popped his nose with the end of her finger, her long, burgundy fingernails, gently scraping his skin. He smiled sheepishly at her and allowed himself to be led away.

"What the hell is going on here?" Losano said, storming into the room, arms flailing, then pointing to the Canadians who had just left. "What were they doing in here?"

"Having a drink Jay, what did it look like?" JP said, taking his arm and leading him to the bar. "Sounds like you could use one too."

Losano tugged his arm away and slammed his hands on the bar top. "I don't want people wandering around the house on their own. And I sure as hell don't want anyone getting drunk and giving away secrets."

"What secrets would that be Jay?" JP said, her voice calm and soothing, though Hart thought Losano was one savage breast that wouldn't calm easily. "Arthur and I are here to provide security, that's all. We don't know anything about BPL, do we Arthur?"

"Ah's is jus' servin' da drinks massir," Hart drawled.

"The morons are just supposed to go to their rooms," Losano raged. "There's nothing stopping them roaming into places they shouldn't be. And who knows what you're yapping about behind the bar."

"Actually Jay," Hart said, slurring his name to mimic JP, "I'm too busy entertaining your guests to drink much back here. And if there are any secrets being revealed it's the, ah... morons doing the revealing."

Losano stared at him momentarily. He was still mad but Hart had his attention.

"Like what?" he said, the red in his face dulling slightly.

"Like the fact that the Canadians won't license BPL unless the signals initiate from their own sub-stations. They won't buy into a cross-border connection without a lot of political ping-pong," he said.

"That's absurd," Losano said, his tone back to relative normal. "The power grids are already interconnected. And they're the perfect candidate for Phase I. All they have to do is flip a switch and *wallah!* they get cheap internet," he said.

"It's the flipping the switch part that's got them nervous," Hart said. "They want that switch on their side of the border."

"I'd say that's pretty good intelligence for you and Lena, don't you think Jay?" JP said, placing a hand on his arm gently. "What's gotten into you anyway? You're so tense."

Losano paced a little, relaxing slightly. "We weren't ready for the Canadians. We should have postponed for a week."

"That would mess up the entire summer schedule Jay, and you know it," JP said forcefully. "Lena said we were ready enough."

Losano harrumphed. "She's not the one who has to get them to sign on the dotted line."

"If you and Lena can work it out that the Canadians can have a little more control, maybe they'll accept a compromise," Hart offered. "If you hadn't known that till you'd offered the license, you would have been scrambling to salvage the all-important first international franchise."

Losano stared at JP, then looked over at him. After a minute he backed away and turned to leave. "This wasn't in the plan. I'll have to talk to Lena."

"The bar is a good idea Jay. You'll see," JP said sweetly.

Losano grumbled as he left.

"Breaks under pressure. Not good." JP muttered.

"You and Sandra were talking about me."

Her face erupted into a massive smile. "Sure."

"And she's no lesbian," he stated.

"Nope," JP said, her smile returning. "But I wanted your take on Francis McLeod without distractions. He's quite a drinker. Sandra knew he'd open up sooner or later. "

"Apparently sooner," he said. "You just want me all to yourself."

"Don't forget to turn out the lights," she said, heading out of the lounge. He was pretty sure her ass was wiggling more than necessary but he wasn't sure.

Robert J. Morrow

Chapter Thirty-One

"It's not design software or an office suite," Jay Losano was saying. "Everybody doesn't get a copy just because they're licensed to use it."

"But it *is* software," Senator Andre Blais insisted. The Senator and Losano were sitting on opposite sides of the centre table in the lounge. Lena was between them, her legs and arms crossed, her gaze focused on some indiscriminate space on the wall behind the bar.

According to JP, the Senator had requested an audience with Castillo and Losano stating it was "of some importance and emergency." She had told Hart it had to do with the component contract.

Hart retreated back to the bar after serving the Senator a whiskey, neat, as per his order. Castillo had a glass of white wine she hadn't taken a sip from. Hart thought she was just being courteous so the Senator didn't have to drink alone. Losano had declined a drink.

"Our technology is software," Lena spoke for the first time. "But it isn't something we intend to make copies of and distribute to our customers, even qualified ones. The very nature of the technology allows us to piggyback on the power grid's hardware and infrastructure. When licensed, we will turn the software on from our location and designate its use to the customer."

"The customer being the cable, phone, and internet companies?" the Senator asked.

"If that's how it plays out," Losano said.

"How else do you see it playing out," the Senator asked, his voice raising slightly.

"Ultimately, our customer could be the US government," Losano said, grinning. "Our only customer."

"That sounds awfully socialistic," the Senator said.

"Also sounds like progress," Losano said.

Lena leaned forward to steer the Senator's attention away from Losano. "President Emerson will be announcing how BPL will be launched at the media dinner," she said. "We really don't know how he wants it to be presented to the public."

"The President does not have the power to dictate how a consumable product is distributed," the Senator said. "The market will create demand and licensee's will provide solutions, don't you agree?"

Hart watched Lena carefully. He'd been wondering about this himself. Clearly, Losano had visions of creating another AT&T or Rogers Cable, providing internet connections to consumers through his and Lena's organization. But had Lena bought into that too? She was a techie, comfortable in front of a computer screen. Hart couldn't see her holding court in some high-rise boardroom in New York. And he definitely didn't think Losano was qualified enough to do it. Of course, there was the lingering knowledge that the whole thing was being funded by the Mob and Hart doubted they would just divest of their investment just because they were asked nicely.

"The President has expressed his concerns about simply selling BPL technology to anyone willing to pay," Lena said. "He feels that any company formed around the technology would be susceptible to antitrust laws almost immediately."

"He has no reason to believe that," the Senator blustered. "The market will generate appropriate competition and pricing structures."

"He is concerned that the current communication infrastructure will be focused on control more than service and his goal is to ensure low cost access to internet throughout the country, especially rural areas currently not connected."

"You seem to know a lot about what the President wants," the Senator snarled.

Lena leaned back again but stared directly at the Senator. "President Emerson shares my vision of providing internet access to everyone--even those who can't afford it."

"We are a democratic nation, my dear, not some South American country where one man gets to determine what it's citizens enjoy," the Senator said. "The President answers to a lot of people and must convince a lot of political groups that his ideas are the appropriate ones for the country."

"The President perceives BPL in the same vein as health care, accessible to everyone at the lowest cost possible, even subsidized if necessary," Lena said. "Big business doesn't work along those lines does it Senator?"

Losano shifted in his seat. Hart grinned. He didn't think Losano was in full agreement with Lena's objectives, despite their joint magnanimous stance.

"President Emerson is a fine leader," the Senator said. "but sometimes he doesn't consider all the options. That's why we have Congress and their ability to debate and decide what is best for the nation."

"Are you saying the President may not be able to determine how BPL is rolled out?" Losano asked.

"My committee will be drawing up a proposed new subsection to current antitrust legislation to be discussed during next Congress session to place BPL technology in the hands of the existing communications infrastructure."

"You mean the phone and cable companies?" Losano blurted. Senator Blais raised his eyebrows.

"Legislation will control the technology--" he nodded at Lena "-- and ensure that all Americans enjoy the ability to experience low cost internet."

"You are assuming, Senator that the technology will be made available to be distributed in such a manner," Lena said coldly.

"If new laws dictate such, then yes, BPL will be integrated into the power grid in such a way that it will be a commodity, not unlike electricity, and automatically available to all."

"As long as the consumer pays the monthly bills to the utility companies on time," Lena said, her tone low, almost a growl.

"It is how a progressive economy functions," the Senator said.

"It is how government and big business control essential services," Lena said. "And it is not always progressive."

"It's the American way," the Senator said, smiling.

"If you'll excuse me gentlemen, I have been away from the lab long enough," Lena said, getting up abruptly. "I am sure Jay will give you a tour of the building and answer any other questions you may have. Thank you for taking time out of your busy schedule to drive up here Senator. I'm afraid there aren't enough hours in the day for programming, however. The press conference is looming closer each day, and there is still work to be done to ensure the success of BPLs launch."

The Senator and Losano both stood.

"Of course Ms. Castillo," the Senator said. "Thank you for your time. I will keep Mr. Losano posted as to our continued efforts in Congress. In the end, everyone will be happy with the results, I assure you. And everyone will have access to your technology."

Lena stared at him for a moment, her face red, her lips tight.

"That is, of course, if the technology is ready on time," she finally said. "One never knows what glitches could cause slowdowns, or even incompatibilities. Good bye Senator." She smiled over at Hart and without looking back at the others, walked out of the lounge. Hart watched the Senator and Losano both follow her departure with their eyes.

Eventually the Senator turned to Losano. "That went well," he said and sat down to finish his drink. Hart could tell from his frown that Lena's inference that the technology might not be ready had him concerned. Was she capable of sabotaging her own project? Just to ensure corporate America didn't control it?

Chapter Thirty-Two

Over the next week and a half, several delegations arrived and departed. Hart was kept busy researching appropriate breakfasts, lunches, and in the case of the Mexicans, an extravagant and spicy dinner: Gourmet empanadas featuring clams marinated in Tobasco™ and tossed in a creamed anchovy and tomato salsa.

The Mexicans were another of the overnight delegations, having taken advantage of the trip so close to the Canadian border. They were heading to Ottawa the next day for a NAFTA conference; thus, the extra meal. Hart was pretty sure that after seeing Lena's BPL presentation, they'd add licensing to the agenda since both Mexico and Canada were the only countries physically connected to the US. He could see Lena's logic that they would be the natural first choices for expanding the operation out of the States. He hoped Lena given some thought to the Canadians' wariness. And, as Losano pointed out later that evening at the bar with Lena, JP and himself, the Mexicans had major security issues to be concerned about since crime and government corruption would be a major deterrent.

"They won't get anything done nationally," he said. "The local city governments are too corrupt. Be like trusting a squirrel to deliver a bag of nuts to a farmer. And that's not taking into account any of the gangs and cartels."

Hart had looked over at JP but her face had been stoney. The talk of cartels and security issues was either behind her or she was putting up a brave front. As for Hart, despite his initial nervousness about cooking such diverse dishes for so many people at once, he had received kudos from everyone thus far and his confidence had spiraled.

The Portuguese were an introverted bunch but the lone female component was a stunning, black haired beauty who, even in her silence, seemed to fill the room with her presence. Hart tried out simple sautéed crawfish in a white wine reduction with a basil-infused yogurt sauce for them since Portuguese are big spicy seafood lovers. Lena's face scrunched while she ate but it could have been her disapproval of the extra attention he was giving the Iberian beauty, rather than the rather intensely spiced crawfish.

He hadn't intended on using crawfish as much in his dishes but it was going over well and Opplefarmer the grocer seemed delighted that he had found so many ways to serve the local catch. Hart hadn't invited the old grocer in yet for a sampling but had promised to do so soon. After wading through international delegations for a week, someone who spoke English as a first language would be a welcome change of pace.

Which brought up the British. The Minister of Telecommunications and some of his cohorts were every bit the stereotypical upper-crust English snobs. They were well dressed though and Hart asked the Minister's aide where his boss got his suits made.

"A little tailor off the Circus. Right charmer he is 'n all. Knits up some fine clobber dun he?" The accent was anything but upper crust. Hart had no idea what clobber was.

The Minister, of course, thought they had every right to take the technology with them now. Losano laughed when the group looked taken aback as Lena told them this was just a presentation, a teaser of sorts.

"We haven't fine tuned everything yet, Minister," she continued. "And we would need to understand how Great Britain would integrate the system nationwide and where the signal would originate from. There is a possibility the initial pulse may need to be initiated on the continent somewhere."

"Oh, that won't do," the Minister said, his chin raising slightly. "And since you're not ready to get things going now, we'll just have to wait until you've ironed things out then, won't we. Let us know and we'll look into it again, then."

And with that, he'd gotten up from the dinner table and, with the lackey's following on his heels, headed upstairs, assumedly to pack."

"Arrogant little shit," said Losano.

Lena had been staring after the man but shrugged, sat back down, and finished her Dover Sole. "You've outdone yourself this time Arthur," she said, munching away.

JP was smiling and sipping her tea. "We really should drink more tea," she said, holding her cup baby finger extended straight out. Hart laughed.

"I'll stick to an expresso thanks," said Losano, walking out.

"Who's up next?" JP asked Lena. She was chewing slowly so Hart answered for her. Losano had given him the schedule early on so he could get supplies ahead of each delegation's visit.

"The Italian, French, Vietmanese, and Chinese," Hart said. Lena nodded and quickly swallowed what she had been chewing.

"That last group will be interesting indeed," she said.

"How so?" Hart asked.

"China is the second largest market in the world after the US. The government there recently announced a three hundred and fifty-billion-dollar investment in the power grid, to move things away from the smog-intense coastal regions like in the south. They plan to lay some 627,585 miles of line by 2020. Approving BPL as part of the investment is one of the most cost effective ways to get communications to outlying provinces," she said.

"I thought communication wasn't high on the priority list for the Chinese?" Hart said.

"It's not really communication they're looking at," Lena said. "Thanks to companies like Alibaba(R) and Yahoo(R), e-commerce is growing at a tremendous rate and is improving the economy literally overnight. They want every Chinese family in every village to have access to the internet so they buy products and services. Wireless requires significant investment but big US companies aren't interested until the Chinese government relaxes internet restrictions.

JP nodded. "Government intervention has always been the biggest drawback to investment in China but as more and more domestic companies integrate western technology into the marketplace, even the old guard recognizes that their future power lies in managing their growing economy. "

Lena stood, wiped her mouth with her napkin and then placed it on top of her plate. "Their wireless network is growing stronger every year but not everyone can afford the technology. Even now, about ninety percent of the total Chinese population have never used the internet, primarily because they can't afford mobile phones and expensive services. But BPL will put the power of online commerce into even the poorest hands, and allow those outlying villages to provide their goods to the wider market too. In many ways, BPL will benefit China even more than the US."

"Why wouldn't Western companies offer to invest in a nationwide wireless system?" Hart asked.

"For the same reason we haven't gone one hundred percent wireless here," Lena said. "Security. It's great for the masses but governments and even some competitive private sector organizations don't want critical info flying around the atmosphere loose so anyone can tap in. And the Chinese government is far more paranoid about that than we are. Using land lines allows the operator to shut it down--or at least limit capacity--anytime they want. And that's something the Chinese understand and appreciate."

"Unlike our friends, the Brits," JP said. Hart arched his eyebrow. "Virgin pretty much owns the phone system in Great Britain," she added. "The British decided it was better for their economy to let big business switch their phone system to wireless, rather than spending immense amounts of taxpayer money on their ancient landline service. Virgin stepped in and built a nationwide mobile service literally overnight. No one under the age of thirty over there owns a land line, they're all on cellular."

"But anyone can tap in to any conversation, anytime," Hart said.

"I'll be looking to Mr. Branson to step up to the plate again if Britain decides to purchase a BPL license," Lena said. "When entrepreneurs get involved, governments lose much of their procrastinating power. And there's no bureaucratic hold ups when one guy runs the show."

"So who's interested in China, besides Google" Hart asked. "Virgin again?"

"Who isn't interested?" Lena said. "But I think Alibaba will be the main player, since they're a Chinese company and bigger than eBay and Amazon combined. They have the experience, the government support..."

"And the money," JP added. "The Chinese are uniquely positioned to be the most important client you will obtain. But they may not agree to license. With infinite amounts of corporate money waiting to be shoveled their way, and a government that is itching to become a world superpower, all that stands in their way is a method to communicate to their millions of citizens quickly." "But most importantly to them," Lena said, standing up, folding her napkin and placing it on the plate, "the government could shut off info going in or out of the country with one flip of a switch. That really appeals to the communist mentality and will be our main selling point."

"You'll have to excuse me then," Hart said, getting up. "It seems I may have my hands full satisfying that bunch." He headed to the little office that he had essentially taken over. He switched on his laptop and began searching out authentic Chinese dishes. After a few minutes, he was overwhelmed and started a new search.

What the hell was Alibaba?

Robert J. Morrow

Chapter Thirty-Three

"Quick, give me your phone!"

JP. rushed through the cafeteria door but stopped it from closing completely with her foot. Hart slid out from under the bar where he was checking a keg line. He brushed dust debris from his hands and reached into his pocket for his cell.

"Come on, come on, they'll be back soon," she said, jerking her head back to the door as if to see if anyone was watching her. She wiggled the fingers of her hands impatiently as he handed his phone over. She huddled over it and began pressing buttons.

"You don't have me on speed dial? Geez Hart!" she said, looking up at him briefly, then back down to the phone. Her hands flew over the tiny buttons as her eyes darted intermittently from the display to the door. Hart could see she was putting her own phone number into the memory.

"I've only called you once," he said in defense. "I haven't had a chance to store it yet."

"Whatever," she said, not looking up. A ringing came from the purse she had slung over one shoulder.

"Don't hang up," she said, handing his phone back. Then she shrugged off her purse, opened it, and pulled out her own cell phone. It had a lime green casing and the ring was some kind of Latino dance riff he didn't recognize. She pressed the answer button and started for the door. Turning back before she went through, she said "Don't...hang...up, okay?"

He shrugged and put his phone on top of the bar. He had been known to pocket dial the kids and send garbled texts unknowingly and he didn't want to risk screwing up whatever it was Lena was doing.

The door slammed shut behind her and he could hear the sound of heels hitting ceramic. But it was a faint sound, not coming from the hallway itself. The sound was coming from his phone. Low voices, and then muffled scratches that hurt his ears. He bent down and went back to the keg, leaving the phone on the bar top.

A minute later, JP. came back, a little slower this time. Hart looked up from the floor. Her face looked funny upside down and he was hoping she'd come close enough to look up her skirt but she stopped just short of his sightline and leaned forward. Her arms were outstretched, her eyes flashing, and her nostrils looked huge from this angle.

"The phone?" She was whispering.

Hart pointed upward and her eyes followed. She jumped to the bar, grabbed his phone and held it to her ear. When Hart finished screwing in the last tap ring, he pulled himself out of the crouch, groaning on the way up.

"Shhh," she hissed, turning and walking over to the window. She wasn't talking, just listening.

He grabbed a stool and watched her. She was staring outside but he could tell she wasn't focused on what was outside. After a while, she turned to see where he was and motioned him over, her finger then going to her lips to keep him quiet.

She pulled out a chair from the table closest to the window slowly, not making any noise, motioning for him to sit. She then pulled out another, sat down, and put the phone gently on the tabletop between them. She then, very carefully, pressed the speaker button.

Tinny male voices popped out of the device.

"You are not one of us and you need to stop thinking you are." Hart didn't recognize the voice. It was gruff and had an Italian accent, which made sense since the Italian delegation had arrived that morning.

"I was under the impression our culture always respected bloodlines."

That voice he recognized. Though thin and nasally through the phone's tiny speaker, it was definitely Jay Losano.

"Macri," JP mouthed. That was the name of one of the Italian delegates, Hart remembered. Each day, one of the techies from upstairs came into the cafeteria and posted the day's visitor list on the corkboard beside the wine fridge. Lena thought he should know the names of each person visiting, just in case they wandered in and engaged him in conversation. She hadn't explained how he was supposed to connect names to faces he'd never seen, but the theory was good. JP had told him three of the Italian group couldn't speak English. Only Eduardo Macri and Carmine Romano had spent time in the West before and were fluent. She had pointed Eduardo out earlier and mentioned he'd studied here one semester as a youth; Yale he recalled.

"You speak to me of culture," the first voice said, the anger evident, despite the treble tone of his voice. "You don't know anything about culture, *saputo*. You have never even been to your homeland. What you know of culture is from your Sicilian mother trying to mold you into a proud American. Instead, you mock your heritage and do your best to associate our heritage with pigrone and criminal activity. You call that a bloodline! Sicilian influence in our homeland died years ago. No one has any use for the familia anymore. It's only here in America that you and your kind are still feared. Italia has shed itself of such old-fashioned methods. We are progressive businessmen, not thugs."

There was a high-pitched laugh which sounded a lot like Losano. The laughter stopped abruptly and Losano's voice came again, his now lower tone menacing and slower. He was emphasizing each word slowly and articulately.

"*Chiudere il becco peasano*," he spat. "You are here at my Father's request because of your connection with his family. Your contempt and disregard for him is laughable. Do you not recall that the lying, corrupt politicians who sent you hear know full well the importance of what we are doing here. And they understand our, ah…needs." There were more muffled noises and sharp intakes of breath. They must have moved closer to JP's phone because Losano's voice became clearer. Hart could almost feel the spittle coming from his lips. "You will respect our demands, or you will be sent packing, your tail between your legs… or between something else."

"Aargh!" Macri's groan was a little higher pitched.

More undecipherable noises, then Macri spoke, his voice softer, more subdued.

"You don't understand. You are standing in the way of Italia becoming a strong voice in the European union. We are prepared to finance the BPL expansion across the Union, but we need the girl and her team there, not here." There was a note of pleading in his tone. "You care of nothing but your code, yet your code doesn't allow for progress in any other way than force. We are trying to be civilized and we had hoped you would see it our way. After all, you are paesano!"

Losano laughed, the pitch loud enough to vibrate the tiny phone's speaker.

"You are sniveling, just as you hand shakers always do," Losano said. "You are right in thinking Italians will dominate in this new technology. But we are not interested in one silly country, or even Europe. My partners and I are interested in dominant markets first. Then we'll see what...."

Just then, the cafeteria door opened and two lab tech's walked in. JP grabbed the phone and pulled it to her, pushing the handset button as she put it to her ear. She looked at Hart and nodded her head toward the men.

He was sure his annoyance was showing as JP then mouthed "Just do it… please!" He got up and waved to the two white-coated tech's.

"Fresh keg boys. Let's try it out."

They both nodded and headed straight for the bar, ignoring JP, huddled at the table, the phone against her ear, her eyes widening as she continued listening.

Chapter Thirty-Four

"I'm coming home this weekend and I was thinking I'd take the kids for an overnight," Hart said into the phone. He was packing up the laptop in the office, checking that he had all his notes for the upcoming week. He had already packed a bag and told Lena and Jay that he would be back on Monday. He hadn't mentioned it to JP yet since she may not like the idea of him abandoning her for a couple of days. But he needed a break and the kids would take his mind off things, at least briefly.

"Umm… That's not going to work, Arthur," Cynthia said.

Cynthia had said many negative things to him over the years and she tended to beat around the bush on most she considered difficult to relay. Hart had always assumed it was a family trait since her brother Frank was a master at offering indirect directives. So, it surprised him when she shut him down so quickly, and so distinctively.

"What do you mean, *it's not going to work*?" the last few words come out with a more sarcastic tone than Hart wanted. "I've only seen them once since I came up here. I thought they'd missed me by now."

"They do miss you Arthur," she said, hesitating for a second. Hart could hear her troubled breathing. "We didn't know when you were going to find some free time, so we've been planning some activities."

"We?"

"Richard loves hanging out with the kids Arthur," she said. "And they like him. He talks to them about things they're interested in, knows their friends, and doesn't mind taking us all out to movies, restaurants, even the amusement park last weekend."

Hart didn't say anything for a moment; wasn't sure if he could without it coming out wrong.

"So you and Richard have made plans for the weekend with the kids then?" he asked.

"Well, Jamie has a swim meet in Pittsburgh Saturday, so we figured we'd grab a hotel and make a weekend out of it. Lucy and I are going to shop for some new school clothes and Richard is going to meet up with some dignitary from Washington. He can write the hotel and some of the food off as a government expense. The kids are excited about it."

She was rambling, talking fast to cover her nerves. Though Hart knew she had no reason to be nervous. Even though they had joint custody, that didn't stop her from planning weekend excursions, with or without a boyfriend. And Hart realized he hadn't given her much warning.

"I had no idea you'd be free this weekend, Arthur," she added. "Frank said you were pretty tied up with feeding all the groups coming up there…"

Thanks Frank

"… and I didn't think you'd mind since you hadn't told us you be able to come home at all. It's not like we expect you here regularly."

The bravado was coming back. She likely figured she'd grovelled long enough. And she was right. Hart wasn't much of a father. Sure, he loved the kids but he didn't spend time with them. He certainly didn't know any of their friends. And an amusement park? He would never have tolerated that; he deplored rides.

"Can you make it another weekend?" she asked, though Hart could tell in her tone that she more likely figured he would stay away another month or so before contacting them.

"I don't know," he said. "Frank's right. It is busy up here." He brushed his fingers through his hair and put his laptop bag back on the desk, slumping back onto the desk chair. "Look, it's okay.

Frank and I had planned an end of summer campout Memorial Weekend. I trust that will work."

"Richard isn't trying to take your place Arthur," Cynthia said quietly. "But you're not here. And even when you are, you're not really here, you know that. The kids need to be active and I can't do it by myself. I work too, you know."

Hart knew, but he needed to end this before she gained more confidence than he could handle at this point. "Tell them I called please."

"Of course," she said, still quietly. "And Arthur, take some time off anyway. Figure out what happens after this. Jamie starts high school next year. He's going to need a father figure even more."

A father figure. Not a father. Message received, loud and clear.

Robert J. Morrow

Chapter Thirty-Five

"I suggest you put something warmer on Senator," the Asian said. "It's a little chilly in the basement."

Blais noticed his semi-nakedness suddenly and reached over to put on a white bathrobe that had been draped over a chair beside the bed. His gaze went to his wife who seemed to be sleeping soundly.

The Asian smiled. "Mrs. Blais is quite comfortable. I gave her a sedative to ensure she has uninterrupted sleep while we, ah... discuss things." He motioned for the Senator to precede him out the bedroom door.

"Why are we going to the basement?" the Senator asked, pushing his feet into furry slippers by the door and wondering where all the security was again. *How did this guy get past them so easily?*

"Oh, I've arranged a little demonstration Senator."

Blais plodded down the wide, circular staircase, across the tiled foyer into the vast gourmet kitchen to a stairway at the end which led to the basement.

Where was everyone? He hesitated once in the kitchen but the Asian prodded him. *Surely he hasn't subdued all of the security.* "I need water," he said, a little groggily.

The Asian stopped, stepped back and allowed the man to reach into the large, stainless steel fridge and pull out bottled water.

"Perhaps I will have one also," the Asian said. The Senator looked at him blankly, then blinking rapidly, reached in for a second bottle. He closed the door and handed the bottle to the

Asian who nodded and then motioned for the Senator to keep going.

The basement was elaborately finished, complete with fireplace, plush couches and a huge television mounted on one wall. At the opposite end was a fully-stocked bar and tournament-size pool table.

The Asian pushed the gun barrel into the Senator's back. "The laundry room Senator."

Blais frowned but shuffled across the carpet to the laundry room entrance. It was more than a laundry room actually as it amounted to all the excess space not used by the builder when creating the recreation room, bar, and games area. Primarily used for storage, only a small corner of the space had been tiled, painted and drywalled. The remaining area, some 800-sq. ft. was used for furnace, water heater, and more storage. The floor was cement and because wooden shelving lined the outside walls, the centre of the area was empty. Except for a chair, an old dining chair that the Asian must have found stacked in the back with other identical chairs. He had placed this one in the centre of the space, just above a drain. About five feet in front of the chair, a large canvas bag hung from the exposed rafters in the ceiling. It resembled a punching bag but was lumpy and all of its contents seemed to have settled to the bottom half of the bag.

The Senator stared at the bag as the Asian motioned for him to sit in the chair. He sat facing the Asian, pulling the edges of his robe over his knees. He wore nothing underneath other than his briefs. He pulled his knees together. It was, indeed cold down here.

The Asian stepped back and bent down to take off his boots and then his socks. He folded up the socks and placed them atop the boots which he placed a few feet to the side. The Senator watched as the Asian then pulled off his sweater exposing a black t-shirt that did nothing to hide the rippling chest and arm muscles.

Senator Blais began to sweat, despite the cold.

The Asian moved his head in a circle, stretching out his neck muscles, and shook his arms and hands in jerky motions. He then put his arms on his hips and began circling his waist. Finally, with a couple of quick jumps, he settled his gaze on the Senator. He had placed the gun on the floor beside his boots but Blais knew he was too far away to make a go for it, even if he was fully alert now. One look at the Asian's physique and Blais knew he would never get near the gun.

"Senator, it has come to our attention that you have been meeting with various, ah, highly-placed executives of late."

Senator Blais just stared at the Asian, then the bag, then back to the Asian.

"We need you to stop doing that Senator."

"Who is we?" the Senator asked, his voice low, groggy. He uncapped his water bottle and took a sip.

The Asian laughed, a quick, short laugh that wasn't particularly menacing, more one of amusement. "It always comes to that doesn't' it Senator? In a world where influence and power rules, it is always important to know who is in charge."

The Senator said nothing.

"As you know, the people I represent strongly feel that America has too much freedom of choice," the Asian said, bouncing slightly, like a boxer.

The Senator scowled.

"Life should be simpler Senator. For example, if I want to communicate with someone on the other side of the globe, I should be able to do so, quickly and cost efficiently, don't you think?"

The Senator's eyes darted around the room.

The Asian started bouncing lightly and continued. "You see, we have no interest in what corporate America's needs are."

The Senator continued to stare at the Asian, not really sure where this was going. Their arrangement had been that he, as Chair of the Senate Judiciary Subcommittee would steer telecommunications debates towards the development of a single conglomerate that could run all communications nationally. TV, radio, cable, wireless, satellite, and internet. One national organization to administrate the various technologies and ensure that the American people received the latest technologies in the most efficient and cost-effective manner. Of course, he, Senator

Andre Blais would head up that conglomerate, but the Asian knew that had been the intention. This was all in line with what he and the Asian had agreed upon. Taking over one entity, when the time came, would be a lot easier than trying to assemble a group of unconnected corporations. Especially during a time of chaos. Didn't he understand that?

The Asian suddenly jumped and while at the apex, about four feet off the floor, lashed out with his right foot which connected with the hanging bag. The contact made a soft *thud*, and caused the bag to swing slightly.

The Senator jumped in his chair. His eyes focused a bit more as the Asian went back to his steady bouncing.

"You have also been assisting lobbyists in their efforts to persuade the Government to pass legislation that will allow the major communications companies to form an, ah.... joint venture of sorts." He lifted up his left leg and while still facing the Senator, thrust out with a side kick, resulting in another thud and somewhat stronger movement of the bag.

The Senator jumped again but noticed a slight shifting of the contents in the bag; The kick was so hard that it had actually reshaped the bag. Perhaps that's why it had such an odd appearance. Of course, the Senator had never seen the bag before and assumed the Asian had set it up earlier in the evening, prior to waking him from his sleep.

"We need you to step back from those activities Senator," the Asian said. The Senator turned his head sideways.

"You're asking me to stop lobbying for a telecommunications conglomerate?" he asked. "I thought that was in line with what your, ah, partners wanted."

The Asian stopped bouncing, lifted his head and formed a huge smile. "You forget our mutual friend in California, Senator."

"I don't understand," the Senator said. "Your friend will become a strong leader, yes. But he will still need a working infrastructure to ensure the country continues to run smoothly once he takes over."

The Asian's smile disappeared. "We don't need your interference in matters of infrastructure, Senator." He began bouncing again. Without warning, he spun around backwards, letting his right foot swing around and out in a sidekick thrust to the centre of the bag. It swung a couple of feet in the direction of the kick this time, then back and forth behind the Asian as he looked at the Senator.

"You are seeking to establish a--what did you call it--a conglomerate, that will control all communications, television, telephone, and of course, internet traffic, thereby forming a monopoly that would hinder any other organization from enjoying the benefits of the American consumer market."

"It will be a strong company, yes," the Senator stammered, "but I would be able to steer it in the direction we seek."

"Ah yes. You see, that is the problem Senator," the Asian turned and performed a front rising kick to the bottom of the bag which jumped this time, then dropped back into place with a snap of the ropes above. "You see, my partners and I feel that indecision during a time of national confusion would serve our purposes much better."

The Senator frowned and shifted in his chair.

"How do I get big business to agree to an international foreign-run conglomerate if we haven't formed a national American one first? They need to see how they can make money as one entity, rather than in an open, competitive market."

"Their concern is profits, yes?" the Asian said, his voice devoid of emotion.

"Well, of course, " the Senator spouted. "That's what capitalism is all about."

The Asian stared at the Senator for a moment, then jumped high into the air, pulling his knees close to his chest. Simultaneously, he spun in the air and at the last second, thrust his leg forcefully out to strike the bag before pulling his knees back in, finishing the spin, and landing smoothly on his feet, facing the Senator once again.

The bag was swinging back and forth several feet now.

The Senator put his hands to the sides of his head. "Will you stop that! I don't understand what this silly demonstration accomplishing. It's clear you have the physical ability to hurt me. But I don't know what it is you want from me!"

The Asian stopped bouncing, leaned forward, his hands on his knees. His breathing was steady, his dark eyes piercing.

"What I want from you is your promise that you will stop trying to form a conglomerate Senator. My partners are not interested in the type of capitalism that only reinforces an elite status for the few, and continued poverty for the masses."

"That's insane!" the Senator said. "Just because you come here and threaten me with violence, you think I'm going to change my entire political strategies, just like that?" He snapped his fingers. "We had an agreement. I can't help it if you misunderstood my intentions." His face was beet red now but he was feeling more confident. "You're crazy. Go ahead, hurt me." He stood up defiantly, his hands forming loose fists, thrusting down to his sides. "No amount of physical abuse is going to make me sabotage my career. You and your, ah, countrymen will never convince American corporations to go along with your scheme without considering profitability, regardless of who is in the White House."

"I see," the Asian said calmly. Ignoring the Senator who was now shaking all over, he turned, picked up his socks, sweater and boots and stood beside the bag.

"It is unfortunate you don't understand the gravity of our situation here Senator. You see, my associates and I, indeed, my countrymen, have no desire to compete or even persuade. We wish to control."

"If this is how you conduct business Sir," the Senator blustered, no longer shaking, his growing anger arising since it appeared the demonstration was over. "Then I doubt anyone will assist in your plans. We are a civilized country."

The Asian, turned the cap off his water bottle with his teeth, spit the cap into the corner, and took a large gulp.

"We shall speak again Senator," he said, placing the half-empty bottle on the ground, and turned to go. As he did, he reached up and pulled one of the ropes free from the rafter. The bag opened with a swish and a body fell to the ground with a loud thud. It was naked, in a fetal position and there were blue bruises all over it's back, legs and side of the head.

"I have no intention of hurting you Senator," the Asian said calmly. "Your function in the new regime will be important."

The Senator was staring downward, uncomprehending, then with sudden recognition, he felt his heart race.

"Your family, however, is not," the Asian said. He then turned then and walked out of the room.

The Senator bent down, oblivious to the Asian's departure. He reached forward and gently pulled the limbs of the body out flat on its back as best he could. He looked at the face and winced, then noticed that the chest was moving slightly. His grandson was still breathing... barely.

Robert J. Morrow

Chapter Thirty-Six

It was Sunday and JP and Losano had left Friday for a trip into Albany for a shopping weekend. Lena was huddled in her lab and Hart didn't want to give her any false encouragement by suggesting they go out for dinner. So, Hart decided to see what Young Oppelfarmer was up to. It couldn't be too boring; they'd have food to talk about at least.

Most of the technicians were either working in the lab, relaxing in the lounge, or quietly relaxing in their quarters, so he didn't lock the door when he left.

It was only a five-minute drive to downtown Oswego where the Oppelfarmer store was located and he wasn't really paying attention to his surroundings as he drove the now familiar route.

He was surprised, therefore, when a dark-coloured Chrysler 300 passed him, then slowed down, forcing him to slow also. At twenty miles-per-hour, it was becoming a little ridiculous, so he looked ahead for a safe place to pass. Instead, the big car skidded to a stop, the back doors flew open, and two men jumped out, racing back to Hart's car.

Hart have never been in the habit of locking his car doors when driving so when the bigger of the two guys yanked his driver door open and started to pull him out physically, it took him a couple of seconds to register what was happening. Lifting his leg to counterbalance the guy's pulling motion, he grabbed his hand with his right hand, placing his thumb into the webby skin between the man's thumb and forefinger and twisted to his right. Wrists aren't meant to go in that direction, so when the big guy felt the tension, he shifted his arm to relieve the pain. Hart kept twisting and the man's body followed his arm and his torso smashed into the open door. Hart jumped out, still holding the guy's wrist and stepped behind him, pushing his arm up behind his back. He let out a yelp and bent over the window.

"Mr. Hart, please let Francis go." The voice was steady, relaxed, and contained an inflection of humour.

Hart looked up to see the other guy, his eyes glittering, a grin on his face, and a large gun in his hand, aimed directly at Hart's head.

"I apologize for Francis', ah… ambitious-like attitude," the man said, his tone that of someone trying to sound cultured but lacking the necessary education, "'cause all we really wanted is to have a little discussion."

Hart pushed Francis' arm up closer to his shoulder blades. He grunted. Hart looked up again at the other guy. He was skinny with greased back hair and no taller than five and a half feet. He didn't seem too worried about aiming a gun at someone in broad daylight which was a little unnerving. Hart's heart was racing but in the back of his mind the whole scene reminded him of an episode of *Goodfellas*.

He had Francis under control for the time being and most of his body was protected by the car door though a bullet would likely go through the thin metal easily. Francis' body wouldn't add much buffer to that either. Regardless, Hart decided to wait and see what happened next.

Skinny guy twitched the corner of his mouth and sighed. He then dropped the gun to his side and quickly walked toward me.

"Okay, Mr. Hart, you're right. I'm not about to shoot you," he said. "And I've become kinda partial to Francis' company, so I'm not going to shoot him to get to you either." He was on the other side of the car door now. If Hart let go of Francis, he could likely grab the gun, perform a similar twist to the wrist, step back and have them both covered. They wouldn't know he'd only shot a handgun in a range, never into a human being.

Skinny guy saved him the dilemma. With a big grin on his face, he holstered the gun and looked up at Hart. At the same time, he felt a sharp prick in his thigh and looked down to observe that Francis had stuck a syringe into his leg. Hart realized too late that he had released the pressure on Francis' arm slightly while watching skinny guy and that had allowed him momentary reprieve from the pain in his arm--long enough to use his other hand to pull out a syringe and poke Hart with something that...

Robert J. Morrow

Chapter Thirty-Seven

The first thing Hart felt was a little chill. Since it was mid-summer in Oswego, he had to assume he was indoors somewhere and the air conditioning was on high. he couldn't remember why he was indoors. Come to think of it, he couldn't remember much of anything…

Then is brain caught up and he grunted. The big guy had stuck him with a needle and he'd blacked out.

How long ago was that?

He slowly opened his eyes and saw a white ceiling. Turning his head he saw a large, familiar structure just outside a large, floor to ceiling window. The Eiffel Tower.

What the hell? Whatever they'd put in that thing had done some damage to his brain.

"Welcome back Mr. Hart."

Hart tried to lift his head to see who was talking to him but a wave of nausea hit him so he dropped back to the pillow and closed his eyes momentarily. After a second or two he opened them again and turned his head to see an older man bent over staring at him.

"That stuff packs a punch, don't it?" he said. His voice was gruff and his face looked funny upside down. Scruffy beard, bloodshot eyes, and thinning hair that appeared to be combed forward--hard to tell upside down.

"Where am I?" Hart asked, surprised that his voice was hoarse. HIs mouth felt very dry, like he'd just taken a shot of Tequila, bit the lime, but forgotten the tomato juice. His head felt like it had been through a similar experience.

"I'll be happy to explain that, Mr. Hart," the man said, pushing a glass toward him. "But for now, you might wanna get a little hydrated, right?"

Hart reached for the glass and the man put his hand behind his back and helped him ease into a semi-sitting position. He took a gulp, relieved to find it was cold, fresh water. The man was in his sixties and the hairdo was, indeed, a comb-over. He was wearing a wide pin-striped, double-breasted suit with a matching vest. His tie was wide and loosened around the collar to allow for a protrusion of excessive neck skin.

"I apologize for the clandestine-like way we've met, Mr. Hart," he said, taking the empty glass from me. "But it was kinda important no one knew we were having this little chat, especially my son Giovanni."

Clandestine-like? --Wait, Giovanni? That was Jay Losano's Italian name, wasn't it?

"You're Jay's father?" Hart asked, his voice only slightly more liquid than before.

The man winced. "Jay, yes," he said. "Giovanni is my son, my legitimate son. I am Antonio Losano." Hart must have frowned because he laughed. "Ah, yes. I apologize. My English is far from perfect; Giovanni tells me this constantly. He is not a bastard son. His mother—God rest her soul--was very proud of him actually. What I mean is that he is the one son I have that is trying to create a legitimate business for the family. That is what I meant."

Whatever nausea Hart had felt moments ago seemed to be receding and he pulled himself fully upright. He had been lying on a plush couch overlooking what appeared to be a balcony on a high floor-looking directly at the Eiffel tower. He looked questioningly up at the elder Losano who had stepped away a bar at the other end of the room. He saw two other men, dressed in similar outdated double-breasted suits. He turned his head to see what was behind him and there stood skinny guy and Francis. Skinny guy smiled while Francis sported a definitive sneer.

Hart turned back and peered through the large window and saw that just beyond the tower was a very large, very bright neon sign advertising Taylor Swift's upcoming shows at Caesar's Palace. The word *Flamingo* was emblazoned in neon pink above it.

Las Vegas?

"I realize it may seem a little much to drag you out here, Mr. Hart," Losano said from the bar. He had poured two dark drinks and was bringing them over to the couch. He sat down beside Hart and offered him one. "You'll find this will take away the rest of the grogginess," he said. "I have found it to be my personal favourite hangover cure."

Hart took the glass and sipped it. Some kind of cocktail; rum and coke he guessed, with a little something sour added which did, indeed, seem to go straight to the part of his brain that controlled balance and cognizance. He felt better immediately.

"I don't get away from town much," Losano said, sitting in a lounge chair opposite me. "My business is here, see. And the hot weather is good for my arthritis, okay. So, I thought since this was an introduction-like meeting, that you wouldn't mind making the trip, right." He wasn't asking a question so Hart didn't respond. He just took another sip and waited.

Antonio Losano was not a large man, wasn't actually intimidating at all in appearance--maybe back in the day. But Hart got the impression he was still used to having people nod and say yes whenever he said anything. The old man watched him without saying anything, his gaze intense and penetrating. Hart gave him his killer smile. He looked beyond him, Hart assumed to either skinny guy or Francis.

"He know why he's here?" he asked them.

The voice Hart recognized as skinny guy said, "Never had the chance to discuss anything boss. Just threw him on the plane and brought him down here."

Losano nodded, then turned his attention back to Hart. "So you cook, eh?"

Hart attempted a smile.

"We got some pretty good restaurants here, right," he said. "But I bet you could give 'em all a few lessons, eh?"

Hart wasn't sure what response he wanted so he tried nodding. It seemed to satisfy him.

"Well, Giovanni tells me that his partner, Lena Lopez Castillo-" he pronounced Lena's name Cast-eelo, "--actually went to see President Emerson. Balsy move. Didn't know the guy would see her but seems she got some Senator to grease the wheels, right. Giovanni says she's worried about some of the people that might be coming to visit our little project and asked for his help."

Hart took another sip of his drink. He figured if he waited long enough, the old man would tell him everything he needed to know.

"Next thing we know, you and a Secret Service agent move in, and our project is now some kinda national security zone or something. That right?"

Hart cocked his head.

"You a spy Mr. Hart?" he said without emotion.

Hart choked on his drink.

"I mean, it seems kinda funny to me that after Castillo goes to see the Pres, suddenly we got all kinda security issues. Are they worried about something in particular Mr. Hart?"

"I'm not sure I understand Mr. Losano," Hart said. Then added, "And I'm not a spy. I just cook. My assistant is the spy."

Losano laughed which caused everyone else to laugh along with him. When he suddenly stopped, so did they. *This was a movie set, right? And I was being punked.*

"Yes, Giovanni told me all about his new friend, Miss Pierce," he said. "And that's why I wanted to have this little chat, Mr. Hart. You see, I know that you be friends with the Deputy Director of the CIA-related to him kinda, right? And he was the one that got you and this Secret Service agent invited to stay up there. Well, I have a lot of money invested in this project and I'm a little concerned that the government seems to feel they need to be involved. I'm sure you can appreciate, Mr. Hart, that although having government interest in my projects is nothing new, I am a little concerned that they seem to feel they need a secret service broad on site all the time."

"JP Pierce is part of the advance team that ensures the President's security when he leaves Washington, Mr. Losano," Hart said. "Her job is to make sure there is no threat to him when he comes to visit at the end of the summer."

"But she's there now," he said. "The President doesn't come for another month. Why does she need to be present every day?"

Was he worried JP would see something she shouldn't? Hart thought. "Her job is to watch the visitors when they arrive and see if any of the delegates may pose a threat to the President at the Press Conference at the end of the summer," he said. "There will be delegations from several countries, some of which are not currently on amicable terms with the U.S.A. The Secret Service is always concerned about possible threats to the President, no matter where he goes."

Losano leaned back in his chair, sipped his drink and watched him. His eyes were steady and though Hart wouldn't call them intelligent, they were cold and concentrated. After a few moments, he put his glass down again. "So this assistant of yours is not worried about our project, you say. She is there to watch for threats against the President when he visits?"

"That's correct, Sir," Hart said.

He thought about that for a moment.

"And when the President leaves, so does the Secret Service?" he asked.

"I would assume so," Hart said. "The President will be officially launching the-ah, project, so when he leaves, everything will become public and there will be no further need for secrecy of any kind."

Losano suddenly smiled, he teeth perfect and gleaming. Dentures. "That is very comforting Mr. Hart," he said. Then his smile vanished.

"Lena-Ms. Castillo-- is preparing to take her technology public at the end of the summer, Mr. Losano," Hart said. "Are you intending to be a part of that?"

Losano eyed him suspiciously.

"We have a vested interest in what Miss Castillo is producing, Mr. Hart," he said. "So, yes, we intend to be a part of the company Miss Castillo and my son Giovanni create."

Well, that was confirmation, if he'd needed it, he guessed. Antonio Losano had fronted Lena's operations. Jay Losano had arranged that financing. In return, the Losano family expected to be integrally involved with whatever entity was formed after the launch. Hart pursed his lips. If Frank was aware of this, he certainly hadn't thought it important enough to let him know. Not that it mattered what he thought, of course. He only hoped Frank had a plan for handling Antonio Losano because it was clear the old man had little affection for government agencies.

"And that then brings us to you., Mr. Hart," Losano said, leaning forward.

"I am sure I will do whatever I can Mr. Losano, as limited as that may be," Hart said, smirking inwardly. Apparently, he had just been dragged over two-thousand miles, unconscious the whole time, in what must have been a private jet since he figured other travellers or airport security would have noticed a comatose passenger. He was not about to tell Antonio Losano--who purported to be an active, though questionably influential mobster--that he was unwilling to lend a hand. Especially since he was five states away from home and surrounded by old school mobsters.

"I would like you to do two things, Mr. Hart," he began. "Firstly, I need you to report to me of my son Giovanni's activities. As you have no doubt determined, I intend to have him run our interests once activated, and I need to know that he is in a position to do so. With all the government interest, including Miss Castillo's unexpected friendship with President Emerson, I have justified concerns. I believe, that Giovanni may be pushed out of a, ah... controlling position, without help from the family."

Hart scratched his chin and waited.

"Secondly, I need you to obtain a copy of the program once it is finalized, Mr. Hart."

Hart stared at him. A lump formed in his throat and he was afraid to swallow.

"You have access to the entire facility, I'm sure, Mr. Hart," he continued. "And if you don't, your assistant Miss Pierce certainly does. My son, Giovanni, seems quite taken with her." Someone by the bar snickered and he gave them a withering glance. "Giovanni also tells me that your relationship with Miss Castillo is, well, shall we say, of a friendly nature. It will be of little difficulty for you to make a copy of the final program on…." He gestured impatiently with his fingers to skinny guy behind Hart who quickly stepped forward and placed a small object into Losano's outstretched palm. He nodded and held it out to Hart. He extended his hand and the old man dropped a USB flash drive into it, smiling. Hart looked down at the bright red cylinder. *Would ArmourNet even fit on this thing?*

"You want me to steal the program?" he asked, wondering why his own son couldn't give him a copy.

Losano laughed again, which resulted in the same cacophony of laughter that had occurred the last time he'd done that. It stopped just as abruptly again when Losano spoke. "I would hardly call it stealing, Mr. Hart," he said, "if I am the one who has paid for the whole operation, wouldn't you agree? Besides, I only want a copy of the program. Kinda for insurance, you know?" he said. "No one will even know I have a copy, right."

"I'll know," Hart said. And Jay won't. Is that why he wants a copy? He doesn't trust his son? Or maybe it's Lena he doesn't trust.

The others laughed again. Losano didn't. They stopped as soon as they realized they'd jumped the gun.

"Mr. Hart, I did not invite you here to *discuss* this," he said, his voice slow and menacing. "And the fact that your friend Mr. Daro would no doubt be upset if he knew you were going to do this for us, is my guarantee that you'll never tell anybody about it."

Hart cocked his head. *Was that even logical?*

"I can see you are not quite sure what I mean, Mr. Hart. Perhaps this will help clarify things." He reached into his breast pocket and pulled out a four-by-five-inch photograph and held it out to him. He took it and turned it over to see a picture of his daughter Lucy playing in the school yard.

He jumped up and threw the photograph into his face. "You're threatening my child?" he yelled.

The men at the bar raced over but Losano waved them off calmly. He pointed his head up to make eye contact. Hart stood seething, staring down at the old man. He could feel Francis breathing heavy behind him and his peripheral vision he saw the other men standing a couple of feet away. If he made a move toward Losano, they would all jump him. He took a couple of deep breaths.

"Sit down, Mr. Hart," Losano said slowly. "Please understand that I show you that photograph of your lovely daughter for one reason and one reason only." He waited. Hart took another breath and dropped back onto the couch.

Losano grinned. "You see, I'm not asking you to do anything illegal, Mr. Hart. As I have already explained, I have paid for the program so it seems only right to me that I get a copy of it before my partners launch it to the world." He reached down and picked up the photo from the floor where it had landed. He grunted as he sat back up. "I'm sure you don't mind making a copy for me, Mr. Hart. And it will be something between you and I, if that's okay with you." He leaned forward again, both hands on the armrests of the chair. "And your friend Mr. Daro--he's the young girl's Uncle, isn't he?" he smiled widely. "Well, he won't need to know about our little arrangement. And quite frankly, Mr. Hart, if Giovanni does, indeed, go on to run the operation once it's launched, then that copy we're talking about will be safely locked away in my safe at home. Nobody will ever know."

"I'll know," Hart said again, trying very hard to keep his voice low and steady.

Losano smiled. "Indeed you will, Mr. Hart," he said. "Which, of course, is the very point I'm trying to make, isn't it?"

Chapter Thirty-Eight

The flight home had seemed surreal considering Hart didn't remember anything about the flight there. He had been to Vegas three times--now four--and was familiar with much of the amazing views below the plane as it traversed the lonely, surprisingly colourful Arkansas landscape. It seemed uncanny that he had no perception of canyons or valleys on the way down to Sin City.

Taking off for the return flight from McCarran International in a private jet was a new experience though, and despite his initial conclusion of Antonio Losano and his crew being stuck in the 1950s, he obviously still had tremendous influence-at least in Nevada--and a fair amount of funding; the Gulfstream G200 was not a cheap airplane, though it could have been leased, Hart surmised. Still, the idea of the crazy old man having unlimited funding was daunting.

They landed in Buffalo around noon and thankfully the warm summer air not usually associated with the northern border city made the transition from one hundred and two degree dry Nevada heat more bearable.

A black airline limo met the plane on the tarmac and Francis escorted Hart to it, even opening the rear door. He was about to thank him, which in hindsight seemed silly--they had kidnapped him, after all--but he shut the door without a word, banged on the roof and loped back to the plane.

With no direction from Hart, the limo breezed across the tarmac to an exit in the high fencing, and after a brief conversation with airport security at the gate, they were speeding along I90.

They would bypass Rochester and aim for Syracuse but somewhere along the way, turn north for Oswego--Hart hoped.

Sure enough, nearly three hours and one uncomfortable car-nap later, the driver stopped at the front door of Lena's complex, jumped out and opened Hart's door. If the guy didn't have a fare to go back, this little trip would have taken a good junk out of his working day, so Hart contemplated what to tip him. Before he had the chance though, the driver shut the door behind Hart and nodded. "I've been looked after Sir. Have a nice day." And with that, he was gone.

"I wondered where you were," JP said, a bright smile filling her face as Hart walked into the kitchen. Hart was about to share his adventure with her when she continued. "Jay and I had a wonderful time in Albany. Lots of shopping, an amazing couple of meals at some places I'm sure you must try, Arthur. And a lovely, cozy evening at an Inn by the waterfront. What have you been up to?"

She was bubbling along and Hart was about to tell her but thought better of it. He needed to think it through. As silly and cinematic the meeting with Antonio Losano had been, the very real possibility that he had enough money to actually fulfill his threat of harming his daughter was enough for him to be cautious at the moment. At least until he had a reason to be worried about what would happen when he didn't provide the old man with a copy of the software.

JP was obviously in a good mood and Hart didn't need to spoil her reverie with his melodrama at the moment either. Later maybe. "Doing a little sightseeing," he said. "Anyone around?"

She pulled a container of orange juice from the fridge and poured a glass, looking up at him questioningly.

"No thank you. I might have a beer, I think," he said and reached around her for a can.

They both sipped our drinks and leaned against the kitchen counter.

"Jay has exceptional taste in women's clothing," she said.

"Of course he does," Hart mumbled.

She looked at him sourly. "Don't be like that. It's nice to have a man around who understands what a woman needs. He actually spent four hours in the mall helping me pick out a couple of new tops. Can you believe it? What man *ever* does that without complaining?"

Hart tried to recall an experience as requested but came up empty. Something else to apologize to Cynthia for, no doubt. Maybe he'd be better with his daughter when she grew up. And Hart would do whatever it took to ensure she *did* grow up.

"I'm glad you had a good time," he said lamely. "Did you discuss anything else other than fashion?"

The corner of her mouth sagged downward and she stared at me. "We talked about lots of things, Arthur. It wasn't all gaiety and frivolity."

"Nice word," he said. Her withering look caused him to grin.

"We talked quite a bit about what he wants to do once Lena finalizes the technology," she continued. "And I think he sees himself as some kind of executive operations manager. He's fairly savvy about government influence and since Lena seems to have befriended President Emerson, the odds are any red tape will be quickly snipped once they are ready to go operational."

"Do you think Losano's father has a lot of influence over him?" he asked, trying to sound nonchalant.

JP gave him an odd look. "Jay is a gay man in a very testosterone-heavy family," she said. "He thinks his father tolerates him because he's trying to do something that will help legitimize the family's business. Jay wants nothing to do with what his father does. He'd be happy to invest everything the family has into Lena's company, and maybe when the old man dies, he'll do that. For now, though, he tries to keep his father at arms length. He knows he owes the old man a lot for financing this, but he thinks that if he can prove himself and create a company that will truly become an international success, he'll finally get his father's approval."

"Wow, you guys got personal eh?"

She sighed. "He's a troubled man, that's for sure. If he wasn't related to a mobster, I think he'd be a lot more flamboyant than he is. But that stigma forces him to keep one foot in the closet when he's around his father, or any of his father's cohorts. I think that's why he loves female company so much. He says he was close to his mother but she died a few years ago." She put her empty cup on the counter. "I think he sees Lena and the technology as his way out from under his father's influence. If this doesn't work, he knows he'll be forced to go back to working for his father. And I think that would kill him… literally."

"He really opened up to you, I gather," Hart said. He was curious about Jay Losano's motives. Did his father pull his strings or was the relationship more of a tug-of-war? And if the latter, how what kind of a risk did that place on ArmourNet?

"I know you find it funny Hart," JP said, "but gay men with his background still find it difficult to assimilate how his lifestyle fits into the grand scheme of things; things being what his very influential father has in mind for him. He's an only son, so his father has some heavy expectations for him. Jay's not afraid of that, he just doesn't know how he could function, let alone run the family business as a gay man surrounded by the most old-school macho-types America could possibly produce."

"Yeah, I know," Hart said.

JP's eyebrow's raised.

"I mean, I could imagine, right? I mean they're Vegas mobsters. How much of a grip on reality could they actually have?"

She frowned but after a moment, started fiddling with a small watermelon. She began slicing it, placing the pieces on a small platter. "Well, he's putting a lot of faith in this thing." She waved her arm around to take in the room, the chef knife loosely gripped in her hand. She had no idea how menacing the motion appeared. "And if it takes off, I think he feels his father will leave him alone and find someone else to run the family business."

Hart doubted that but now wasn't the time to discuss the Losano family hierarchy. He motioned to the knife with his head. "You're pretty good with that thing. Maybe I'll turn you into a sous chef yet."

She looked at the knife in her hand and gave it a little circular swing that was definitely not a move taught in any culinary school Hart knew of.

"I could impale a chicken at twenty feet," she said, the edge of her mouth twitching as she turned, flipped her wrist, and sent the twelve-inch knife speeding toward a bag of potatoes sitting in the corner. The blade sank in about halfway, shuddering slightly from the impact.

Hart walked over and pulled it out, grabbed a dish towel from the stove handle, and wiped the blade clean. He slowly placed the knife on the countertop and winked. "Okay, so maybe sous chef is out. Next time I make pheasant stew though, I'll know who to call."

He turned and walked back to the main corridor. "I'll be in the office if you need me. I have to plan for the Chinese delegation. They arrive day after tomorrow, right?"

JP nodded and picked up her plate of watermelon slices. Hart assumed from the number she'd cut that she planned on surprising the tech's upstairs with a mid-afternoon treat.

The Chinese were going to be a challenge for many reasons. Not only had Frank told him in the beginning that the Chinese delegation were the most concerning for the President, but he was not sure what he supposed to feed them. Gourmet was not a Chinese term. Their tastes were simple for the most part, though Hart was sure those from the metropolis' and those who travelled extensively had acquired more sophisticated palettes. But what, exactly, would they expect from an American chef serving Chinese cuisine? Hart was losing sleep over it actually. Apparently, so was Frank but for completely different reasons. If the Chinese bought in, the political nightmare that would stem from sharing a technology that could potentially allow either country to dominate internet communications was an issue Hart knew was rocking the conference rooms all over the Pentagon.

He closed the office door behind him and pressed the speed dial number for Frank on his cell. While it rang, he dropped into the desk chair and threw his legs up onto the desk.

"How's the weather up north?" Frank said, in place of 'Hello'.

"Not as warm as Las Vegas," Hart said, settling in for a mostly one-way conversation. For the next few minutes he related his escapade with the Losano's and after Frank peppered him with questions for the next fifteen minutes, they had exhausted all Hart's recollections of the adventure.

"So, does this change anything for the press conference?" Hart asked.

"I don't think so," Frank said. "I'll let the President's personal team know about the possibility of Losano and his crew showing up, but otherwise, there's no real threat to our original plan."

"I didn't know we had an original plan."

"The original plan was for you to keep an eye on Ms. Castillo as various visitors from around the globe descend upon the complex and negotiate the rights to use the technology," Frank said.

"I thought the original plan was for me to cook great food for Lena and her guests," Hart said.

"Yeah, that too."

"And isn't JP the spy in this arrangement?" Hart asked.

"Sure she is Hart, but she's Secret Service. You, on the other hand, work for--"

"Don't say it Frank."

He was quiet. But not for long. "You know I trust your judgement Art," he said. "And that means I knew you'd get a feeling about what's going on there. Whether Castillo and Losano are really trying to do something good for America, or whether they're just out to make a million dollars and sell the technology to whoever writes a cheque."

"I think the jury's still out on that one," Hart said.

"Yeah, well, I still think you'll let me know when there's something to worry about, right?"

"I just did."

"He's worried about not getting control," he said. "Making you get a copy for him is a simple solution in his mind."

"And when I don't provide a copy?"

"I'll have my techies work something out Hart," Frank said. "Maybe we can come up with a realistic fake piece of software."

"Just don't forget that Lucy's related to you too, Frank," Hart said.

"Ouch!"

"Just so you keep the guesswork in perspective," Hart said. "If anything happens to Lucy, I'll kill him, and then you."

Frank was silent. The conversation was frivolous, as were most of their conversations. But Hart knew Frank had gotten the message. They would have to deal with the older Losano's expectations before the company went public.

"There's lots of people looking into his other exploits: Justice, FBI, and DEA, even the NSA. He'll slip up sooner or later," Frank said.

There was no question the facility in Oswego ran smoothly due to Jay Losano's operational skills. Lena spent all her time cocooned in her private lab/office and rarely conferred with the other techs. Losano was the glue that kept the whole thing running smoothly day-to-day. He also seemed to be the one who looked after schedules, payroll and most of the other administrative duties. He might just be the logical choice to run things once it all went public. Daddy would be happy and he wouldn't need a copy of the software, right?

Hart didn't feel too confident actually.

It seemed logical that Frank would see Jay Losano as an unwitting asset to whatever he had in mind once Lena launched. Was he thinking of pulling Losano into the fold? It seemed unlikely but Frank had surprised Hart before. The CIA didn't adhere to rules, or even logic for that matter. And Frank had reiterated many, many times: The end justified the means. Hart guessed that included recruiting mobster's sons, if indeed, that was Frank's plan. Hart doubted supplying a copy of the priceless software would ever be part of the deal though.

"So, you're counting on Losano playing ball then?" Hart asked.

"Which one?"

Good question. "Both, I guess."

"I need Jay to keep Castillo in line," Frank said. "Antonio is dispensable. If he causes friction, I'll get the FBI to take him out of the equation with tax, racketeering, vice, or something."

"But if he goes along."

"Then the American taxpayer saves money because I'll make Losano finance the thing indefinitely," Frank said.

Hart could feel his mischievous grin without seeing it. Frank was a master manipulator. And although Antonio Losano had impressed him with his own persuasive skills, Hart had no doubt he would be no match for Frank Daro in the long run. Mobster or not, Losano had no concept of the depths to which Frank would go to in order to achieve his goals. And because his motives were supposedly always altruistic--for the good of the country--Hart knew he had the support of an army of *associates* that Antonio Losano could never match, even if the latter recruited every *paesano* in the country.

Hart felt reasonably comfortable that his daughter was safe for the time being.

Well, reasonably safe.

Chapter Thirty-Nine

Americans love Chinese food but the food eaten here isn't authentic Chinese fare. Schezuan and Canton, for example, have differing styles of cooking as well as unique sets of ingredients. They also focus on locally grown foods and a lot of fish--strange fish. If Hart was going to please the Chinese delegation at lunch he had known he would have to prepare a virtual smorgasbord of small plates, originating from various Chinese cultures. He had annoyed Opplefarmer enough for him to bring in some supplies from a reputable Asian grocery outlet in Syracuse.

When they arrived, the Chinese were the epitome of old and new, traditional and modern. Three older ones wore what looked like brown track suits that had been starched and pressed. It must have been some kind of official uniform because they all had several stars and other emblems stuck to their breast pockets. Possibly, the People's Armed Police, infamously known as the Gestapo of China.

The other three younger Chinese wore western suits with bright coloured ties, had Hollywood style haircuts and brandished smiles right out of a toothpaste commercial. They were all male. Hart guessed Chinese women still couldn't get high-profile government jobs.

"We are very excited to see your technology," the leader of the younger set said in perfect English with no hint of an accent. They were drinking green tea in the lounge shortly after their arrival. Lena had met them personally and led them into the room, knowing as well as he did that no business would be conducted prior to morning tea, or without being welcomed by the head honcho, even if the boss was a female.

They were all standing and sipping away when one of the older Chinese men spoke to the younger one who was apparently the spokesperson. His speech was loud and accented with a lot of guttural noises. He reminded Hart of pictures he'd seen of Mao Tse Tung, only shorter and not as intimidating. He was obviously the leader and was used to having all conversation stop when he spoke. JP watched him intently, smiling incessantly as if to assure the old man that whatever he was saying, it would be met with agreement and understanding. JP understood that, as a woman, her role would be more in the background during this visit. Even Lena had quickly deferred to Losano during the initial introductions, sensing the Chinese group--at least the older ones-- were more comfortable with a male lead.

"General Honsu asks if there are any Asian personnel in your organization, Mr. Losano," the younger one said.

Losano's smile faded slightly. "We have several technologists who are of Asian descent, Mr. Lee," he said. "But I believe some were born and educated in America." Hart knew who was talking about and they were all Korean. And he doubted any of them were American citizens.

Younger one translated and the older one snorted, turned and headed to the door, his high-pitched voice insistent.

"General Honsu is ready to see your technology," Younger one said, his expression flat. He was obviously used to Older one's abruptness and was not about to apologize for it.

"Of course," said Losano, quickly putting his tea cup down on the bar and following the Older one down the hallway. "Please have dinner ready in an hour, Mr. Hart," Losano said to Hart as he turned to leave. Hart guessed he wanted to show the Chinese he had things under control. The other older ones nodded. Hart shrugged. Dinner was already cooking.

Younger one bowed slightly to Hart and followed, the younger Chinese delegates on his heels. None of them had said a word.

Half an hour later, JP came in, frowning. "I've been dismissed."

Hart laughed. "I gather the Chinese have no tolerance for female input."

She sat on a bar stool and pouted. "Jay is treating that old fart like he's Jesus in the Second Coming," she said. "Lena might as well not even be there."

"It's important to both of them that the Chinese like what they see," he said. "With China on board, the other delegations won't be as vital to the project's success. The licensing fee for China's millions of users will be substantial enough to pay back any debts they've incurred. Deep down, Lena knows that. She'll suffer through it."

"I hope they piss her off enough that she'll never consider moving operations elsewhere," JP said. "The President needs BPL to be an American product, licensed overseas, not the other way around." She eased up onto a bar stool. "With pressure from Congress to squelch any successes here, he's afraid Lena and Jay could consider moving operations to somewhere like China."

"You're kidding."

"China is not the online desert everyone thinks it is. Look at Alibaba, Jingdong, Tencent, and other leading companies there. China boasts one of the largest e-commerce societies on the planet and they still haven't reached a third of the population. And Lena knows that. China would pay dearly to have the base of operations on their soil."

"Lena and Losano wouldn't last ten minutes in China with all the government interference," Hart said.

"But if the young officials suggested Hong Kong or even Macao or Shanghai as a destination, it wouldn't be quite as harsh, would it?" she said. "Look at this group; how well the young people are integrated into the old regime. When the old dogs die, who do you think will be running things?"

"You think Lena is thinking about it?" Hart asked.

"If she isn't, Losano is," she said. "And President Emerson considers the Chinese delegation a real threat." She pointed at a glass and he poured her a sauvignon blanc. After a sip, she looked up at me, the squiggly lines on her tense face slowly dissipating. "Lena would never put up with being a second-class citizen," she said, the right side of her mouth pushing upwards, forcing her nose to raise slightly in conjunction. "This is her baby and I don't think money is her motivation."

"It's most likely Losano's though," he said.

"Gays don't last long in a communist environment," she snorted. "Once he understands that, no amount of money will convince him to shift it all over there."

Hart cocked his head and frowned but JP was too absorbed in her wine to notice his look. Something about the way she'd said that was unnerving. He shook his head and poured himself a glass of red wine. He'd had enough tea for one day.

"If BPL is launched here, does the President have support for nationalizing it? I mean, since corporate America seems bent on prying into BPL, is he confident the government will be able to maintain control of the new, ah... utility?"

She looked up from her glass, her lips glistening from the moistness. "It can provide hundreds of jobs nationwide, so the Democrats are pushing to create a national agency that will license the technology and control its distribution. The Republicans, of course, have communications companies in their back pockets and are aiming at private sector administration."

"So it may all come down to who gets into office next election?" Hart said.

"Ever since President Obama signed that executive order, every internet provider, cable, phone, VOIP, or anything yet to be invented would be legally bound to comply and cede control to Homeland. Even the Republicans can't get past that. If they take power, and even if they manage to de-nationalize BPL. if it's initially set up as another agency within Homeland's directive-- while Emerson's in power--it will be even harder to pry it loose to become a publicly-traded company. Why do you think Frank's so invested in us being here?" she said.

Hart thought about that for a minute and then he got it.

"Frank wants to run that agency," he said. JP's eyes opened wider and one side of her mouth raised upwards into a grin.

"No shit Sherlock!"

Chapter Forty

Hart was cleaning glassware and filing them on trays behind the bar counter when he heard something that grabbed his attention. The older members of the Chinese delegation were at a table by the window, conversing loudly, as they always did. Hart had ignored them. Younger one and one of his companions were huddled at the end of the bar, a little more hushed. They were using the same staccato verbal click so common to Asian languages, but it didn't sound Chinese.

Hart listened carefully but didn't let on he was paying attention. Younger One was listening while his taller, thinner counterpart spoke urgently. Hart automatically translated what he was hearing in his head.

"The Air Force has spread four divisions over various airfields. By the end of the month, we will have close to one hundred thousand troops staged and ready."

Hart bent to rearrange bottles in the small bar fridge below the bar, keeping his eyes focused on the interior of the refrigerator. The conversation continued for a couple of minutes, then Younger One shifted to the centre of the counter.

"Would you have any Japanese Sake, Mr. Hart?" he asked in English, leaning over to get my attention.

"Japanese?" he queried.

He laughed, nervously Hart thought.

"Please do not tell General Honsu," he said, turning to make sure no one could hear him. "But Japanese sake is far superior to ours. Whenever I travel, I try to enjoy as much as I can."

"I believe I have some Nabeshima," Hart said. The Japanese were due to arrive in the next week so he had ordered a few bottles through Oppelfarmer. Sake wasn't a rural New York staple but it was common enough in larger towns.

"That would be perfect, thank you," Younger One said. "If you don't mind, we'll take it out to the terrace. It's a peaceful evening, don't you think?"

Hart nodded his head. The guy he'd been talking to had already meandered over to the patio door and was obviously waiting for Younger One to join him. Did he somehow sense he'd been listening?

Hart poured a couple of ounces of sake into two Chinese tea cups and placed them on the bar.

"Thank you Mr. Hart," Younger One said, picking them up and taking them out to the terrace.

Hart went back to polishing the glasses and watched the two men continue their conversation outside. Younger One seemed to be on the defensive, his partner gesturing impatiently with his hands.

"Does Al make you do that at home?" JP asked as she strode in wearing a stunning two-piece pale yellow pant suit. Her hair was down in the bob which made her appear several years younger.

"We have machines at the *Hart*," he said, putting the drying cloth down and pouring us both a glass of 7 Deadly Zins, a fresh and fruity zinfandel from California. "The dishwasher here is a household one, leaves spots."

"You're so domesticated," she said. "You'll make someone a great...."

"Don't say it," he interrupted. Then he nodded toward the terrace. "See those two?"

JP looked over her shoulder while taking a sip of her wine.

"Yeah, looks like the General's translator may be in trouble," she said, watching the other one continue to berate Younger One.

"He's not Chinese."

"Who isn't, the translator?" she asked.

"No the other one," he said.

"How do you know? "

"Notice that he's taller, has a more traditional athletic build, and his hair is thicker," he said.

"Okay, I admit, most Chinese are dumpy and round faced," she said. "That guys dateable, for an Asian. But how does that mean he's not Chinese?"

"He's speaking Korean," Hart said.

JP watched for minute, tapped her glass with her forefinger, and thought that over.

"Shit," she finally said.

*   *   *

"How do you know it's North Korean?" Frank asked. Lena and Hart had gone into the office and called Frank on the secure cell phone he'd given me.

"The dialect," Hart said. "He's from the province just east of Pyong Yang," JP stared at him.

Hart shrugged. He had been immersed in Taekwondo training since his youth. Unlike other martial arts, there were only two styles of Taekwondo: North Korean and South Korean. It was invented in what is now the North and that was the style Hart had learned as a teenager and practiced for nearly twenty years. Back then, part of that training included learning Korean.... North Korean.

"He's tall and good looking too," Lena said, grinning. We were on speaker phone. Hart gave her a withering look and waited for Frank to comment. He chose to ignore her.

"You have to watch his every move," he said finally. "We told Castillo North Koreans weren't to be included and she readily agreed."

"Lena has no idea," JP said. "She thinks they're all Chinese, just like everyone else. Including Losano, no doubt."

"Losano's a loose cannon," Frank said. "Maybe he knows."

"It doesn't make sense Frank," JP said. "Losano want things to go smooth in the States. He's not going to risk that by showing the North Koreans what he's doing."

Frank was silent for a moment. Maybe he was contemplating whether JP's female intuition was strong enough reason to believe that Losano had no idea there was a North Korean on the grounds.

"It would be nice to know why the Chinese brought him," Frank said. "It doesn't benefit them either. They don't need the NK to make BPL happen in the homeland. It would risk getting the license and they should know that."

"Maybe they don't know either," Hart said.

"Well, at least one of them does," JP said.

"Asians all look alike to most Westerners," Frank said. "But there's no way a Chinese General would be fooled, especially that particular General. He knows he's brought a North Korean with him. What I want to know is why?"

"I don't think they're going to let me overhear any more conversations," Hart said. "They haven't caught on that I understand what they're saying but they seem paranoid. They've already left the bar and gone outside to talk once."

"Okay, so you watch him for now," said Frank. "There's not enough to go on for me to go to the Director with. I can't afford to create an incident right now. If the Chinese go for BPL, that's our door for infiltrating their communications. We need that licensing agreement."

"And if they suggest moving operations there as part of their investment?" JP asked.

"Then we move the FBI in and build a virtual wall around that facility so fast no one will be able to go anywhere. It'll make the Great Wall look like a toy fort."

Hart loved it when Frank got hot under the collar. He was so Clint Eastwood. He hadn't missed the part about infiltrating Chinese communications but was smart enough to know not to ask any questions, especially over the phone, even if it was a secure one.

"The Chinese have ousted JP," Hart said. "They don't like women around when men are doing men's work." She tried to punch him but he turned and her jab hit thin air. He smirked at her.

"Jesus, what a backwards country," Frank said. "It scares me that they could be the next super power."

"Wait till their women get the internet," JP said. "Once they discover what Susan B. Anthony did, they'll have a modern-day sufferance movement on their hands."

"They'll be too busy monitoring shopping online," Hart said.

"The NK is there for a reason," Frank said, stopping our jostling. "And since we can't officially ask anyone, I need you to find out why he's there. They've had the presentation already?"

"Yes, this afternoon," JP said. "They're staying the night and catching a charter in Rochester tomorrow morning."

"He was there for a reason," Frank repeated.

"Maybe he likes dim sum," Hart said, confident it was JP who was supposed to find out why the NK was there.

Frank hung up.

Robert J. Morrow

Chapter Forty-One

Hart wasn't sure what awoke him but since he was a light sleeper, it didn't have to be much. He sat up and listened.

There was a rustling downstairs.

Damn it.

It seemed to be an international malady. No matter where people came from, there was always someone in the group who couldn't sleep and raided the fridge during the night. He had gotten annoyed the first time it happened with one of the Mexican guys and when Hart mentioned it to Lena, she didn't like the idea of strangers wandering around the house without supervision. Since he was in charge of the kitchen, it was his responsibility to ensure that stuffing their faces was all they were doing.

Hart got up, pulled on his jeans and a t-shirt, and headed down the stairs to the kitchen. He didn't want to risk waking anyone else so he was barefoot and treading lightly.

Which turned out to be a good thing because the noise wasn't coming from the kitchen. It was coming from the living room. His eyesight was pretty good in the dark and he didn't want to scare anyone by turning on lights, so he leaned against the entranceway and peered around the corner into the large room.

A figure, about five and a half feet tall, completely dressed in black, was leaning over the double patio doors, as if gently shutting them. Hart watched as the figure turned and slowly crept across the room toward him. Hart had nowhere to go except the hallway, which he backed into quickly and quietly, so as not to be seen. It was a fifty-fifty chance the intruder was coming his way--

to get to any of the other rooms--or the opposite way toward the front door.

As Hart was preparing to defend himself if the figure came his way, he heard a thump and a low groan. Then quiet. He looked around the corner and saw two black clad figures, one bent over the other one who seemed to be sprawled out, face down, on the hallway floor.

Two intruders?

Actually, the bent over one looked familiar somehow. The shape of the head or maybe the curve of the waistline.

It was JP.

Hart didn't want to startle her since he knew what he would do if someone startled him in that position. So he watched as she checked the downed figure's pockets, found what looked like tiny tools and a small black box, slipped them into her pocket, then stepped around in front of his head. She leaned over and pulled the intruder's arms over his head and began dragging him down the hallway.

Hart stepped out as quietly as he could but had his hands out in front of him so JP noticed him immediately.

She dropped the guy's arms and crouched into a fighting stance. Hart stepped closer until he could see her face clearly. Black smudges covered her cheeks and forehead. When she recognized him, she frowned and reached down for the guys arms again.

"Don't stand there, help me," she hissed in a whisper. "I'm making too much noise."

"Who is it?"

"Your friendly neighbourhood Korean," she said. "Grab his legs. We'll carry him up the stairs to his room." Seemed a little silly and Hart wanted to ask more questions but she was already standing tall, the guy's arms trapped behind her forearms, almost in a sitting position. He bent and grabbed the crook of his knees and lifted up till the guy's rear end was a few inches off the floor. He nodded for JP to lead the way, backwards.

Luckily the stairs were wide and the steps not very steep. They half carried, half dragged the inert Korean up to the second level and down the hall to one of the guest rooms.

"How do you know this is his room?" Hart whispered.

"I followed him," she said.

"Is anyone else in there?"

"Yes, but he won't be hearing anything for a while," she said. "I gave him some GHB." He'll wake up with a headache, maybe have a wet dream, but he won't remember anything else.

"Is that what you gave this guy?" Hart said, holding the guy's back half while JP dropped his arms and opened the door.

"No, his treatment was a little more personal," she said. "But I don't think he'll complain to anyone since he was breaking into the presentation centre."

"One, two, three..." Hart said and they heaved him up and dropped him onto the bed. Hart looked over to the other single bed and saw Younger One, eyes closed, sleeping soundly. "What was he doing there?"

"He was taking pictures of some documents on Lena's computer screen in her private lab," she said, tapping her pant pocket. But I've got the camera."

"You didn't see what he was looking at?" Hart asked.

"I was kind of busy," she said, pushing the Korean, so he rolled onto his side, facing the wall. "Come on, let's go."

Hart checked the hall to see that they hadn't roused anyone, took one last look at the two sleeping Asians, and closed the door after Lena walked out.

"My room's closest," he said, pointing down the hall.

"Not now," she said. "I don't want to be seen in this second-floor thief outfit. We'll talk about it tomorrow. I have to go back to the lab and shut off Lena's computer."

"Catwoman," he said, and grinned.

"What?" she hissed, clearly wanting to get to her own room.

"You look more like Catwoman than a burglar," he said. "Much sexier."

She was too far away for Hart to notice but he was sure he felt her roll her eyes.

Robert J. Morrow

Chapter Forty-Two

The next morning, they all gathered at the front door, as had become custom, to say farewell to the delegations. Losano seemed agitated and Lena looked pre-occupied, glancing at her watch every few seconds, wishing the Chinese to hurry up and leave.

The old General had been escorted to the limo by two of the younger clerks and they were all inside, the door still ajar, when Younger One came out, his arm around the Korean's waist. The Korean's face was ashen, his mouth in a grimace. He was obviously still feeling the effects of the drug JP had administered.

"What did you give him?" Hart asked. He and JP were off to the side observing. Lena and Losano were the ones who did the official shaking of hands in farewell.

"It's called RX351." she said. "He'll be dead within twenty-four to forty-eight hours."

Hart stared at her but she was watching Younger One push the Korean through the door. No one in the car appeared to be helping him and the Korean bumped his head getting in. It didn't seem to add to his already obvious pain and Younger One didn't stop but kept pushing until the Korean was clear of the doorway and was able to get in himself.

"What's up with him?" Lena came over and asked.

"Food poisoning, most likely," JP said.

Lena looked at Hart who shrugged. "No one's perfect," he said. She shook her head, turned and went back into the house.

Losano watched as the limo pulled away from the curb. Once the car had disappeared, he went inside also, obviously distracted with his thoughts.

"Do you think killing him was necessary?" Hart asked, astounded that they were talking about taking someone's life in such a casual manner.

"The military came up with RX-351 last year and it's only been tested a handful of times. As far as I know Military Intelligence wanted exclusive use for combat situations but someone high up in the CIA convinced them one or two field ops could use it in a pinch." she turned to walk back inside but began talking again. Apparently, Hart was supposed to keep up.

"North Korea is the new big bad wolf" she said. "It's bad enough he was here but to be clandestine, and get caught trying to infiltrate Lena's private sanctum?" She shrugged. "It was a no brainer. Besides Frank sanctioned it."

"We don't know why he was here, or why the Chinese brought him," Hart said.

"Although it would be good to know that, we didn't know what he was looking for, or what he actually found for that matter. Frank just assumed since it was done this way, whatever secrets he was after weren't something they could obtain through diplomatic circles. So it was sabotage, or technology theft. Doesn't matter. He was an enemy spy and has been dealt with accordingly."

"I didn't think you were, ah... well, a killer," he said. "Your story about the drug lord boyfriend made me think you weren't the killing type."

She looked at me, her eyes narrowing, taking on a dull, dark hue. "Frank didn't want to risk that he'd memorized important data that could be taken back to North Korea. It was his decision. And it's why he sent me here with you. I'm the government employee, not you." She paused and turned away. "Be thankful he didn't ask you to do it."

"When he dies, they'll know it happened here," he said to her back.

She stopped and turned slightly without fully turning to face him. "Sure they will but they won't know how, or why," JP said.

"If the Chinese knew what he was doing, they'll assume he got caught. If they didn't know, they'll just figure we knew who he was and took him out anyway. Or they'll blame you for bad food." She smirked. "Regardless, they won't turn it into an incident because he shouldn't have been part of their delegation."

"Because by bringing it up, even through diplomatic circles, they'll be admitting they brought him with them."

"Yep," she said.

Hart looked up at the sunny, lightly cloudy sky. As each cloud passed over the house, a shadow trailed across the front lawn like a spotlight raking a prison yard.

"I have to meet Frank for a debriefing," she said. "I'm going to Syracuse. Wanna come for the ride?"

"I could use the break but I need to research the South Korean menu." he said, not sure why but realizing he just didn't feel comfortable around JP at the moment. The woman had just technically killed someone in cold blood. Besides, something about JP's dark mood made him feel it would be best to let her spend some time alone. Hat stepped up beside her and put on a smile. "Some of the ingredients will be hard to find. I may even call you, get you to pickup some things if it's not too late."

"I'll be done with Frank by late afternoon, so catch me before four pm or so."

"Sounds good." he said. They walked to the front door side by side. "By-the-way, did you notice Losano seems a little antsy the past couple of days?"

"Pressure, probably," JP said. "It's all coming together and he has to make sure all the kinks are out by the time the President arrives for the big shindig. Right after that, the system goes national."

"It's as if he's worried about something though," he said. "I wonder if the Korean did something in the lab?"

JP's head snapped around and she looked at him sharply.

"He didn't have time," she said but her eyes squinted a bit in thought. "All he did was take pictures of the active screens. He didn't touch anything while he was in there. No more than a minute, tops."

"What did he shoot?"

"Whatever was on the screen, I'm assuming. It was an encrypted flash drive camera, so nothing can be opened. I sent the files to Frank last night. He'll have it decoded by the time I get there. Maybe it'll make sense then."

As JP continued inside to get ready, Hart watched the shadows cross the lawn again in a non-stop parade of darkness cutting a cooling path across the hot, brightly lit grass. It would be a good day to go into town on the bike, see if Oppelfarmer can find him some eel.

Chapter Forty-Three

Hart was in the office, finalizing his grocery list for the South Korean visit when Losano tapped on the door.

"Was JP staying over somewhere?" he asked, his usually intense face marred with concern.

Hart looked at his watch. Ten pm. It was a little late though maybe Frank had splurged for supper after all.

"She's probably just tied up with something," he said.

"Please have her come to the lab when she arrives," he said. "If it's not too, too late, of course."

"Is there something I can help you with?" Hart asked. The poor sod seemed upset. He realized JP was likely one of the only friends he had up here. Everyone else was an employee. Hart had left JP to deal with him so we hadn't developed much of a relationship. He wasn't particularly good with gays; had nothing against them, just didn't know what to talk about or how to handle myself. His flaw, he realized. But his background hadn't included much feminine influence, so he really did feel uneasy around them.

"No, no, it's nothing important," he stammered. "I was just concerned. She is, after all, my bodyguard, of sorts." He blushed and left quickly.

Hart pulled out his cell and dialed.

"Yo!"

"You're kidding," Hart said. "You chide me for answering the restaurant phone with 'Yeah' and the best the super spy can do is 'Yo'?"

"What do you want Art? Has JP filled you in?" Frank said.

"Actually, she's not here yet. Losano was worried. So I thought I'd check."

"She left here several hours ago," Frank said. "Maybe she went somewhere on the way back. She doesn't punch a clock you know."

"I was just checking to make sure you hadn't had a bout of chivalry or something and taken her out for a late supper," he said.

"She wouldn't go if I asked," Frank said.

"Don't mingle with the boss syndrome?"

"In our business, it's a good way to get compromised," he said.

"Is that what they call it now?"

"Listen, if she's not back by midnight, let me know. She's a big girl with an active libido. We'll give her till then, just in case."

"Is that her curfew?"

"You've had no luck getting into her pants have you," Frank said. "Don't worry, she can't stray far, I have her on GPS. If she isn't back by then, I'll check it."

"Why not check it now?"

"Because she would feel it and I don't want to embarrass her," Frank said.

"Her phone vibrates when you activate her GPS locator?" Hart asked

"The GPS is embedded under her skin," Frank said.

"I thought they only did that in the movies," he said.

"By the time technology shows up in a movie Art, we've been using it for five years," Frank said.

"I'll text you when she gets home Daddy," Hart said and hung up. Unconsciously, he rubbed his arm. Then he shivered. Where the hell would Frank embed a chip in a woman that has spent considerable time naked with the enemy?

Chapter Forty-Four

Consciousness came slowly. JP's first vague thoughts were that she was tired. No, not tired, groggy. And sore. She tried to stretch her legs to alleviate her discomfort but she couldn't move them. As if as an afterthought, she slowly fought an unusual bout of fatigue and forced herself to open her eyes.

Her eyelids fluttered open and the sight brought her brain to full-functioning capacity immediately.

Two of the ugliest Italian guys she'd ever seen were a couple of feet in front of her, sitting in chairs, leaning forward, heads in their hands, elbows resting on their knees. They were leering at her with stupid looking grins on their faces. She tried to move but realized her ankles were tied to the chair she was sitting on and now that she was slowly gaining clarity, she realized she couldn't move her arms either

The room was cement block and a little damp. A tiny window at ceiling level was boarded up and a fluorescent light in the centre of the room was the only illumination. A basement. The chairs were the only items in the roughly twenty by twenty room, other than unfinished wooden stairs leading upwards at one corner of the room. There was no flooring, just poured concrete that had been painted gray. An unfinished basement somewhere in a suburb, no doubt. But a suburb of where?

Her gaze came back to the two Italians who were still glaring…no not glaring. They seemed mesmerized by her for some reason.

That's when she realized she was naked. Well, nearly naked; they'd left her bra on but it was up around her neck and still strapped around her back. Her breasts were completely exposed. She looked down and saw that her skirt was crumpled on the floor and her panties were around her ankles.

A quick scan of her body, that which she could see by moving her head around at least, told her there were no marks or cuts.

She looked up at the two monkeys. One had a round face, was around forty-five, with a two-day old stubble that probably made him feel like he was still in style. The other one, maybe twenty-five, was thinner but bore a similar Brad Pitt-esque stubbly beard. Old guy's hair was nearly gone but he had the comb over thing going. The younger one's hair was long but was wrapped into a man bun that stuck up like a duck's butt above his head.

"You boys enjoying the view?" she said. She didn't particularly feel confident--what woman would stark naked in front of two strange and very ugly men--but since her panties and bra were still attached to her that meant they had tied her up first, then stripped her to expose her female parts. Nobody had raped her yet. Though they'd likely felt her up.

"Mr. Losano's a lucky man," Old guy said, his eyes studying hers, then roaming down to the hairless mound between her legs.

"Mr. Losano will kill you when he finds out what you're doing," JP said.

"Oh, I don't think so Miss," old guy said. "You see, we don't work for him and he don't know who we are from Jesus."

The young guy leaned forward and with his forefinger pushed one side of the bra up a little farther.

"Must be cold in here," he snickered.

"Actually, they're always like that," JP said, staring at the kid. His eyebrows raised in surprise. "When I'm cold, my entire breast lifts an inch or two."

The young one cocked his head, thinking. Then he lurched forward, his hand open, ready to cup the breast closest to him.

Before he could though, the old guy grabbed the kid's wrist and pushed it away.

"We can look, maybe even touch a little," he said. "But no rough stuff. If she don't go back happy and comfy, the boss'll have your nuts."

"The boss?" JP asked. "You mean you boys didn't think up this highly original episode all by yourselves?"

The old guy snorted. "Yeah, he said you were a tough one, and we weren't to be taken in with your, ah, obvious charms."

"And he will be okay with this?" she pointed her chin downward, her eyes noticing that they'd used plastic ties to attach her legs to the chair legs. She assumed her wrists were attached to the chair back in the same way. They hadn't used long ones like the police use but the type you picked up at a local hardware store. They'd had to put two together in order to get around each of her ankles. Where the two links attached would be a weak point.

"He just wants you out of the way for a while," Old guy said. "So don't worry your little head off, we're not going to hurt you at all…"

"But we might have a little fun before we let you go," the young one interrupted, sneering. The old guy rolled his eyes, for her benefit, JP assumed but it was little reassurance. She didn't think he'd try too hard if the young guy got pushier.

"I wonder how wet you can get if I finger ya a little bit," the young one said.

"You'll have to wash your hands first," JP said, putting on the best smile she could muster.

The young guy was getting heated. Obviously, he wasn't used to women making fun of him. The old guy snickered. "She'd probably swallow your finger paesano," he grunted.

JP continued to smile, holding the young guys stare until he broke it and jumped up, slapping his knees in frustration. He began pacing back and forth behind the old guy.

"So we're supposed to sit here staring at each other until the boss tells you we can all go home?" JP asked.

"Somethin' like that," the old guy said.

"This is bullshit!" the young one exclaimed. "What makes her so special? We always have a little fun on these jobs Mickey."

The old guy stood up quickly and grabbed the younger one's arm, pulling him close until they were practically nose to nose.

"You called me Mickey. Now she knows my name... Dillon," he hissed. The younger one's face went red.

"Sorry Mi... man," he stammered. "But now you gone and told her my name."

Mickey smiled broadly. "Yeah, and if you keep acting the way you are, she's gonna remember your name a lot better than mine, eh?"

"No one will know," Dillon pouted.

"She will, you idiot," Mickey said. "And she's goin' back, remember? You wanna do work for this guy again, you don't fuck up the first job he lays on us, eh?"

Dillon looked longingly at JP.

"Go take a walk around," Mickey said. "Construction crews are all gone for the day but they usually have a rent-a-cop on site. He's probably made a bed somewhere for the night. See if you can find him so we'll know where to keep an eye out."

Dillon kept staring at Lena, his eyes raking over her from top to bottom.

"Go!" Mickey said forcefully. Dillon shrugged and went up the wooden stairs. JP heard a door close after him, then a few seconds later, another door, farther away was shut also.

"Thank you," Lena said quietly.

Mickey sat down and stared at her breasts for a moment before shifting his gaze to her eyes.

"If I were ten years younger, you'd be fightin' me off miss," he said, laughing. "But I've been doing little gigs like this too long to play around with the merchandise. Lot of things have changed with the mob but mistreatin' someone's woman is still a death wish. Even if she ain't really his woman."

"How do you know I'm not Mr. Losano's woman?" Lena said.

Mickey's neck jolted inward, a look of incredulity crossing his face. "We both know the answer to that," he said, grinning. "I'll keep young Dillon off of ya miss if you just keep your smart mouthin' to a minimum, eh? Get him too riled up and.... well, I ain't about to get in the way of true lust, know what I mean?"

JP nodded, and then shivered.

"They do firm up don't they," Mickey observed. JP frowned and cocked her head sideways.

"He wouldn't get so riled up if he wasn't constantly reminded of what he's missing," she said.

"Good point," Mickey said and leaned behind him to grab her sweater that had been scrunched up behind his chair. He held it in his hands and looked at her, tied to the chair.

"Hmmm," he muttered. He leaned over her and draped the arms over her shoulders so that the sweater hung down in front, covering her breasts. He then reached back, grabbed her skirt and threw it onto her waist.

"Ain't perfect but boss said not to let you loose while your awake," Mickey said. "Figures you could be quite a cat, since you's federal and all." He grinned.

"Wow, chivalry isn't lost on you, is it," JP said.

Mickey frowned. "See, now there's that smartmouthin' again," he said. "I'm telling ya, keep that up and I go for a walk and leave Dillon here to watch you. I can't be held responsible if I ain't here, right?"

JP fidgeted her knees so the skirt covered most of her waist to the tops of her knees. The nakedness didn't really bother her but damn, it was cold down here.

After what seemed like at least an hour, Mickey looked at his watch.

"Where the hell is that kid?" he said and got up.

Tires crunching on gravel caught his attention. To JP it sounded like the vehicle was just on the other side of the wall, meaning that if this was a new home construction site, someone had just driven into the driveway of this house.

Mickey's chin lifted as if perking up his ears to hear better. He said nothing but slowly walked behind her and reached down for something.

JP thought about screaming but if the person outside was an old security guard, her screaming would cause him to blunder in here and probably get shot or something. No, she'd be better off waiting to see if he investigated further. If she could distract

Mickey at the right moment, it might give the security guard enough time to aim his gun and, hopefully, fire.

She heard a rip and then Mickey's hands came into view with a piece of duct tape stretched between them. Before JP could react, he firmly slapped it onto her mouth and pressed the corners down.

Should have screamed after all, she thought.

Mickey went to the stairs, took a look back at JP who simply stared at him, and then pulled a switchblade from his pocket, it's swoosh upon opening echoing in the confined room. With blade in hand, he went up the stairs and quietly opened the basement door.

Chapter Forty-Five

"She's not back yet Frank," Hart said into his cell. Losano was on the other side of the desk, pacing back and forth.

"It's only just midnight," Frank says. "I don't think we need to be concerned."

"Jay Losano is here with me and he seems to think JP was planning to be back sooner," Hart said. Losano didn't acknowledge him but started nodding his head, muttering "Yes, yes..." under his breath.

"With all due respect, she's only faking to be his BFF Art," Frank said. "She could be anywhere, with anyone."

"True, but she would have told me Frank," Hart said. "She was going to grab some items for me. She knows I'd be looking for her by now and she knows what that means."

"That you'd call me," Frank said.

"Yep."

Losano gave Hart a wary look. He hadn't told him he and JP had prior arrangements. He may have had other ideas for her.

"I left a couple of guys in Syracuse," Frank says. "I'll send them up the 481 Highway. See if they notice anything on the way."

"I can go the other way, meet them in the middle," he said. "Save time."

"I'm afraid that won't be possible," Lena Castillo said as she stepped into the office. Her face expressed concern but it could also have been frustration. She stepped past Losano and leaned on Hart's desk, arms straight, her gaze drilling into him. "I just heard from the South Koreans. They're coming a day early. I need you here to get ready for them."

Losano stopped pacing and stared at Lena.

"She might be in danger Lena," he said quietly.

Lena turned to face him. "She's a big girl Jay," he said. "And she's Secret Service for Christ's sake. She can take care of herself. I don't need to remind you that the Koreans are one of the most important groups coming. We can't afford any screw ups."

"Surely a couple of hours won't make a diff...." Losano said but Lena put up her hand to interrupt.

"They've put in a special request for kimchi, when they arrive, whatever that is. They'll be here early tomorrow evening now." She looked at Hart but spoke to Losano. "I don't think Arthur will have time to be gallivanting Jay. My understanding is that kimchi prepared from scratch is extremely time consuming, at least according to Yoshi upstairs in the lab. Isn't that right Arthur?"

Hart was still holding the receiver but hadn't said anything. He could hear Frank's breathing on the other end. "She's right Art," Frank said in my ear. Obviously he'd heard the conversation. "There's nothing you can do that the guys can't do. It's only a ninety-minute drive from Syracuse to Oswego. She can't have gone far. Besides, like you said, she would have told you if she was going off the plantation. It's protocol."

"If that's Mr. Daro on the line there Hart, be sure to tell him the Koreans are very important to this project, thanks to Jay," Lena said. Losano was just staring at the wall now, lost in thought, the creases on his forehead evidence of his concern.

"JP is fine Art," Frank said. "Your priority for now is to keep things going according to schedule."

Hart gave Lena a hard stare but it didn't seem to phase her. Then he glanced at Losano who seemed not so much concerned as consternated over something.

"Call me when you've got her Frank."

"Yeah," he said and Hart heard the click in his ear. He put the phone in his pocket and sat down, opening his laptop.

Lena straightened up and turned to Losano who was still staring at the wall.

"I won't be ready for them Jay," she said. "I've got that MS variance problem still. I need your help."

Losano's forehead crinkled and his eyes narrowed as he dropped his gaze from the wall, turning to grab Lena's arm.

"We'll talk about it in the lab," he said, steering her toward the office door.

Just before they turned into the hall, Losano turned back to me.

"Tell me when she shows up, ok?" he said. Hart couldn't tell if his expression was worry, annoyance, or nervousness. He was a hard guy to read.

Hart nodded. The South Koreans coming a day early, demanding a meal that most Korean nationals he knew would never trust an American to do properly, seemed odd. But Losano had been right. Kimchi, though a relatively simple dish--and not one he would have thought world-travelling diplomats would desire--was very time consuming. In the old days, Koreans would ferment the ingredients underground in large jars for weeks or months. But there was a northern version that could be accomplished overnight, he recalled, using fresh fish and oysters. He picked up phone and dialed Oppelfarmer's. He'd leave a message, hoping it wouldn't take all day to fill his order. They were right on Lake Ontario for heaven's sake. Surely, some of the fish was edible.

Robert J. Morrow

Chapter Forty-Six

JP heard nothing for quite a while. She wondered if Mickey and Dillon were experienced enough to incapacitate a security guard without doing any real harm to him. But the longer she waited, the more she figured something had gone wrong and all three of them were probably lying in pools of blood somewhere on the street.

She hadn't heard any shots or grunts from being stabbed, though she wasn't sure she would unless they were right above her. She started to hotch the chair toward the stairs. She wasn't sure what she'd do once she got there but maybe there was a loose piece of masonry or discarded wood chip there that she could use to cut or at least loosen the plastic ties.

About halfway there, she heard the front door open, then shut. She heard footsteps come toward the basement then stop in front of the door.

She tried to shout but it came out as a muffled grunt with the tape securely stuck to her skin. She blew between her lips, trying to push the tape outward so she could make a louder sound but it hadn't been on long enough and wasn't pliable yet.

The door opened and a dark figure came slowly down the stairs in a crouch.

He was dressed in all black, complete with full face mask and blackened eyes. He held a gun in front of him as, still in a crouched position, he edged down the stairs, stopping just under the ceiling level scanning the room with both the gun and his eyes.

JP had been quietly watching him and when their eyes connected, she grunted. She was aware she had become exposed again since all the hotching had dislodged her sweater and skirt. The man must have noticed but he continued looking around the room still in a crouch.

Satisfied with what he saw, he came down the rest of the stairs, stuffed his gun in a holster that was around his chest and stood up to his full height which was roughly five and a half feet, JP figured. He was stocky and had a full chest. He walked straight toward her and, without warning, ripped the tape from her mouth. JP gasped and twisted her mouth around to get the blood circulating in her lips.

"You can scream if you like but there's no one around to hear you," the man said. His voice was stiff, monotone, and American. "Besides," he continued. "I think I just rescued you so that makes me a good guy."

There was no smile in his cadence. It was tough to tell from the loosely fitting camouflage outfit, but she sensed he had a lean, muscular build. Not a thug like Dillon, more sophisticated, more trained. His biceps and triceps were unusually defined and since he seemed natural in his crouching stance on the stairs, he obviously worked his leg muscles extensively. The shape of his head didn't tell her much and although the mask looked to be made of nylon and was tight fitting, she couldn't tell if he was bald or just had short hair. There was no way to guess his age although someone this well-defined was likely not middle-aged.

"Who are you?" JP's voice was a little hoarse from not being used for a while. She coughed and tried again. "What happened to the Italians?"

"Hmmm," he muttered as he gazed at her. JP didn't sense a leer, more of an appraisal of her figure. Since he'd already declared himself as her white knight, she didn't think she should be threatened by his gaze, though she knew with most men that could change in an instant.

"Are you going to untie me?" she asked.

"Your friends are sleeping in their car for now," he said slowly, pulling a long curved knife from a sheath that had been hidden inside a pant leg. "And actually, no, I'm not going to untie you."

"Then what are you doing?" she asked, exasperated and wary.

"I'd call it evening the odds actually," he said. His eyes glittered and JP could imagine him smiling beneath the cover of the mask.

He kneeled down in front of her and with a quick flick of his wrist, cut through the ties on her one ankle. Then he shifted to do the same with the other ankle. He then got up, walked over to JPs sweater and skirt, picked them up and brought them back to her.

She was waiting for him to cut the ties that held her wrists to the chair but he dropped the clothes in front of her and turned back to the stairs.

"We're about an hour Southwest of Oswego, a place called Clyde," he said, starting up the stairs. He crouched at the top. "It's a new subdivision. There's a high school down the street and if you hurry you might make it into town before the gas station closes for the night."

"You can't leave me here like this," JP said.

"I'd worry about getting out of the chair first, get some clothes on. It's a little chilly out there," he said and got up.

"Wait!" JP exclaimed. "This is the dumbest rescue I've ever heard of. Why don't you untie me? I'll let you leave ahead of me, I promise. You've got secrets and the whole Delta Force thing going on, I get it. But why put me through more torture?"

"You're just lucky I was in the neighbourhood," he said. "The skinny one looked like he was ready to do a little dancing with you. Might not have been fun." He went up the rest of the steps and closed the door behind him.

"Wait! Don't leave me here, you idiot!" JP shouted after him, no longer concerned about any amorous undertones. She wanted out of here. She stood but since her wrists were still attached to the chair, she was forced to lean forward.

Silence.

"Come on," she shouted. "This is stupid. How am I supposed to get out of here?"

There was no answer. "Shit!" she exclaimed. She set the chair down again and looked around the room for anything sharp. She got up and limped around looking for anything, a piece of wood, glass, whatever.

As she came close to the stairs, she noticed a glittering on the top step. Light from the other side of the basement door was leaking in and shining on something silver.

JP manipulated the steps by bending forward and walking up. If she lost her balance, she wouldn't be able to break her fall and would go flying backwards to the cement floor. Oh well, at least the chair would probably break on impact and she could get her wrists free that way. Extremely painful but it would achieve that much at least.

When she got closer to the top of the stairs, her head bowed down almost to step level, she saw that her rescuer had dropped his knife.

No, he left it there on purpose for me to eventually find. Asshole.

She leaned forward, grabbed the knife between her teeth and debated whether to go back to the basement or break the door down and head upstairs. Breaking through anything in her current position would be impossible so back downstairs it was. On a whim, she pushed her head against the basement door. It opened.

It isn't even locked!

With the knife still in her mouth, she got to her knees on the top step and crawled through into what looked like a half-finished kitchen. The light was coming in from street lamps through the kitchen window.

She listened but heard nothing. She dropped the knife on the kitchen floor, then rolled on her side in front of it, the chair bottom forcing her to stay in a bent position, knees up. She hotched a little until her hands found the knife. Turning it so the blade was between her wrists, she started cutting the nylon tie, all the while debating whether to kill the Italians first, or just go and chase after Delta-man.

In the end, after her adrenaline subsided from the exertion of cutting herself loose, she decided to get dressed and figure out a way to get back to Oswego.

Chapter Forty-Seven

"I want more security here."

Jay Losano stood with his arms flailing around, fists clenched. His mouth was thin, his lips tightly clasped together. Lena stood behind him, arms crossed, watching him.

"We've been doing fine so far," Lena said calmly.

They were sitting in the lounge at the center table. Hart could see the waves gently rolling into the shore as the light breeze wafted over Lake Ontario, dropping the warm July temperature by about ten degrees. Inside the complex, the AC was running full blast and it was a somewhat unpleasant sixty-five degrees throughout. Still, Losano looked like he'd just come in from the outside.

"The South Korean delegation were quite disturbed that we'd allowed the North Koreans to infiltrate the lab," he said.

"I didn't tell them so how did they know?" Lena said, turning to Hart. He shrugged and took a sip of his first afternoon bottled flavored water.

"You knew one of them." Losano accused, pointing his finger at Hart.

"No, I merely recognized that he wasn't speaking Chinese," he said.

Losano looked at him quizzically.

"They were speaking Korean," Hart said.

"And you didn't think that important enough to tell me?" Losano spouted, his face reddening.

"In retrospect, it might have been a good idea," Hart conceded. Lena cocked her head. "But since JP is the resident security expert, I told her."

"JP's disappearance may have a connection to this Korean-speaking Chinese man then," Lena said. "Do we know where he is now?"

"He's dead," Hart said. "At least I think he is. And yes, that may have something to do with why JP has gone missing." Hart hadn't really thought that initially but saying it out loud certainly made it more plausible.

Losano spun around and gave him a squinty-eyed look.

"I would imagine Mr. Daro is doing something about all this?" Lena asked.

"There are search parties looking for her as we speak," Hart said. "They started in Syracuse where she left after meeting with Frank and are heading this way."

Lena looked at Losano. "Well then. There's nothing we can do that the US Government can't." She turned back to Hart. "I'm sure it's upsetting for both of you but we can't just stop because one person is missing. We have delegations coming."

"All the reason I want more security here," Losano said, tilting his head to the side and pursing his lips. "I...I just mean that since the South Koreans are so important to our venture," he stammered, "i..it's important that they feel they're investment is safe."

"What investment?" Hart asked

Losano jutted his chin and puffed out his chest. "The South Koreans are the obvious choice for developing and manufacturing hardware needed to get BPL up and running in end user environments," he said, his voice raising in volume.

"End-user environments," Lena mimicked. "Sounds like an ad-agency term Jay. Are we that far ahead?"

Losano's bluster waned slightly as he realized his smugness was controlling him at the moment. He took a couple of deep breaths quickly, turned toward the panorama window and stared out for a few moments. Then he turned back to them.

"The South Koreans will begin manufacturing the hardware consumers will need to run their computers off electrical outlets," he said. "It's all part of the launch process. In order to be successful, we need to have units ready for sale as soon as the public realizes the technology is up and running."

"And who are the South Koreans selling these units to?" Lena asked, her voice still soft but with a little more edge now.

Lena and Losano looked at each other, the latter's eyes flickering nervously.

"We are merely setting the, ah...stage, so to speak," Losano said. He looked over at Hart, his eyes pleading. "We know we will need those units to execute a full launch nationwide," he said quickly. "It only makes sense that we be prepared, regardless of what entity runs the operation in America."

"Congress might want to be in on that decision I think, Jay," Lena said, striding over to him slowly, bypassing Hart. She took Losano's hand and tapped it lightly with the palm of her hand. It reminded Hart of when his father used to tap his hand when he had said something ridiculous or stupid as a kid.

"It is part of the launch process," Losano said sternly. His bluster had diminished and he was all business now. "We can't hope to be successful if the consumer has no way to plug in," he said. "So it was our obligation to make sure that all the pieces are in place."

Losano stood up, ran his hands down the fronts of his pants as if to straighten them and stood erect.

"Your concern is to make sure none of the technology is leaked to our competitors," he said, looking at Lena. He then turned to me. "And your job is to make sure none of our potential customers go hungry."

Hart gave Lena a quick glance and saw her head shaking softly. She was still holding Losano's hand, but loosely. His gaze was a bit stupefied. He obviously wasn't very good with conflict.

Lena turned and gave Losano an exasperated look. "We need to run that voltage test again," she said. Which broke the spell and Losano pulled away from her, offering a quick smile.

"Perhaps we can have a quiet dinner tonight, just the two of us," she said quietly. And discuss this further. "I'm sure Arthur can create something simple and not too filling. I've been eating very well of late."

Hart nodded at both Lena and Losano, the nod meaning different things to each of them but seeing by their smiles that they both understood their respective messages. He guessed it was crackers and cheese in the office for himself again tonight. Good thing Young Oppelfarmer had packed a jar of Branston pickle and seaweed-flavored rice crackers in the last grocery delivery.

Chapter Forty-Eight

"Nice to see I was missed," JP said as she strode into the kitchen. Hart was heating up some oil but took off his apron and went over to give her a hug.

"Frank called. Told me you'd been picked up," Hart said. "But he didn't say what happened, just that you were okay." Her hair was more mussed than usual, her skirt had a couple of innocuous stains on them and her sweater could have used a wash. Of course, he wasn't about to voice any of this.

"Thanks to your friend Carl, I didn't have to wait for the pickup team," she said. "Which was a blessing. It's friggin cold at night up here."

"Carl?" he asked. Which is when Old Oppelfarmer walked in carrying a small box of fresh tomatoes and cucumbers.

"Figured you were taking too long to invite me so I'm invitin' myself," said Oppelfarmer, his grin stretching the width of his wizened face.

"Carl, huh," Hart said.

"You never asked," he replied. "Smells good. What's on the menu today?" He walked to the stove, lifted the lid on the stewing pot, leaned in and took a good long sniff.

"Ahhh," he moaned. "Don't know what it is but it smells delightful."

A Korean version of clam chowder... Sort of," Hart said, then turned to JP. "So where were you?"

"Having a little party with a couple of Italian gentlemen," she said, grabbing a beer from the fridge. She offered Carl one but he shook his head. She didn't offer Hart one.

"By Italian, you mean mafia?" Hart asked. She took a good long gulp of the beer then hotched herself up onto the counter, swinging her legs.

"That'd be my guess," she said. "Right out of *Goodfellas* too. Unbelievable."

"I'm assuming you put them straight?" Hart said.

"Actually, a superhero came to my rescue. Even wore a superhero outfit, sort of," she said.

"Your young friend here has had quite an evening," Oppelfarmer said, grabbing a small tomato and taking a big bite out of it. Remarkably, no juices squirted, showing how firm and fresh they really were. "Hart handed him a small side plate. You could never be too careful.

"No thanks to you," JP said. "Where the hell were you, my knight in shining apron?"

"Frank told me about your homing device, though he wouldn't tell me where they embedded it in your body," Hart said.

She opened her arms and shrugged.

"Said he had a team nearby and they'd just pick you up," he said.

"I was freezing my ass off out on the highway waiting, when my second hero of the night..." she pointed to Oppelfarmer who gave a slight bow. "...drove by in his truck and was kind enough to give me a ride."

"So the team's still looking for you?" Hart asked.

JP nodded. "It'll give them some practice. They should show up here any minute."

"You didn't call Frank?"

"Let him stew, the little shit," JP said. "Maybe next time, at least he might send the team a little sooner."

"Losano went anal on me," Hart said, his hands up in front of his chest in defence. "Said I had to stay here and work up kimchi for the Koreans. They're coming early."

"Is that what that is?" Oppelfarmer said, pointing to the stew pot. "Asian fixins?"

"Actually just vegetables and that fresh fish you sent up earlier. Apparently, it will remind them of their childhoods," Hart said. Oppelfarmer grimaced, then shrugged and pointed to the box he'd brought in.

"Oysters from the coast too," he said proudly. "Betcha didn't think I could pull that off so quick, did ya?"

Hart smiled and nodded his approval. Then he turned to JP. "So who was the superhero?"

JP jumped down from the counter. There were voices coming from the foyer and Hart heard her name mentioned. He heard Losano trying to stop them from going any further. Seemed the team had tracked JP all the way home.

"Don't know. American though, very abrupt actually. Well put together though a little short for my tastes," she said ambling out of the kitchen. "Needs to work on his superhero manners though."

Hart gave her a quizzical look but she just said "I'll tell you later," and went out to rescue the team from Losano.

Oppelfarmer opened the fridge door and checked the contents. "Didn't know you had a pretty assistant," he said. "Maybe she can do the shopping from now on, eh?" He grinned.

Hart turned his attention to him. "She's not really much kitchen help. More of an operations gal."

"What the hell's going on up here?" he asked. "Not that I mind, I mean this is the most excitement I've seen since old Maggie Felton yelled at me for selling her rotten tomatoes."

Hart wasn't sure but he didn't want to alarm the old guy any more than necessary. "A little corporate espionage, I'll bet," he said. "We've got some pretty high-level technology here. A lot of people would like to know how it all works so they can get in on the action."

Oppelfarmer thought about that for a minute.

"Got something to do with that power line internet thing we were talking about?" he asked.

Hart nodded.

"Think it's going to work that well? Enough for some big conglomerate to start foolin' with common folk?"

"It's my best guess," Hart said. "But give me a day or so. I'll get my boss to look into it. It's kinda what he does for a living."

"What, industrial espionage?" Oppelfarmer asked.

"No, chasing down deadbeat kidnappers," Hart said.

Oppelfarmer grunted. "You know, your guys aren't turning it on till late at night," he said, changing the subject.

"Turning what on?"

"That power line service or whatever it is," he said. "Me and the boys know what the interference looks like and we don't get any all day or evening. But Ivan over on Route Twenty says he was powered up around two am the other morning and he got a spike knocked him off the net for about an hour."

"You mean interference like you used to get with IBEC?"

"Yeah, exactly the same," Oppelfarmer said. "So, they's either only powering up when they think everyone's asleep, or it just doesn't work as well at night, which I'm pretty sure doesn't make any sense."

"Interesting," Hart said. "That means they're probably running proprietary service during show and tell." He looked at Hart quizzically. "I'll look into it. Do me a favour. Keep a log of when you and your buddies go on and if and when they get interference. Might be something the lab's missing."

"Sure thing," he said. "Boys are antsy. They don't want a repeat of the last time. Kinda ruins all our fun, ya know?"

Hart nodded. Lena had said right from the start that the interference problem had been dealt with. "I'm on your side, ah... Carl. If the interference is still happening, my guy will want to know." He nodded. "Maybe I'll call the airport, see if they've noticed anything," he added.

"Well they won't if the thing's only powered up in the wee hours of the morning," he said.

"Oh?"

"No flights after eleven pm. It's a small airport. Lights out between midnight and seven am," he said.

"So no one would notice any spike's during the night then," Hart said.

"No one except hammers like us," he said smiling. "No one else is on the waves at that time of the night."

"Exactly," Hart said.

Robert J. Morrow

Chapter Forty-Nine

"Okay, I see what you mean," JP said after they shook hands with the South Korean delegation. She and Losano had escorted the group to the second floor so they could freshen up. Losano hadn't left JPs side since her return and he seemed genuinely concerned that she'd been put at risk, almost apologetic. Hart was pretty sure JP had assured him she was a big girl and could take care of herself. He could also tell she was taking advantage of his concern and was lapping up the attention. He sensed a shopping spree coming up shortly.

"What I mean about what?" Hart asked while cutting the last few thin slices of beef from a well-marbled sirloin steak.

"How you can tell the difference between Asians," she said. "These guys are dressed like Wall Street power mongers, kind of act like it too."

"Yeah, the South Koreans are the new aristocrats of the East," Hart said. "Though the Japanese and Chinese would disagree. But unlike other Eastern cultures, South Koreans have successfully blended Western tastes with Eastern ideals. It's an interesting dichotomy; many political scholars believe they have created the best of both worlds, better adapted than the Japanese ever did during their heyday in the 1960s and '70s. I'll bet most of these guys are corporate types, not scientists; probably exchange students to the States during their university years."

"They do have that *it* look don't they?" she said. "Especially the tall, well built one with the longish hair."

"I wondered if you'd notice him," he said.

"Why, do you know him?"

"I'll tell you all about it after cocktails," he said. "Bring the hot pot on the counter, will you?" Hart walked out of the kitchen with the large platter, heading for the lounge where he'd already set up service for a quick Korean barbecue brunch.

Chapter Fifty

The South Koreans came in later looking exactly as JP had described, complete with pin-striped suits, prim white shirts and power-colour ties, each one different: yellow, red, sky blue, neon green, mauve, and orange. Only the seventh guy was dressed differently. Although wearing a custom-tailored suit, as were all the others, his was a deep black--no pinstripe--and his tie was off white, a subtle attempt at blending in and easing attention away from him.

His eyes roamed the room slowly as if checking for hidden surprises, eventually resting on Hart who nodded. After a moment, the Korean returned the nod, almost imperceptibly.

JP had noticed though and she cocked her eyebrow in Hart's direction as she met the group and seated them at a large round table in the center of the lounge. The platter was in the middle and both ginseng tea and sake was set in front of each person. Red tie bowed at JP and then Hart who bowed slightly but never took his eyes off red tie. JP observed this and did the same. They all sat except for the black suited one who moved to the bar and perched himself on a stool, twisting it round so he had a good view of the group.

Hart watched as JP began pouring tea and saw that the Koreans were enamoured with her. He walked over to the bar and sat beside the black suited one.

"Sonny," Hart said.

The man nodded. "Arthur," he mumbled. "It has been a while."

"At least fifteen years," Hart said holding out his hand. The Korean shook it firmly, never taking his eyes of the group.

"You're security?" Hart asked.

He smiled. "I'll save you the trouble of checking," he said. "I'm with the KCIA, babysitting diplomat duty." When he saw Hart cock his head, he smiled and added "To this bunch I'm the Liaison for Singun Industries, New Business Development, Consumer Products Division."

"That's a mouthful," Hart said, lifting his eyebrows and curling the edge of his lips. Singun, Hart knew was the up-and-coming competitor to Samsung, being present in all consumer markets the latter company was currently dominating worldwide.

I had last seen Sung-jin "Sonny" Kim in Kuala Lumpur for the Indonesia Martial Arts Finals in 1999, an international event attracting three-point fighters from many countries. Winners were determined by points and/or knockouts. This was around the time of the *Bloodsport* movie, long before the advent of Mixed Martial Arts (MMA). In these tournaments, when an opponent fell, the bout stopped and continued only when both competitors were once again on their feet. Sonny and Hart had made it to the quarter-finals that year, Sonny as a modified Olympic-style Taekwondo and Hart competing as a traditional international-style Taekwondo. They had faced each other three times during the competition, both of them winning one of the fights, but Hart had come to the conclusion in tournaments leading up to this one that he lacked the competitive *killer* instinct necessary to achieve top ranking in sport fighting. It had been one of the reasons he had joined a bike gang later on; to gain a little more edge.

Sonny had no such reluctance. Olympic-style TKD was the official sport of South Korea, introduced during the Olympics in Seoul in 1988 but had only recently taken the world stage with vigour. The country considered TKD a political tool as well as a recreational one and supported training heavily. They also couldn't abide failure which they had instilled in Sonny. Hart lost the semi-final round to Sonny who was later disqualified in the final match for using an illegal spinning back fist. They met by accident after the tourney at a local bar and fell into discussing their supposed shortcomings. They quickly concluded that if either of them was to make a living using their skills, it wouldn't be in the sports environment. There were too many rules, too many cautionary restrictions, too much consideration for the opponent. They parted assuming each of them would likely become some kind of security specialist in the coming years.

Several years later, Hart was using his unique skill set at The Farm in Virginia. Now, it appeared Sonny had done something similar, though if he was with the KCIA then he was, essentially, a spy.

"You're a little overqualified to be a bodyguard," Hart said, leaning over the bar and pulling out a bottle of Santa Carolina Reserva, a wonderful Chilean Shiraz that just happened to be inexpensive. He grabbed two glasses and poured each half a glass. He wasn't worried that if Sonny was on duty, so to speak, that he wouldn't drink. When they'd been on the circuit, they had both admitted to taking a shot of whisky before a fight to give them a little extra bravado. Hart figured he still wouldn't have any reservations about having a little alcohol in his system, even if he was working.

"They're just industrialists," Sonny said, tapping Hart's glass with his, swishing the ruby liquid gently, and then taking a small sip. He nodded his approval. "They represent Hyundai, Samsung and, of course, Singun, he said. "No spies there, I'm afraid." He grinned.

"You knew I would be here?" Hart said, noticing he hadn't excluded himself as a possible spy.

"Of course, we were briefed before leaving," he answered. "And I must say, they can't be too worried about the technology if they've put you in charge of security."

Hart grinned and swept his free arm around the room. "I am simply the chief cook and bottle washer, nothing more. My involvement with security--if you could call it that--is in a support capacity."

"You refer to the lovely JP Pierce, I presume?" he said, nodding toward the table where JP was holding court with all of the very attentive Korean businessmen.

"She's with Losano," Hart said.

Sonny smiled, took another sip and turned his chair around, facing the bar. Hart sat on the one beside him but faced it toward the table. Their faces were inches apart.

"She's Secret Service and she's here to make sure none of us get too close to the action," Sonny said, downing the last of his wine with a gulp, then reaching for the bottle and pouring another half glass. "And she's already dealt with one, ah.... overt attempt at someone finding out more than they were supposed to."

Hart tried to keep a stony face and watched as JP played hostess to the men at the table. The BBQ appetizer seemed to be a hit.

"You knew the North Koreans had infiltrated?" Hart asked.

"No, we didn't," Sonny said quietly. "Not until after the fact. We have our own communication problems with the Chinese, if you recall."

Hart did. The Chinese had almost refused to visit because Castillo had also invited the South Korean delegation. Only when someone--presumably Castillo or Losano--had assured them that the Korean delegation consisted mostly of hardware manufacturers, not government representatives, did the Chinese relent and book their excursion. They had, of course, insisted upon being first to view the technology.

"I don't think the Korean made it," Hart said.

"I heard," Sonny replied. "Thought it was a little harsh on your part."

"Not me," Hart said, nodding toward JP. "Her."

Sonny's eyebrow's raised. They both sipped their wine. Sonny turned back to look at his charges.

"So is the technology legit?" he asked, not looking at Hart but continuing to watch the group as they munched, sipped their drinks, and fought over each other to impress JP.

"I really don't know," Hart answered honestly. "There's something to it for sure. It's impressed enough scientific-types already. But I'm not one hundred percent convinced it's as good as she says it is."

"Will it work though?" he asked. "These guys are prepared to spend millions re-tooling manufacturing plants to build hardware that the consumer will use to transfer power from the grid to the computer."

"Is it your job to find out?" Hart asked, surprised.

"No, I'm no scientist," he said. "But I don't want my country to suffer because these buffoons commit too much future income to a technology that will be out-of-date in a decade." He turned to look at Hart. "They've done it before. We don't plan on following in Japan's footsteps," he said.

Hart nodded and finished his glass.

"If I thought it was a scam," Hart said, "I'd tell you. But the truth is I think it's legit... just not perfected."

He raised an eyebrow again.

"I'm working on it," Hart said, smiling. "If I find anything worth worrying about, you'll be the fir... well the second to know."

"The Secret Service being the first," he said.

Hart shrugged.

"So if it works, it's the next big thing," he said. "And if it doesn't, we all lose face."

Hart smiled.

Just then, Jay Losano strode in. He wore a grey suit and white shirt, though no tie. Hart had never seen him in a tie and figured it was too restricting for him. He was all smiles and worked the table, patting backs so the men didn't stand up, and shaking hands all around. He leaned over green tie and snapped up a tuna roll, plopping it in his mouth ceremoniously, then nodding his head in agreement with the others that it was, indeed, delicious.

"He's why I'm here," Sonny said.

Hart watched Losano. He was truly out of character, much too cordial and accommodating. It was almost like he was sucking up which was something he hadn't done with any other delegation so far.

"He's Lena Castillo's right hand man," Hart said. "Loosely connected to the Mafia but we don't think they're pulling his strings." Hart caught a grin from Sonny but it faded quickly.

"We're not so sure," Sonny said. "Last time I saw him, he'd raised a couple of million for lab equipment and had purchased this place."

"Last time?" Hart asked. "You've met Losano before?"

"He met with representatives of a consortium of manufacturers in Seoul last year," Sonny said. "The government sent me to get a handle on what he was looking for. Turned out he was looking to nail down contracts for the design and manufacture of various hardware components he would be selling to consumers who signed up for BPL."

"Signed up to who?" Hart asked, not missing the fact that Sonny obviously knew enough about the technology to use the abbreviation BPL.

"He was elusive about that," Sonny said, "saying he represented a conglomerate that would operate the BPL system and purchase the hardware from our group. He gave us exclusive rights for hardware and first rights for software updates"

"And your guys bought into that?"

"To prove he was serious, he left a half million-dollar deposit so the consortium would begin designs," Sonny said. "So, yes, they bought into it. "He pointed at the men around the table. "All these guys brought blueprints to show Losano and, I presume, Ms. Castillo. The consortium sorted out which company would manufacture specific components, based on current factory tooling, and they're ready to press the button on the assembly lines."

Hart thought about that for a few moments. He didn't think Frank knew the South Koreans were that far into it and wondered how Losano had managed to develop so much infrastructure without anyone noticing.

"These guys represent the factory divisions of our top manufacturers. If they get the go ahead today, Korean engineers will be building moulds for the parts by the end of this month."

Hart watched as Losano continued to interact with the Koreans, patting backs, munching small strands of blackened steak and laughing along with whatever they were saying. JP turned and gave him a quizzical look. That's when he realized they were all speaking Korean.

Including Losano.

Robert J. Morrow

Chapter Fifty-One

Sonny had explained to the delegates that he was taking a walk for fresh air.

Though not familiar with Oswego, he didn't really care. Privacy was what he needed in order to make this call, so he simply walked down the street from the facility, the crisp breeze and musty lake smell redolent of an early summer evening at his Father's cottage on the island of Jeju, just off the southern coast of Korea.

He pulled out his new burner phone and dialed the number from memory. It amazed him that these cheap phones could actually work so well with international calls. One prepaid card was used up every time he made the call but that was nothing compared to the convenience of being able to report in using an everyday cheap phone he could purchase anywhere.

"Report." The voice was gruff and to the point. As usual.

"We are on schedule. There are no major concerns," Sonny said.

"Your contacts. They are aware of the timeline?"

Sonny sighed. Jay Losano hadn't been his contact initially but if anything went wrong, Sonny knew that General Hwang would blame him for any failures due to Losano's possible miscalculations. It didn't matter. According to Arthur Hart, the technology was working as well as could be expected at this point, so he had no real concerns. Once the delegation left, he intended to stay in Oswego, out of site somewhere, but close by to keep an eye on progress. Senator Blais hadn't seemed to get the message and Sonny felt further, more aggressive, actions might be required on that front. But not yet. The CIA, FBI, and Secret Service were ramping up their surveillance on all parties involved and any mishaps involving participants would be investigated thoroughly at this point. It was just under a month till the launch with the American President and Sonny knew he would have to operate under the radar until then.

"The timeline has not changed," Sonny said and waited. He could hear heavy breathing on the other end of the line, which in itself created an efficacy of nervousness, even fear, in most who came into contact with the General. But Sonny had spent too much time overseas. The General's impact on both Sonny's thoughts and actions had diminished over time and distance. If something went wrong with the plan, he knew he could disappear, finding refuge in several places across the globe. The General, though enjoying almost God-like status in North Korea, had never been outside the virtually walled-in country and his knowledge of the World, therefore, was based on reports he received from field agents, and the library at Pyongyang, which everyone knew was so heavily censored that it was of little significance.

On-the-other-hand, should the General and his associates actually succeed in their world domination ploy, Sonny would be elevated to high position in the new regime. He would still live out his days in some remote Caribbean island somewhere, but at least he wouldn't be chased for the rest of his life by the megalomaniacs who would suddenly become the pre-eminent governing force on the Earth.

"The Chinese are anxious," the General said. "They know that the gathering of our troops at various transport facilities will not raise too many eyebrows. But when they begin to amass their own troops close to our border, the Americans will know instantly. They are already asking questions about our reduction of forces at the national border."

Sonny waited. He knew the old man was just catching his breath.

"Timing will be critical. All transports will depart within a two-hour period, making arrivals during midday when least expected."

Sonny hadn't liked this part of the plan but had been powerless to convince the General otherwise. The mentality was that with the Americans virtually blind to incoming air traffic, there was no need for cover of darkness. They would invade during the daylight which not only lent an element of surprise, but would also reduce casualties and increase landing success by the joint Syno forces.

It was entirely dependent upon Sonny being able to ensure the Americans were, indeed, blind to the coming onslaught. Daunting as that idea was, he wasn't overly worried about his part in the plan. Ever since meeting Jay Losano three years ago at a gay bar in San Bernardino, he had been developing his end of the coup, colossal in its audacity but so simple in execution.

And it all hinged on a young, female, Mexican immigrant technology whiz.

Sonny smiled. Thankfully, the General was several thousand miles away. He didn't really understand how precarious the whole thing was.

"Your team will be able to control the project once launched?" the General said, interrupting his thoughts. The old man was talking about the group of young people Sonny had infiltrated into Castillo's complex. Known in the hacker world as Bureau 121--the Sony hackers--the group of young computer geniuses had never been out of the country before. Not that it mattered. Losano had them so busy at the lab there was little time for them to get out and enjoy any form of freedom. Sonny had made it clear that no one from the group could leave the premises, ever. So far, Losano had managed to keep them entertained at the complex. Not that there was much to entice them in Oswego, but Sonny knew even a trip to McDonalds would have them salivating over other western delights so close at hand. The ever-present threat of retaliation on their families back home had long been the quintessential leverage required to keep them in line. Losano reported that the group happily played video games and watched American television whenever they had time off. Hart had even unwittingly offered his aid by creating a bar and games room in the lounge of the facility. The Koreans happily played pool, drank beer, and discussed video games most evenings, he was told.

"The team will be ready to take over control once the girl launches the technology," Sonny said matter-of-factly. "And will liaison with the government to ensure compliance during the transition."

"And the girl?"

"Once she has launched the code into the ethernet, she is dispensable," he said, knowing full well the General had only a passing understanding of what an ethernet was.

"When we have confirmation of initial success, then eliminate her," the General said. "We don't want anyone alive who can replicate the technology elsewhere once we have control, correct?"

"Yes, Sir," Sonny said, grinning. He had thought about keeping a copy of the code as insurance but that type of negativity only bred defeatism. He believed in the cause and as such, he would eliminate the girl and destroy any copies of the ArmourNet code. It would be up to the new leaders to ensure this one chance at Korean supremacy succeeded as planned. Destiny. That was what this was all about. Korea had risen from oppressive occupation prior to World War II to become the fastest growing, most successful industrial nation on the planet, surpassing even Japan's brief jump to pre-eminence in the consumer products field during the last half of the twentieth century. In just over seventy years, millions of people all over the world drove Kia and Hyundai cars, communicated with Samsung phones, watched LG televisions, and worked with various other world-leading Korean technologies. It was only natural to assume that the intelligence and hard work which had created such dominance in the commercial world could easily be turned toward the political world.

There was no doubt in Sonny's mind that it was his country's destiny; indeed, his own destiny to play a pivotal role in the future of the New World.

"You have done well Captain Kim," The General said. "We will meet very shortly on the shores of our new land, our new future."

"Yes General," Sonny said. The old man considered himself an antichrist of sorts. Oddly enough, he knew the American Senator had similar ambitions. Ironic really. Neither would last long in the new regime, he knew. The Bible, of course, had no place in Korean culture but the General knew what influence biblical teachings had on the masses in Christian countries. Sonny knew that the old man's goal was to use that influence to further his own political status within the new regime. He and the Senator would be ideal figureheads, for a while. Ridding the world of the Supreme Leader would be the first act of the new political force. And putting in his place a rejuvenated King as an internationally-acceptable figurehead would allow the old man and his cronies to build their empire behind the scenes and indeed, rule the world. For those who followed the teachings of Revelation, he was playing into the hands of the belief that one political leader would rise in the end times to rule the world. The General didn't believe these were the end times; indeed, he strongly felt it was the beginning of a resurgence of wealth and prosperity. But he knew that the new King would be welcomed as a world leader due simply to his ability to dominate the United States so swiftly and completely. Once that was accomplished, Sonny knew, both he and the Senator would become dispensable themselves. There were others, younger Korean politicians, currently struggling under the oppressive regime, who would pop up during the chaos of an emerging world order, eliminate anyone representing old ideas, and begin forming a new superpower: A single political force that would return the earth to a truly tranquil place to live and prosper. Korean's had long felt they had the answer to global restructuring. The idea had been suppressed again and again by more brutal cultures, cultures that understood nothing more than power and control. The new Korean regime would revolve around the perfect communist ideals. Where others had failed, this regime would succeed, primarily because the first act would be to control the world's strongest economy. And as rulers of the world's only remaining superpower, the world would listen to what the new regime had to say, and would follow its lead.

"I look forward to that day, General," Sonny said. "I will be in contact again once I have finalized the launch procedure."

He waited for a moment to be sure the General had nothing more to say. The white noise emanating from the phone told him the old man had already hung up. Sonny dropped the phone to the pavement where he stood and stomped on it once, crushing it beyond use. Then, using the edge of his shoe, he swept the remnants over to a sewer grate, pushing it between the metal tines. As he turned to head back to the facility, he heard a faint splash.

Chapter Fifty-Two

"Which delegation is there now?"

General Wade's voice sounded slightly higher pitched than normal, Hart thought, and he didn't think it was because they were on speaker phone or that he had been conferenced in with Frank.

"The South Korean's," Frank said. "Why?"

"The NSA just captured a call to a village just outside Pyongyang," the General said. "And it came from Oswego."

"When was that, Sir?" Hart asked.

"About thirty minutes ago, give or take," the General replied. "Any ideas?"

"Someone calling family, perhaps?" Hart suggested. He expected a quick reprimand and was surprised when Frank concurred.

"Possibly," he said. "There are a dozen or so Asian's working here and I know some of them are Korean. One of them could be a North Korean informant."

"Too coincidental not to be," the General added. "Do you have any concerns about anyone in that delegation Hart?"

Hart didn't have to think about that one.

"Sonny Kim is a possibility," Hart said.

"I agree," Frank said. "He's a known intelligence officer for the KCIA."

Hart arched his eyebrows though he knew Frank couldn't see.

"You knew this Kim fellow back in your competition days, didn't you Hart?" the General asked.

"Yes Sir. But I haven't seen him for over fifteen years."

"Can we safely eliminate the others?" the General continued.

"Probably," Hart said. "They are supposed to be manufacturing representatives and certainly act the part."

"Until Sonny Kim is proven otherwise, he's the logical choice then," Frank said.

Frank seemed adamant that Sonny was the culprit and Hart wondered how much more about his old nemesis he knew that Hart didn't.

"Why would he call the North?" he asked. "Especially if he's a South Korean intelligence officer?"

Both men were silent momentarily. Then the General spoke, his voice slower, more reflective. "Korea is a political dichotomy Hart, always has been. Though North and South oppose one another adamantly on the world stage, even in commerce, their cultural influences are congruent. The dominant structure of Kim Ill Sung's original republic has been diluted twice now, and the reigning Great Leader is not perceived by either side as someone capable of leading Korea into a unified future. And remember, that's the goal of every South Korean politician: to unite the country again."

"It's not a stretch to have Sonny contacting someone in North Korea," Frank added. "Most likely it's a member of one of the underground resistance groups working within Kim Jong Un's regime. A coup is decades overdue."

"But what does that have to do with ArmourNet and the South Korean visit?" Hart asked.

"Maybe nothing," Frank said. "Sonny is an active agent who was sent primarily as security we think. Perhaps its concerning something else he's involved in."

"I don't like it," General Wade said, his gruff voice clear and menacing. "We've already had one incident with a North Korean. It's possible this Sonny Kim character is simply picking up from where the last agent left off. Hart, you knew the man. See if he's changed politics over the years."

Hart thought about that for a moment. It seemed paranoid but he had to admit it was possible. Sonny was a mysterious entity; a man who clearly represented the interests of his country. Was that country South Korea, or just Korea? If the latter, then anything was possible, as the General was implying.

"I'll see what I can find out, Sir," he said.

"Good," the General replied. "Then I leave it to you gentlemen to try and establish why Mr. Kim called North Korea while visiting our facility. Need I say that as we are getting closer to the launch date, the last thing we need is an international incident, especially with that imbecile of a leader in charge over there."

"Understood General," Hart said. All the *Sir* stuff was starting to get to Hart and he decided to stop doing it.

Both men said quick goodbyes and Hart tapped the end button on his cell. He had hoped to have a little time catching up with Sonny anyway. What bothered him most about that whole conversation though was that General Wade knew so much about Hart's past.

Robert J. Morrow

Chapter Fifty-Three

"Let's go to the office."

"Why?"

JP rolled her eyes and walked out of the kitchen heading down the corridor to the office. Hart was putting the final touches on hoevres d'oers for the main event in a few days and needed to get it done prior to giving his pre-event speech to the serving staff. JP knew he was extremely busy so whatever she wanted must be important. When he walked through the doorway, she was pacing behind the desk, hands on her hips. Hart leaned on the door jam. She looked over at him.

"Okay, so there's no good way to tell you this," she said, her lips pursing. "President Emerson's Personal Protection Detail will be arriving at eight o'clock tomorrow."

"I understand why that might make you nervous," Hart said, "but what does it have to do with me?" His face scrunched up when it dawned on him. "Don't tell me I have to feed the cretons?"

JP sighed and dropped into his chair, putting her elbows on the desk, head in her hands. She was still, however, looking straight at him.

"No. You don't have to feed them. But they'll want to know all the details about the ingredients, the presentation, the scheduling... all of it," she said.

"Why aren't you doing that? I mean, you're Secret Service," he said. "We could do it tonight; save time. And isn't that why Frank sent you here anyway?"

She dropped her eyes. "That was mostly a pretense and you know it. I'm Secret Service, but I'm not PPD detail. Someone else you know is."

I cocked my head.

"Richard Hattis was recently appointed lead agent for President Emerson's Personal Protection Detail. He'll be in charge. And he'll be here tomorrow."

Hart stared at her for a moment, thinking. Then he pushed himself off the wall and turned to head back to the kitchen.

He heard JP mutter "Shit!" under her breath as he left.

His sentiments exactly.

Chapter Fifty-Four

With the sun shining brightly and no clouds to alleviate the intense heat, Hart knew it was going to be one of those colossal upstate New York summer sizzlers.

So, you'd think everyone would have been in a better mood. Not today, apparently. FBI agents with dour faces mingled with sweating Secret Service agents, all vying for the best vantage points within the sweltering heat of the tent. It was easy to tell which was which by the telltale white earpiece cords worn by the Secret Service. The fibbies relied on old fashioned walkie-talkies, their low, tinny conversations causing reverberations within the confines of the fabric-covered dome. And even though the Secret Service were better dressed--wearing suits that had been purchased within the past couple of years as opposed to the more Amity-style wear of the fibbies--all of them looking ridiculous sweating profusely inside the tent that was at least fifteen degrees hotter than outside.

Richard Hattis was making the rounds of his men, leaning in close, gesturing with his hands and occasionally pointing at what he must have thought were vulnerable access points inside the tent. He stationed several agents at the various plastic windows on the east and west sides of the structure. Of course, the sun's rays were intensified through the plastic which made the mens' cheeks glisten, sweat beading on the ends of their noses.

Hattis' eyes were wide, his cheeks flushed and his head moved like a chicken, searching the interior for more places he wanted coverage.

Hart grinned. This was a big day for Richard; his first outing heading up the Presidential detail on an out-of-town visit. He wondered if the man was up to it. For President Emerson's sake, he hoped so.

"He's scheduled to arrive at two pm," Frank said, interrupting Hart's thoughts. "You ready?"

Frank had arrived early in the morning, meeting with Lena and another young, skinny man. Hart assumed the guy was a CIA operative but after inquiring, Lena told him he was an aide to the Director of Homeland Security. So, Homeland was represented too, Hart thought. No doubt, the NSA, DND, and a host of other alphabets were also here.

"Food is in various stages," Hart said. "Aiming to serve the first course Fantasia Salad at two-thirty." Frank nodded and wandered off. Hart knew he didn't care about what we were eating, just that we were on schedule.

JP strode through the open flapped entrance and stood just inside scanning the room. When she saw Hart, she smiled and headed over. She looked stunning in a cream pantsuit, red blouse and matching red high heels. A custom wood floor had been laid inside the tent overlain with a very thin, weather-resistant dark blue carpet. Her heels made no sound as she glided over. Hart wondered if her make-up would run in the heat, and perhaps to compensate somewhat, she had placed her hair back in a stylish pony tail, the knot high atop her head, hair pulled back from her face, exposing her long neck and pronounced cheekbones.

"You'd think they could come up with something a little better than a tent, no?" she said.

"Easy to pack and transport," Hart said.

"I've been in hay barns that are cooler than this," she said. Hart thought about that for a moment, picturing scenes out of old Playboy magazines, and decided not to ask.

"The air-conditioners haven't been turned on yet," he said.

"What are they waiting for?"

"The cold air dissipates pretty quickly," he said, "so they wait till just before it starts and turn them up full blast so it stays fairly cool for about an hour. You'll know when they turn them on. Sounds like a jet taking off."

"With all these so-called geniuses around, I would have thought someone would have come up with a better plan," she said.

"Apparently the President likes it. Keeps speeches short since everyone wants out as quick as possible," he said. "Frank said Emerson's been using tents for that very reason since campaigning for Governor back in Texas. Apparently, he commissioned the first one the company that builds these made."

"Only a politician would research that," JP said.

He gave her a wink and pointed to the entourage that had just entered. All in uniform, they looked like a squad of high-ranking military who'd made the wrong turn off a parade route. General Wade led the group to the centre of tent. He had a lot more sparkly and dangly things on his uniform than the others. He scanned the room much like JP had and only stopped momentarily to nod when his gaze reached them. He continued his quick assessment of the empty tables and chose one to his liking. He turned and whispered something to a younger, similarly uniformed officer to his right who promptly nodded his head, took the General's valise, and marched to a table near the front, off to the right of the lectern that had been set up on at centre stage.

Frank must have noticed the General's entrance, because he quickly strode over to him.

"General Wade, glad to see you made it Sir," Frank said, extending his hand. The General looked at it then promptly saluted. Frank smiled and stepped back, leaning casually on the edge of one of the tables. Hart would have liked to stay and listen in--as JP obviously was doing while pretending to adjust utensils and place settings--but he had food to organize. He gave her a quick nod and left.

*　　　*　　　*

"I assume security is all in order?" the General asked.

Frank smiled and crossed his arms. "General, the Secret Service, FBI, local police and yours truly are all in place and suitably briefed. No harm will become the President."

"I wasn't worried about him," General Wade said, his expression staunch and hard. "I was referring to Castillo's secret technology. With all the foreigners wandering around, I would have thought the CIA would be playing one-on-one with their counterparts from God knows where."

"I don't think it's a secret anymore," Frank said, grinning. "Especially since, as you say, nearly every intelligence agency in the world will no doubt have a representative attending today."

General Wade was about to say something else but Frank held up a finger to stop him.

"I have taken every precaution to ensure that Ms. Castillo's software is suitably protected," Frank said. "Once this little dog and pony show is concluded, I will be taking her and her technology to a safer laboratory nearer Langley where she can continue to oversee the national release of BPL."

"You don't approve of President Emerson's press conference Frank?" The General said, the edge of his mouth curling upward ever so slightly.

"I think by making the launch of Castillo's BPL a media event, he has brought unneeded attention to this particular location yes," Frank said. "It was secure while under development, but using Castillo's lab as a staging point for regional distribution, even initially, is now too much of a risk."

"A risk for who Frank?" The General said. His aide had returned and stood behind him watching the conversation. The other members of the entourage had dispersed.

"For DHS and everyone else involved in running the BPL system once it's operational nationwide," Frank said. "If anything happens today that in any way puts a negative spin on the technology, consumers and other end-users won't be as willing to adopt it as the next progressive step toward a single national supplier of internet."

"There are some who think having one supplier is tantamount to a monopoly, much like the telephone or oil companies of years gone by," the General said.

"Are you one of those who think that way, General?" Frank asked.

"My concerns lean toward maintaining national security," the General said.

"Then I should think you would support a one-tier national internet supply system," Frank said. "That way the government can control the system's stability and, of course, use it to benefit national security efforts."

"Normally, I would agree," General Wade said. "However, nationalizing any widely-used utility--which internet no doubt has become--has its drawbacks because the government cannot always be trusted to keep national security first and foremost."

"I suppose you feel military control would be better?"

Wade grinned. "You'd think so, wouldn't you. And based on past experience, I would have been proven correct." He straightened his tie and stared out to where the podium was being placed atop the stage, the nearly invisible teleprompters set up to each side at a forty-five-degree angle. "But in this case, I believe you are right Frank. DHS would be the logical choice. I fear, however, that with adversaries like Senator Blais--" he cocked his head toward the Senator's table set at the front of the tent "--your hardest task may yet be ahead."

"And he would sacrifice security for a more profitable, tax generating vehicle, wouldn't he?" Frank asked.

The edges of General Wade's mouth curled even higher at this and Frank noticed a slight sparkle in the older man's eyes.

"Competition has always been the ultimate leveler," he said. "It's one of the foundations of democracy, isn't it?"

"Agreed, for the sake of commerce, General," Frank said, standing up straight. "But for purposes of national security, having one switch to turn internet usage on or off when required is an opportunity we simply cannot ignore." He turned to look at Senator Blais briefly, then turned back. "Besides, he wants to head it up himself and the only way to do that would be to make it a public company. And since the public wouldn't understand the subtleties of national security, we cannot allow that to happen.

"Spoken like a true spook, Frank," the General said, then turned to his aide. "Michael, I believe Mr. Daro here may have aspirations of becoming Secretary of Defence."

"I believe that is a military position General," Michael said.

The General turned back to Frank and stared him straight in the eyes. "Yes, I believe it is, Michael. Perhaps Mr. Daro here has other aspiration in mind. If you will excuse me Frank, I wish to have a conversation with the Canadian Ambassador." And with that, the General nodded at his aide who lead the way out of the tent again.

"I get the feeling Military Intelligence isn't completely on your side Frank," JP said, sidling up to him as they both watched the General and his aide walk toward a black SUV.

"General Wade is a complicated man, and even though he's liaison between Military Intelligence and the Company, I'm never really sure who's side he's on," Frank said.

"But he's a General in the United States Army," JP said. "He's automatically on our side."

"Yeah, but I haven't decided who's side we are yet," Frank said, grinning. "Excuse me, I have to find a Senator," he said, heading toward the exit. As he strode through the entranceway, he turned his head back slightly. "Shouldn't you be keeping an eye on Castillo?" He kept walking, not waiting for a reply.

JP gave a curt salute to Frank's retreating back, muttered "Shouldn't you be giving orders to someone who works for you?" under her breath and followed him out.

Forty-five minutes later, and as is custom, the press secretary rose first to speak. It was a well-prepared dissertation on why BPL was to be so important to he American economy, it's people, and, most importantly, its security. The journalists in attendance were quiet, if not detached from the proceedings. They all knew there would be no Q&A until after the President had spoken. Besides, this was all background fluff which most of them were already aware of. They appeared impatient as they sat in silence awaiting the main event.

Hart had scurried the staff back to the kitchen where the after-event cocktail sandwiches and drinks were awaiting distribution. The tent held just over one hundred people and for the most part, they were paying various levels of attention to the press secretary. His comments were circumspect and inwardly and Hart hoped President Emerson would be a little more forthcoming about BPL's future. He noticed the line of secret service agents at the rear of the tent, as well as those of to the side of the podium, including Richard Hattis. He felt wary, though he wasn't sure if that was due to this being his first outing as a caterer, or because of the realization that there were a large number of dignitaries in attendance. How easy it would be to fly a plane across the Lake, or even drive a container ship onto shore, demolishing the tent and taking out vitally important politicians from several nations: A terrorist's wet dream. He stepped out of the tent and to the north. The lake was calm and only one or two white sails of recreational boats could be seen in the distance.

He could rule out the ship anyway.

Robert J. Morrow

Chapter Fifty-Five

Within minutes the air conditioning was losing the battle. After the press secretary, one or two other dignitaries had already spoken, including General Wade. They had taken a short break before President Emerson would speak. Several of Castillo's technicians were checking the large screen to the left of the podium along with all the cords leading from it to a computer on the podium itself.

Tables represented either a conglomerate, a state, or a foreign country, with delegates seated around in a circular fashion. Most had taken advantage of the break to catch up with colleagues or to run back to the open bar at the rear for a fresh drink.

Sonny Kim was talking to a senior vice-president for Singun about the consumer units that various Korean companies were gearing up to manufacture in time for the full launch of what President Emerson had nicknamed *National Net*.

"And the software will all be proprietary to the joint conglomerate," the VP was saying. Sonny was vaguely listening. Although he was interested in understanding that America would, indeed, have one national internet service, it wasn't critical to the first phase; the phase he was about to unleash later tonight, here at the warehouse.

"Once Ms. Castillo provides the additional coding for her final safeguard," the VP was continuing, "we will install a switchable chip inside each unit allowing the provider full control of access."

Sonny's eyebrow raised. "Additional coding? What additional coding?" he asked.

The man leaned forward, his face opening up into a huge grin. "It was a brilliant last minute inclusion," he said, excited now that it was clear he had caught the attention of someone so obviously important. "It is a few lines of special coding that will be burned into a chip which can be switched on or off from the provider source."

Sonny leaned in. "And what exactly does this chip do?"

The VP slapped the table, his excitement growing. "It's remarkable actually. The units are functional all the time, but without the special chip, no information would go further than the power line coming into every home or building. Data would literally disintegrate once it left the house system because of the intense heat that's always present on high voltage lines."

Creases were forming on Sonny's forehead. "But I thought ArmourNet ensured data was protected from the intense heat," he asked cautiously.

"Oh yes, it does," the VP assured him. "But without the coding on the chip being enabled, ArmourNet is never switched on inside the unit." He clasped his hands together. "Don't you see? It's the perfect way for the provider--the government in this case, I presume--to turn off the power, so to speak, to anyone who is in payment default, or mis-using the system--you know for porn or whatever. It would be the ultimate Big Brother control on who uses the internet, when, and what for. It's absolutely brilliant!"

"And you say that although ArmourNet is installed in every unit, it won't work without that additional chip," Sonny said, rubbing his hands restlessly.

"Yes, that's right," the VP exclaimed. "In fact, Ms. Castillo has arranged for all of us--" he extended his hand to the other Korean delegates at the table, "--to meet with her later this evening to deliver the prototype chip to us. Oh, I can't wait to test it back in our own labs."

Sonny leaned back and placed one fist inside the other. He brought them to his lips and gently chewed on his knuckle as he thought over the implications of what the man had just told him.

He had a problem. And he needed to speak with Jay Losano. Now.

He was about to excuse himself when General Wade stepped up to the podium and began introducing the President. Sonny looked all around the tent. Secret Service men and women were stationed at every entrance and exit. He wasn't going anywhere at the moment.

Robert J. Morrow

Chapter Fifty-Six

At first, when the shot rang out, nothing happened.

For about three seconds.

Then all hell broke loose.

Secret Service men bounded onto the platform and surrounded President Emerson who had been in the middle of his speech but had taken a step back in surprise. It didn't look like he'd felt anything but was no doubt sure the bullet had been for him. His expression of surprise was the last anyone saw before he was completely obscured by black-suited agents--all taller and larger than the President--encircling their leader and shuffling him toward a creased exit behind the stage that has been held open by Supervisory Special Agent Richard Hattis. In less than 20 seconds, the President was gone.

Frank took a moment to decipher that the President was okay, then quickly realized no one would miss their target in this tight a venue, so obviously the President hadn't been the target. He looked around frantically, focusing his attention momentarily on each table. Some of the guests were crouching under tables, others huddling in corners talking. The General's table was blocked by a wall of uniformed personnel facing outward. The General was likely behind the men, safe and sound, otherwise they would have been facing inward, yelling orders at the top of their lungs, and administering first aid.

His gaze went to the other side of the room to another front row table where several people were bent over, covering up something, or somebody, now lying on the floor. He ran toward them, pushing chairs and people out of his way, his gaze never leaving the now growing circle of onlookers. One kneeling man turned and gave a curt nod as Frank approached. He lifted a hand with three fingers extended. Frank noticed there was dripping blood on the agent's hand and stopped quickly to begin scanning the room again. Three fingers meant the third threat. The President had been the first possible target, General Wade the second, and Senator Blais the third. That meant Senator Blais was down and injured. His agent knew the protocol and would follow it. There was no need for Frank to get involved. He could go after the shooter.

*   *   *

Bullard heard the shot and watched as Senator Blais grabbed his chest and dropped to the floor in a heap. He quickly calculated the trajectory and turned to his left just as the shooter slipped through the waiters' entrance near the right rear side of the tent. He thought he recognized the squat man but wasn't sure. It didn't matter. His orders were clear in a situation like this. He got up and headed over to the wall of military men.

*   *   *

JP had been watching a macho guy with an army crew cut throughout the press conference. He seemed to be on his own, not talking to anyone. Obviously, he was somebody, or he wouldn't have been allowed in. There was something about him that kept drawing her attention. She couldn't quite place it but the man's posture, his mannerisms, seemed familiar. Yet she knew they'd never met. JP never forgot a face, ever, so it was really bugging her. This guy was so real in her mind. He'd even caught her staring once and given her a sly grin and a quick nod, as if in acknowledgement.

When the shot rang out, JP had been focusing on the man, but she turned her head quickly to assess the situation. When she saw the circle of federal agents around a downed body at the front, saw that the President had been evacuated, and watched as Frank raced toward the victim, she turned her attention to the stranger again.

But he was gone.

Frantically, she scanned the room and saw him moving toward General Wade's group, quickly and with purpose. He was reaching into his inside pocket for something. A gun? Was he taking advantage of a diversion to go after his own target, General Wade?

JP ran after the man, reaching behind and under her jacket and to pull the Glock from the holster that fit snugly against the small of her lower back.

*   *   *

Sonny was tentatively listening to the President while trying to devise a way to leave without causing a stir, when the shot rang out. Having been trained to decipher trajectories by sound alone, he immediately turned to his right and saw the shooter duck into the makeshift tunnel leading to the kitchen. Then he saw Frank Daro, racing toward the Senator, then quickly changing direction and chasing after the shooter.

Sonny turned and watched the group circling the downed Senator, then shifted his gaze toward the other side of the tent where the military contingency had formed a human wall in front of their table, effectively blocking the view of who or what lay behind them. He had seen one of the two people he was concerned about heading toward the General, and his other concern, Daro's Secret Service girl and Arthur Hart's partner, was chasing after him. They would be busy for a little while.

More complications. Did this ever end? He resigned himself to what he now knew had to be done. He looked around. The majority of the secret service personnel had raced toward the President so this disturbance was the diversion he'd been waiting for. Without excusing himself, he got up, and headed toward the tent tunnel that lead to the kitchen.

*   *   *

It was a fluke that Hart actually saw the shooter but he recognized him instantly.

The kitchen crew was bringing in plates of ours 'd oeuvres through a tee-pee'd entrance at the rear of the tent structure. He had ordered an entrance canopy from one of the event companies in Syracuse and set it up to connect the tent to the back door of the warehouse. Usually used for restaurants to emulate a red-carpet entrance, complete with velvet sides, the canopy ensured that waiters could deliver food to the tent unharmed regardless of weather conditions. Though no one was guarding the entrance to the tent, none of the guests had used it to get outside for a cigarette break or bathroom break because there was no access to the outside from the makeshift tunnel.

So Hart had been surprised to find a short, older man who seemed familiar, crouched behind the flap on the canopy side of the entrance to the tent, his back to Hart. The man was watching what was going on inside but kept his body out of sight from those inside, almost as if hiding from view.

"Can I h...." Hart began. But before he could finish, he saw the man step quickly to the centre of the entrance, form a wide stance and lift a small object steadily with both hands, directly in front of him.

A moment later, Hart heard the shot and watched in amazement as the guy quickly spun around, shoved the gun down the front of his pants, and lurched toward him.

Now normally--with his background and training--he would instinctively jump into a fighting stance, ready and able to take on King Kong. But with a tray full of painstakingly prepared hors d'oeuvres straddling his arms, he was initially more concerned about the food than he was about protecting himself or stopping the assailant, whom he now recognized.

The guy ploughed into Hart's shoulder, grunting on impact and Hart went down like the centre pin at a bowling alley, food flying in every direction, creating a mosaic of splattered lettuce, tuna, eggs and watercress on the walls and floor. Despite Hart's efforts at containing the foodie artwork by keeping his arms straight during the descent to the floor, virtually everything left the tray.

His only thought as he slid down the velvet wall was how long it will take to replace the forty or so lost sandwiches.

Frank pounded through the entrance a moment later and lurched to a stop. He was about to say something but Hart just pointed his thumb over his shoulder and mouthed "It's Losano. Go!" He gave Hart a pained look and rushed toward the kitchen. Hart slowly get up and begin brushing off loose pieces of tuna and lettuce that had attached themselves to his pants when he heard Frank yelling.

"Hart, get your ass in here!" It was faint as he was obviously still running further into the warehouse. But Hart get his drift... along with his sense of urgency. So he finally let go of the tray to take chase.

*   *   *

"Freeze!"

Bullard heard the female voice yelling but it didn't register that the command was being addressed at him. He was too busy concentrating on the young Corporal directly in front of him. They had locked eyes moments ago and Bullard knew the man was sizing up the threat and choosing the method by which he would stop Bullard from breaking the ranks and getting past him. Bullard grinned as the Corporal balled his hands into fists and prepared to strike. But three steps out of reach, Bullard pulled out his ID, the Military Intelligence insignia large and clear. The Corporal visibly relaxed for a moment, then quickly drew his gun.

Bullard frowned, then burst forward and down as what seemed like a block of cement hit him squarely in the back.

"Stay down asshole!" JP yelled.

The Corporal wasn't sure where to train his gun but since he'd already seen the woman talk to the CIA guy in charge earlier, he figured the guy on the ground must be the bad guy.

JP had her knee in Bullard's back, his arms pulled back behind him and had the barrel of her gun lodged tightly against the back of his leg.

"Move and I'll shoot," she growled. "You won't die but you'll walk funny from now on."

"Agent Pierce, I do believe your attention--impressive as it is--might be better served elsewhere. This man works for me." General Wade stared down at JP, his arms crossed, his face expressionless.

JP looked up at the General and in that instant, Bullard, feeling the slight release of pressure on his back, jerked his body into a roll, pulling JP forward until she let go of his arms. She jumped up quickly and aimed her gun under the table but Bullard had rolled out of view. General Wade placed his hand on top of JPs revolver and gently pushed it downward.

"I realize Mr. Bullard is not in uniform but he is, in fact, a Captain in the United States Army," General Wade said. The Corporal gave the General a strained look and quickly put his gun back in his hip holster. JP hadn't been the only one to mistake Bullard for an assailant.

Bullard popped up on the other side of the table, shook himself off and gave JP a grin. She stared at him then turned her attention to the General.

"I apologize General," she said. "I saw him racing toward your table and with all the confusion here I thought you might have been in danger."

General Wade took her arm and steered her toward the other side of the table where Bullard stood motionless.

"Admirable actions my dear," he said. "And I sincerely thank you for your diligence." He then stepped in front of Bullard. "May I introduce Captain Garrison Bullard," he said, nodding and pushing JP closer to the other man. JP was forced to put her gun away so her right hand was free to shake Bullard's extended hand. His grip was firm, almost crushing and JP found herself unwittingly enjoying the childish competition of seeing who winces first.

As they both squeezed harder, the General's calming palm pressed gently atop their hands and they reluctantly broke apart. Bullard was still grinning.

"And what exactly does Captain Bullard do for you General, that requires him to be out of uniform, and sitting at another delegation's table," JP asked.

General Wade smiled and leaned in conspiratorially. "Sometimes I need eyes where Uncle Sam feels I don't need eyes, if you know what I mean Ms. Pierce."

"I'm sure Agent Pierce is aware of clandestine operations, Sir," Bullard said, his grin widening. "After all, she is with the Secret Service is she not?" It was the first time the man had spoken and JP looked at him sharply.

"Indeed," The General said but he wasn't really paying attention. JP had been momentarily distracted by Bullard's voice but turned to see what had caught the General's eye. Across the room, just past the entrance for the serving staff, Hart was pulling himself up from the ground and shaking himself free of what looked like sandwich ingredients.

"If you'll excuse me General," JP said, stepping away.

"Of course, Agent Pierce, I understand completely," the General said, turning toward Bullard and pulling him away from the table.

JP quickly stepped to her right and spun around, her tightened right fist blasting into Bullard's stomach, pushing it inwards an inch or so. Bullard didn't quite double over and in the back of her mind JP acknowledged that the man's stomach muscles were stronger than she had imagined. But he did pitch forward far enough for JP to lean down quickly and whisper in his ear.

"That's for not untying me before you left the house," she hissed before walking away. Out of the corner of her eye she noticed the General shaking his head. "Some friggin' super hero," she muttered under her breath as she briskly headed to the tunnel leading to the kitchen.

*　　　*　　　*

Moments earlier, Frank had passed through the kitchen and was headed toward the centre staircase. He could hear raised voices upstairs and figured the shooter had run up and had either bumped into staff or some straggling guests. He chastised himself for not being in better shape while running up the stairs but managed to keep his gun aimed forward. He could hear steps thudding behind him and hoped they belonged to Hart, who was undoubtedly in better shape than he was.

At the top of the stairs, he followed the sounds and turned left but quickly stopped short as he saw a group of men he didn't recognize, standing in an informal circle, talking. Although their ages ranged from young to old, all were clad in tailor-fitting, double breasted suits. And all appeared to be of Italian descent.

Frank let his gun drop to his side as he slowly approached the group who had, as if on cue, all turned to look at him.

"The shooter?" Frank yelled, breathing heavily. "Did you see him?"

"Who?" one of the men at the front says.

"He had a gun," Frank says. "Hard to miss."

They all reached into their jackets or behind their backs and produced pistols of all shapes and sizes, holding them up in a guarding pose in front of their chests.

"Like this?" an older man in the front asked, holding up a 9mm. The others chuckled. He must have been the leader. And he looked vaguely familiar.

Frank suddenly realized who all these Italians were but was distracted by a shuffling sound behind him.

*   *   *

Sonny knew there were two staircases to the upper levels on opposite sides of the building, both leading to the centre foyer on each floor. When he saw Frank Daro take the first one he headed across the lounge to the other staircase. He took them two at a time and headed for the second floor where he could hear several voices. As he rounded the top banister, he saw Frank on the other side of the foyer. He slowly crept up the remaining few stairs, pushing himself against the wall, keeping low.

*   *   *

Hart had heard steps racing up the stairs and figured Frank was heading to the second-floor landing. As he approached to follow, he caught a quick glimpse of a tall guy in a dark suit swinging around the banister head of the other staircase, heading up to the second floor.

It looked like Sonny Kim but he couldn't be sure. Everyone was in dark suits today. It didn't matter though. Either way both staircases were covered so if Frank had followed the shooter upstairs, he wouldn't be coming down without running into someone. Hart took the stairs two at a time and headed for the voices. As he hit the landing he saw Frank just inside the entrance to the foyer, bent over a bit, out of breath. He was talking to someone beyond Hart's view, his gun loosely pointing at them as he spoke.

Then Hart saw the other guy, though he was in the shadows, pushed up erect against the wall, edging himself toward the foyer, gun in two hands against his chest. It was Sonny.

Frank was exposed and Hart was trying to figure out what Sonny was doing when the Korean suddenly stepped out from the shadows, levelled his gun, and shot into the room.

Hart quickly peaked around the side of the opening and noticed Frank standing stock still, his gun in his hand but by his side. There was a group of men in the middle of the room, and one was lying in a pool of blood on the floor in front of them. It looked like the shooter, Antonio Losano. Hart quickly looked over to where Sonny had been but saw that he was running up the staircase to the third floor. When Hart turned back, Frank had dropped to the ground for cover and a herd of dark-haired men were jumping over him, racing toward the foyer, every one of them armed and pointing their weapons upwards.

"Who the hell was that?" Frank exclaimed when Hart appeared in the room.

"Sonny Kim," Hart said.

"Dumb fuck. What'd he do that for?" Frank said. He wasn't looking for an answer though because he took chase behind the herd up to the third floor.

Hart didn't follow them but thought about what had just happened. Sonny's shot hadn't seemed impulsive. And Frank hadn't been in any danger, so why shoot? But Sonny had purposefully aimed at the head guy and shot him. And now they were all after him, Frank included.

But running up to the third floor was a dumb idea. You never ran upwards to escape.

Debating what to do, Hart thought about that for a moment. *Unless you knew of another way down that no one else knew about.*

Of course Sonny did. He'd been here before with the delegation.

There was a tiny service elevator serving all the floors at the far end of the building. It was never used and when Losano had shown Hart during his initial tour of the facility, he'd told him they used it to bring up computer hardware, etc. It saved them carrying it up the stairs. Hart recalled that it was just big enough for a human to squeeze into. Just. Sonny would be cramped and out of breath by the time he reached the first floor, which Hart assumed was where he was headed.

Frank and most of the Italians were sprinting up the stairs taking chase.

Hart turned and ran back down the stairs heading to the east end of the building where the elevator came out at the back of the kitchen.

Chapter Fifty-Seven

"Why aren't you at the press conference?" Losano asked Lena as he quietly entered Lena's private office and lab.

"I had to be sure everything would work when he pressed the switch," she replied, her faltering voice relaying her nervousness.

"I thought we'd done that two days ago," Losano said coldly. He moved to stand behind his college pal and peered at the same screen Lena's eyes were glued to.

"The interference is stronger when more power is streaming through the lines," she said, not taking her eyes off the screen. "And with all the TV crews and extra lights in the tent, there's a lot more wattage drawing through the final phase than during any of our tests."

"I thought you were able to filter out low-level surges," Losano said.

"I can but with this much high draw running through the first two hundred metres of our wiring there is an intense load on the sleeve mechanism."

Losano didn't pretend to understand what his friend was talking about since Lena often made up terms to describe systems and computer programming she'd invented.

"You guaranteed me you'd done everything you could to ensure a successful launch," Losano said slowly. Lena hadn't noticed her friend's change in tone. "I assured the President's staff that you had holed yourself in here for the past twenty-four hours to tweak things a little, that everything was set and there was nothing else to do put turn the switch."

Lena turned to look at her friend. She had now noticed the unusual edge to his voice.

"Why are you so concerned about whether the system is fully operational?" she said. "It's important it works today, I understand, but we've got time before we launch to the whole Eastern grid."

"Actually we don't Lena," Losano said, staring at his friend. "You assured me two days ago that everything was ready and it was just a formality to get through this press conference." His voice was rising slightly as he continued. "You told me that the interference problem had finally been put to bed. You said there was nothing to worry about now and that it was just a matter of attaching more units along the power grid to get the whole East Coast on line. You said we'd be there by the end of the month."

Lena stared up at her friend. She tried to push back her chair to stand but Losano didn't move so she couldn't push it away from the desk. She gave Losano a puzzled, hurt look.

"Jay, I know we've committed to a lot of people," she said, "but they all understand that so far, everything we have done is conceptual. We've never actually turned it on full blast and have no idea if it's powerful enough to sustain the surges indefinitely." She turned in her chair. Losano wasn't letting her up but at least she could shift around so she could see her friend better. "I knew it would work today, at least until all the TV trucks showed up and plugged in that is. Mr. Daro and I had a plan. But I'm not going to be sure about the region until we actually turn it on and take over the existing load."

"The region!" Losano burst out. "We should be able to launch nationwide within days. Of course it's ready!"

Lena was confused. Technically, a signal could be sent around the nation in one direction but no customers could utilize it to return data until they installed their own modems, those specially designed to filter the strong current coming into their homes and offices.

"Jay, I know your job was to promise dates and success," Lena said calmly. "And I understand that. But you and I both know that this is an unproven science. We can build models, run tests, make educated projections, yes. But we can't guarantee anything until we actually run it live. And we can't do that until after we get the President's blessing. Which is why today was necessary."

"Today was necessary to get everyone here," Losano said. He ran his hand through his greased back hair and shook his head a little. "You don't get it do you, Lena?" He spat out her name and reached into his pocket, pulling out a small syringe.

"Today is the day we take over!" he shouted. Lena turned her head sideways, a quizzical and fearful look clouding her face. Losano continued, building up to a rage. "Today we show the American people, and the world, that we control their very existence."

"I don't understand, Jay" Lena said, pushing harder to stand up now. Jay's tone of voice was really scaring her. Losano stood his ground and brought the syringe around so Lena could see what he was holding. Inside, a light blue liquid shone as though incandescent. Lena's eyes stared hard at the syringe, then up at Losano.

"What are you talking about--and what is that?" she said, pointing her finger at the syringe.

Losano grabbed Lena's outstretched arm with his left hand, gripping the muscle in her upper arm tightly. Then, with one swift movement, he jabbed the syringe into the underside of her forearm and pushed the stopper to the hilt.

Lena pulled her arm back quickly and Losano let go. The syringe came out too but one glance showed Lena that whatever the blue liquid was, it was now in her body. She rubbed the spot where the needle had penetrated and looked up at Losano angrily.

"What the hell is that?" she demanded, though her voice was shaky.

Losano stepped back and grinned.

"That was your walking papers my friend," Losano said, the grin sinister to Lena' eyes. "We have been together a long time but your services are no longer required, as they say." He stepped to the door and started to open it. He watched as Lena's eyes stared at him, pleading for help. Then they glazed over and her head slumped to her chest. Her body, now off-balance, slumped forward, her forehead crashing onto the keyboard.

Losano grimaced but turned, pulled the door open and headed out to the corridor.

*   *   *

Hart arrived to the dumbwaiter just as Sonny was crawling out. He leaned against the kitchen counter and crossed his arms.

"You killed Losano's father, you know," Hart said.

Sonny's head snapped around to look at Hart but he continued to slowly unfold himself out of the small elevator.

"You don't understand, my friend," he said calmly as he straightened up.

"You're right, I don't," Hart said. "And I'm beginning to think we're not really friends, are we?"

Sonny stood straight making no move toward Hart or to get away from him. Hart slouched a little more but kept his knees bent, ready to shift quickly in either direction.

"He was about to… ah, take Jay out of the picture," Sonny said. "And I simply couldn't allow that to happen."

Hart wasn't sure how the mob boss had planned to do that, or why, but surely it hadn't required what was essentially, a professional killing. He couldn't believe South Korea would sanction such a move.

"So Losano's father is a mob boss, so what?" Hart said. "You don't think our guys knew that? As far as I know, the old man had stayed out of the picture. Just because he showed up today with all his cronies doesn't mean he was going to get physically involved, not with all the Feds and Secret Service around."

"Not to mention the CIA," Sonny said.

"The CIA was asked to stay close to Lena until she was ready to launch," Hart said. "Once the President made his announcement today, the FBI was going to take over, an internal matter from there on in. JP and I were going home."

"But Antonio Losano did come," said Sonny. "And he made a mess of things."

"Having Senator Blais shot, you mean?" Hart asked.

"For starters, yes. He's now caused a delay in the President's announcement," Sonny said. "But we can't wait any longer."

"Who's we?" Hart asked. "Your government is supplying the retail components, I get that. But a couple of weeks won't make a difference."

Sonny smiled then. Hart thought it an unusual smile and not just because of the timing. In fact, it could easily be construed as a sneer.

"Actually, time is very much of the essence, my friend," Sonny said, stepping away from the elevator, coming toward Hart. "It is unfortunate the President won't be making the gesture in front of all the media, but the switch will be pulled within forty-eight hours, with or without his or anyone else's interference."

"If it's so important to you and your country, you could have explained it to me, or Frank. We could have dealt with Losano's mob other ways," Hart said.

Sonny laughed. "You are so American, my friend. Your country always comes out on top, doesn't it? You and your people have been brainwashed by Hollywood to assume that any challenges to the American Way would be met with defeat." He stepped closer. "Unfortunately, to someone not in this country but having spent a lot of time here, I have to tell you, your loyalty is that of a child to an abusive parent. Unconditional love, unconditional trust. Yet your country is lying to you. Your country needs to be brought to its knees, to understand that it is not the only power in the world. In fact, soon, it will no longer be *the* power." He took another step closer. Hart tensed his legs slightly.

Hart thought Sonny was going to continue, like a professor in a university lecture hall, but he stopped and shook his head.

Then he quickly lurched foreword and with a speed Hart had not been expecting, his hand shooting toward Hart's face and surrounding his throat, his forefinger and thumb pressing inward, closing on his Adam's apple, causing a sharp jolt that went straight to his brain.

Hart lashed up with an arc hand under Sonny's elbow, hoping to release the pressure on his throat by eliminating his ability to bend his arm, flex his muscle and keep a tight grip. But he was already seeing sparks in front of his eyes and the constant pounding under his elbow wasn't relieving the pressure enough to stop him from slowly seeing darker and darker images of Sonny's face looking down at him. Hart tried to kick out for Sonny's ankle but the movement caused Sonny to lurch sideways out of the way, inadvertently causing him to press just a little harder. Instantly, everything went very black.

Chapter Fifty-Eight

JP was racing down the hallway, looking for Frank or Arthur. She had heard voices upstairs but also muffled voices in the kitchen. As she approached from the main corridor she saw Sonny walking briskly away from the kitchen and down the opposite corridor.

"Have you seen Arthur?" she yelled out. He turned, startled, then without answering, walked faster down the other hallway toward the lounge. JP thought that was strange but then everyone was acting strange today. As she ran past the kitchen, she saw two legs protruding out from behind the counter. Recognizing the pants, she rushed over and found Hart lying in an awkward position, out cold. She checked his pulse, then pulled out her cell phone and pushed the speed dial button for Frank's cell. Then she ran after Sonny.

"Yeah!" said Frank. He sounded exasperated. JP spoke quickly as she hurried down the hall and saw Sonny duck into Castillo's office.

"Arthur's down," she blurted. "In the kitchen. He's out cold. Send someone." She pressed the end button and didn't hear Frank's reply. As she picked up speed, Sonny dashed out of Castillo's office, gave JP a cold stare, and took off in the opposite direction.

JP slowed as she came up to the door leading to Castillo's private office.

She pushed herself up against the wall, gun in two hands, then jumped forward, her legs landing in a wide, low stance, ready to clear the doorway.

*   *   *

Hart was pretty groggy when he opened his eyes but he'd been knocked out before. He sensed there was nothing wrong. Two guys were hovering over him, one in a suit who he recognized as one of Frank's guys, and another in a military uniform who was wiping Hart's forehead with a damp cloth.

Hart slowly got up, with the help of the uniform and shook his head a little to relieve the remaining dizziness.

"How long was I out?" he asked.

"Agent Daro called me at one-oh-five or so," Frank's guy said, checking his watch. I got here in less than a minute, so I'd say no more than five or six minutes.

Hart's legs were a bit wobbly but he didn't have time to fully recover. He had to get to Sonny and find out what the hell was going on. He hobbled out to the corridor and headed deeper into the house. Frank's agent followed behind but the uniform headed the other way, likely back to the tent.

"Thanks!" Hart yelled to the uniform.

"He's a medic, it's what he does," the agent said, shuffling along behind him.

When they reached Lena's office they found JP bent down in the corner, picking up a small object. Lena was slumped over her keyboard at her desk.

"What happened?" Hart asked. The agent moved past him to check on Lena's vitals.

JP looked up, then stood up, staring at what looked like an empty vial in her hand.

"She's been poisoned," she said, still staring at the vial.

"How do you know?" Hart asked.

"The numbering on the vial. It's RX-351," she said.

"Which is?"

"The same stuff I used on our North Korean friend," she said, looking at Hart.

"I'll get the medic back here," the agent said.

"You needn't bother," she said, smiling at them both. "I have the antidote."

Hart looked at her. "You had an antidote all along?"

She nodded.

"So you could have saved the Korean?"

"If I'd wanted to, yes," she said. "Good thing I didn't though. I only have one vial in my suitcase upstairs."

"I'm going after Sonny," Hart said.

"He couldn't have done it," she said. "He didn't have time. He was only in here a couple of seconds. Someone else caught Castillo off guard."

"Who?"

"I'll ask Castillo," she said. "When, and if, she wakes up."

Hart dialed Frank's cell.

"What the hell's going on there?" He sounded breathless.

JP leaned closer and said loudly, "Someone gave Castillo RX-351."

Hart heard Frank exhale sharply. "Someone? That's military grade, unsanctioned. No one else has it," he said. Hart pressed the speaker icon on his phone.

"You saying someone on our side poisoned her?" Hart asked, holding the phone between JP and himself.

Frank didn't reply right away. JP stepped back a pace, her face scrunched up in thought. Hart stared at her. "The North Koreans invented it," she said.

"That's why I sanctioned it for JP to use on your intruder," Frank said. "We were sending a clear message to the DPRK that we were aware they were developing weapons-grade chemical weapons."

JP grinned.

"You're saying a North Korean did this?" Hart asked.

"Well, nobody on our side would," JP said, smirking. "I'm the only one Frank's given permission to use it. Right Frank?"

"General Wade controls our supply and stores it at Fort Meade," Frank said.

"General Wade?" JP's smirk disappeared. "The same General Wade out there?" She pointed toward the tent for Hart's benefit, he supposed, but he was sure Frank understood.

"Coincidence. Wade's been in on this from the start." Frank said.

JP looked at me. "Where's Bullard?" she asked.

"Who's that?" Hart said.

"A mutual friend of mine… and General Wade's," she said to me, then leaning into the phone, she said "I need to get the antidote."

I heard Frank breathing for a few beats, then he said, "I'm tied up with the Feds and these mob guys up here. I'll be down soon. Where's Sonny Kim?"

"We had a disagreement," Hart said. "Lena's going to die if we don't get that antidote."

More silence. Hart blew out a series of short breaths.

"I know. I'm thinking," he said, "I'll call you back in a minute."

Hart looked at Lena then at JP. She was holding Lena's head and had her palm gently placed on her exposed neck. "She can't die," Hart said.

JP watched him curiously. "Your eyes are watering Hart," she said quietly. "I thought you weren't involved with the girl."

"Where's the antidote?" he asked.

*   *   *

Frank was just turning the corner on the second floor when he noticed Jay Losano hurriedly walking toward the main lab. He looked to be in a hurry and when he briefly turned to look over his shoulder, Frank saw deep creases stretching out from his eyes. Losano hadn't noticed Frank and continued into the lab. Frank followed to the doorway and watched through the window as the other man went up to a large area of screens at the far end of the room, sat down, and began furiously pounding onto a keyboard. Frank watched as Losano furiously typed away. Was there something wrong? Was that why Losano seemed to be losing it? He didn't know about his father yet, so it had to be something to do with BPL.

And why would Sonny shoot Losano's father? What did that gain anyone, especially the South Koreans? It wasn't like the Mob was competing for the hardware business.

Sonny had some of the answers. But Frank thought Losano had some too. And Losano was right here. He opened the door and stepped inside.

*   *   *

JP had just told Hart where she had hidden the antidote and he opened the door to leave and saw a guy he vaguely recognized heading toward him.

"Castillo in there?" the guy asked.

Hart stood his ground. "She's kind of indisposed at the moment," he said.

The guy's eyes narrowed and he reached behind him, pulled out a gun and pressed it into Hart's stomach.

"Let's just see, shall we?" he said pushing the gun harder into Hart's stomach. Hart stepped back into the room, watching the stranger's eyes constantly. He'd had a lot of training over the years and one thing you learn very quickly is that very few maneuvers beat the speed of a bullet at this close a range.

Apparently JP disagreed.

With a downward chop connecting with his forearm and a sharp front kick to his shins, JP effectively disabled the guy long enough for Hart to turn, brace his bruised arm, twist it into a double arm lock behind his back, and push downward till he was forced to his knees.

"Careful, he's an Army Captain, don't you know," JP hissed, leaning down to put her face close to Bullard.

"Where'd you get the RX-351?" she spat. He flinched but Hart's hold kept him on his knees.

"What are you talking about?" Bullard hissed.

"General Wade controls the supply and you have access to General Wade," she said. "And since you like playing Ninja, I figure you're probably the one who did this. Now you're just checking to make sure we don't give her the antidote."

"Why the fuck would I do that?" he gasped, trying to free his arm. Hart leaned forward slightly and pushed it up higher till he grunted. After a moment, he gritted his teeth. "Look, I have no idea what RX whatever is but I came here to take Ms. Castillo to a safe house. She's an important asset to the US government and there's a good chance what happened just now was a diversion to get to her."

JP looked up at Hart. "He's right about that," she said, then looked back at the guy she knew as Captain Garrison Bullard. "But I still think you're a loose cannon and there's a good chance you've got your own agenda."

Bullard groaned.

"She's been given a lethal poison but your boss has the antidote," JP said.

"How long's she been out?" Bullard asked.

Hart looked at JP.

"She was like this when I got here," she said, looking at her watch. "Eight, ten minutes or so."

"But we don't know how long she's been here like this," Hart pointed out.

"The General likely has an antidote vial in his case," Bullard said. Hart released the pressure on his arm slightly. "He carries stuff like that just like the President carries launch codes."

Hart looked at JP again. She nodded. Hart released his hold on Bullard.

He stood up, shaking dust off his knees and rubbing his forearm. "If I'd taken your course, I'd know how to get out of that, wouldn't I?" he asked, straight faced.

"You should know anyway Captain," Hart answered.

"Touché," he said, smirking, pulling a cell phone from his pocket. "What was she given again?" he asked JP.

"RX-351," she said. Bullard stepped out into the corridor as he dialed.

"So how does a North Korean drug get to Northern New York state," Hart asked JP. "Especially if the US Army can account for all their vials?"

"It has to be a North Korean product," she said.

"And the closest place to North Korea..." he said

"Is South Korea," she finished.

"Sonny," he said.

"Sonny," she replied.

Robert J. Morrow

Chapter Fifty-Nine

Bullard helped the army medics lift up Lena Castillo and place her on a serving cart that one of them had jerry-rigged as a gurney. Hart touched her arm as four guys wheeled her away, still unconscious and lacking colour. The plan was to get her to the lounge where she would be more comfortable while the medics applied the antidote and basically waited for her to come around.

Hart would have liked to go too but he needed to find Sonny. He had answers and besides, Hart had a score to settle for the coldcocking.

Problem was, Hart had no idea where to look. Obviously, Sonny wasn't going to be waiting for people to find him after shooting Antonio Losano and attacking Hart. But would he run away from the facility, or just hide somewhere?

President Emerson had been whisked away right after the Senator had been shot, Richard Hattis taking charge right after the team had pushed and shoved him out of the tent and into the waiting Presidential convoy. He seemed to have convinced the President that it was the right decision for now and the convoy of five vehicles, lead by four motorcycles, had left the compound heading to Albany and Air Force One. Hart could imagine the curious farmers and small town residents along the mostly rural route watching as the train of black vehicles sped along at high speed, ensuring the President wasn't a sitting target. While en route the President had called JPs cell and expressed his concern about delaying the launch of BPL.

"He wants me to get a team together and bring Castillo to Washington," JP said when she returned.

"Why you?" Hart asked.

"I'm Secret Service, Arthur, he can ask me to do anything, anytime he wants."

"All her equipment is here," Hart said. "And Losano seems to know what he's doing for the time being."

"I think there's something the President's not telling us," she said. "He said he wants to talk to her as soon as we get her there, then he wants us to get her to Langley. He's ordered General Wade to organize a platoon to move all this stuff--" she spread her arms out taking in the whole building--"and get it to one of their portable labs near the Farm. She's to get things up and running and then he's going to arrange another press conference, but down there."

"So he's pulling the plug on this facility?" Hart said. "Can he do that?"

She shrugged. "He already has." Her phone buzzed and she reached into her pants pocket to retrieve it. She put the phone to her ear but said nothing, then after a few moments she said, "I understand Mr. President."

She stared at the phone for a second then put it back in her pocket.

"The President now wants Castillo in Washington by the time he gets back to the White House," she said.

"You didn't tell him she'd been drugged."

JP lowered her head and gave him a harsh stare. "One doesn't tell the President about minor setbacks when he has a plan worked out in his mind."

"Oh, and if she dies?"

"Then I might have to dress up Losano to look like her."

She'd said it with a straight face so Hart figured she might have been half serious. "Why the urgency?" he asked. "Emerson was prepared to do a high-profile media launch today and then slowly across the rest of the country over the next few weeks through the network Losano had set up. Why does this change things?"

"I don't know, but it does," she said, then headed out the door. "Castillo's now my new assignment. The second she's strong enough to move, we're headed to D.C."

Hart followed her to the corridor but turned in the opposite direction. "I'm going after Sonny," he said. "Something's not adding up and Sonny's got answers."

She stopped, turned and pushed her hair back with one hand. "We don't understand everything that's going on with Sonny," she said. "He's just proven he's very dangerous and has some kind of agenda we haven't figured out yet."

"When I find him, I'll ask him about that," Hart said.

Robert J. Morrow

Chapter Sixty

Sonny had every intention of getting out of there. But not without Castillo. She was now the key to everything he'd worked for. But, as agreed, Losano had tried to kill her. Luckily for Sonny, the idiot didn't know there was no antidote. He'd been watching the Secret Service detail take the girl into the Lounge from down the hall and knew they were trying to revive her. That meant an antidote was near by. After a moment he realized that since General Wade was here, that's where the antidote was coming from. He headed out to the parking lot in search of the South Korean delegation's limo.

Sonny pondered his dilemma. It wasn't too late. The deadline was looming but he still had twenty-four to forty-eight hours to complete the assignment. Besides, he was as good as dead if he didn't get that new coding from Castillo. He thought she might have a copy of it locked up here at the compound somewhere but with the place crawling with FBI, Secret Service, and CIA, he would never be able to search for it. No, his best bet was to shift to Plan B. And that meant Castillo would have to go with him.

Everything he'd done for the past two years depended upon there being open access to the entire Eastern Power Grid by Friday morning at seven. That was two days from now. He knew the schedule had been tight, and had told his superiors that when they'd dreamed up this scheme. But they didn't care; they never did. The Great Leader had chosen the date--based on Sonny's original intel--so now it was carved in stone. Sonny admonished himself for not allowing for more contingencies, though admittedly, he'd never expected Antonio Losano to go after Senator Blais.

He even had to do it himself instead of ordering one of his monkeys to do the shooting. The idiot probably thought he could muscle in and be some kind of boss in a new world order of his own.

Sonny looked at the tools he'd put in the trunk of the limo before they'd left the hotel this morning. He put the pieces in various pockets and slammed the trunk lid down heavily.

The old mobster had served his purpose regardless, Sonny reflected. He wasn't necessary for future success and would, indeed, have been trouble fairly quickly, with his attitude and outdated methods of getting things done. Sonny had done the new regime a favour by eliminating him early on.

He headed back to the front door, eyes roving left to right looking for anyone who gave him too much attention. Only Frank Daro and Arthur Hart had seen him shoot Losano and they were both busy at the moment and likely hadn't raised any alarm about Sonny yet. He knew Daro wouldn't involve other agencies or local police; he'd want to handle Sonny himself, maybe capture him and take him to some un-registered safe house for some unauthorized interrogation.

Sonny smiled. That actually might be fun. There weren't many agency operatives here, he knew. This was a Secret Service venue, with support from the FBI. The CIA couldn't be active on domestic soil, and though Daro had an argument for presence due to the number of foreign country representatives here, Sonny didn't think that's where Frank Daro's focus was.

Daro wanted BPL to work as much as Sonny did. And for much the same reasons.

No Sonny could handle the CIA presence here...

Unless Hart got involved.

He hitched his shoulders and stretched his neck, considering the prospect of having to meet up with Arthur Hart again. After catching him off guard in the kitchen, he knew it wouldn't be easy to take his nemesis down that easily a second time.

Hart wasn't a player in the game, Sonny knew. He'd been a trainer, not an operative. As far as Sonny knew, Hart had never even been in field. And he'd suddenly given it all up a decade or so ago.

So that put the American at a disadvantage. Deep down though, Sonny knew that Hart was an adversary not to be underestimated. He looked good, obviously still trained. But had he ever developed that killer instinct that had eluded him in his youth? Sonny seriously doubted it; Hart played by the rules, always had.

Sonny, of course, stopped following the rules long ago.

Surprisingly, since the quick exit of the President, things had died down a little. An ambulance, already on site, had quickly whisked away Senator Blais and a large group of his entourage.

General Wade and his contingency had jumped into their army green Humvees and Jeep SUVs and disappeared down the highway, following President Emerson's route but at a much more civilized pace. A troop carrier was waiting at Albany, ready to fly them back to Fort Meade.

So, for the most part, the only people left wandering around the tent and the grounds were media people, catering staff, Losano and Castillo's people, and a few distinguished guests and their parties. Most of the media had veered toward some of Blais' lingering entourage since that was clearly the only story left to explore at the moment. The caterers were quickly scrambling to clean up after a semi-finished meal, and the VIP guests were hovering around their limos waiting for a reason to leave, or a more likely, a chance to grab a soundbite with one of the many reporters running back and forth from their mobile hook up vans.

Sonny simply walked through the front door and up into the lounge. One or two staff members walked by but gave him little more than idle glances.

He took the steps to the second floor two at a time and when he reached the foyer at the top, leading to the lounge, he pulled a small canister from his back pocket and twisted off the lid.

He then pulled a small, thin tube from another pocket and attached it to the end of the canister.

The lounge doors were closed but Sonny could hear voices inside. Hopefully, they'd administered the antidote to Castillo already. If not, he had one too. It had come with the RX351 vial he'd given Losano. It would be better if they'd administered theirs already and were simply standing around waiting for the young genius to wake up.

He bent down and pushed the open end of the tube under the door and into the room about two inches. He then held the canister up and let the liquid drip down the tube.

He could hear hissing as the liquid turned into vapour as soon as it exited the tube and was bombarded by oxygen. This combination of the liquid inside the canister and breathable air instantly became a toxic steam that would render the entire room uninhabitable within a minute or so.

Sonny held the canister up with one hand and looked at his watch with the other. He listened with his ear close to the door, still crouched down, occasionally checking to ensure the tube was still spilling its contents inside the room.

With one more glance at his watch, he reached into his left jacket pocket and pulled out a simple nose plug and a Draeger Ray rebreather, the latter being a small cylinder placed inside the mouth--much like a snorkel--and a thin hose leading to a tiny canister behind his head, held in place by a wire apparatus resembling a stethoscope. This allowed him to rebreath unused oxygen from his exhaled breath while absorbing carbon dioxide. This tiny version would only last about ten minutes but that would be enough. With rebreather and clip in place, preventing him from breathing through his nose, he entered the lounge.

Two men lay prone by the large window facing the lake while a third was slumped over an armchair, face down. Lena Castillo lay on the couch, here face calm and serene, as if sleeping. Two men were slumped on the floor beside the couch, one of whom Sonny recognized as General Wade's man, the one he'd tried to stay clear of since arriving back in America. The man's arms were hooked behind Castillo's legs, caught there when the gas had hit him no doubt. Sonny lifted the girl's legs slightly allowing the man's arms to slip off the couch completely. His head made a thud as it hit the floor and his eyes opened, staring straight up at Sonny. Then, just as quickly they closed again and his head slumped sideways. Sonny bent to lift up the girl.

With gun in one hand--silencer attached--and his other arm supporting Castillo in a fireman's carry, Sonny headed down the stairs to the side entrance and the four-car garage. The gun was aimed directly ahead.

No one blocked his path. He could hear animated voices down the corridor in the opposite direction, toward the main entrance, staircase and beyond, the tent. But no one was paying attention to anything going on at this side of the building. As he passed by an office, he had a thought and slipped in, nudging the girl higher on his shoulder. He placed the gun on the desk momentarily as he searched the drawers with his free hand. Finding a set of keys and fob he grinned. *Faster than hotwiring.*

The side entrance door was a big metal fire door with a push bar in the centre. This type of door would be permanently locked to those trying to get in but easily opened by someone trying to get out quickly. Sonny smiled at the irony. Then, with a quick front push kick, he slammed the centre bar in and the door whooshed as it swung open to the gravel side driveway.

The side entrance to the garage was locked but with one quick *pffft* from the gun barrel, that door slowly swung open too. Sonny had to turn sideways to get them both through the narrow doorway but once inside, the entire garage came into view, dimly lit by sunlight coming in from the four or five windows along the back wall.

Sonny pulled out the keys and fob he'd taken from an office and pressed the door open button. The rear lights on an older-model green BMW convertible flashed. Sonny grinned and carried Castillo over to the passenger door.

It was a tight squeeze with the canvas roof up but Sonny managed to manhandle the still-unconscious Castillo into the passenger seat and strapped her in. He searched the cavernous room for a switch that opened doors but couldn't see any panel anywhere. Then he studied the doors again.

Built in the mid-to late 1800s, the garage had originally been a carriage house for the work horses which pulled barges into the warehouse from the Lake. Each garage entrance boasted two huge wooden doors with cast iron door jams mounted in the centre. A large wooden pole crossed behind the doors, mounted on wooden racks, preventing the doors from being opened from the outside.

Sonny strode over, putting his gun in his back pocket. The pole wasn't heavy and he easily lifted it off the racks and leaned it vertically against the front wall. He appreciated the simple technology and how well preserved all the wood and iron parts were, despite there being close to two hundred years old. He inwardly thanked the architect who had chosen to maintain its originality rather than upgrading it to something electrical, and more complicated or at the very least noisier to open. It would make his escape a little less noticeable.

He went back to the car and started it up, the ignition catching instantly and the three-litre engine quickly settling into a steady rumble. Putting the car in gear, he slowly backed up until the rear bumper touched the huge wooden doors. With a little more gas, the doors slowly opened as the stubby rounded rear end gently pushed them wider. Once the doors cleared the edges of the little car, Sonny kept backing until the front bumper cleared, then pushed the tiny shifter into first and slowly drove out onto the road.

As he drove down the tree-lined laneway toward the main lake road he checked the rear-view mirror. No one seemed to be running out frantically waving arms so he had gotten away unnoticed. He looked over at Castillo, her head safely lodged between the seat headrest and the canvas of the roof. She would come to in the next fifteen minutes, so with his right hand he adjusted her head and brushed back her hair so that the side of her neck was exposed, including the large, sinewy artery. When the girl regained consciousness, Sonny would be able to quickly put her under again by pressing just below the internal carotid artery and gently closing off the carotid sinus below the jaw line. That should give him enough time to get to his destination, especially if he raced along back roads. Even if an APB was placed out on the car it would take a while for the local police to find him. If he got stopped or speeding, he'd deal with that when the time came. It would get a little trickier as he got closer to bigger cities but he was ad-libbing now anyway. He had no choice. The girl had to give him the code so he had unhindered access to the entire eastern power grid. And he had two days to convince her to do it. He looked at her again. It would be a lot easier to do the *convincing* if Castillo had been an obnoxious American engineer or something similar--Sonny didn't enjoy torturing women--but he would do whatever it took to get that code.

Robert J. Morrow

Chapter Sixty-One

By the time Hart had reached the third floor, he had seen no sign of Sonny. Bullard, a couple of FBI agents and General Wade's medical officer had taken Lena to the Lounge on the second floor. Hart had seen her lying on the couch just before one of the agents had closed the doors.

He continued up to the third floor where the computer lab was. Basically, a cubicle farm set up in one large loft-style room, there were a dozen or so young people manning various sized screens. There had been no attempt to make it appear like an office environment and wires ran everywhere from under desks, along the edge of walls, even up into electrical outlets screwed into wooden beams across the ceiling.

At the back was a long table which Hart knew was Jay Losano's desk. Thicker wiring ran from his main twenty-seven-inch monitor, through a hole in the thick brick wall and out to a post which hosted a direct line to the main trunk line coming past the building from the nuclear plant just further down the road. Lena had told him this was the main reason she'd chosen this site for the lab. Being so close to the trunk line meant she could not only test high voltage data transfer but also, with permission from the plant, have access to the whole grid, from a major source of generated power.

Frank was talking to Losano by the desk, both men huddled over the keyboard as Losano fingers flew frantically across the keys.

"She didn't tell me he was going to do that!" he cried as his lucid eyes darting back and forth from the screen to Frank.

"So we couldn't have accomplished a complete launch even if we had wanted to," Frank questioned.

Losano threw down mouse and ran his hands through his hair. "Of course we could," he said, "but she's added blocking code that stops the programming mid-stream."

"Meaning?" Hart asked as he came up to them. Frank gave him a curt nod and turned back to Losano. He didn't seem to acknowledge where the question had come from but he answered it anyway.

"Meaning she's got a line--or a series of lines--of code that has to be input into the programming at a certain point which enables the software to continue running. Without it, the program stops right here!" He pointed his finger at the screen emphatically. Frank and Hart looked at each other. Frank's eyebrow raised as Hart shrugged.

"What are we looking at Mr. Losano?" Frank urged calmly. Losano's head bobbed up and down and he rubbed his arms quickly.

"This is the entrance code for the launch," he said. He turned when neither Frank or Hart responded. Shaking his head in frustration he looked back at the screen. The white cursor was flashing on and off after the last line of what clearly looked to Hart like HTML code.

"Various data signals are generated here," Losano said, swiping his arm around, presumably to take in all the techies at their desks. "It's then funnelled to this computer where it is encircled by ArmourNet." He brushed his hand through his hair and sighed. "It's like a knight covered in armour going out to war. When arrows and stones bombard him, he's protected by the shielding covering his body as he rides across the battlefield. Lena's code acts the same."

Frank rolled his eyes. He knew the basic idea behind Castillo's technology. Explaining things seemed to calm Losano a little though and so Frank let him ramble on, sitting on the edge of the desk, his hands in his lap. "It's a kind of electronic shield that envelopes the data being transmitted and stays with it as it travels along the wires. That way, the intense heat from over thirteen-thousand watts of high voltage can't destroy the data. When the data reaches its destination--the end user--it is filtered out from the shield's cover and sent unencumbered along lower one-twenty or two-twenty voltage lines into the home, office, or wherever it's going."

"So that, ah, armour code, is missing?" Hart asked.

"No, no, it's integral to the BPL software we've perfected," he said. "It's what makes the BPL work when it never worked before. But Lena has added additional code to enable it, to turn it on. Without that code, the shield doesn't embrace the data and anything transmitted over high voltage power lines would fry almost instantly."

Frank shifted his weight from one foot to the other. Hart could tell he was getting agitated. He didn't need a science lesson. He needed answers. Hart knew that squinty look he got when he just wanted people to cut to the chase.

"So no one here can figure out Lena's code?" Hart interjected.

"I don't know," Losano cried, standing up and pacing. "I didn't know she'd put one in. She must have done it last night, or early this morning maybe. Everything worked fine last time I ran the program yesterday. All the President had to do was press the switch we'd wired to the podium and the whole grid would have been online."

"The whole grid?" Frank said slowly, an edge to his voice. He leaned forward and caught Losano's attention. "What do you mean, the whole grid?"

Losano stopped pacing and shook his head. "I didn't mean the whole grid, you know just the northeast NY portion, that's what I meant." He emphasized this by flinging his hands in front of him in a *you know what I mean* gesture. Frank hadn't liked the mis-statement, Hart could tell. He grabbed Losano's shoulders and stopped him from moving. He pressed his own face to within a few inches of Losano's and spoke slowly.

"You said the whole grid. You meant the whole grid. That wasn't the deal Losano." Frank held onto the man who started to shake a little.

"No that's not what I meant," he said, trying not to look into Frank's eyes which was difficult due to his proximity to them. Frank was relentless.

"Castillo knew that if it worked properly there was a risk the entire grid could be exposed, so she put in a safety code, didn't she?" Frank said.

Hart waited for Losano to keep reiterating he'd not meant the entire grid but instead he stopped shaking and let his head flop forward, looking toward the floor.

"And she didn't tell you she was doing it, did she?" Frank continued.

Losano stared at the floor, oblivious to Frank's grip on his shoulders, oblivious to his continued questions.

"She was afraid someone was going to open up the entire eastern seaboard, wasn't she Losano," Frank continued. "She was afraid that our soft launch to the north coast would somehow become a major launch in the Eastern States, even Canada, and she wanted to be sure that couldn't happen until the powers that be said they were ready."

I watched Losano. He stared sullenly at the floor, not answering, indeed, seemingly not paying attention.

"She was afraid someone would open up the whole country in one instant, before the country was ready, didn't she," Frank said, his voice louder now. He began shaking Losano's shoulders. "She was afraid that someone would be able to do that without her being able to stop it from happening. Now who would have enough knowledge about the program to do that? Who would have access to the right computer to be able to do that, hey Losano?" Frank pushed the sullen man against the desk and tightened his grip on his shoulders. Losano winced, and seeming to only just notice that Frank was holding him, tried to shake off the hold but Frank shook him harder.

"She was worried about you Losano, wasn't she," Frank said. "You would know how to open up the grid wouldn't you? And you have access, don't you?" Frank's head bobbed toward the monitor. Losano's gaze followed.

"I can't believe she did this!" he exclaimed. "Why didn't she tell me? What am I going to do now?"

"You could always get Lena to come up and put the code in Jay," Hart said quietly, watching to see his response. Frank let go of the man's shoulders and stepped back.

"Yeah *Jay*," Frank emphasized the man's name with a sardonic grin. "Why don't we just ask Lena to come up here and release the blockage?"

Losano's eyes darted from Hart to Frank nervously. He was rubbing his right arm with his left and shifting his feet from one to the other. Hart's son Jason had that same look whenever Hart would catch him stealing an extra cookie from the cupboard.

Clearly, Losano knew Lena was out of commission. But how could he know? JP had gotten to Lena right after Sonny had ran from the office. Frank and Hart looked at each other. Losano had been the one to drug Castillo. He had tried to kill her.

"Right, well there's nothing more you can do here, then is there?" Frank said, grabbing Losano's arm and leading him past the cubicles to the door.

"What! Wait, I can't go anywhere. Not now!" Losano exclaimed, trying to pull himself free.

"Hold him will you," Frank said to Hart, pushing the straining man toward him. "I'll be right back." He strode to the door, pulling out his cell as he went.

Losano looked stricken and tried to bat off Hart's grip on his arm. Hart placed his thumb on the backside of his hand, between his thumb and forefinger, pressed, and twisted his hand backwards toward himself.

"Yeow!" Losano exclaimed while twisting his upper body in the same direction, meaning he was now facing the ground, bent over at the waist.

Frank came back, three other men in tow. Hart assumed they were either FBI or CIA. By the looks of their semi-casual dress, his guess was CIA. He had seen them lingering around at the back of the tent during the press conference.

"I told you to hold him, not hurt him," Frank said, grabbing Losano's flailing arm, pinning it behind his back, which was simple to do since he was already bent over. He then raised his eyebrows to Hart, his free hand extended. Hart pulled the hand he had toward the one Frank had and let go. Frank quickly snapped on handcuffs and stood back while Losano uprighted himself. His demeanor suddenly changed.

"What is this?" he demanded. "You can't arrest me."

"This is not an arrest, you idiot. I'm not a policeman," Frank said, grabbing his arm again and pushing him toward the other two men. They each grabbed an arm and led him past the bewildered crew of techies who had stopped tapping keyboards to watch the show.

"Where are you taking me?" Losano squealed. The pitch of his voice evidenced the level of fear he was experiencing at this point. He kept talking but Hart couldn't hear what he was saying as the two agents lead him down the stairway.

"Where are you taking him?" Hart asked.

"Somewhere quiet," Frank said. "Where there are tools and preferably sound proofing."

"Frank," Hart said slowly, tipping his head. "Really?"

"I know a lot of what's going on here, but not everything. The grid was never at risk, Castillo and I made sure of that. But he doesn't know that." Frank said.

I lifted the corner of my mouth and squinted.

Frank shook his head. "I'll fill you in later. It still doesn't all add up. And with the girl out of commission for the time being, I need answers." He turned to go then stopped. "You haven't found Sonny yet?"

"No."

"Consider that your new assignment," he said and left.

"I don't work for you, remember?" Hart said. Frank ignored him.

Chapter Sixty-Two

Hart bent over Losano's screen and tried to make heads or tails of the programming code.

Nothing.

He was pretty proficient with a computer, but only when he used software designed for certain purposes. This was like a foreign language and there was no friendly interface.

Besides, everyone was staring at him, wondering what the hell he was doing, no doubt.

Hart smiled and followed Frank.

As he approached the second floor, he saw a commotion in the lounge. The door was open and several people were milling about looking like they didn't know what to do. Hart saw Frank talking to the Captain, JPs buddy, whoever he was, and he didn't look too good; kept shaking his head and combing a hand through his hair as he spoke. As Hart walked in he noticed the two agents holding Losano between them. Losano seemed subdued and was listening intently to the Captain.

"...some kind of knockout gas," the Captain said.

"And you're sure it was the tall Asian guy?" Frank asked, nodding at Hart as he approached and gesturing for him to come closer. Hart nodded at the Captain who gave a quick nod back.

"Yeah, the one with the South Korean delegation," he said. "Pushed me out of the way, picked her up like she was a pillow, and took off."

"How can you be sure it was Sonny?" Hart asked.

"Captain Bullard wasn't completely out," Frank said. "Says he's had training resisting chemical deterrents."

"Of course he has," Hart said. Bullard didn't catch the sarcasm. Just looked at Frank.

"Listen, he can't be far. It's been less than five minutes," Bullard said.

Frank stepped back and addressed everyone in the room. "Search the building," he demanded. "Tall Asian, in a dark suit. Can't miss him, he'll have a young woman in his arms."

"Why would he want Lena?" Hart asked no one in particular. Frank was busy giving orders so Bullard lifted his head and answered.

"Because he's been a part of this from the beginning, I figure," he said. "Working for the other side. He knows too much about our security, has too many James Bond-ish tools, and knows this place like the back of his hand."

Hart looked at him. "What other side would that be?" he asked. But before Bullard could respond, four uniformed policemen ran into the room, followed by a couple of suits, FBI most likely.

"The garage is open, and one of the cars is missing," said one. He had a couple of stripes on his shirt, whereas the others didn't so he was likely the leader. "We've been monitoring all departures since the President left, you know the limos and buses, etc., checking trunks for weapons, whatever. But we were in the parking lot. No one was watching that side of the building."

"Which car is missing?" Hart asked

"Now how would I know that mate," the officer said. "I didn't see it leave, did I." He gave Hart a withering look.

"What cars are left?" Frank asked. The leader looked taken aback, his lips curling down. He turned to his men.

"An SUV and a... a Mercedes I think," one of the other men said.

Frank glanced at Hart. "Officer, put out an APB on a green BMW Z4, license number...." he looked at Hart.

"No need," Hart said. "There is GPS installed."

"And it's always on Sir?" the lead officer asked.

"Actually it's a separate unit in the trunk," Hart said. "I had it installed in case the car got, ah, stolen. I can activate it via an app on my phone. It'll tell us where the car is, as long as it's not in a garage, underground parking, or anything like that."

"I see," the officer said. Everyone nodded. And stared at Hart.

"Oh, yes, of course," he said. "My phone's in the kitchen."

Frank motioned to the two agents holding Losano. "Get him out of here. I'll catch up."

Losano suddenly came alive. "Wait, no, you can't take me away." He struggled against the two men holding him, to no avail. "My father will not let you do this. Where is he? I demand you tell him where you're taking me."

Frank, Bullard and Hart stopped and looked at Losano. Of course, he didn't know. They'd taken Antonio Losano away right after he'd been shot. Most, if not all, of his entourage had piled into a couple of old town cars and taken off, presumably to a local hospital, though they all knew the man was dead.

All but Jay, his son, of course.

"We'll talk about your father when we get to the house," Frank said, then nodded to the men who dragged Losano out.

"The house?" Hart said.

"People lived there once," Frank said, leading the way and waving his arms for the policemen to follow. "Has a great wine cellar."

Robert J. Morrow

Chapter Sixty-Three

Driving along Lake Road just west of Oswego, Sonny realised no one had immediately noticed their departure and relaxed a little. He maintained the speed limit and surveyed the older model sports car. The radio had no satellite function and a quick check of the Bluetooth feature showed pairings with a phone and a device belonging to the owner, no doubt. There was a GPS unit stuck to the lower driver's side of the windshield but it was turned off. He reached up and pulled out the power plug at the rear just to be sure.

There were no other electronic gadgets in the glove compartment or under his seat and, after searching behind his seat in the small space allotted for what would have to be very small passengers, he felt confident there was no way to track them.

He looked over at Lena, still unconscious, her head bouncing slightly against the metal frame of the canvas roof. He frowned, slowed the car and pulled over to the side of the road.

He reached over and put his hands into the girl's pockets, pulling out the contents: A tissue, two coins, and lipstick in one; a five-dollar bill, a folded piece of paper, and a USB stick in the other. He thought about the USB for a moment but then threw it out the window and dropped the other items onto the floor between her sprawled legs. He then did a quick external body search, pushing her forward gently to rub her back for any protrusions. He noted that her breasts were firm which shouldn't be surprising for a woman in her late twenties. He felt a little ridiculous pushing his fingers between the two mounds to see if she wore a necklace--possibly an electronic tracking device--beneath her shirt.

Nothing.

If she had a cell phone, it was probably in her purse. He didn't remember one in the lounge and figured it was probably in the office where she had been when he'd found her unconscious.

Losano caused this, he thought. Some mobster. He couldn't even kill someone properly. His father would have been disappointed. That thought brought a thin smile to his lips as he recalled the astonished look on the old Losano's face as he realized he'd been dealt a deadly blow.

General Wade's people had given the girl the antidote and she would live. Sonny smiled. *It was a good think Losano screwed up.* Apparently, he still needed her. He leaned back in his seat, sighed, and looked around to be sure no one was following.

Satisfied that they couldn't be tracked electronically, he put the car in gear, and pulled back onto the road, accelerating quickly but slowing until he reached the speed limit plus five miles per hour. It was a couple of hours drive to his destination but through mostly rural country. If the police put an APB out for this car, they'd not get the search organized fast enough for each community to be on the lookout. This wasn't the movies, nor was it a major city centre. Rural New York State wasn't swarming with police cruisers and if he stayed off the major highways, he'd likely get through without notice.

It would get riskier the closer they got to Buffalo but he wasn't particularly worried. Police enforcement travelled in two's in this country. Two at a time, he could dispatch without too much trouble. But if they formed some kind of road block, his escape would have to become a little more dramatic.

Chapter Sixty-Four

Once Hart had checked his *Gotcha!* tracking app and discovered that Sonny and Lena were heading west--in his car--Frank tossed him the keys to his rental car along with orders to follow them.

"We know where he is so as long as he stays in the car, we don't have to worry about Castillo at this point," he said. "But if he abandons it anywhere, we need to be close. We can't risk losing her." He gave JP a withering look which Hart didn't understand but she shrugged it off and headed to the passenger side of the car.

Hart knew Frank. He wasn't concerned for Lena's safety. He was protecting a highly valued government asset. That's why Hart's hidden GPS chip in the old BMW worked whether the car was running or not. It had its own tiny solar power source. Apparently Frank considered Hart a valued government asset too. Or at least his car was. Maybe he just wanted to know where Hart was all the time. He'd have to think about that when this was all over.

"Where do you think he's going?" he asked JP as they raced outside to Frank's car.

"Only thing in that direction is the Canadian border," JP said. "He can't turn north or he hits Lake Ontario. He must be planning to cross over and get lost on the other side."

"He could have gone south and achieved the same thing; Mostly cottage country and small towns till Syracuse" Hart said. "He just kidnapped somebody. Why risk a border crossing?"

"Unless he's going somewhere else," Frank said. "The I90 also leads to Detroit, Philadelphia, even Chicago."

"He wouldn't assume he could get that far," JP said. "He'll be expecting an APB on the car at least. He doesn't know we have a way of tracking him. And he knows that even if he switches cars along the way, sooner or later, he'd be picked up because everyone will be looking for an Asian and a Latina travelling together." She shook her head. "No, he can't stay on US roadways and he knows it."

"More likely he's gambling that since we have no jurisdiction across the border it would take time to authorize a Canadian APB," Hart said, "and he'd have a better chance of slipping through the net."

"Agreed," JP said. "He needs to find a safe place to interrogate her, or whatever."

"So, we're heading to the border?" Hart asked.

"I'll call Frank and get him to put eyes on all the crossing points," JP said, pulling out her cell. "As soon as we know where he's crossing, we can head up the detaining committee."

Turns out there are only three places you can cross into Canada from that part of New York--four if you included the frequent-user Nexus bridge which required a special pass--and all are isolated around Buffalo and Niagara Falls. The international boundary is the Niagara River connecting Lake Erie and Lake Ontario and all access points to cross into Canada utilize bridges: The Peace Bridge in Buffalo, Rainbow Bridge in Niagara Falls, and the Queenston/Lewiston Bridge closest to Lake Ontario. Sonny was headed along the 104, a northerly route which ended at Lewiston, a tiny town a just north of Niagara, directly opposite Queenston, Ontario, the historic site where British repelled an American invasion during the War of 1812.

If Sonny wanted to get to Buffalo or even Detroit, he would have to veer south at Rochester and pick up the I90.

As Hart pressed the gas pedal into the floorboards of Frank's surprisingly sprightly Chrysler 300, JP scoured local maps they'd downloaded and printed before leaving. A police cruiser had lead them out of town with flashing lights and siren but once they hit the open highway, he'd let them pass. If they needed Police along the way, Frank would contact them.

About thirty minutes in, Frank called JPs cell to tell them that the BMW had been spotted entering Rochester. Once it had passed over Irondequoit Bay, the car had stayed on the 104 which ran north of the city centre, confirming Sonny's destination as Lewiston. Frank had informed the local authorities along the route to confirm sightings but not to interfere or make contact with Sonny as they couldn't risk his harming Lena. Frank didn't trust local police, Hart knew. He also had ulterior motives which Hart was also aware of.

Unless there was something else along the coast--which he didn't think was likely since he couldn't have planned this little excursion--Sonny was almost certainly heading to Canada.

But why?

Robert J. Morrow

Chapter Sixty-Five

Sonny almost missed the turnoff; he'd been keeping one eye on the road and the other on the girl. She'd stirred just after passing through Rochester and he'd gently pushed his two forefingers against the pressure point at the junction of her collar bone and neck which had caused her to lose consciousness again. He didn't want to risk giving her any more drugs so he would have to keep using pressure points to keep her knocked out. There was a risk he could do minor brain damage if performed too many times but at this point, he had little choice. He just needed her to function enough to type in her code once they reached their destination.

The highway they were on was also known as Ridge Road and he had been watching for the North Ridge Road cut-off since the little jog south on Highway 78 just north of Lockport. He hated risking everything on the Google Maps(R) app on his cell phone--it had let him down before when it hadn't registered newly constructed roads--but he had little choice. Once across the border, the tool would be more accurate since he felt confident his final destination hadn't changed much in the last decade.

If it hadn't been for the sign showing that the next right would lead him to the town he was looking for, he might have whizzed past it. The road was more a class B surface but Sonny was still able to maintain a speed of sixty mph as he now headed in a more northwest direction.

Thirty minutes later he crossed Highway 18, the main coastal highway, then the Robert Moses Parkway, a thoroughfare named after the famed master builder which lead along the coast from

Old Fort Niagara directly south to Lewiston and the bridge to Canada.

But he wasn't heading for Lewiston.

As an exchange student visiting the University of Buffalo in the early 1990s, he and three Seoul National University friends had visited the Falls, heard about an amateur yacht race farther up the coast, and had signed up to crew on a forty-two-foot yacht owned by a retired airline pilot. The race was the Fifth Annual Youngstown Level Regatta, which took place on the Niagara River and Lake Ontario. The course crossed the Canadian/American border several times, back and forth. The experience had left a lasting impression on the young athlete, not the least of which was the lackadaisical attitude toward borders, unlike his own country. He had experienced firsthand how easily teenagers from Canada and the US had crossed borders via boat to attend parties, concerts, and the like. The authorities didn't really patrol that often as boats went back and forth to restaurants and entertainment venues regularly. Of course, travellers were supposed to declare their crossings but locals rarely worried about that minor detail. Large homes dotted the shoreline on both sides of the river and the river itself was only a few hundred yards wide in places. Despite strict attention when crossing using the three bridges in the vicinity, Sonny knew it was relatively easy to cross the border via the waterway, especially in daylight when recreational boats were everywhere and no one was paying close attention.

The highway ended at the Youngstown Yacht Club but Sonny turned left onto Main Street. The Niagara River sparkled between the trees and buildings as he slowly drove south. Just outside town Main St. turned into River Road which Sonny knew followed the coastline all the way down to Lewiston village. Luxury homes on vast riverside lots dotted the road all the way but he knew he couldn't go too far if he wanted his trip across the river to be short. He slowed the car, allowing one or two vehicles behind to pass, then crept along the road looking for a house with a visible dock and boat. Most of the homes had docks on the river but since this was early evening, many of the owners would likely still be out on their boats enjoying the summer heat. He needed a home where he could see a boat still docked, preferably a motor boat but a sailboat with motor would do just as well; he wasn't going far. He had to find something within the next mile or so if possible.

As he took a bend in the coastline avenue, a New England-style two-storey home came into view. Sonny could see through the trees to the back deck with stairs leading down the escarpment edge to a dock below. Tied to the dock was a late model bowrider, sloughing gently in the mild waves created by a pleasant summer breeze.

Perfect.

Sonny turned into the long driveway and eyed the house for any sign of movement as he rolled the car to a stop in front of a two-car garage. Checking to see that Lena was still unconscious, he got out and looked through the garage window. One car on the left, a station wagon. The other side was empty.

He strode up to the front door, looking around to see if any neighbours or passers-by were paying attention. There was no one in sight. He rang the doorbell and heard a faint chime come from somewhere inside. If anyone answered, he'd push them inside and detain them from moving around for half an hour or so.

He waited patiently, one eye watching the car to see if there was any movement from the girl, the other looking through the lightly veiled door window to see if anyone was approaching. He knocked to be sure, as loudly as he could, then walked past the car, around behind the car, and into the rear yard.

The house boasted floor-to-ceiling windows on both floors, the upper ones being adorned with decks allowing the occupants to enjoy the view of the yard and river beyond.

He peered into several windows on the main floor and noticed that most lights were out, a fireplace at one end was empty, and the kitchen appeared to be spotless. He stepped back and stared at the upper floor for a while.

No movement.

With a smirk, he checked the lawn behind the garage, then got back into the car and slowly edged it beside and then with a tight turn, behind the garage. It was now parallel to the garage wall, unnoticeable from the road.

He then turned his attention to the boat tied to the dock. It looked to be about twenty feet long or so, a modern bowrider with covers off, exposing the bow area seating clearly. The motor was an inboard which was good because Sonny had little experience with outboard motors.

He reached in to the tiny car and gently pulled the girl out and laid her on the ground beside it. Her head lolled to one side but she lay still.

Sonny then jogged down the angled stairway to the dock and jumped into the boat.

Three minutes later, the engine roared to life and Sonny jumped to the steering column where he placed the shifter into neutral and let the engine settle into a low idle.

"Hey, who are you?"

Sonny turned to see a man, dressed in a Hawaiian shirt and dark shorts standing on the edge of a dock about forty feet away.

"A friend," Sonny answered, his voice friendly to match his huge smile. "Just taking her for a little spin."

"I'm calling the police," the man said and he pulled a cell phone from his pocket.

"I wouldn't do that if I were you," Sonny said, reaching behind his back and pulling out his 9mm, pointing it straight at the man's chest. From this distance, he'd likely miss but the guy didn't know that.

"Ah, shit!" the man exclaimed, dropping the phone to the deck. It bounced once, then dropped into the water. "I knew you were stealing it. Frank and Glenda are away for the weekend. I told him he should have covered it up and put a lock on the wheel, you know one of those theft-deterrent things from the hardware store?" The man was nervous but he hadn't made a move to come over to his friend's property. And now that his phone had disappeared, he wasn't much of a threat.

"I'm not stealing the boat," Sonny said, still smiling, but holding the gun steady on the man. "I'm just borrowing it, to go there." He pointed to the other side of the river.

"You're trying to get to Canada without going through customs?" the man said, incredulous.

"I am," Sonny said. "And if I make it, you can tell your friends their boat will be waiting for them tied up along the shore somewhere between here and Niagara Falls."

The man lifted his head and squinted into the sun. "And if I call the authorities as soon as you leave?"

"Then, once they release me, I will come back here and shoot your family. I'll start with your wife, any children you have, then any pets. And I'll make you watch. Then I'll shoot you in the arms and legs and throw you in the river to drown."

The man stepped back abruptly.

"Your shittin' me," he said.

"Look at me," Sonny said. "I'm a foreigner, I have a rather big gun, and I must be desperate, otherwise I would have figured out a much smoother way of crossing over the border, don't you think?"

The man seemed confused. He had probably expected a thief to stop what he was doing and run once confronted. Clearly, he hadn't anticipated a conversation, and certainly not a threat on his life. The intruder was over forty feet away for God's sake, what could he do?

Sonny's quick shot convinced the neighbor that standing perfectly still was probably the best choice at this point.

The silencer was still attached to the gun from the last time Sonny had used it to kill Antonio Losano, so the noise was minimal. But although the spurt of water about two feet in front of the deck had plainly shocked the man, Sonny was disappointed; he'd been aiming for the deck but the silencer had caused the bullet to drop sooner.

The man threw up his hands and stared at Sonny.

"Tell you what, ah..." Sonny said. "What's your name?"

"Peter, ah, Evans...Peter Evans, why?"

"Well, Peter, I just had a change of heart. I don't think I'm going to borrow your friend's boat," Sonny said. "You are."

The man cocked his head which looked funny since his hands were still stretched out to the sky.

"Why don't you come over here, Peter," Sonny said. "I need some help." The man just stared. "You can put your hands down, you know. Someone might see you and wonder what's going on." The man didn't move. Sonny aimed the gun barrel an inch higher and pulled the trigger. A splinter of wood burst from the deck just inches from the Peter's feet. He jumped, and with his hands still raised, walked quickly to the end of his dock, onto the grass, and headed toward Sonny.

Sonny left the boat running and jumped out, heading toward Peter, his gun still aimed at the stunned man's chest.

Up close, the man looked to be in his late thirties, a little overweight--mostly in the belly, likely from beer--and had receding red hair. His eyes darted from Sonny's face to the gun and back again.

"I need some help carrying something," Sonny said, and motioned with the gun barrel for Peter to go to the car.

As they got closer, Peter stopped quickly when he saw Castillo's body on the grass.

"Is she dead?" he asked, his voice shaky.

"No, just sleeping. It's very important I get her to Canada before she wakes up," Sonny said. "So you see that's why I can't drive across the border with her."

Peter didn't see but it didn't matter.

"We're going to carry her to the boat Peter," Sonny said. "You take her head and I'll handle the legs."

Peter kept staring at the prone woman.

"Peter?" Sonny said, his voice lower and menacing.

"Oh... ah, okay."

"Just lift her by the shoulders and bring her head to rest in your lap as you walk," Sonny said. "And Peter..." the man looked up. "Remember, I have the gun. I am quite capable of carrying her myself, so don't try anything. I do appreciate your help though."

Peter nodded and the men picked her up horizontally and began walking down toward the dock and the boat slowly, staggering occasionally on small rocks. Peter never took his eyes off the unconscious girl and Sonny used one hand and one wrist to hold up her legs, his right hand still clutching the gun.

When they got to the dock, they laid her down beside the boat and Sonny jumped in.

"You can get her in here Peter," he said. Peter looked like he was thinking about that for a minute, then jumped into the boat and pulled Castillo's legs over the side.

"Don't let her head bounce Peter," Sonny said. Peter looked at him, nodded, and awkwardly pulled the rest of Castillo's body into the boat by holding her head and shoulders against his chest as he dragged her off the dock and onto the edge of the boat where she slid the rest of the way on the vinyl seat covering. He lay her head gently on the rear bench seat, then pulled up her legs so she was stretched out.

"Okay, I did what you wanted," Peter blurted. "Now, you don't need me any more. I won't say anything, I promise."

"I'm sorry Peter but that's not going to work," Sonny said, motioning for Peter to go through the gap in the window and sit in the bow. The man reluctantly obeyed.

"You see, this way, your friends, the..."

"Matheson--Frank and Glenda Matheson."

"The Mathesons won't have to recover their boat," Sonny said. "You will have brought it back to them safe and sound."

Sonny watched Peter as he leaned over the girl and unwrapped the stern line. He pointed the gun and raised his eyebrows until Peter understood he wanted him to untie the bow line.

"When we arrive on the other side, the young lady and I will get off and you can bring the boat back to your friends the Mathesons. You'll be a hero, Peter. And I'll have a head start before you can call the authorities and tell them about your adventure."

Peter thought for a moment then nodded his head. "Where are you going to land?"

"Right there," Sonny said, pointing the gun to a steep hill on the other side covered with trees right to the water's edge.

Peter nodded his understanding, almost as if agreeing that it was a good plan.

Sonny wished he had the same confidence.

Chapter Sixty-Six

The GPS monitoring application on Hart's cell phone was set to beep as soon as the target changed direction, so the second Sonny turned onto the road that lead to Old Fort Niagara, he and JP knew.

"What the hell is he doing?" she asked, checking the phone, then verifying what it said against the open map on her lap. "This road doesn't go anywhere near a border crossing. Are we missing something?"

Hart squinted and shrugged, knowing he had nothing to contribute at this point.

"He can't have arranged a boat or something to take him across the Lake," JP said. "He hadn't planned this little excursion--at least we don't think he did."

"He didn't plan this," Hart said.

"How do you know?"

"Because I know Sonny. If he'd planned an escape, I think it would have been a lot simpler than this," he said. "No, I think he's playing this one off the cuff. I think he has a Plan B but he has to get somewhere before he can go to it."

"Somewhere in Canada?"

"It appears that way, unless he stops somewhere between here and the border. Is there anything of any significance?"

"Not that I can see. Just small towns, old shipping ports, and a lot of lighthouses," JP said. "It's got to be the border."

"Okay, so how do you cross the border here?" Hart asked, trying to remember his geography and history lessons but coming up pretty much blank. He'd only been to see the Falls once as a kid and had no memories of how he had gotten there.

"He has to cross the Niagara River somehow," JP said. "It's the border. And you go over by bridge, but there's no bridge up this far north."

"Well, I don't think he plans on swimming, at least not with an unconscious Lena on his back," he said. "So what else is up there?"

JP leaned forward and studied the map for a few minutes.

"A lot of yacht clubs," she said finally. Hart could feel her eyes on him. He turned.

"And yacht clubs are full of..."

"Yachts," Hart said.

"The river isn't very wide up here," she said. "If he had a boat, he could be on the other side in a matter of minutes."

"But like you said, he didn't plan this, so what's he going to do, rent one?"

"He's a spy on the run," she said dully. "He'll just steal one."

The cut-off was well sign-posted and Hart followed Sonny's route as fast as he could. The road was a little rougher here but still two lanes. He maintained a steady eighty mph and passed everything that he came upon as they travelled, only slowing for long curves in the road.

They were silent for half and hour or so until they started seeing signs for the Old Fort, Youngstown, and Lewiston. The GPS has shown that Sonny had passed over the Robert Moses Parkway, a faster way to reach Lewiston and Niagara Falls, but instead went into town and turned south on River Rd. JP confirmed the road followed the shape of the shoreline all the way to Lewiston and Niagara Falls beyond.

It took a couple of minutes for it to register that the blip representing his Z4 had been stationary for a while. "He's stopped somewhere along the shore," Hart said.

JP looked at the phone, then at the map. "There's nothing along here till we hit Lewiston," she said.

"Except big houses."

"And big houses usually mean lots of money," she said.

"Enough to buy a boat or two," Hart said. They both grinned. He wanted to go faster but traffic was leisurely and would be too dangerous to pass. Besides, they now knew where the car was. Once they had a visual, they could decide what the next move would be.

As the blip got closer, Hart slowed. They couldn't tell which side of the road the car was on but it seemed logical it would be the river side.

"These are mini-mansions," JP said admiringly. "And some of them look pretty old."

Hart nodded. He wasn't really in the mood for discussing architecture, despite recognizing what was clearly an affluent neighbourhood; old money, no doubt.

Suddenly, his phone began beeping faster until, while rounding a curve in the road, it became a steady hum. He hadn't read the manual but it was pretty obvious that meant they were very close to the car. He pulled over and looked ahead. There were only two houses within 100 yds. or so. One was a wooden, Muskoka style cottage which looked like it had experienced several additions. Lights were blazing and smoke was coming from the chimney.

The other house, more of an East Coast design with shutters and white paint, looked uninhabited. There were no lights and no smoke coming from the chimney. A dock could clearly be seen through the trees. There was no boat tied up there but Hart still thought it was the better choice. He turned into the driveway. Without a word, JP folded up the map, pulled out her glock and checked the magazine. The snap as it clicked back into place seemed loud in the interior of the car.

Hart stopped about twenty feet from the house and they both got out. Hart didn't have a gun, so he stood behind the car door, using it as a shield for at least the lower part of his body. JP crouched in what Hart assumed was her Secret Service stealth crouch: arms outstretched, both hands holding the gun aimed directly in front of her.

After about ten feet, she turned to look at him and said in a low voice, "If he's going to shoot you, he won't aim for your genitals, more likely your head. So the door won't help."

Hart stepped away from the car and walked, semi-crouched till he was right behind her. It seemed silly and he didn't like the idea of hiding behind a female, but since he was unarmed he didn't really want to be a sitting duck. JP didn't sense his dilemma and seemed satisfied that he'd joined her. They both duck walked to the front door where she assumed the beside-the-door stance you see cops do on TV. She nodded her head toward the door. Not sure what she wanted him to do, Hart pushed the doorbell. It must have been normal protocol because she nodded for him to stand on the other side of the door. They waited for a minute.

"Nobody's home," Hart said.

"Or Sonny has them hostage," she said.

Not wanting this to turn into some kind of SWAT operation, Hart started toward the garage.

"Where are you going?"

"I'll check around back," he said. "Homes like this have picture windows for the view. I'll be able to see more. You stay here though; in case someone comes out."

"You don't have a gun," she said.

"I wouldn't shoot anyone if I did," he said and walked around the side of the garage.

Two minutes later they were both staring at Hart's car, parked parallel to the garage and hidden from view of the road. It was obvious there was no one inside. He checked the door. It was open, and the keys were lying on the driver's side floor mat. Either Sonny had been thinking of him, or he just dumped the keys because they were no use to him anymore. Likely the latter.

"There's no boat," JP said.

"Which means he probably already took it," Hart said. "He wouldn't stop here for any other reason."

The sound of an outboard motor racing at high pitch broke into their conversation and they bent down to see below the tree line. A sleek, blue and white speedboat was heading for the dock at the house at high speed.

JP raced to the closest tree and crouched low beside it, her gun aimed at the dock and the approaching boat.

Seemed like a good idea to Hart, so he took refuge behind another tree. He didn't crouch, just hid from view.

"Whoa!" JP exclaimed.

Hart peered around the tree to see the speeding boat burst onto the tiny sandy beach beside the dock, it's bow slamming into a grassy knoll marking the edge of the lawn. It balanced for a second or two, then tipped sideways.

A man in a brightly-coloured shirt popped out and began running across the lawn. It looked like he was headed next door.

"Freeze!" JP yelled. She stepped out and in her same Secret Service crouch, quickstepped closer to the fleeing boater.

The man turned to look at her but kept running, his disheveled red hair bouncing. It wasn't a haircut designed for joggers.

"I said freeze!" JP yelled again. "Secret Service! Stop now or I'll shoot your leg."

That got his attention.

He quickly stopped and, shaking, turned to them.

"What is it with guns today?" he blurted. "I have to call the Police ma'am. It's important. We can talk after, ok?" And he looked like he was going to run again but by then JP was within five feet and her gun, pointing low to his leg, seemed to stop him in his tracks.

"Why do you need to call the police, sir?" she asked, less menacingly, but still with authority. Hart thought she was very sexy when she was in her control mood.

"I was just kidnapped," he spurted. "Some Asian guy just made me steal my friend's boat and take him across to the other side-- some white slavery thing, I'll bet. I gotta call the cops, before he gets too far."

"Wait, sir, please," JP said, in a not-so-menacing voice. Hart edged around to the right so that he could block his path if he decided to run again.

"I think you're talking about someone we're looking for," she said, putting her gun back in the holster behind her back and holding up her hands to show him she had no weapon. "As I said, I'm Secret Service. This is a matter of national security."

The man cocked his head and nervously shifted his weight from one leg to the other. He really wanted to make that phone call.

"The Asian, did he have a young girl with him?"

The man stopped shuffling and his gaze narrowed. "Yes, how would you know that?"

"Like I said, Sir, he's someone we're looking for," JP said. "We've been chasing him and the girl. Did you take them somewhere in that boat?"

"Well he made me!" the man exclaimed. "It's not like I get kidnapped every day. I didn't know what else to do."

"That's ok, sir, we understand. Of course, you had no choice." JP didn't break her eye contact with the man as she stepped closer to him. "Where exactly did you take them?"

"He just wanted across the border, and quick. I took him to Fort George--well the shore just below the old Fort. He just threw the girl over his back and started climbing up the hill. I don't even know if she was alive!"

"I'm sure she was sir, our friend the Asian would not want to harm her, I assure you."

Hart stared at the spot where the man had pointed to. It was densely forested almost to the shoreline and was almost a 90 degree climb upwards. Sonny would have had a difficult time carrying Lena up there. Why would he choose a spot like that, unless he felt he could get lost easier?

"What's at the Fort?" Hart asked. The man's head jerked to him as if noticing him for the first time.

"It's the Old Canadian Fort from the War of 1812," he said. "They have nostalgic shows, concerts, sometimes fireworks at night. It's a pretty active place; enough parking for a small town. Buses by the dozens come every week."

A huge parking lot with pre-occupied and harried tourists.

The perfect place to steal a car.

Chapter Sixty-Seven

Traffic was light this time of day but once across the bridge, JP instructed Hart to bypass the rather long lineup of cars waiting to go through Canadian customs and head straight to the customs office.

"I'll get us clearance to go straight through. Give me your license," she said and once he handed it to her, she jumped out, fishing in her jacket pocket for her own credentials. Hart wondered how much pull the US Secret Service had at the Canadian border. He dialed Frank's number.

"Where are you?" came the gruff voice.

"Crossing into Canada. Sonny snuck over without going through customs. He's got about a thirty-minute head start and has probably stolen a car by now. We figure he's heading north, he'd have no reason to go south; it just goes back into the US at Buffalo, or into cottage country. There's only one main highway out of here and it heads toward Toronto so we figure that's where he's headed."

Hart had wanted to steal the boat and then a car on the other side but JP had told him that if they got stopped by authorities in Canada without going thought proper protocol to cross the border as agents of the US government, all hell would break loose and they'd lose Sonny for sure.

"I'll get Wade on it," Frank said.

"The same General Wade of Military Intelligence?" Hart asked.

"He's the MI liaison to the CIA remember," Frank said. "He's on our side--more or less."

"That's reassuring."

"Wade has resources I don't have, so just play along for now Hart, ok?" Frank said. He took a breath and continued.

"Losano has been singing like a bird. Interesting stuff too but we'll get into that later. For now, head north."

"I agree but why does Losano think that?"

"There's a couple of scenarios I'm working on with Losano, both north of where you are, so just go. When I get an exact destination, you'll be the first to know."

"Not General Wade?" Hart asked.

"Don't be an ass," Frank said, then a moment later, "He'll be second."

Chapter Sixty-Eight

Sonny had been a little winded after carrying the girl up the steep hill, dodging roots and other shrubbery. But once at the crest, the forest gave way to manicured lawns stretching in both directions for hundreds of yards. In the near distance, low buildings formed a semi-circle and were interspersed with small hilly and grassy mounds. Sonny had learned a little about the war that enabled Canada to become a country instead of another US state, but in his mind, he'd imagined more elaborate military establishments. Fort George was little more than a few wooden barracks, man-made hills, and a few cannons interspersed atop the grassy knolls, aimed across the river at the Americans. There was also a large parking lot on the opposite side, hidden from the main road by the small hills. Hard to believe such a tiny encampment had held off the mighty US but, of course, two hundred years ago, America was little more than a colony rebelling against the mighty British empire.

Sonny knew from history lessons how his own countrymen had rebelled against stronger powers. While the English and Americans were waging gallant war with one another for vast lands, his own people were fighting for their very survival against the Japanese, a race of animals that maimed, beheaded, raped and pillaged every land they invaded. Korea had succumbed to them, off and on, up until the Second World War when, of all things, the Americans had finally crushed the ruthless enemy. But it had taken two unearthly bombs to do it, which proved the arrogance of the Japanese in thinking they would survive such an ordeal.

The Americans had then brought their own ideals and democratic attitudes to his homeland which had, of course, caused a rift in the country itself. Even now, Korea wasn't a sovereign nation. Half of it was a westernized capitalistic puppet, while the other half was a communistic, socialist republic run by a dictator who's only claim to power was the blood running through his veins.

Not much longer, Sonny thought. In a matter of months, maybe even weeks, Korea would be united again and it would be free to become the superpower it was meant to be. But now they had the nuclear prowess to be the conquering nation. And if Americans were brought to their knees during the process, so be it. South Korea had proven its ability to lead in a modern world. In the south, automobiles, electronics, even emerging technologies were becoming the international standard. North Korea boasted one of the world's largest active military, after the US and China, a fact most Americans didn't seem to be aware of.

At least not yet.

There would have to be a few changes in his country, of course, not the least of which was ensuring cohesive union of the two warring nations. But the Silla Court were all leaders of industry, commerce, even politics, and were poised to create a single, united country, ready to lead the world. There would be a new President, a new government, and a new peace. Korea would be united, strong and powerful in the world, both as a military force and as an economically-stable society.

Sure there would be a few uprisings along the way. But it wouldn't take long for the world to see that Korea really did possess everything necessary to be a world leader, a superpower.

Sonny casually strode across the manicured lawn, staying close to the small grassy hills which acted as walls surrounding the Fort. Although in the wide open he felt he was far enough away from any public areas that no one would pay him much attention. As he reached the edge of the parking lot, he dropped the girl to the ground in front of a car and headed into the lines of vehicles.

Canadians are very lackadaisical with their possessions, cars included. Several had been left open and when he came across a white panelled van with its rear door unlocked, Sonny figured the Gods were looking after him. Despite being a late model vehicle, he had the ignition connected within a few minutes and quickly drove around to where he'd left the girl. With the engine still running, he manhandled her into the empty rear compartment. Calling upon his memory of maps he had perused while setting up his secondary plan, he pulled onto the Niagara Parkway, and headed west into town. He stopped once at one of the wineries that lined the Niagara Parkway leading into the tourist village of Niagara-on-the-Lake. The parking lot was huge and he had spotted a similar looking van at the back near one of the out buildings. He switched license plates, using a screwdriver he'd found in a small fold-up tool kit in the glove compartment. The blue and white Ontario plates were odd looking and the crown in the centre made Sonny smile. Even Canada paid homage to a monarchy that did virtually nothing to aid in its economic growth. In the new Korea, the leader would be a real King. And someday, a cartoon rendition of his slender face would adorn the centre of license plates all over the world, homage to a returned dynasty.

Before leaving the winery--and knowing that the girl would regain consciousness again soon--he jumped into the back cargo area, where she was stretched out on the floor. There was a crumpled material tarp in the corner which he spread out along one side of the van, then rolled the girl on top. He found two stretchy tarp straps and used them to tie both her hands to one of the chassis' exposed cross-ribs on the side of the van. She would be able to maneuver herself to sit up but that would be about it. But at least he wouldn't have to keep using pressure points to keep her unconscious; he was concerned about doing permanent damage.

He jumped back into the driver's seat and drove back out onto the parkway.

On the other side of the busy resort town, he stopped at a gas station and quickly bought a map, a couple of chocolate bars, one of those tightly wrapped pre-packaged sandwiches, and two bottles of water. He'd checked the gas gauge which was half. Should be enough to get him to his destination. After checking how much cash he had on him--all American, of course--he decided to hang onto it for as long as he could. He had credit and debit cards but now that he was on the run, they were useless. He would use them only if absolutely necessary.

"Ohhh!"

Sonny turned to see that Castillo was coming to. He crawled into the back, checked the dilation of her eyes, then untied one of her hands. She was groggy and uncomprehending but when he pushed an opened bottle of water into her hand, she stared at it blankly then instinctively took a sip.

"You're a lucky girl Ms. Castillo," Sonny said, taking the bottle away before she spilled the water. Her arm was a little sluggish due to lack of circulating blood. "You can thank me for saving your life. Jay wanted you dead. But I need you alive, for now." He watched as the girl's colour slowly returned, though he could see her mind was lagging behind a little.

"We can talk later," Sonny said. "For now, I suggest you eat. One by one, he held the sandwich and chocolate up to her eyes."

"I, I.... don't under...." she started to say, but her voice was grumbly and low.

"Don't try to talk now. We won't be driving for long but I don't know if there's food where we're going, so just eat." He knew he was taking a chance leaving her one hand free but was counting on the fact she wasn't fully cognizant and wouldn't think to undo her other hand for a little while; at least long enough for her to feed herself. Sonny figured that appeasing her hunger would supersede any urge to escape at this point. After two hours of being unconscious, her stomach should be growling. After she satisfied that basic urge though, she'd start thinking about her predicament and he'd have to tie her hand back to the metal ribbing again. He wished he'd bought some duct tape because he knew any minute she would start asking questions, or worse, start screaming. Not that anyone would hear her while they were driving down the highway but it would drive him crazy and cause another headache for sure. Then he'd be forced to knock her out again.

For the next ten miles or so, Sonny checked in the mirror and watched as Castillo munched the sandwich hungrily, stopping only to take gulps of water. Once finished, she got on her haunches and tried to look out of the front window.

"You were with the South Korean delegation," she said, quietly.

Sonny caught her gaze in the mirror but said nothing. The girl looked around the van but thankfully didn't become hysterical as he'd thought she might. Perhaps she understood that screaming in a van wouldn't alert anyone. If so, he was impressed. He had found most females to be emotional first, rational later. This one, however, had a higher than normal intelligence, and seemed more curious than scared, at least for now.

"Where are you taking me?"

Sonny kept looking straight ahead, regularly watching her in the mirror to be sure she wasn't trying to free herself. She was looking out the front windshield, no doubt trying to determine where she was. Sign posts whizzed by so Sonny knew she'd soon realize they were in Canada. But unless she'd crossed the border before, she'd have no idea where they were, despite seeing the names of towns go by: St. Catharines, Grimsby, signs showing distances to Hamilton and Toronto. She would know the latter major city but they weren't going that far. It didn't matter anyway. Once she did what he needed her to do, she wouldn't be necessary anymore.

"What happened back at the press conference?" she asked. "Is President Emerson dead?"

Sonny watched her intermittently for a few moments then made a decision.

"He wasn't the target. They shot Senator Blais."

"What....why?"

"It's a little complicated but suffice to say the Senator was playing both sides against the middle," Sonny said. "And the middle didn't think he was playing fair. So they tried to eliminate him."

"So the Senator is dead?"

"Actually, I have no idea," Sonny said. "But those who represent the middle are out of the equation for the time being,"

Sonny said, wondering if Losano knew his father had been injured or even killed.

"I don't understand."

"It's not important, " Sonny said. "What's important is that you and I complete our mission."

"You want me to give South Korea a copy of ArmourNet," she said matter-of-factly.

Sonny laughed.

"I won't do it, so unless you plan on... killing me, you should let me out right now," she said. Sonny thought her stuck-up chin and strong jawline did her justice, especially when she had to wrench her arms oddly in order to present that adamant face to him.

"My dear girl, as admirable as your stand against injustice may be," Sonny said. "This has nothing to do with South Korea, nor do I want a copy of your software."

Her head dropped and she furrowed her brows.

"What we are about to do, you and I, will change the economy of this country, well not this particular one, but the US, Europe and the Far East anyway. It will, in fact, alter history." He gave her a broad smile. "You'll be famous Ms. Castillo, though perhaps not in a way you had hoped."

She began pulling at the rubber bands holding her wrists to the side of the van. Any second, she would start yelling for help.

He pulled over to the side of the highway and squeezed himself between the front seats into the cargo area. Rummaging around the box at the back, and the built-in-cupboards, he eventually found another rubber band. The girl was mumbling something incoherent and it wouldn't be long before she found her voice and started yelling. He knelt in front of the her and held the band in front of her face. Her eyes were darting around the van but eventually she focused on the black strip of rubber in front of her.

"No! Please don't," she said. And then she let out a loud "Awww! Help!" which made Sonny flinch. He placed the wide side of the band in her mouth as she was yelling and pushed the clip ends to the side of the van where he attached them--one on each side of her head--to the ribbing.

She shook her head back and forth which only forced the rubber to bounce the back of head against the metal. After a few seconds, her eyes flickered and she stopped.

Sonny found an old rag in the box, folded it and placed it between her head and the metal side of the van, creating a cushion of sorts.

"We don't have far to go," he said. "Once we arrive, I'll explain everything. Then it will be your turn."

She started to shake her head again, but a jolt from the metal stopped her.

"Oh, and don't worry. Once we're done, I'll release you. Of course, by then, it won't matter if you run back to the States, even to the President himself. " He reached forward and stroked her hair gently. She winced and turned her head, as best she could against the restraint.

"Because by then, there will be nothing anyone can do. It will be too late for anyone to stop us."

Robert J. Morrow

Chapter Sixty-Nine

After about twenty minutes of cred-flipping, arm gesturing, gun checking, and finally a call to Frank from the Customs Shift Supervisor, the Canadians finally let JP and Hart cross the border.

Frank had promised to inform the RCMP and OPP about their pending chase and after exchanges of cell numbers, they were on their way.

"Criminals and terrorists can cross the border faster than law enforcement for God's sake," JP spat as she dropped into the passenger seat.

"Head north, toward Toronto," Frank said. JP had him on speaker phone.

"How's the interrogation going?" Hart asked.

"Gays have a higher tolerance for pain than regular assholes.... pardon the pun," Frank said.

"Does that mean you've got some answers," Hart asked, not wanting to go there. He'd noticed JP rolling her eyes.

"Some, but not all... yet," Frank replied. "So here's the highlights so far: Sonny is his partner...."

"What!" JP cried out. Hart frowned.

Frank continued as if he hadn't heard her outburst. "Apparently, while Jay and Lena Castillo were in University, some of Castillo's published articles in techie magazines got the attention of the Koreans and they sent Sonny over to see if there was any validity to her BPL trials''

"Sonny has been in the US recently then?" Hart asked. "I mean before coming with the South Korean delegation."

"The way Losano tells it, they met about three years ago when Sonny came over with representatives of Samsung and Singun and worked out a deal with them to manufacture the demo models of the various BPL components in exchange for the rights to manufacture all hardware components once it was released in the States."

"He can't make those kinds of deals without FCC approval," JP said.

"The deal was for prototypes, nothing illegal about that. Foreign companies do it all the time. Everything was agreed on a handshake," Frank said. "Once they got to the manufacturing of actual products, the government might demand tenders and Losano would simply make sure the Korean manufacturers won the bid."

"And Sonny could take home some hefty manufacturing contracts," Hart said.

"But that's not the best part," Frank said. "Part of their deal was to let Castillo develop the software programming but have Losano keep track of what she was doing, or at the very least, understand how it all worked. Then when it was up and running, Losano was to maneuver himself into the CEO position and push Castillo out of the way."

"Out of the way, where?" JP asked.

"Initially, they would just take over and keep her in place as the head techie. But Losano would run operations."

"So where does Sonny fit in?" Hart asked

"Seems he's tired of being a secret agent for the monkey administration at home, so he was setting himself up as the logistics guy. He would oversee the installation of hardware nationwide and manage the new BPL grid as it slowly grew."

"Sonny and Losano see themselves as the next Brin and Page?" Hart asked.

"So it seems, though a lot of it doesn't fit," Frank said.

"It's really out of character for Sonny, Hart continued. "Sonny's not a people person. I mean, he's been a spy most of his life.

That's not exactly a prerequisite for being COO of a major corporation."

"Which is why I think there is more to this than a couple of guys trying to create the next Microsoft or Facebook. This is political somehow," Frank said. "By the way, Losano doesn't know Sonny has taken Castillo. He thinks she's dead."

"Why?"

"Took a while but he finally admitted to giving her the RX351."

"I knew it wasn't Sonny," JP said. "There wasn't enough time for him to do it."

"Why did Losano want Castillo dead?" Hart asked.

"He got agitated at that point," Frank said. "Insists Sonny gave him an ultimatum," Frank continued. "If Losano knew how to control the ArmourNet, then either they got rid of Castillo permanently, or he would."

"Didn't Losano balk at murder?" JP interrupted.

"He grew up in a mob family," Hart reminded her.

"So he wouldn't be squeamish about doing it," JP said, pursing her lips.

"And, of course, Sonny had access to RX351 which he likely thought was so new, no one would know what to look for in a toxicology exam during an autopsy."

"Foolproof," JP said.

"Except we had an antidote," Hart said.

"Losano doesn't know anything about that. He figures she's gone. That's why he finally broke down," Frank said.

"I don't understand," JP said.

"When I found him in the lab earlier today, he'd just realized that Castillo had put in some extra programming to initiate ArmourNet. Without it, the system doesn't work. He thinks he's a dead man once it gets out and with Castillo out of the picture, the thing unfixable."

"I can understand his frustration, but why is he a dead man?"

"Because the mob financed them so far and if it doesn't work, they won't write off the loss--"

"No, they'll cut off the loss," JP interrupted. "Permanently."

"That's what he figures," Frank continued. "Of course, he thinks his father would hold off any action and give him a chance to work out the programming, before higher ups forced his hand."

"He doesn't know his father's dead then," JP said.

"No," Frank said, pausing for a moment. "I'll tell him when we've got Castillo back. Until then, he thinks his father can save his ass."

"But if you let him out on the street, the mob will kill him," Hart said.

"Most likely," Frank said. "They don't care at this point. With Antonio gone, there'll be a power struggle in Vegas and they'll want to remove any, ah... issues relating to this investment."

"They'll write it off and move on," JP said.

"And write off everyone involved while they're at it," Hart added.

"Including Sonny," Frank said.

"He might be hard to kill," Hart said.

"Let's hope so. Until we get Castillo back, he's as valuable as she is," Frank said.

"Because he has the answers Losano doesn't have," Hart said.

"Exactly," Frank confirmed.

Chapter Seventy

For the past hour or so, it had seemed to Sonny that Canada was a prosperous country. Most of the buildings on the edges of the highway boasted successful businesses, several roadside hotels, even a couple of wineries. Occasionally, closer to the major centres, there were large subdivisions with two storey homes, many of which faced Lake Ontario. He envisioned the stupendous views each home would have from their backyards.

But now, driving through the centre of what he thought would have been a more substantial town, he was surprised to see many empty storefronts. Even occupied stores had makeshift signs and sold items like second hand clothing and used electronic equipment. The odd restaurant spouted life with flashing neon signs but they were mostly eateries appealing to ethnic cultures.

Sonny knew there was a casino here, owned by the native Indians. He smiled. There was no such thing as a native in Korea which, in his mind, was the reason South Korea had progressed so rapidly since the Second World War. Everyone embraced western ideals so everything took second place to progress.

Towns in North Korea were far worse than this, of course, but that would all change soon. Once South Korean progressive culture mixed with North Korean prowess, the united country would stop concerning itself with its own internal conflicts and concentrate on dominating the world.

He turned into the parking lot of a large grocery store that appeared busy and parked near the back. He crawled into the back and checked the girl's bindings, then pulled the rubber band out of her mouth. She coughed, then sputtered a bit, drool sliding down her chin. She took a couple of deep breaths and looked up.

"Where are we?" Her voice was hoarse and she cleared her throat.

"Would you care for steak or chicken?" Sonny asked.

Her eyebrows furrowed. "What?"

"We haven't eaten since early this morning," he said. "I'm sure you're hungry. I'm not quite as accomplished as your friend Artichoke but I can put together a great Korean BBQ."

She shook her head as if to clear it, then stared at him. Then her eyes opened wide, her chest expanded, and she lifted her chin, opened her mouth, and....

Sonny slapped the band back in place before she had a chance to scream for help. The noise she made instead was a muffled groan which she maintained for about ten seconds, then gave up, here head slumping downward.

"I'll take that as a steak," Sonny said and backed out of the side door, closing it quickly behind him.

Ten minutes later, he jumped back into the driver's seat and threw two plastic grocery bags on the seat beside him. He'd picked up the cheapest cell phone he could find at a kiosk by the entrance--just over sixty bucks-- and was told he needed some pay-as-you-go time cards, $50 each if he wanted to make a long-distance call overseas. Didn't Canadians believe in disposable phones? At least the kid had given him exchange for the American cash he used.

"I forgot you can't buy booze in grocery stores here," he said into the rear mirror, watching for Castillo to lift her head. "Not to worry though. There was a wine kiosk in the store so I picked up a white and a red--wasn't sure which you preferred. They only had domestic though, Niagara I think, but I'm sure it will suffice."

Her eyes watched him as he put the van in gear and headed back to the road.

"Not long now, Ms. Castillo," he said, watching the road, not her. "Providing I can find the right road, we should be at our destination in about fifteen minutes. You'll be happy to know we won't need your vocal restraint once we arrive. You can probably scream all you want but I assure you no one will hear you and I can also assure you that I won't put up with it for long. I'm truly hoping we can be civilized and enjoy a nice meal together before we get started. It will taste much better than that rubber, I guarantee you."

Lena's head jerked up. She'd been trying, unsuccessfully, to chew through the thick rubber band in her mouth. Whenever she'd managed to get a piece dislodged, she hadn't been unable to spit it out of course, and Sonny had watched carefully as she nearly choked on the small remnants as they trickled down her throat. He didn't think she'd manage to chew through before they arrived but if he had to, he'd take it out of her mouth. Once they left the town proper they would be surrounded by farmland as far as the eye could see.

No one would hear her.

Robert J. Morrow

Chapter Seventy-One

The last time Hart had been in Canada, it was to attend an annual event called The Taste of Toronto. Ninety percent of the country's head offices were located in and around Toronto so it boasted a culinary culture that rivalled New York or London.

But right now they were driving through wine country, along the Niagara Peninsula. Canada had embraced wine production in the early seventies and over the decades since had won international awards for the ability to combine fertile soil with cool breezes emanating from the Great Lakes.

"What else is here besides endless fields of grapes?" JP asked, admiring the never-ending parallel lines forming the vineyards on either side of the six-lane highway.

"Fruit trees I think," Hart said, pointing to the side of a warehouse on the other side of the highway with the familiar logo of an internationally famous jam company.

"Where could Sonny be going?" she said. "I mean, we're not even sure he came this way."

"There's nothing in the southern direction, except back into the US at Fort Erie," Hart said. "The Lake is due east and west is Lake Erie-- a lot of cottages and small farm towns. He could have gone there, to some secluded place, I guess. But he could have had seclusion in upper New York, if that's all he wanted; he wouldn't have had to cross the border for that."

"So we think he's headed somewhere specific?" JP asked.

"I think so. The farther north we head, the closer we come to the financial hub of the country," Hart said. "I don't know where exactly, but it just feels right. Almost half the population of Canada--and the majority of its influential companies--are within fifty miles of where we are right now."

"Sandra Breis has a cottage just north of Toronto somewhere," JP said. "She says it takes her about six hours to get there from Ottawa.

"Hopefully we're not going that far," Hart said. "The antidote will have coursed through Lena's body by now so she'll be awake. That means Sonny has to keep her tied up, or otherwise occupied, until he gets to where he's going. Something tells me he wouldn't travel too far with her in that condition. He needs her for something."

"What makes you say that?"

"Why would a South Korean intelligence officer risk kidnapping a known protégé of the US President, then cross the border into another country--making it an international felony--unless he needed that specific person for some reason?"

JP raised her eyebrows then reluctantly nodded her agreement.

As they passed the cut-off to Beamsville, JP's phone rang. She pressed the speaker button.

"Hart, Pierce, I just got off the phone with General Wade," Frank said. He sounded pumped and his words spilled out quickly. "Military Intelligence has been doing background work on BPL since this all began and they think they've stumbled on something that may have relevance."

"Wade seems awful close to the action Frank. What aren't you telling us?" Hart asked, turning to give JP a quizzical look.

"General Wade had that guy Bullard dogging us back at Oswego," JP added. "Why are they suddenly anxious to help us now?"

"It's not sudden," Frank said. "Look, Wade is the Military Liaison to the CIA, as I keep telling you, so he's been in on the project from the start. Captain Bullard is his man, yes, and admittedly, I don't know what he's got the guy doing, but they're on our side. You can trust me on that."

Neither Hart or JP spoke. JP stared out the windshield. Frank continued, not waiting for a response.

"Anyway, it seems Blackberry--you know, the cell phone company--had some interest in BPL back in the early 1990s. When they were first creating their own private messenger service, they were looking for any way to make it unique and self-contained. The US government was their biggest client and they were demanding a platform for operating a completely separate server system that would be exclusive to users of their phones."

"We all use them in the Service," JP said. "Custom models I think. Ever since Obama ordered a special one, every President since has a custom-built Blackberry."

"Yeah, but back in the early 1990s, Blackberry was having trouble coming up with a better system than Motorola which was the standard at the time. Apple and IBM were still working on their own systems but that was more for the consumer. Blackberry held the patents for most of the secure technology surrounding messaging and emails via hand held devices, and the others were already licensing their innovations. That was what Blackberry did best--research. Even though the world didn't perceive them as the leaders in the new multi-billion-dollar industry, they were spending the most money and manpower on the future of secure messaging using phones."

"Company wasn't called Blackberry though, if I recall. Some other weird name," Hart said.

"Research in Motion, RIM for short, yeah," Frank said, "which, like I said, is what they were all about, research. But the Blackberry was their breakaway product. They couldn't make them fast enough. However, the messenger network still hadn't satisfied the government's purposes fully. So they were researching every possible option for delivering secure emailing capabilities."

"And they discovered BPL?" JP said.

"No, BPL has been around for decades but there were problems with it," Frank said. "Interference radiated for distances up to four-hundred meters from power lines when data was sent through them. That meant BPL operators would have to voluntarily design their systems for reduced emissions or risk interfering with communication services of essential services like Fire, Police, other short wave emergency providers and government safety systems. So, even though a few companies tried, in the end that's what stymied them. "

"But RIM found a way around that?" Hart asked.

"No, they gave up after attempting trial after trial and spending millions in the early nineties," Frank said. "Their future lay in wireless devices, not landlocked systems."

"Is there a point to this technology lesson then, Frank?" Hart asked.

"One of the techies involved in the BPL experiment--kid named Michael Powless--was convinced BPL was the ultimate platform for desktop communications. It was cheap, the infrastructure was already there, the cost of hardware needed would be minimal and could be paid for by subscribers, not the government or even business. It was perfect."

"What happened to him?" JP asked.

"RIM created a lot of millionaires in the early days," Frank said. "When they went public, half the company's employees were worth seven figures overnight. A lot of them left; retired, bought big boats, houses, whatever. But some used the windfall as seed money for new start-ups."

"So this Gauge kid kept researching BPL?" Hart interrupted.

"He did, but not the way you'd think," Frank said. "Kid new he'd blow through all the money if he started a research company. So instead, he buys a small farm not far away from the head office, in the middle of nowhere, but along the path of a major high voltage transmission field. He sets himself up a lab right next to a rural power substation and connects himself into the grid.

There's no emergency frequencies nearby, no airport for miles. All his uploading is done in the middle of the night and whatever interference he projects goes unnoticed for the most part, except for a handful of short wave operators in the area."

"Did he have success?" JP asked.

"We don't really know," Frank said. "He was killed in a car accident five years later. And no one was able to pick up where he left off."

"Get to the punch line Frank," Hart said, exasperated. They were passing a town called Grimsby now and he could see Lake

Ontario to the right a couple of miles away. It looked more like a lake from this viewpoint as they could see a large spiked tower on the horizon, surrounded by grey outlined skyscrapers. That would be the CN Tower in Toronto, some fifty miles away, around the bay.

"Seems he had no family, kind of a recluse, so the property went to the government after probate. They tried to sell it but the kid had gutted the farmhouse and had insulated electrical wires laying on the grass all over the place. There were some interested buyers but no one brave enough to try and fix the unknown."

"Where is this farmhouse Frank?" Hart asked.

"That's the ironic part," Frank said. "He didn't want to go too far from RIM's headquarters in Kitchener. He had friends in the area--other ex-RIM employees--who he sometimes hired on contract to perform certain tasks for him. But the kid had a flair for the melodramatic. He bought a farm just outside Paris--"

"France?" JP exclaimed.

"No, Paris, Ontario. It's where Alexander Graham Bell made the first long distance phone call back in the 1800s. From his lab in Brantford to the tiny river town of Paris, about five miles away. Gauge's farm is just outside Paris, about two miles off Highway 403."

"I just saw signs for Brantford," Hart said.

"I know. Cut-off's in Hamilton. You're less than an hour away Hart," Frank said smugly. "General Wade's detoured a drone from an Intel and Sustainment Regiment in Buffalo to fly over and give us a bird's eye view of what's there. I'll download the video to you soon as I get it. I'm sending you coordinates now for the farmhouse."

JP and Hart looked at each other as she pressed the button to hang up on Frank and then another to open up the file with the coordinates.

"He didn't say anything about backup," Hart said.

JP looked at him and thought.

"We're in Canada Hart," she said. "Back up may take a while."

He stared at the highway and the lights of hotels and rest stations as they passed. He had a momentary vision of red-clad Mounties chasing across the fields on horses to meet them.

Chapter Seventy-Two

Sonny almost missed the turn as it had become dark over the past hour and only a small green post at the side of the road designated the address as 4116, stencilled in white on a small post at the edge of the road. The trees had overgrown part of the entrance causing him to break a few branches off as he slowly turned into the laneway.

There wasn't much light out here. There were no streetlamps and by the looks of things, the closest neighbour was a good half a mile away; Sonny could see several lights in various rooms of a similar farmhouse in the distance. The laneway was a few hundred yards long, winding around small gatherings of trees and a large pond before opening up to a clearing with a two-storey brick farmhouse facing the lane from across what had once been a manicured front lawn. Wild grasses now crowded the area but he could still make out the outline of civilization's efforts at keeping forest growth at bay.

To the left were open fields. It was too dark to see if anything was growing other than wild shrubs but the three-quarter moon shone bright enough on the clear night to make it possible for Sonny to find his way to the front door without searching for a source of portable light.

"I'll be right back," he had told Lena. She just stared at him, her pupils large, dark and watery as he slid the van door closed.

He didn't expect the front door to be open but he tried it anyway, and wasn't surprised that it was locked. He then walked around the side of the house, looking in the windows, conveniently set at waist level.

There were no lights on inside which was good. Sonny hadn't expected anyone to be in residence. But the moonlight provided enough light for him to determine which room was which. He went from window to window noticing sparse furnishings, a clear kitchen--though he was happy to notice pots and pans hanging from a rack above a kitchen island. At least he had tools for cooking, though he wouldn't be here long, so he wouldn't require much.

The living room had two couches, a chair and a small, old model television. The dining room setup, however, made Sonny smile. A large oak table near one wall was laden with numerous pieces of electronic equipment, various coloured wires streaming from them, along the floor and out into the hallway.

A window at the rear of the house revealed a mud room leading to the main foyer. Through what must have been patio doors at one point--but were now boarded up with holes in various places--Sonny saw a stream of thick, black wires running from the makeshift wall across the rear yard and out toward a barn that was about 50 yards away. He frowned at the sight of the wires which, though rubber coated, didn't look to be outdoor gauge and may have been eroded by weather and lack of use.

He followed them to the barn, confirming they were the types of wires used for power transmission a couple of decades ago. Looking over the roofline of the barn he could see additional wires and cables running from a post sticking out of the roof leading directly to a transmission pole just behind the barn. This confirmed that the house was still hooked up to the grid. The moonlight allowed him to see beyond the barn and he smiled as he saw that three or four cables ran from the transmission pole to a large high voltage tower in a wide field beyond; a hydro tower corridor. He squinted to confirm that the tower was just one in a long line of power line towers stretching as far as the eye could see in either direction.

Michael Powless had chosen the location well.

Breaking into the house via the small window in the mud room, Sonny searched the main floor, the second-floor bedrooms, and finally the unfinished, low-ceiling basement, using the flashlight app on his cell phone to see in the now pervading darkness. He found the main breaker in the corner of the basement behind the ancient oil furnace and pulled the switch to the ON position. Immediately a light came on in the room--a single bulb hanging on a fraying wire in the centre of the room. There wasn't much in the basement other than the heating and water equipment, what looked like a tiny cellar, an old, brown-stained sink with an ancient looking washer and dryer beside it.

Back upstairs, one or two lights had come on and Sonny turned the switches in other rooms on the main and second floors. Most rooms were empty but one had an old bed with no covers. The kitchen, as he'd noticed before, seemed to be well stocked with utensils and cookware, etc. The refrigerator was unplugged, the door open showing an empty interior. Sonny reached down and plugged it in. It wheezed a bit but settled into a quiet hum. He shut the door so it could start to get up--or down as it were--to temperature. He then checked cupboards and saw a few cans of fruit and vegetables, some pasta boxes, and what his research had discovered to be a young Canadian's favourite: Mac 'n Cheese--at least a dozen boxes. Everything would be stale dated he knew, so he didn't disturb them.

The dining room beckoned since it was obvious that was where Michael Prowess had set up operations. There was one reclining chair under the main window and one or two office chairs against the wall. But facing another window was the large wooden dining table he'd seen from the window, piled with pieces of electronic equipment and monitors, albeit ancient ones.

Sonny walked around the table and saw that the wires coming into through the patio door in the family room next door led straight to a big black box set underneath the table. From that box, standard computer and telephone wires ran up to various pieces of equipment which had been spread out in a semi-circle on the table top.

Sonny pulled up a chair and pressed the power switches on everything he could see. Some lit up immediately while others flashed momentarily and went dark again.

For the next ten minutes or so, he inspected the equipment, the wires, and the connections. Then he remembered the girl, got up and went out the back door.

Ten minutes later, he dragged Lena into the dining room and allowed her to see the table and equipment. Her hands were still crudely tied behind her back but Sonny had taken out the rubber band that had been in her mouth. He could see a little bruising on her cheeks where the band had rubbed but her eyes widened at the display on the table. He was surprised she hadn't yelled for help as soon as he'd pulled her from the vehicle but her curiosity seemed to be overpowering her desire to escape at the moment. He hoped that was a reflection on his treatment of her so far.

"What is this?" she said. "Where are we?"

Sonny was glad the girl had decided he wasn't a threat to her physically--for the time being anyway. She seemed to be distracted by the table's contents.

"This is your new lab," Sonny said.

She looked up at him, a quizzical look on her face.

"You've probably never heard of the guy who set this all up--before your time--but he was a lot like you Ms. Castillo."

She walked over to the table, leaned over and studied the pieces of equipment. She looked a bit awkward with her hands bound and Sonny thought for a minute, then reached behind her and untied the band. She didn't seem to notice but rubbed her wrists subconsciously without looking away from the screens, and began pushing buttons and typing onto one of the keyboards.

"How old is this stuff?" she asked over her shoulder.

Sonny smiled. Potential for a Stockholm syndrome moment, he thought.

"The kid who set this up--probably around your age, I think-- was killed in an automobile accident in 2006, and he had no relatives so it's all been sitting here for over a decade. The bank took over the property but there were some litigation issues concerning the hydro company and money owed for past billing, so it's been vacant, awaiting someone brave enough to take on all the problems."

"What kind of litigation issues?" Castillo asked, pulling up the chair and sitting down.

Sonny smiled. She was perceptive--and easily distracted. That was a good thing as it would make the next few hours go much smoother than he'd thought they would.

"Apparently, Michael Prowess--that's the guy who bought the place and set this up--plugged into the local grid but never paid for his usage," Sonny said. "By the time Ontario Hydro caught up with the irregular voltage bursts, he was dead."

Castillo nodded. She was typing furiously. "Damn!" she said suddenly. "The software is workable but the hardware could never handle the necessary upgrading."

A sudden click on Lena's belt brought her attention away from the monitor and she reached behind her to investigate. "What... what are you doing?"

"I'm sorry Ms. Castillo," Sonny said, stepping back his hands holding a leather tether attached to the eye bolt that he had clipped to her belt. "For the time being, this is necessary. I can't afford to have you escape."

Lena looked down at her waist. She could easily unclip herself or even undue her belt, drop her pants, and run away. So what was the point?

Sonny noticed her confusion. "As I told you, Ms. Castillo, I have no intention of harming you. However, I need you to do some work for me, specifically get this lab up and running like you did in Oswego." He attached the other end of the tether to a pipe extending from the old radiator in the corner. The old farmhouse was heated by water and every room had a radiator that was connected to the piping running under the floors. It would take someone much stronger than a young girl to pull that pipe out of the floor. However, it would still be relatively simple for Lena to escape at her end.

He could see that he'd broken her concentration. She was once again concerned about her well being. He needed her to focus on the scientific possibilities.

"You know Jay Losano was prepared to sabotage the Oswego facility?" he said.

She slumped in her seat and although her eyes showed a little fear, Sonny could tell she was also processing thoughts.

"Jay gave me an injection," she said quietly.

"A deadly one," Sonny said, noticing Lena flinch. "He felt you were no longer necessary. He figured he knew enough about ArmourNet and the grid coding to recreate what you had prepared for the President's launch earlier today. But he was wrong wasn't he Ms. Castillo?"

Lena stared at Sonny for a moment, then brushed back her hair with both hands, blowing out a long breath of air.

"I had my concerns about Jay," she said quietly, looking at her hands, now clasped together in her lap.

"You knew he was planning some kind of takeover, yes?" Sonny asked.

She looked up quickly. "I didn't think he would try to hurt me," she said, her voice shaky.

"He was trying to kill you actually."

Her head shot up quickly and her eyes burned into his.

"What was in that syringe?" she asked.

"A deadly virus called RX351, known only to a select few," he said.

"Deadly?" Her voice quivered.

"If it hadn't been for me, you would have died Ms. Castillo." A little white lie, he knew, but since she had been out cold, she wouldn't know who had applied the antidote. Had General Wade's team not done it, Sonny would have, so the clarification was mute.

"Why?" she exclaimed. "Why would he want to kill me... he was my friend."

"He was your friend in the beginning, Ms. Castillo," Sonny said, his voice low, reassuring. "He had latched onto your balloon, so to speak. Jay thought you were the answer to his future. But he didn't think you needed to be a part of it once it was clear his life was about to change dramatically."

"Change, how?"

"He decided he was going to run the company formed when the President approved ArmourNet as the primary national internet service provider."

"We were going to do that together," she said, her eyes tearing slightly.

"He had other partners who he felt would build a stronger, more profitable corporation," Sonny said.

"His father?" she spurted. "I had an, ah... arrangement with President Emerson that Jay and I would run the software administration and he would establish a government-run agency to handle operations and licensing. His father would benefit financially, reward for his original stake, but the President would never have allowed mob involvement. We were going to find a new partner to integrate the software and hardware for installation."

"Actually, that's where I came in," Sonny said, surprised to hear about President Emerson's direct involvement.

She tried to stand but Sonny put his arm gently on her shoulder and she sat back down but stared up at him.

"You're with the manufacturers, the ones who make the hardware," she said. "Why would you be interested in the operations?"

Sonny smiled and patted her shoulder.

"Why don't we just worry about whether we can get this system up and running, even for a short time," he said soothingly.

She furrowed her brows. "Why... why would I do that? I have a perfectly good operation in Oswego. Why don't you just take me back. I'll forget all this---" she swept the room with her hands. "I just want to go back." She began to sob.

Sonny didn't want to escalate his compliance methods with her just yet, so he maintained his current demeanour. "Ms. Castillo, I need to know that I can access the power grid, even for a very short period of time, and right now the only way to do that is to get this particular system up and running here. Then we can incorporate your special code so that ArmourNet can initiate and protect the data signal I will eventually send."

She looked up sharply. "How do you know about my initiation code?"

Sonny smiled. "I wasn't really aware, till just now," he said, patting the back of her hand in a friendly manner. "But it's exactly what I would have done, especially with Jay as a partner."

"What do you mean?"

"Jay Losano is controlled by his father," Sonny said. "Eventually, he would have demanded control."

"Once we were established he was to receive 33% of the company," Lena explained. Until then, he was just providing foundation money.

Sonny smiled and stood. "I'm afraid you're a little naive dear, which is understandable. You are young. Very intelligent, yes, but not well versed in the motivations of men of the world, especially the likes of Antonio Losano."

"I don't believe that," she spurted. "I met with him myself and he convinced me that our business arrangement was legitimate and mutually beneficial."

Again, Sonny was surprised. She had met with Jay's father and Jay hadn't known about it.

"You made a deal with the devil, Ms. Castillo," he said. "And now you have to rectify that."

"What are you talking about?"

"Well, if you recall, it was Jay who injected you with a poison meant not to keep you out of the way for a while, but to eliminate you permanently."

"Jay w...wanted to k..kill me? Tears formed at the edges of her eyes.

"As I said, if it hadn't been for me, you would have died Ms. Castillo," Sonny said, reaching out for her hand again, but this time taking it in his and holding it. "I had an antidote you see. And I gave it to you after Jay left you in your office to die."

"But then you kidnapped me!" she blurted.

Sonny held her hand and stroked the back of it with his other. "I know it looks like that to you but I had no choice at the time Ms. Castillo. You see there are a lot of people interested in your invention, and despite many being representatives of various government agencies and interests, there is a question as to how much they can be trusted too."

"The President assured me that...."

"Ah, the President," Sonny interrupted. "I'm sure the President has you and the American people's interests at heart, but unfortunately, he is surrounded by members of various agencies that may not feel the same way about government operated national internet service. In fact, they are more interested in control than they are about providing low cost access to everyone."

"We could have spoken with him instead of you.... you kidnapping me." The tears were dripping down her face and she pulled her hand away from Sonny's to wipe it with the back of her hand. Sonny walked to a sideboard and grabbed a box of tissues from a pile of boxes. He'd noticed them earlier and assumed young Michael had stocked up on supplies so he wouldn't have to leave the house often. He came back and handed the girl several tissues from the box. She took them and dabbed at her eyes and cheeks.

"I realize my actions seem rather, ah... harsh to you Ms. Castillo," Sonny said soothingly. "And, in hindsight, perhaps I was a bit rash. Had I taken the time to explain my plan to you, I'm confident you would probably have chosen to come with me of your own free will. However, the people I represent are very interested in ensuring your project gets launched without any political issues hindering its success, and it was clear to me that I had to get you away from all those groups quickly, before someone else swooped in and buried you away in some clandestine safe house somewhere."

"What people?" she said, her voice quieter now.

Sonny turned his head and gave her a quizzical look.

"I mean, who do you represent?" she asked.

"Ah, well that's best kept a secret for the time being Ms. Castillo." Sonny said. "But I assure you, the President will be one of the first to know that you have successfully initiated the launch of ArmourNet. It's just not going to occur the way everyone had originally planned."

She looked at him and he could see she was trying to figure things out.

"Why should I believe anything you say?" she asked finally, her eyes glittering with determination, though she was nervously tapping her foot on the wooden floor.

"Well, at this point, I'm not asking you to believe me," Sonny said, eyeing her carefully. "But I do need you to see if this old set up here will suffice to at least launch your beta test, just like we were going to do in Oswego."

"But we crossed the border," she said. "We're in Canada. I don't have any kind of arrangement with the hydro companies here, at least not yet. I know they were very interested, but Jay never finalized any official agreement."

"You see, all you have to do is set up the beta test, on their home soil," Sonny said. "When they see how well it works, they'll be the first international partner. In many ways it's a better plan than the original."

Lena shook her head. "No, President Emerson would never involve a foreign nation to test something of this importance."

"Canada is hardly a foreign nation Ms. Castillo," Sonny said softly. "In fact, look at what our friend already established here. Had he not suffered an untimely death, he may well have beaten you to the punch, so to speak."

At that, the girl turned back to the table and the array of equipment.

"He was going about it the wrong way," she said matter-of-factly.

"Oh? And why do you say that?" Sonny asked, smiling inwardly. He was intrigued by her sudden confidence. Her devotion to technology clearly outpaced her fear of breaking international rules, or the fact that she was still a kidnap victim.

She pointed at one of the units on the right side of the table. Several wires ran from an exposed front panel into a port on the side of what Sonny knew was the mainframe computer running the system.

"That looks like a transmission filtering device; homemade by the looks of it," she said, brushing her hand over the face of the thin component. "He was trying to eliminate the interference radiating from the high voltage electrical current."

She looked up and Sonny nodded for her to continue.

"That was what IBEC and the others did back in the 90s and it never succeeded. The FCC didn't allow for any risk of signals floating around near the power lines, interfering with emergency bandwidths and such."

"And your solution doesn't interfere with those transmissions?" Sonny asked tentatively. He knew some of the technology behind Castillo's invention but he had never actually seen the coding for ArmourNet itself.

"It was simple really," she said, trying to hide a smile. "Rather than trying to suppress digital data or even electrical pulses so they didn't interfere with other bandwidths, ArmourNet simply surrounds the signal, protecting signals from getting in or out. It allows data to ride along with high-voltage electrical currents inside a shell of protective electrons. It doesn't share the power line as much as it becomes embedded in the current. There is no interference because the data is encased within the current itself."

"And ArmourNet ensures the data isn't burned up by the high voltage current?" Sonny said.

"More or less," she said, smiling. "There's a little more to it--such as filtering the data out from the current when it reaches the recipient--but essentially, that's the gist of it."

"I'm sure you are simplifying for my benefit," Sonny said, purposely humble. "However, Jay said that you had, indeed, achieved success in local tests."

The girl frowned suddenly.

"You're not sure it will work over greater distances, are you?" Sonny said, leaning forward and staring her in the eyes.

She returned the stare then turned her head away.

"I've never sent a signal farther than a few miles," she said. "I was worried the protection would eventually erode as the intense electrical currents bombarded the ArmourNet coding as it travelled longer distances."

"I see," Sonny said, thinking.

She turned and began fiddling with some of the wires, checking to see what ports they led to and which components were on and which ones weren't working any more.

"Perhaps we should do a test here to see if your theory does, in fact, work," Sonny said.

Castillo stood up abruptly. "I'm not doing anything for you, not here, not anywhere!" She stomped her feet childishly. "You kidnapped me."

Sonny wasn't really surprised with the sudden outburst; in fact, he thought it was overdue. He stood, with his arms folded and looked at her intently. He thought about the punching bag and how much he wished he'd brought it with him instead of leaving it at the Senator's house. It wouldn't take long he knew, to make the girl do what he wanted. Actually, just putting her in the bag would probably scare her into compliance.

Her glare suddenly softened and her demeanour relaxed as she dropped back into the chair just as quickly. Sonny knew she'd seen his eyes and understood--as most people did--that there wasn't much behind his eyes in the way of compassion. His general conciliatory attitude was fake and she had recognized that in an instant. He would be a gentleman as long as she did what he wanted. When she stopped being compliant, he would become a monster, instantly. Sonny knew his eyes conveyed that message. And now he knew the girl had seen it and understood.

She turned and put her arms on the table, her head in her hands.

"What are you going to do when it's working?" she asked through her hands.

Sonny smiled.

"Let's worry about getting it to work first, shall we?" he said, stepping over and pulling her to her feet. He held her arm tightly and began steering her out of the room into the kitchen.

"Where are we going?" Her voice was shaky, fearful. She had been expecting some kind of force, he knew, but she had been distracted by the farmhouse setup.

"This equipment hasn't been turned on in over ten years," he said, pushing her ahead of him through the basement door and down the stairs. Castillo struggled to keep pace. "I need to go shopping for a couple of new items, don't you agree?"

He was pushing her down the wooden stairs quickly and she didn't answer as she was too busy trying not to hit her head on the low ceiling.

Once in the basement, Sonny lead Lena across the sparsely lit, dank basement to the old wooden door that opened into the cellar. She resisted as they approached but Sonny took her other arm and kept pushing.

"What are you going to do to me?" she squeaked as Sonny opened the thick door, its hinges creaking from lack of use.

"Not to worry. You're not my type," Sonny said, pulling the string attached to the only bulb in the centre of a small wine cellar. With the room suddenly illuminated, she could see that all three walls were lined with floor to ceiling shelves designed for wine and about two thirds were occupied by dusty, dark bottles.

Lena coughed as Sonny gently pushed her inside.

"It's the best I can do on short notice," he said, motioning for her to sit on a tiny stool in one corner. "It seems our friend Michael was a bit of a connoisseur. There are some awfully good vintages here. Help yourself. I'll be back in an hour or so."

"You can't leave me in here!" she exclaimed.

"There is nowhere else I'm afraid," Sonny said. "This is the only room in the house with a reliable lock and until you and I come to some kind of an agreement as to what you are going to do for me, I have to consider you a flight risk."

He stepped back into the doorway, his tall and wide frame casting a dark shadow over Lena as she cowered in the corner.

"Why don't you wile away the time choosing a good wine for dinner," he said, smiling. "When I return, we'll have an indoor barbeque, so make it a robust cabernet or something similar." He bowed slightly, quickly stepped back and abruptly shut the door.

"No, don't leave me here!" Lena screamed as the door slammed shut.

As she jumped up and banged on the door with both fists, she didn't hear the click of the old latch dropping into place.

Robert J. Morrow

Chapter Seventy-Three

"It's too quiet," JP said, as they crept along the edge of the small forested area which separated the Gauge farmhouse from the neighbour's farm.

"You were expecting cops on horses with big brown Stetsons?"

"They don't still do that, do they?"

"Saw it on TV at some Senator's funeral couple of months ago," Hart said. "Maybe just ceremonial."

"Well I don't see anyone, horses or not."

"Call Frank," he said. "I'm going to check it out."

"We should wait for backup."

"You wait. We didn't race up here, hot on the trail of a Korean CIA agent who may have turned bad, just so we could sit and wait for the cavalry. He could be torturing her, or forcing her to do things against her will."

"Like raping her," JP said straight-faced.

Hart watched her carefully. "Sonny may be many things but Genghis Khan isn't one of them. I was thinking more like making her reveal her code."

"If he even knows about that yet."

"I think that's why he abducted her," he said. "I think he found out she has a safeguard and he hadn't counted on that."

"Don't go in Hart," she said. "Just do some reconnaissance. We need backup."

"It's one guy," he said.

"It's Sonny Kim," she said. "And your last tangle with him wasn't too positive for you."

Hart frowned. "Lucky punch." He reached up to switch off the dome light, jumped out and ran, crouched over pushing small branches and tall ground cover out of the way. Once in the clearing, he raced toward the rear door of the farmhouse.

He edged along the sides of the house, peering in windows as he circled around from the left, eventually disappearing around the front then, a few moments later, emerging again at the rear. He looked over to where he knew the car was hidden, just beyond the trees. He figured JP was probably now calling Frank.

Hart noticed the broken glass from the back door and wasn't surprised when the knob turned freely. This is how Sonny had gained entry.

The only light he had seen was coming from the dining room and hall leading to the front entrance. But he hadn't seen anyone inside or any sign that anyone had recently been there, other than the lights. He knew that due to the age of the house, once he entered creaking noises were going to occur no matter how stealthily he tried to sneak in and around the first floor. So, against his better wisdom, he simply opened the door and walked in, as if expected, with fists raised and clenched, ready for an ambush.

The floorboards did groan and creak but Hart continued striding down the hall, past the kitchen and into the lit dining room. He quickly surveyed the table and vaguely recognized some of the components on display as older model CPUs and routers. Other pieces he couldn't fathom but assumed were various resistors and condensers used for the transmission of broadband internet several years ago. No doubt modern equipment which performed similar tasks were now housed in apps used on smartphones but back in the day, each of these components likely only performed one job each. Thus, the need for so many bulky metal boxes hooked up to computers and monitors semi-organized in a half circle on the tabletop.

He continued searching the main floor but saw no evidence of occupancy, recently or otherwise. Taking the stairs up to the second floor two at a time a quick search revealed a similar state of un-use on that floor.

Of course, if I were hiding someone against their will, I wouldn't do it out in the open anyway. I'd hide them somewhere unseen, the most logical place being the basement, if there was one.

A quick search of the kitchen revealed a door beside the ancient refrigerator which opened up to a dark, unrevealing wooden staircase heading downward.

He searched the wall on either side for a light switch, found one, and flicked it upward.

Nothing happened.

That's when he heard a tapping noise.

*   *   *

"What do you mean he's gone in by himself?" Frank said, his frustration evident in the terseness of his words.

"Sonny couldn't have planned this too far in advance Frank," JP said. "If he had, he would have had a better way to get into the country than stealing a boat in Youngstown and high jacking a van in Ontario."

"Your point being?" Frank spat.

"My point being that only Sonny and Lena are here," she said. "And Hart is worried he's torturing her, trying to get her to give him the code."

"An RCMP special task force team is no more than twenty minutes away," Frank said. "He should have waited."

"If attacked in force, we don't know how Sonny will react," JP said. "He might harm Lena permanently if he thought he had no way out."

"Why would he do that?"

"Because if he can't get the code, I think he'd make sure we, or anyone else, couldn't get it either."

"You think he'd kill her?" Frank said incredulous. "He's a South Korean agent for Christ's sake. He's supposed to be on our side; well, sort of anyway. His country would benefit immensely just from the hardware contracts alone."

"There's more to Sonny Kim than we think," she said. "You said Losano called him his partner. Why would a Korean agent get involved with a gay Mafioso offspring like him? It just doesn't add up." She thought for a minute. "What else has General Wade's team come up with about the work this Gauge character did?"

"Nothing more than what you know now," Frank said quietly. JP waited.

"What aren't you telling me Frank?" she asked finally, reading into Frank's hesitation. A few seconds passed.

"The kid actually got the servers to connect to the grid," Frank said. "Just for a few minutes," he added quickly. "But it was long enough for him to send an email message with no traditional internet connection. He wrote 'Mr. Chretien come here, I want you!'"

"Who's Mr. Chretien?" JP asked.

"The Canadian Prime Minister at the time," Frank said. "But it was a play on words from the first message Alexander Graham Bell sent in 1874 to his assistant: 'Mr. Watson come here, I want you!'"

She'd seen the signs on the highway coming into Brantford that hailed itself as the Telephone City but she hadn't made the connection. "I thought Bell invented the telephone in New York?"

"Actually he was in Boston when he made that call but Canadians like to think one of their own invented the thing," Frank said. "Bell prepared the patent application at his parent's home in Brantford. Doesn't matter. The point is that Gauge managed to get the attention of the government and they sent a group of scientists down to investigate his claim."

"And?"

"And three months later, Matthew Gauge was dead."

"Whoa! Are you saying the Canadians snuffed him because he'd found a new way to communicate? I thought Canadians were mild mannered, vanilla versions of Americans?"

"My ex-wife is Canadian," Frank said.

"No offence," JP said.

"She's an ex, no offence taken," Frank said. "The kid's death was likely legit. Covert activities in Canada weren't that sophisticated back then. I don't think they had him eliminated. It was more like providence and misfortune. The RCMP checked everything out at the farmhouse, saw nothing threatening, and literally walked away. Case closed."

"And nobody's been here since?"

"The bank sold it to a low-ball investor a decade ago and he's just sitting on it, waiting for the town to grow toward him. Eventually the farm will become a suburb full of towns and singles."

"But they left it intact?" JP asked, incredulous.

"So I'm told." Frank said. "Canadians don't worry about reuse like we do. They've got a lot more open empty land that's cheaper to develop. When they need the space, they'll deal with it. Until then, the property's insured as vacant and no one has bothered to clean out the house. Gauge had no living relatives."

"Meaning that whatever Gauge achieved back in the nineties is probably still possible now," JP said.

"I think Sonny believes it," Frank said. "That's why he's there."

"And that's why he brought Castillo," JP said.

"The question is why is it so important for Sonny get access to the internet via power lines? Despite Castillo's claims, it's still slower than wireless or even optics. And the equipment here is decades old."

"That's what Wade and his team are working on," Frank said.

*   *   *

The tapping was coming from the rear of the basement. A heavy door with an old-fashioned bolt latch was set into the wall in the corner of the back wall; some kind of cellar. Perfect spot to keep a prisoner.

But where was Sonny?

He could be behind the door, waiting for him to barge in. Heaven knows Hart hadn't been quiet since arriving. Was it a large room and was he now interrogating Lena as Hart contemplated what to do next? Sonny wouldn't have heard him walking around behind this door.

Hart leaned his ear against the heavy wood and listened. Nothing. He was about to try the latch when he heard the tapping again.

Looking around the basement for something he could use as a weapon, he grabbed an old piece of lead pipe that had fallen off the hot water tank. About the size of a baseball bat, he held it up with one hand, ready to strike.

Then, using his knuckles he returned the tap.

*　　　　*　　　　*

JP decided to get out of the cruiser and move closer to the house in an effort to see what Hart was doing. He'd been gone fifteen minutes which wasn't really that long if he was searching the whole house. But she was getting nervous.

Frank had told her the RCMP task force--a group of elite police similar to a SWAT team--was gathered at a farm equipment dealership about two miles down the road. They all agreed they needed more intel on the situation at the farmhouse before they came rushing in with all barrels blazing. The Captain was being dropped off a few hundred yards away from the farmhouse laneway and would hike in to meet JP and make an assessment on site. By then, Hart should have returned with more information.

The night was quiet and a little cool. She wrapped her arms around her body and shivered. The lights inside the farmhouse were the old, incandescent style. The mild yellow colour invoked a felling of warmth. At least Hart wasn't freezing to death.

A rustling behind some bushes on the other side of the road caught her attention and she turned to greet the Captain.

The man striding toward her, however, wasn't wearing a uniform. And he was presenting a set of credentials out toward her.

"Hello Agent Pierce," the man said, saluting half-heartedly.

JP had been reaching for her gun but she sighed when she recognized the man. "Where the hell did you come from?"

*　　　　*　　　　*

Hart wasn't sure what to expect when the thick door opened but he hadn't expected to see Lena Castillo crouched down against the rear wall, surrounded by hundreds of bottles of wine. He could see the fear in her eyes but as she realized who was standing in the doorway, her fear turned to relief and she started to get up.

"Where's Sonny Kim?" Hart asked her.

"He left me here," she said, moistening her lips. "Said he was going into town to get some equipment. A lot of the units upstairs are very old and won't work properly."

As he helped Lena shake the dust and grime from her clothes, he couldn't help but notice some of the bottles on the shelves. A 71 Penfolds Grange stood out on an upper shelf, and an early seventies Ramos Pinto Vintage Port about halfway down. Unbelievable. They would have been avant-garde when Gauge first put them here. But now, more than a decade later, the Grange was nothing short of astounding, though the port was likely vinegar.

Lena was heading for the stairs, so with one longing last look, Hart followed, slowly changing focus to the fact that Sonny could return any minute.

He wondered if the RCMP task force Frank had promised was nearby. If so, he needed to get Lena safely out and let them know Sonny wasn't on the premises... yet.

"It doesn't really make sense," Lena said, as she led Hart through the kitchen into the dining room. She sat at the table and typed on one of the keyboards.

"We need to go Lena," Hart said. "He'll be back any time."

She nodded but kept typing. Hart reached for her but she put up her hand to stop him. He watched as she plugged a cord connected to a small box into the main CPU in the centre of the table. She tapped some more on the keyboard and turned to Hart.

"Who owns this place and where did they go?" she asked.

He cocked his head. "Why?"

"Because whoever it was he or she was onto something but from the looks of things they just suddenly stopped one day. This stuff hasn't been in use for a few years."

"He died," Hart said.

Her eyebrows raised. "That would explain it." She disconnected the small box and handed it to Hart.

Hart looked at it. There was no label, just the manufacturer's logo. It was some kind of removeable data storage device. The word *Zip* adorned the side of the unit. Hart recalled the Zip drive was an early version of a portable disc drive, albeit one of the earlier models based on its thickness. "What do you want me to do with this?"

"Just keep it somewhere safe till this is all over," she said.

Hart reached for her hand. "Come on, we can't wait around here anymore. We need to get you to safety and I won't be able to do that if I have to confront Sonny on the way out."

"I'm not going," she said, staring at me.

Her eyes bored into his. *Where had the fear gone?* A moment ago in the cellar, she looked like a rape victim. But now, she was sitting on a chair, hands in her lap, telling him she wanted to stay. *Stay for what?*

"Lena, you're not safe here. Sonny will come back and once he gets you to do whatever it is he wants you to do, he will likely kill you." He saw her take a deep swallow but her eyes didn't waver.

"That's what I need to know," she said.

"Know what?"

"What it is he needs from me. She stood and faced him, her hands on her hips. "He knows ArmourNet," she said. "I mean really knows, like what the coding does and everything."

"Your partner Losano," Hart said.

"There's more," she said, pulling her arm free. Hart sighed. "The guy who owns... owned this place," she said, putting one hand on his chest and looking into his eyes. "He found something, something nobody else thought of. I need to know if Sonny Kim has figured it out too."

"He didn't plan this little excursion Lena," Hart said. "Kidnapping you was a last resort, believe me. If Anthony Losano hadn't shot the Senator, your press conference would have gone off as planned and the President would have launched ArmourNet."

"It doesn't work."

Hart frowned and watched as she took another step away from him, back to the table. "What doesn't work?"

"ArmourNet," she said, sighing. "Oh nobody would have known today. I set it up so the test never left the immediate press conference area. ArmourNet works well... until it reaches the pylons."

Hart looked down at his watch, a maze of thoughts passing through his head. What was she talking about? Why was that important? And where the hell was Sonny?"

"He wants me to activate my code so he can run some kind of internet message across the power lines," Lena said, interrupting my thoughts. "But even if I did, it wouldn't work."

He grabbed her arm again and this time pulled her out of the living room into the hallway. "If you run to the edge of the clearing, JP is there. I'll be right behind you."

Lena stared at me, the fear in her eyes evident. But there was something else there too.

"We need to go..." he urged but stopped as Lena dug in her heels and began pulling away again.

"I need to stay," she said.

"Lena!" Hart had had enough. This was getting silly. He looked out the windows, searching for any sign of Sonny returning, or a bunch of black-clad policemen racing in en force.

Lena was leaning against the wall, her one hand rubbing her forehead vigorously. "Why is it so important for him to be able to send messages across the power lines?" she said, more to herself than Hart. He felt sweat running down his back and raced to the kitchen window. There was no movement in the back yard. The bushes beyond looked inviting, safety being assured in the darkness that lay beyond.

"Even when BPL is up and running, it won't be the fastest network available," Lena was saying. "It will be the cheapest, and the most widely accessible, but no one's under any delusion that it will be any more than a national service only slightly better than high-speed DHL is now. No business requiring speed will use it.

Fibre optics, cable, even wireless will always be more efficient, even if they're more expensive."

Hart was only half listening to her, the other half listening for any sound inside or outside the house that would mean someone was coming.

"It doesn't matter," he said. "We need to get you to safety. We can figure out motives later, once you're safe and we have him in custody. And if there's something here you want to experiment with, we can come back later, when Sonny is captured."

"I can't go," she said, her eyes suddenly darker, her focus boring into his eyes. "There's something here that I'm missing. I don't know if he knows that and came here on purpose or not. But I get the feeling Sonny's tech-savvy enough to figure it out if he has to," she continued. "Clearly, he, and maybe Jay, were planning something that they didn't want me involved in." She banged the wall behind her with the edge her hand. "I need to know what that is."

"Do you forget he kidnapped you?" Hart said, trying to pull her away from the wall. "And locked you in the cellar?"

She walked past him, to the door leading to the basement.

"Exactly," she blurted. "Jay tried to kill me..." she caught her breath when she realized what she'd just reconciled. "...But Sonny doesn't want me out of the way. At least not yet. He needs me." She stamped her feet. "I have to know why. It could be vital to the future of BPL."

Scientists, computer geeks, whatever... it never ceased to amaze Hart that regardless of what physical harm may be eminent, those who were obsessed with their earth-shattering breakthroughs were always oblivious to the dangers of the world around them. Especially when that world included the antics of a foreign government agent who had clearly gotten a couple of wires crossed.

"When he's used you for whatever he needs you for," Hart said, putting his hands on her shoulders and leaning in so he could stare directly into her eyes. "He will kill you."

She shook a little but stared back.

"Maybe," she said, then shook her head. "Okay, he will. He would have let Jay kill me, I know that." she took in a quick breath. "But I... no we... have to know why what I'm doing is so important to him."

"No, all I have to do is get you safely back to Oswego where I can protect you and let you finish your job for the President," Hart said.

"Don't you see!" she said, her voice louder, more adamant. "Sonny may know something I don't; something that may make ArmourNet work. And I think the answer is here. This is too important. And it's too risky to not find out what he knows. If he's figured it out, I need to know. I think he's been here before. It could take me weeks to catch up to what he obviously already knows. It's a matter of national security!"

Had we not been in the middle of a foreign country--albeit a friendly foreign one--waiting for a foreign agent to return and take back his captive back, that last comment might have been funny.

"Have you been talking to Frank?"

She turned her head sideways, her eyebrows furrowing. "Actually it was the President who said it was a matter of national security," she said.

Okay, I'm out of my league here, Hart figured. *Time to just get her out of here.*

"Come on, enough talk, we need to get you safely back to Oswego," he said, pulling her away from the door.

She pushed his chest in an attempt to escape. "No, we need to know what Sonny's doing!" she shouted.

Hart let go and stared at her.

"Listen, he doesn't know you're here," she said. "Lock me back in the wine cellar and let's find out exactly what he wants me to do," Her voice was confident, any fear she'd been experiencing a few moments ago dissipating completely. "You can hide somewhere and listen."

"I can't do that," he said.

"Of course you can," she said. "You can hide upstairs somewhere..." she was thinking quickly, her arms pumping up and down with excitement. "And make sure he doesn't hurt me."

Hart stared at her. She stared back.

"We need to know," she said finally.

Hart stepped back, took a long look outside into the backyard. The SWAT team, task force, whatever they were, wouldn't move in until they'd heard from him... he hoped. JP would be nervous but she'd trust his judgement. Another hope. He looked at Lena. The fear was gone for the most part. Determination and focus seemed to have invaded her being. He had no intention of carrying her out arguing or even screaming, especially if Sonny was nearby.

He grabbed her hand and walked her back to the basement stairs.

"I will never be more than ten feet away," he assured her. He wasn't sure how he could guarantee that but he'd figure it out somehow. Lena's life depended on it. Of that, he had no doubt.

Chapter Seventy-Four

Once Lena was securely back in the wine cellar, the big heavy door sealed and locked, Hart raced back up the stairs to find a vantage spot near the dining room where he could remain hidden from view but also be able to see what Sonny and Lena would be doing once her freed her from her makeshift cell.

A closet in the hallway provided enough cover that when the door was closed, he had a sliver of a view right into the dining room. It was, of course, the dumbest hiding spot he could think of, and if Sonny searched the house it would be one of the first places he looked. However, with Lena back in the cellar, Sonny wouldn't have any reason to search the house. If he arrived before the task force he would still think he was undiscovered. Hart's only hope was that whatever it was he had in mind, what he had in store for Lena, it would happen in the dining room where all the equipment was. Hart was in the closet less than ten minutes when he heard the sound of the back door open. His heart pounded as he heard several heavy steps and then Sonny walked into view. He dropped a couple of large boxes on the dining room table, turned and headed to the kitchen. Hart heard footfalls get fainter as he went down the stairs to the basement. Then he heard what sounded like the heavy cellar door creaking open...

And then nothing.

Hart kept his breathing low and steady, trying not to sneeze. The dust accumulation in the closet was immense; you could smell it. He crouched against the back of the closet wall. There was still no sound from the basement.

What was he doing down there?

Suddenly his--actually Lena's--plan seemed absurd. He should have taken her away from here when I'd had the chance. The task force could have come for Sonny once she was safe. But because he'd listened to her, bought into her idea about finding out what Sonny was doing, she was now down in the basement with Sonny and Hart had no idea what was going on.

After another couple of minutes of silence, he decided he would have to risk being seen and, as quietly as possible, get to the top of the basement stairs and see if he could catch what was going on. If Sonny was torturing Lena, or doing any other unspeakable acts, he would have to attack. Strangely, he felt no fear at the idea; Sonny and Hart had rumbled before. But that was fifteen plus years ago, in a controlled tournament environment, and neither of them were breaking any laws at the time. Hart had to believe Sonny's motivations today were a little more sinister and his intensity during a battle would draw from resources Hart wasn't sure he possessed anymore, if he ever had.

He pushed the closet door wider slowly, cringing as it made a slight squeak. He crept along the corridor, keeping as close to the wall as possible as this is where the creaky old floorboards would be nailed tightest to the subfloor. Crouching down as he neared the basement, he pushed his torso forward, leaning into open space, trying to angle a view into the lower level. The bulkheads and old piping obscured most of his view. All he could see was that the cellar door was open and the light from inside was illuminating the basement floor. He couldn't see anyone or anything else.

He strained to hear any movement but heard nothing. Frustrated, he slowly stood up and stepped onto the wooden steps leading down.

At the bottom, he still hadn't heard anything but as he crept across the cement floor, more of the cellar came into view. He could make out Lena's jean-clad legs jutting out on the floor. Her ankles had been bound with what looked like grey duct tape. What the hell was Sonny doing and where the hell was he?

There was still no noise coming from the cellar meaning Sonny may have knocked Lena unconscious and was somewhere else down here; it was a huge basement. Could there be another way out, back up to the main floors? Hart hadn't checked. He decided to forget the original plan and get Lena out of here. If Sonny was upstairs setting up equipment or something, then he still had time to free her and head out through the kitchen to where, hopefully, a group of mounted or unmounted RCMP were waiting.

Hart took one more look around the dark basement room and moved into the light.

Lena hadn't been knocked out but she did have more duct tape across her mouth. Her arms too seemed to be pulled behind her, no doubt taped together behind her back.

He edged closer and was about to enter when Lena's head shot up, her eyes wide and staring straight at him. She began shaking her head from side to side violently but before Hart could register the warning, a long, thin, dark shape came racing toward his head. He tried to duck but it landed with a thud against the side of his temple. It felt like someone had struck him with a red-hot iron and then everything went dark.

Robert J. Morrow

Chapter Seventy-Five

Sonny smiled when Hart finally opened his eyes.

"Welcome back Arthur," he said, crossing his legs. He had tied Hart's arms and legs to a dining room chair with extra electrical cords he had found lying around the dining room. A smaller cord was wrapped around Hart's neck, tight to the top rung of the chair, forcing the man to look slightly upward. "I'm assuming that since you are here, other official authorities won't be far behind you," he said. Not waiting for an answer and not really requiring one, he continued. "Though even Frank Daro won't be able to make the Canadians move very quickly, will he? Once he's explained what's going on, there will be all kinds of official discussions and meetings; diplomatic protocols to consider and all that."

Sonny checked to see if Lena was listening but she seemed preoccupied, leaning over the table, concentrating on the keyboard and the main monitor. Good.

Hart appeared to be a little groggy still but Sonny was enjoying himself. "Just to be sure, I have taken the liberty of sending your boss a little photograph." He leaned forward, showing the screen of his smartphone to Hart. It was a picture of a young woman, naked from the waist down. She was tied to a wooden chair, not much different to the ones in this dining room, which was, in fact, what had given Sonny the idea in the first place. Black wires wound around each of the woman's legs and led to her genital area which, though somewhat dark in the picture, was clear enough to make out. The ends of the wires had been flayed about two inches and the exposed copper jutted out from under the tape, both pieces being attached to each of her thighs just shy of her labia. The black electrical tape gleamed as it reflected light from an unknown source. It was clear that if the woman shifted her legs together, the exposed wires would touch, the assumption being that something electrical, and not very pleasant would take place between her legs, less than an inch from her exposed vagina.

"Who is that?" Hart said, his voice muffled as though he had something in his mouth.

Sonny smiled. "An unfortunate playmate of my superior's, but no one you know. Fortunately for us, they won't know that," he pointed to the window.

Sonny watched as first confusion then slowly comprehension dawned on Hart's face.

"Though I am a little surprised you somehow followed me here Hart," Sonny continued. "I think you probably came alone. But that meddling brother-in-law of yours has no doubt been in contact with the Canadians and is probably at this very moment attempting to amass some kid of rescue mission to save our young friend here." He nodded to Lena who was still in her own world, her eyes darting from one screen to another. Sonny was happy she had understood the dilemma she was in. Once he had brought Hart upstairs and tied him to the chair, he had then brought her up and explained that if she didn't sit down and finish preparing the code for launch, he would begin torturing Hart. He sensed she hadn't needed much persuasion, though whether it was for Hart's safety or her own curiosity at what she was finding here, he wasn't sure. He knew she would find some interesting materials amongst young Michael Powless' files but of how much value it would have he didn't know. Nor did he care. Regardless, she seemed focused for the time being. He would have to kill her once she was finished, of course; Hart too. They had been competitive adversaries years ago and Sonny had always had a fondness for Hart's aptitude in the ring. The man didn't have the killer instinct so necessary to winning big tournaments--something that had been drilled into Sonny early on during his training at the Kukkiwon--but the man didn't seem to have any qualms about hurting his opponents when he had the chance. It would have been nice, perhaps under more suitable circumstances, to sit and explain the Great Plan with Hart and maybe convince him to join forces. There would no doubt be room for men like him--skillful, malleable, and a little heartless--in the new regime. And the great leader would certainly enjoy his skills as a chef, perhaps at the Whitehouse once it was the home of the new Korean administration.

He watched as Hart closed his eyes, mustering up strength to ward off pain. Having him handy to elicit threats upon only ensured that the girl would remain intent on doing her job quickly, not worrying about her own life. Sonny felt like laughing. He hadn't wanted to hurt the girl because she may have lost focus for a while. But he had been prepared to if she hadn't agreed to finish the coding. When Hart stumbled in, it had given him another body to taunt her with. It was perfect actually because Sonny could continue to instill a threat to the girl without harming her physically, thereby achieving his goal without slowing down the process. Hart was the perfect pin cushion, much like a voodoo doll. And Sonny knew Hart would be able to take the pain for a while. Whenever he threatened Hart, the girl would get back to work.

Sonny could see that Hart's current pain was intense, the growing dark bruise just to the left of his eye was proof of that. He leaned forward and put a bottle of water against the other man's lips. Hart opened his mouth and the water trickled in.

"I found some Tylenol upstairs in the bathroom," Sonny said. "It's a little outdated but I gave you enough to dull the pain somewhat." Hart just looked at him, his bleary and unfocused. "You'll be fine, for now," Sonny said smiling.

"The new CPUs are working fine, I trust?" he said, turning to the girl. She nodded, her intense gaze riveted to the screen as numbers and symbols scrolled down almost too fast for Sonny to comprehend.

"I need it to be live before the morning," he said.

Castillo jerked her head around. "I can't do that," she stammered. "There are still bugs in the system. If you try to send a message before it is ready, it will burn in transit."

"You were prepared to launch at Oswego today," Sonny said. "So it is ready. All you need to do is configure it to this hardware."

She watched Sonny for a moment, then turned and put her elbows on the edge of the table, her head in her hands. She was breathing heavily. After a few seconds, she looked up. "General Wade insisted on launching today and the President reluctantly agreed," she said. "Senator Blais and his corporate partners were gathering strength and he was concerned that if we didn't go public soon, the Senator would entrap the whole thing in a long and drawn-out legal battle. The President didn't want that."

All of which is fascinating, but of no importance to me," Sonny said. "Just get it ready. I will send a message, and we will be finished."

"I can't!" she exclaimed, her eyes boring into Sonny's.

Sonny turned toward Hart and reaching for his left hand, grabbed his baby finger and wrenched it up and backward quickly until he heard a faint pop.

"Aargh!" Hart's eyes popped open, his mouth stretched outward in both directions and his head snapped back.

When Sonny let go of the finger, it dropped limply and didn't align properly with the other four fingers. Hart's cheeks rose forcing his eyes to squint. He began breathing rapidly through his mouth.

"Please do not make the mistake of thinking I do ·not understand what you are doing," Sonny said to Castillo who was staring in horror at Hart's broken finger. Sonny glanced at his watch. "In an hour, I will review what you have done and if you have not secured your software to the level I require, then I will demonstrate my disappointment on Mr. Hart here once again. We can do that nine more times, as you can see: Once every hour." He checked his watch. "If you have not readied the system by four o'clock this morning, we will have to move elsewhere on Mr. Hart's body." Her eyes watered. She stared at Sonny for a few moments, then leaned back.

"You don't understand," she said quietly, her eyes never leaving Hart.

Sonny smiled. "Then perhaps you had better explain."

Castillo continued to look at Hart. His eyes fluttered then closed but his chest was rising up and down. He was either unconscious or just resting in an attempt to ease the pain.

"It doesn't work," she said flatly.

Sonny cocked his head and leaned in toward her. "What doesn't work?"

"ArmourNet. It's only good until it hits the high-voltage power lines. Messages are safe from the source to the transmission lines, then onward to the substation, but as soon as it hits the high-voltage wires for long distance, it slowly disintegrates. The heat intensity is too strong."

"That is what your ArmourNet is for, is it not?" Sonny said.

"Yes, it is. But it can't keep the heat out for more than a few miles of high voltage line. Eventually, the armor code breaks down under the heat."

"And the message is lost?" Sonny asked, his eyes narrowing.

"Sometimes it goes a few miles, other times, less than a mile. But sooner or later, the armor data breaks down under the intensity and it all burns up."

Sonny jumped up. "Then how were you going to launch today? Losano said it was ready."

At the mention of Jay's name, Lena's expression hardened. "What has Jay got to do with this?"

Sonny ignored her and began pacing. "How were you going to achieve that?" he said, not looking at Castillo, talking to himself. "With all the media, the military, the Senator's people… how were you going to sell them on a product if it didn't work?"

Lena pushed her chair back away from the desk until it hit something hard on the floor. She was trying to get farther away from the pacing Asian.

"The electronic billboard was the key," she said. "It was Frank Daro's idea."

Sonny stopped pacing, standing right behind Hart, staring at Lena. He said nothing so she continued. "Smoke and mirrors, he told me; what the CIA does best. When the President typed in a message on the laptop at the podium, it was hooked up to a large television beside him so everyone could see what he typed. They never told me what the message would be; it was a big secret only he knew so no one could claim it wasn't happening live."

Sonny put his hands-on Hart's shoulders and squeezed. Hart tried to shrug him off but Sonny's thoughts were elsewhere.

Watching Sonny closely, Lena quickly continued. "Over at the plant, they'd erected a huge electronic billboard that was connected to the transmission lines. The message was going to be displayed on the billboard as soon as the President pressed the *send* button. Media had been invited to station cameras at the plant, focused on the billboard, all the substation wiring and high-voltage connections in the background. It was to create the illusion that the message had gone over the lines and was ready to go further into the grid."

"But there were no high voltage lines between your lab and the nuclear plant," Sonny deadpanned, trying to understand what this all meant.

Lena nodded. Hart stirred slightly, his legs shaking. Sonny dropped his hands, slowly walking back to the table where Lena sat.

"The message would go over the transmission lines, but it would stop at the billboard," she said.

"A media stunt," Sonny said, dropping into his chair.

"We are close," Lena implored. She glanced at the monitor she had been working on, then down at the floor to see what had impeded her chair from moving back further. She looked back up at Sonny. "And I think I have a solution. But I haven't tested it and I don't know if it will work."

"You failed and President Emerson was going to cover it up until you succeeded?" Sonny asked.

"I didn't fail!" Lena stood quickly, hands on her hips. "ArmourNet can transmit data regionally for miles. We eliminated the interference problem, we configured the code so it would embrace large, terabyte sized files, and all at no additional cost to the end user."

"But it wouldn't be a national transmission," he said.

Lena shook her head vigorously.

Sonny came around beside Hart, lifted up another finger and stared at Castillo. "Then you have about nine hours to perfect it Ms. Castillo… or our friend Hart here may never be able to cook a delicious meal ever again."

Castillo stepped closer. "I can't do it that fast, just because you say so!"

Sonny dropped Hart's finger, and quickly stepped to within a few inches of her face, his eyes boring into hers. "You can and you will. Because if you don't you'll be coming with me to a place you will not like; a place you will never leave." Sonny knew that if he went home without a successful version of ArmourNet, he was as good as dead. If he had to, he would take the girl with him and she could work from one of the camps. If he was able to convince General Hwang that she would eventually perfect it, then the abduction would be worth any international outrage. They would know she was in North Korea but they wouldn't know where and short of an unprecedented CIA extraction, they wouldn't be able to do much about it. And, of course, General Hwang would be salivating over such a young, fresh, American plaything.

He turned with the intent to take one of Hart's fingers again, just to emphasize the importance of the moment to the girl… but out of the corner of his eye he noticed a blur coming at him, aimed at his midsection. He lifted his hands to block but it was too late.

Hart's body felt like a brick wall as it connected with his stomach and he felt himself losing balance and falling backwards.

Robert J. Morrow

Chapter Seventy-Six

JP sat in what was essentially a tricked out panel van, complete with surveillance equipment, communications set-ups, and a round table near the rear; a command post unlike anything she'd seen in the States.

"So why are you here?" she asked the man seated across from her, the American Military Intelligence officer who had accosted her by the car. The same man who had rescued her from the suburbs near Oswego.

Bullard grinned. "Ms. Castillo is a valuable asset to our country," he said, his voice low and the words strung out slowly.

"I'm aware of that," she said. "Which is why Hart and I chased Sonny Kim up here. We're trying to get her back."

"Your efforts are commendable Agent Pierce," Bullard said, still grinning. He seemed to be enjoying himself. "Without you, we wouldn't have known where to come. But now we do, and the good Captain there--"he nodded toward a tall, thin haired man decked out in SWAT-like gear "--has been kind enough to arrange this task force so we can go in and get her out safely."

JP looked around. The van resembled ones she had seen and used herself during surveillance assignments during her training. There were minor differences which she chalked up to the difference between Canadian and American manufacturers, but for the most part it was a well-equipped mobile command station, complete with computers, video monitors, recording equipment, and various other pieces of mechanical and electric equipment that JP had no idea of their use.

"Where is Hart now?" Bullard asked.

She pointed out the side of the van toward the forest and the farmhouse beyond. "We saw no signs of Sonny, so he went in to try and get the girl. Sonny is back now and I was about to go and help Hart when you showed up." She scowled at him. "Now they're both in there with him and I have no idea what's going on."

"All the more reason for the task force to establish--"

"We have contact sir." The operator at the console interrupted. They both turned to look at him. "Sort of," he added.

They leaned down to see the monitor he was pointing to.

"It was put out on the internet about twenty minutes ago, Sir," the operator continued. "NSA picked up the tag words *Castillo*, *Hart*, and *ArmourNet* which were attached to the picture on a known Facebook page sometimes used by North Korean hackers. US Military Intelligence just sent it to us."

"Who is that?" Bullard asked.

"The message with the picture states that it is Ms. Lena Castillo, Sir," the operator said, pointing to the paragraph below the picture. He read from the text: "*Ms. Castillo is in my custody and will be instantly and irrevocably damaged should any task force attempt to take the farmhouse.*"

"What the hell?" JP said.

The operator continued. "It's signed Sung-jin Kim," he said.

"What is that wire taped to her, ah...her thighs," JP asked.

The man looked at the American, then JP, and since no one seemed to be talking, he answered. "It appears to be an electrical charge ma'am," he said, pointing to the part of the screen showing the inside upper thighs of the women in the picture. "If she closes her thighs for any reason, the exposed wires will touch and, I assume, an electric charge will pass through the wire..."

"Doing what?" JP demanded

The man shifted in his seat and kept his eyes on the screen. "It would burn that part of her anatomy ma'am. Pretty badly, I would think."

"Jesus!" Bullard exclaimed, turning and stomping to the back of the van.

"He knows we're here," JP said, staring at the picture on the screen. She couldn't see Lena's expression as the picture showed only the naked genital area. She was sure the girl would be horror stricken.

"Ya think!" he said, jumping up and heading to the van's back door.

"But where's Hart?" she asked.

The American stopped. He came back and looked at the picture again. After a moment he said, "He doesn't know Hart's in there."

"Or he's already killed him and just didn't bother to mention it," JP said.

"He'd mention it," Bullard said.

JP looked at him quizzically. He seemed so sure of that. "Why?"

The man squinted and began pacing back and forth in the tiny space. "He just would have. They have a history. He'd want to brag, trust me."

"So you think Arthur is hidden in there somewhere and is just biding his time?" JP asked.

Bullard scratched his forehead. "I'd like to assume that until I have a reason not to."

JP sat on the stool behind the operator, looking at the picture again. Something wasn't adding up but she couldn't put her finger on it. She shook her head. It would come if she didn't ponder on it. She thought of Hart, what he might be planning. How could he possibly rescue the girl without setting off that horrific torture depicted in the text picture? Did he even know Castillo was trussed up like that? He wouldn't make a move until he knew he could get her out safely. Or would he? It wasn't like he was a trained government operative. A combat trainer, sure. But for God's sake, he had been a chef for the past decade.

"We have to figure out a way to get in there without Sonny knowing," she said.

"I'm open to any and all suggestions," Bullard replied.

She looked at him and sighed.

"We can't risk him harming her to the point where she can't

function," he said. "I think we should wait until we see or hear something from Hart. He's in there. Maybe he can do something that will change the odds enough that we can send in the task force and disable Kim before he can harm the girl."

"If I didn't know better, I'd think you actually cared what happens to *the girl*," she emphasized the last two words.

Bullard stared at her. "I do care," he said simply. No emotion, no additional supportive comments.

"You care because you need her to complete the launch," JP said.

"Yes," he said. "That and the President has taken a liking to her. Reminds him of what his little girl may grow up to be."

JP laughed. "You're a piece of work." She stood and stepped to within an inch of the other man's face. "You couldn't give a shit about the girl's well-being. You and Wade just need her to finish ArmourNet so the Army will have a new weapon against terrorism. But as sad as that makes you, it still means you'll help me keep her alive through this because you need her alive as much as I want her to be alive."

The American didn't shrink away. But he didn't say anything either. After a moment, JP stepped back and sat down again.

"What can Arthur possibly do?" she said, her voice low.

"He can disable Sonny Kim," he said. "Given the right circumstances."

JP cocked her head.

"Not going to get into it," he said quickly, shaking away her stare with his hand. "We just need to be ready to storm the place when we get a signal."

"What signal?"

"If I knew that I'd be a bit more confident than I am right now," he said. "I'm going out to brief the Captain, get his men ready. You watch the house. If anything changes, come get me immediately." He turned, opened the back door and stepped down into the dewy grass outside.

JP stared outside. She watched Bullard address the Task Force Captain, and using hand gestures, it was clear he was asking the man to get a team ready to rush the farmhouse at a moment's notice.

She stood, took one last look at the picture that was still on the monitor, scratched her head for a second, then turned and stepped out of the van and into the darkness. She'd hadn't asked if Bullard cared whether Hart survived or not. She thought she already knew the answer to that one.

Robert J. Morrow

Chapter Seventy-Seven

Hart knew he only had one shot at this. If he didn't take Sonny down with the initial attack, he wouldn't get a second chance. His forearms were still tied to the chair arms, his one broken finger aching and throbbing. But Sonny had tied his ankles to the chair legs quickly, using one piece of old extension cord. It's coating was plastic and by moving his feet around, Hart had managed to stretch the cord enough to loosen the knots enough that he knew one last push and they would drop away. By concentrating on this endeavor, he had been able to push the pain of a broken appendage away momentarily. Even now, with adrenaline pumping full bore, any pain he felt was secondary.

All he could think of was knocking Sonny over so he could get his foot across the other man's throat and press down on his Adam's apple.

Hart's shoulder plowed into Sonny's stomach, which was as he had anticipated, hard as concrete. But surprise and momentum gave him the upper hand momentarily.

Sonny lost his balance and fell across a small coffee table, shattering the glass centerpiece and banging his head against an old CPU lying on the floor. He was dazed but not out. Hart kept going, his momentum launching him into the wall, his shoulder taking the brunt of the impact. With no hands and the bulky chair hindering his posture, he was momentarily stuck trying to gain balance and turn toward his fallen foe.

Castillo lunged at Sonny, a stapler in her hand. She smacked the side of his head and was about to repeat the performance, probably several times, when Hart got her attention.

"The Kitchen!" he yelled. "A knife. Get a knife" He pointed his chin to his still bound forearms.

She jumped up, dropping the stapler, and ran to the kitchen, coming back a few seconds later with a Japanese chef's knife. Hart stood as straight as he could, which was still a bent over posture, the back of the chair preventing him from standing fully erect. He winced as she approached, the sharp end of the huge knife coming for his arm.

"Careful!" he exclaimed. She looked at him, her eyes wild, her hair completely disheveled. At least her hands weren't shaking. "Put the knife edge under the wire sideways, then slowly turn it upwards and then…" Hart watched as she followed his instructions. "Now quickly jerk the blade upward." As she did so, he pushed against the chair, the result being a clean cut through the wire and its plastic coating. Thank God the knife had been sharp, even after all this time.

Hart grabbed the knife from her hands and cut the wires on his other arm.

The chair dropped behind him and he stood upright, bending slightly backwards to get the blood back into his muscles.

They looked at each other, then down at Sonny. He wasn't unconscious and his head lolled from side to side. He wouldn't be out of commission for long.

Could Hart take him?

He wasn't sure. It was clear Sonny was a professional spy. He'd probably killed. At best, Hart was an instructor, never having proven any techniques in the field, just tournaments, and later at The Farm. He'd hadn't used his skills recently. In fact, except for a brief period of idiocy when he'd joined up with the bike gang he'd never been in a real fight. Hart didn't think that matched him well with someone who could very well be an international assassin.

But Hart couldn't risk Sonny taking Castillo.

"You have to escape," he said. "JP's out there somewhere in the bushes, probably with the RCMP by now. They won't storm the place till they know you're safe, so you need to go."

"What about you?"

Hart looked at Sonny. His eyes were open now, not quite focused, but coming around. The combination of hitting his head against the table and being at the receiving end of Lena's stapler attack had put him down for a few minutes but he had no delusions that it would last long.

"Go!" Hart implored, pointing to the kitchen door. Just run into the bushes and yell. JP will find you."

He turned to look for something heavy he could hit Sonny with again, maybe this time putting him out for a while longer, so he could tie him up, at least until JP and the Canadians could get here. He looked down at the knife in his hand, then at Sonny. No, he couldn't do it.

Just then the kitchen door slammed open and JP careened in, a gun in her hand sweeping the room and the hall as she advanced. She grabbed Castillo who stood dumbfounded watching her from the edge of the hall. She pushed her head down, forcing Castillo to crouch. Gun still in hand, JP hovered over her while her eyes darted around the inside of the kitchen and hall until they found Hart staring at her.

"You made it," Hart said

She cocked her head.

"Where'd you get the gun?" he asked.

She looked at Sonny, groggy but still prone on the floor. "There's a Canadian task force outside waiting to storm the place," she said. "But they couldn't risk getting Castillo injured or killed."

"It wasn't her in the picture," he said.

"I know. Whoever that woman is has skin too light to be a Latina," she said. "I couldn't figure out why Sonny would send a picture if it wasn't Lena but had to assume it was a stalling tactic. But I didn't want to waste time convincing Bullard so I decided to come and get you myself."

"Bullard? What's he doing here?" Hart asked.

"He just showed up. Frank was using Wade's drone so it's not too much of a stretch to figure Bullard knew where we were too. The guy has a habit of showing up everywhere," she said.

"We can't let him take Lena," Hart said. If Wade gets hold of her, she'll disappear into a bureaucratic wormhole where even Frank can't find her."

"But if I take her out there, Bullard has likely convinced the Canadians he can take over custody," JP said. "Military Intelligence trumps Secret Service, assuming the Canadians know the difference."

"Then we have to get Lena out of here ourselves," Hart said, looking out the window to the bushes beyond the rear yard. There was no movement, no sign of anything behind the wall of green.

"But we need to know what this is all about," JP said. "Maybe Bullard isn't here for Lena, maybe he's here for Sonny."

"Possibly," Hart said.

"And if he gets him, they'll whisk him away to some European interrogation site and we'll never know why he kidnapped Lena," she said.

"I know why Sonny kidnapped her," Hart said. "Well, sort of. He looked at Lena. She nodded and looked up at JP

"He wanted me to give him the code for ArmourNet," she said quietly. "I think he had a military use for it. He's North Korean you know."

Hart looked at her incredulously. "How did you know?"

"Many of my friends in University were Korean but their language was different. Sonny uses old terminology, old slang. He was obviously educated in the South but more recently, he has been in the North and picked up the nuances."

Hart grinned.

"How long have you known this?" JP asked her.

Lena shrugged. "Since he arrived in Oswego," she said. "I figured he was just part of a united Korean organization that was going to manufacture the hardware for BPL in America."

Hart looked at JP and rolled his eyes. She grinned.

"You have to stay close to him," JP said, pointing her gun at Sonny who was still prone but letting out low moans now. "You have to make sure Bullard doesn't get him away from the Canadians. Call Frank. Tell him what's going on. He may have to let the RCMP have a shot at him first but eventually we'll get him to a safe house someplace and figure this all out."

Hart nodded. "But how are you going to get her out of here without anyone noticing? The car's back there." He pointed to where the task force was supposed to be gathered beyond the bushes.

"I know a way out," Lena said, her eyes large and animated. "I found it when Sonny locked me up. There's a big door behind the wine racks in the cellar. It opens up to a tunnel. I don't know where it goes and I couldn't see the end. Maybe it goes out into the forest."

JP smiled and pushed Lena toward the basement staircase. "Wherever it comes out, we can double back behind them and get the car. The majority of the task force will be creeping up here. There will only be monitoring technicians at the trucks."

Hart nodded. It was possible. He needed to stick close to Sonny when the task force arrived.

"I'll drive a couple of hundred miles east, find a hotel and call Frank for an extraction," she said. "We'll be back in Langley by tomorrow morning."

Just then, Sonny's moaning grew louder and Hart turned to see him trying to get up. He had one arm on the half-broken table, the other steadying himself against the wall.

"Go!" he urged and pushed the women down the stairs. "And shut the damn door behind you so the task force don't find it too quickly and come after you."

Hart then turned to face his nemesis. As he watched Sonny slowly rise it dawned on him that maybe he should have asked JP for the gun.

Robert J. Morrow

Chapter Seventy-Eight

As Hart watched Sonny slowly shake off his drowsiness, it dawned on him why Frank had felt he was the ideal person for this job. Frank may have known about Sonny's involvement from the beginning, or at least before Hart had. And even though he wouldn't have known the level of involvement, he did feel that, short of a bullet, Hart was the only person who could stand up to him one-on-one if it became necessary. Hart knelt down and without taking his eyes off Sonny picked up the stapler Lena had dropped.

He knew he had to do something to spark the attention of the task force. For whatever reason, something or someone had kept them from simply attacking in force, probably the graphic picture of the trussed-up woman they thought was Lena. But if they saw or heard conflict, they would assume a change of control was taking place and-hopefully race to assist. JP had said they didn't know she'd come to the farmhouse alone. That meant they would need some persuasion to feel confident they weren't putting Lena, or himself in harm's way.

If they even know I'm here.

Damn! he'd never asked JP that. This spy stuff definitely didn't come naturally.

Sonny stood up fully and turned. His eyes were still a bit misty but Hart could see he'd be fine in a moment or two. There was no sign of the task force. And, of course, Hart realized they wouldn't be coming anytime soon since JP had gone with Lena into the basement. No one was telling them to come in and help him out.

Hart felt a lump in his throat as he became aware that the one-on-one thing had just become necessary.

"We're done Sonny. It ends now," Hart said and stepped close to Sonny's left side. The Asian's eyes focused suddenly and in an instant he swung his left arm around for a back-fist strike. Hart's eye caught some color and he realized Sonny was holding something. Somewhere in his head, he was amazed that their minds had thought alike at this moment. Hart aimed the stapler at the upcoming wrist and using it to block Sonny's back fist, depressed the lever when it struck the base of the other man's hand, sending a tiny staple into the flesh.

It was by no means a serious strike, nor one that would hurt much. But it did surprise Sonny, long enough for Hart to twist inward, lift his elbow and slam it down into the side of Sonny's neck. The Asian staggered back but lashed out with his foot, the tip of his shoe connecting with Hart's broken finger. Pain shot up his arm as if he'd been electrocuted.

Though pushed off balance, Sonny quickly regained his footing and stood in a fighter's crouch, staring at Hart. Then he grinned.

"Where's the girl?" he asked.

"Gone."

He grimaced. "That's unfortunate. However, she likely hasn't gone too far, and I have to assume that since we are not under attack, you have asked her to escape on her own, leaving the only obstacle between me getting her back to be... you."

Hart shrugged.

"We don't have to do this Arthur," he said, stretching his fingers and twisting his wrist around to loosen the joints. "You see, regardless of whether I find the girl or not, there is enough data here--"a grand sweep of his arm took in all the equipment on the table--"for me to reasonably accomplish my initial goal."

"Which is?"

He smiled, though his eyes weren't in on it. "Let's just say it's time for change in this country. Actually, I meant the United States but this country will be affected also, no doubt."

"You wanted Lena to send a message out using her armor code, right?" Hart asked. "Something that would disable communications, perhaps put a virus into the power grid that would wreak some kind of havoc on the eastern seaboard?"

Sonny laughed. "Admirable goals, indeed. But sadly, lacking in vision." He moved sideways, still maintaining a classic loose fighter's stance common amongst martial artists. "What I am doing is setting the stage for worldwide change. It begins with disabling communication; on that score you are correct. But it goes much deeper my friend. Within hours of sending my signal, the United States would no longer hold the monopoly on superpower status. It would be at war, a war it could not win because of its inability to not only communicate, but even activate much of its defense technology. My signal would render your weapons systems themselves inoperable. America would be completely open to conventional attack... and she wouldn't see it coming."

Hart heard what he said and didn't doubt for a second that some of it was probably based on possibilities. But still, the man sounded a little crazy.

"But you still need the girl, don't you?" Hart asked.

The edge of his mouth curled up and his eyes glittered momentarily.

"It would make the process considerably simpler, I admit." Sonny said. He stepped closer, his legs pushing away a chair and some loose debris on the floor. He was clearing the ring. "So we should get this over with, as unfortunate a situation as this may be. And one to which I would rather not pursue."

Hart moved a little to his right ensuring Sonny's front leg was always facing him directly.

"There would be a place for you in the new regime you know," Sonny said, his fingers no longer flexing but forming tight fists. "A man of your skill, your knowledge. My superiors would listen to me if I told them you had, ah... stepped down from being an adversary and assisted in my mission. All you have to do is call the girl and ask her to come back."

"Sorry, I don't have a phone."

Sonny smiled. "You can use mine."

Hart shook his head and felt his smile, however fake, disappear.

"Then I can't let her get much farther," Sonny said. "Because I really don't want to finish my mission without her input."

Even though Hart saw Sonny's shoulder shift slightly, he was still faster than he anticipated and the Asian's spinning hook kick caught Hart's blocking arm and slammed it against his own shoulder even as he attempted to duck out of the way. Sonny had been aiming for Hart's head and Hart's slow reaction had only saved him for a few seconds. A second kick from Sonny's other leg shot out, a crescent kick aimed once again for the side of Hart's head, but this time coming from the other direction.

Hart countered with a spin side kick of his own but rather than making contact with Sonny's midsection, it swished through mid-air, its momentum sending the rest of his body along with it.

This was a good thing as Sonny executed a series of hand blows to the space Hart had just been occupying. When Hart's forward motion decreased, he used what was left of his momentum to twist back in the direction he had just come and threw out his leg in a reverse crescent to the general direction of Sonny's torso.

It connected with Sonny's kidney and the force of the kick sent him sideways, into the table. Monitors and CPUs slid across the surface and over the edge, crashing onto the floor.

Sonny was crouched over the table and he turned his head to look at Hart. His eyes were dark and glazed, a tint of red at the edges.

"Enough," he growled. "She is getting away." He stood, flexed the muscles in his arms, clenched his fists, and strode quickly and confidently toward Hart.

Hart stood his ground, waiting for the tell. Whatever attack he had in mind, it would show in his eyes first. He was angry which was a good thing because the tell would be clearer. Whether he was an assassin or not, his training was primarily taekwondo initially and all those years of training wouldn't be disregarded, despite what he may have learned since. Martial Arts was the basis for many a professional hit man, as Hart well knew from discussions with Frank. Killers could learn other combat skills, including weapons, but the basic actions ingrained into every man who was raised in the martial arts--that automatic reaction borne from repetition--would always be present. For those trained in the arts, it was survival; reacting without thinking. But if your opponent was a martial artist also, there was always the risk that he or she would also know what your reaction would be, and anticipate it.

These thoughts raced through Hart's mind in milliseconds, the realization of which caused him to lose focus on adequate responses to Sonny's offensive moves.

For the first minute or so, he concentrated on, well, not concentrated, rather thoughtlessly reacted to--whatever attack came his way. When Sonny came from one side of his body--a hand thrust or elbow strike-- Hart would instantly retaliate with an appropriate counter from the opposing side of his body.

To a spectator, it would no doubt have been dazzling. But to the two adversaries, it was a warm up. One of them would occasionally break the pattern and a strike would connect. Then they would begin the process again, the only hope being that the successful strike wasn't powerful enough to inhibit continued combat.

In the back of Hart's mind he recognized that he should be doing something to alert the task force just outside. If he could make noise, or otherwise create a disturbance, those watching would realize things were in flux and they would hopefully come running. Part of him knew it would be the right thing to do. But the other part was morbidly enjoying the engagement.

As one of Sonny's swinging legs connected with the side of Hart's ribs, he realized his focus needed to be on the task at hand. Whether he was a match for Sonny or not was irrelevant at this point. This wasn't some kind of Van Damme movie; it didn't matter if the good guy won the fight. It mattered that the bad guy couldn't go after the girl until she was far enough away not to be found. Hart wasn't sure he could prevent that alone, so assistance from the outside seemed imperative. Sonny was going to tire of the back and forth soon and would escalate the fight to its closure, one way or the other.

Hart stepped to the desk and picked up a monitor, raising it above his head. Sonny watched and he took a step backward anticipating a throw. Instead, Hart threw the screen through the front window, the shattering glass adding a new element to the relative silence of the encounter thus far.

Sonny lunged and Hart dropped to the ground in a crouch as the Asian's leg sailed above his head. Hart thrust out with an arch hand strike to Sonny's groin but he twisted away and Hart hit the side of Sonny's thigh instead.

A bright light suddenly burst through the window and a series of loud voices were heard from the general area of the forest.

Sonny's attention was diverted for a second and Hart jumped at him with a travelling front snap kick which connected just under his sternum, propelling him back into the wall behind him.

Just then Hart heard a scream--a female scream. It came from the front of the house, near the van. Hart ran to the front window and looked out to see JP and Lena racing across the gravel parking area from the barn toward the driveway. He could see them clearly because they were brightly lit from a harsh light coming from the sky. The noise from the task force racing across the lawn and breaking down the kitchen door had hindered his hearing the chopper until it lowered into his view.

As he watched, four men dropped from grappling lines on either side of the helicopter, unhooked, and chased after the two women who were only a few yards away. One of them must have yelled because JP stopped and turned, her arm holding Lena's and forcing her to stop running also.

The soldier motioned with his arm to the chopper and Hart saw JP shake her head. The soldier's rifle rose slightly, not really aimed at JP but the intention was clear. Hart thought he saw her glimpse his way but he couldn't be sure. She nodded and pulled Lena toward the chopper that had now landed on the front lawn. The two women followed the soldier and his comrades back to its open door. Hart saw another man inside reach for the women but he was obscured by the soldiers jumping in. Without hesitation, the chopper blades accelerated again, and with a loud whine, the machine left the ground, its side door still open.

"No!"

Hart turned to see Sonny yelling while leaping onto the table and then jumping out of the semi-broken front window. He landed and rolled on the grass, came up from a crouch and raced toward the chopper.

"Freeze! RCMP" came a gruff yell from behind Hart. He turned to see several black-clad soldiers filter into the living room, dispersing into a single line, all guns up and aimed at him.

"On your knees, hands behind your head," the leader growled.

"My name is Hart, Arthur Hart, I'm..."

"Right now Sir, I don't give a shit who you are," the man said. "Just get on your knees and we'll sort it out in shortly."

"But Sonny is--" Hart had turned toward the window to point out where Sonny was, the guy they really should be going after, but one of the men grabbed his arm from behind and gruffly forced him to the ground. He deftly pulled Hart's arms behind him and clasped a nylon tie around his wrists, pulling it tight. Hart's finger was already steadily throbbing and he let out a short yelp as his hands bounced together.

"Guys!" he yelled in exasperation. "The Asian out there, running. That's the guy you want. Please don't lose him," he urged. The leader followed Hart's gaze, caught sight of Sonny racing hopelessly toward the helicopter, and barked orders to his men to take chase. Two of them jumped on the table as Sonny had and after executing a similar jump and roll. They were quickly racing across the lawn, rifles drawn.

Robert J. Morrow

Chapter Seventy-Nine

JP had heard the grunts of the two men engaging upstairs, and the occasional thump as one of them hit a wall. She drew her attention back to Lena who was inside the wine cellar--her former prison cell--and was pulling aside a large wine shelf, exposing an old barnboard door. JP took one last look behind her, hoping Hart wouldn't get caught in any sort of crossfire when the task force rushed in, then followed Lena into the darkness of the tunnel beyond the door.

Just as JP was about to turn the flashlight app on her phone on, a light suddenly appeared in the distance. Lena was at another door, this one flat against the ceiling. JP worked her way underneath beside Lena and they pushed together until the door opened into an enclosed space with the distinct odor of freshly-mown grass. JP figured it was the barn behind the house.

They climbed out and looked around to see bales of dried hay, an old green tractor, and wires. Everywhere there were wires. Some led to the roof and out through a large hole, others snaked along the dusty floor and out a similar hole on the side of the barn facing the house.

The interior was lit completely with an almost fluorescent glow and a thumping noise initially had JP thinking there was a huge generator somewhere illuminating the building.

She followed Lena to one of the huge barn doors and pushed. The door creaked but didn't budge. They both put their shoulders to it and with a loud crack, it opened a foot or so.

The mystery of the bright light and thumping noise was cleared up when they both watched as a dark-colored helicopter hovered over the front lawn on the other side of the house. A high-intensity light on the nose of the chopper highlighted large portions of the ground as the pilot slowly swung the machine around in a tight circle.

"Let's go," JP urged, grabbing Lena's arm and propelling her out from the barn and in the general direction of the driveway.

"Isn't that the police or something?" Lena asked, resisting JP's pull away from the chopper. "They've come to rescue us."

"I don't know," JP said. "And until I'm sure, we need to make our own plans of escape. If we get into the forest, we can double back around the other side of the house where we parked the car."

Lena looked at JP. "But Arthur, What about Arthur?"

JP frowned. "He's a big boy, he can take care of himself. The important thing is to get you out of here safely and back to the US where Sonny and his cohorts can't find you."

Lena looked into JPs eyes. JP became uncomfortable with the stare and she pushed Lena's back, aiming for the forest. The chopper light was swinging around to their direction. If they didn't go soon, they'd be spotted. Lena relented, thankfully, seeming to trust JP at least for the moment.

The women were twenty feet from the safety of the trees when the light caught them, passing over at first, then quickly coming back as the pilot reversed his circle, pinpointing them in bright array. Lena looked up, a deer in headlights, but JP kept her head down, grabbed Lena's arm and pushed her toward the safety of the trees.

The helicopter accelerated toward them and JP couldn't hear anything as the chopper blades hammered the air, causing waves of grass to undulate. Lena stumbled, her hair whipping around her face blinding her. JP fell to her knees beside her and looked up to the light, trying to see past it into the fuselage. Four shapes emerged from both sides of the chopper, and quickly dropped to the ground. They dispersed and circled the women. JP threw her gun in front of her so they could see it, then raised her hands in the air. Lena's head was bowed and she was trying to pull back her hair so she could see.

"No need for that ma'am," a low voice said loudly. He was obviously used to speaking over the noise of the rotor blades. "Sergeant Blake, 914th Airlift Wing, Niagara Falls. We're here for Ms. Castillo. Which one of you would that be?"

JP put down her arms and stood, pulling Lena to her feet with her. "It doesn't matter Sergeant. We're both coming with you." She walked toward the four men. "How the hell did you get here so quickly?"

The Sergeant cocked his head. "We were dispatched here an hour ago Ma'am, and were ordered to follow Captain Bullard's instructions." He pointed to the chopper which was now just landing about twenty feet away, on the back lawn. The rotors slowed slightly and the Sergeant motioned for them to head toward it.

"I'm afraid we won't be going with you Sergeant," JP said, stepping back to pick up her Glock.

"Don't do it Agent Pierce," came a voice from the direction of the helicopter. It was loud and gruff, and recognizable. Bullard. "I don't want to have you arrested but I will if you don't bring the girl and come along with us in an agreeable manner."

"Agreeable?" JP snarled. "You're kidnapping us." She noticed out of the corner of her eye that the Sergeant was grinning at that. Two of the men had taken each of Lena's arms and were escorting her to the chopper. She wasn't resisting, and following the lead of the soldiers, bent slightly at the waist as they neared the open fuselage door.

"Actually, it's an extraction JP," Bullard said, standing by the door and gesturing her over. "Ordered by General Wade. Are you coming?"

JP swore under her breath but strode over to the helicopter, stubbornly refusing to bend over for the rotating blade wash. She allowed one of the soldiers inside to grasp her arm and pull her up. No sooner had Bullard, the Sergeant, and the other soldiers jumped in that the rotors revved up again and the chopper alighted.

JPs stomach clenched as the chopper ascended and angled sideways toward the front lawn. From fifty feet up, she could see a man racing toward them, fully lit by the chopper light. She squinted and recognized Sonny. Behind him, like ants, several of the task force members seethed through the front window. They were chasing after Sonny, widening their line of attack as they ran outward into the lawn. The chopper turned sideways again so that they could all see the scene through the open side door. Another man jumped through the window, following the task force but he was dressed differently.

"You plan on leaving Hart here?" JP said, her voice straining to be heard over the noise of the wind and the motor.

"He's not a member of any government agency," Bullard said. "I have orders to extract US service personnel only. I have no jurisdiction to take civilians on foreign soil."

"Asshole!" she muttered. He didn't hear what she said but got the gist of it from the formation of her lips. He smiled.

"He'll be fine," he said. "Someone has to explain this to the Canadians."

JP stared at him, then turned to the scene below. Lena was watching too.

"They'll look after him, won't they?" she said to JP.

JP stared as the task force men surrounded Sonny and closed in. He seemed oblivious, just staring up toward them, hands on his hips. The last thing she saw before the chopper turned away was Hart casually walking toward the group, his eyes also fixed on the chopper.

Chapter Eighty

Was Castillo safe? Hart wasn't sure. She was with JP which was a plus. But she was also with macho army man Bullard which was a minus. God knows where he was taking them.

As long as JP was with her, Lena couldn't simply disappear into Army bureaucracy, right?

He stopped watching the chopper once it's lights became a tiny speck on the horizon and turned his attention to the excitement on the front lawn.

"I have diplomatic status from the country of South Korea," Sonny was telling the leader of the group, who was clearly a Captain because of the bars on his shoulders.

The Captain nodded as Hart approached. Six other task force team members had formed a circle around Sonny and the Captain, guns loosely aimed at Sonny's torso.

"Captain Bullard informed us of your identity Mr. Hart," he said, nodding to one of his men in the circle. "However, until we can verify what's going on around here, you'll have to come with us too, Sir."

"And exactly where might you be taking us?" Hart asked watching as the man the Captain had nodded to approached him with plastic cuffs in his hand.

"For now, the local RCMP station in Hamilton, Sir," he said, not looking at Hart but concentrating on putting cuffs on Sonny.

"I told you I had diplomatic immunity," Sonny said drily.

"You have been unable to identify yourself Sir," the Captain informed him. "You have no ID on you depicting any status of any kind, other than an international driver's license.

"He'll tell you," Sonny said, nodding to Hart.

Hart shrugged. "If they're holding me for questioning, you're coming too," he said.

"It's not jail gentlemen," the Captain said. "Simply a holding cell until we can sort this all out. Shots have been fired, we have been informed that a kidnapping took place, and quite frankly, if you guys are foreign agents of some kind, neither of you can prove it to my satisfaction at this point, so as far as I am concerned you are involved in criminal activity in our country. And I will detain you until I am satisfied otherwise. Is that understood?"

Sonny sighed.

Hart shrugged again. He didn't have a phone and Frank, of course, hadn't thought to call ahead to tell the Mounties that he was a good guy. All in a day's work for the CIA, even though Hart couldn't prove he was with the CIA... because he wasn't.

Of more interest though was whether Sonny could prove diplomatic immunity, especially since they all knew he was actually North Korean, posing as a South Korean diplomat; they being JP, Lena, Frank, Hart, and Hart assumed, General Wade, all four of whom were not here to vouch for him. Hart was beginning to understand the CIA mantra that when performing clandestine activities in a foreign country... you're on your own if you're caught.

Sonny's disposition had mellowed since he'd watched Lena being whisked away with Bullard, JP and the Army extraction squad. He didn't quite bow his head but his body showed no other outward signs of resistance. He allowed the Captain to lock the plastic wrist band around his hands. Hart noticed his hands were outstretched when the Captain tightened the clasp; an old but useful trick he remembered from their younger days, but otherwise he showed no resistance.

Inwardly, Hart thanked Sonny for reminding him of the technique and did the same as the soldier clasped his hands behind his back and applied the plastic cuff.

"This really isn't necessary," Hart said, knowing it was a waste of time. "You said Captain Bullard vouched for me."

"I didn't say he vouched for you," the Captain said. "I merely asked him who you were and he told me."

"An agent of the US government?" Hart said, widening his eyes and applying his biggest grin.

"He said you were a Chef," the Captain deadpanned. "And a personal friend of President Emerson."

This time Hart sighed.

"If I were you," the Captain added, his mouth turning up at the edges; the first sign of any sense of humor I'd seen. "I'd make my free phone call to the Whitehouse. Might get you home sooner." He laughed heartily as soon as he said it.

As dumb as he obviously thought that was, Hart considered it wasn't such a bad idea; President Emerson seemed a more reliable friend than Frank at this point.

The task force hustled them to the parking area where several vehicles, all with flashing lights, though with different paint schemes, had assembled. Some were blue and white with the words *Brantford Police* on the doors. The one Sonny and Hart were led to, however, was traditional black and white with the letters O.P.P. emblazoned on the doors. Sonny was lead to one side, Hart the other. They both ended up in the back seat, arms clasped behind them--a very uncomfortable way to sit--while two officers jumped into the front. One wore a black uniform, the other a dark blue one. Canada was definitely a strange place. Hart thought this was an RCMP operation. But there were no horses in sight. And they wanted to figure out who we were?

Robert J. Morrow

Chapter Eighty-One

Hart thought it odd that the squad car he and Sonny had been placed in left the farmhouse on its own; no escort, no backup.

The Captain had rounded up his men near a black utility van and was talking to them as we left. Two of the other patrol cars, the blue and white ones, had followed them down the laneway but had turned in the opposite direction when hitting the main road.

The other uniformed officers had been heading toward their black and whites as they left but didn't seem to be in too much of a hurry to follow.

So, after three or four minutes, when they were racing down the highway, lights flashing, horn blaring occasionally to get vehicles out of the way, Hart began to feel concerned about his safety. It was late though and traffic was minimal, even on the main artery.

It would take very little for Sonny to break out of his cuffs, the flexing of his fingers and palm at the time when the officer had been applying the band creating the illusion of being a tight clasp when in fact, once Sonny relaxed his hands, there would be ample room to slip at least one hand out of its confinement.

Of course, Hart had done the same thing, and would be equally able to release his hands when and if necessary. But at the moment, they were in the back of a squad car complete with no door handles or locks and metal caging between them and the officers up front. If Sonny was going to try something before they got to the station house, Hart would be his target.

He began twisting his wrists behind his back, loosening the plastic cuffs. He needed to be prepared.

When Sonny did make his move, however, it wasn't what Hart had expected.

As the patrol car slowed to enter onto a ramp entrance leading to what the signs said was Highway 403, Sonny lurched his body forward so his rear end was on the edge of the seat. He then lifted his legs up and placed his feet against the cage behind the officers and then pushed his back into the seat. He was bracing himself for some sort of impact.

Hart turned to see what he was up to and saw him playing with his mouth, as if trying to work a piece of meat that had gotten caught between his molars. Hart cocked his head and stared but Sonny didn't acknowledge him. He saw the driver look through the rear mirror and raise his eyebrows but Hart was sure he had seen a lot of weird things in the backseat of his cruiser and didn't seem too concerned yet.

Sonny played around with his mouth some more. Hart could see his tongue working something free, pushing against his cheek occasionally. After a minute or so, he must have found what he was looking for because Hart could see he'd moved whatever debris he'd located toward his lips, looking like he was ready to spit.

Hart manipulated his own hands to the point where he was pretty sure one quick pull and he'd have one hand out of the cuff. He didn't want to release himself completely in case whatever Sonny was up to didn't work and he would need to show his compliance for a while longer.

As the cruiser began to speed up and the driver was looking into the mirror to see that he could merge into traffic safely, Sonny spit out what looked like one of his teeth. The white projectile hit the metal caging and exploded. Dark, heavy smoke suddenly appeared everywhere, soaring into the front cab and filling the rear area where Sonny and Hart sat. Within seconds, the entire cabin was filled with a dense fog that smelled a little like lavender.

The driver braked hard and Hart's body flew forward. He turned his torso quickly just in time to allow his shoulder to take the impact against the back of the front seat and the metal caging. He turned toward Sonny but could only make out the outline of his shape in the same braced position.

The car swerved left and then right as it's speed decreased and with a small jolt, left the pavement and came to a quick stop on the gravel shoulder.

Both front doors flew open and the air cleared a little in the front. Both back doors opened and arms reached in for both Sonny and Hart from opposite sides. Sonny's form suddenly exploded into movement and as the smoke cleared out through his door, Hart watched him launch himself at his captor.

With no other choice, Hart ripped his own hands free and rolled out of his doorway, shoving the driver's arm out of the way. Hart rolled into his legs, knocking the officer backwards and down into the culvert beside the ramp way. In his peripheral vision, he saw the man roll clumsily down the ten-foot man-made hill into the darkness. But Hart continued out of his roll into a crouch and watched as Sonny--his hands now free also--dispatch the other officer quickly with one chop to the back of his neck.

Without looking back, he headed down the ramp a few yards then darted sideways down the culvert and into the heavy bush that bordered the highway on both sides.

Hart could, of course, go and help the officer who had rolled to the bottom of the culvert, or the one lying beside the cruiser.

Or he could go after Sonny.

It took about five seconds for him to decide that if he stayed to help the officers, the odds were they would just take him back into custody and call for backup to go after Sonny.

Hart took one last look to make sure the officers were moving about. Then he took off down the low rise after Sonny.

Robert J. Morrow

Chapter Eighty-Two

At first Hart didn't know which direction Sonny had gone. He had no idea where they were and assumed Sonny didn't either. After a moment of reflection, he realized that probably wasn't true either since he'd obviously known all about the farmhouse. Was there a subdivision on the other side of the forest? A road? There was a three-quarter moon shining through the trees and Hart could just make out footprints in the soft ground cover.

A flash of movement caught his eye about a hundred yards ahead and to the left. Looking down he saw that the ground was soft and muddy, even mushy in places. Footprints headed in the direction of the movement he'd seen. Ducking to miss low hanging branches and vines, and swishing other saplings out of the way, Hart followed the tracks, his eyes darting between the loose ground cover and the spot he had last seen movement.

Hart figured that once the officers got back to the cruiser they would call for backup and, if possible, surround the forest. If Sonny had a plan of some kind, Hart had no idea what it was yet. The forest wasn't getting any lighter and the few feet he could see ahead was more of the same. Somewhere in the back of his mind he recalled geography lessons concerning Southern Ontario. Full grown forests half a mile wide often ran between densely populated areas; Canada's attempt to preserve as much natural wildlife as possible while it eagerly grew in population.

"Aargh!"

The exclamation had come from further in the forest. It had sounded like Sonny but Hart couldn't be sure. Had he tripped and injured himself? Or had he come across a stranger on a hike and harmed them? No, he had no reason to do that. In fact, he'd be better off just running past someone noiselessly. Did he know he was being pursued?

Hart slowed, trying to weaken the noise he was making when his feet hit slushy spots. Brushing aside shrubbery and long grass he edged forward. He saw something shift just ahead and then he heard heavy breathing. He moved forward and pushed aside a branch stepping into what appeared to be the edge of a small gully. At the bottom, illuminated in moonlight, Sonny sat awkwardly against a dead tree stump, his one leg straight out in front of him.

And he had a gun aimed at Hart's head.

Chapter Eighty-Three

The chopper landed less than an hour later in what JP assumed was an obscure reserve base somewhere near Niagara Falls. It was dark now but she had seen the lights of the illuminated, world-renowned waterfalls a few minutes before landing.

The Captain and his men left the chopper and escorted Castillo across the tarmac to what looked like a base command building.

JP started to follow but Bullard pulled her back.

"We'll take it from here," he said.

"I go where she goes."

"She's getting on an Air Force jet to Dulles and straight to see President Emerson. You're not invited."

"Like hell. How do I know that's what you're doing? You're not even on the books, I checked."

"You'll have to take that up with General Wade."

The pilot leaned back and interrupted. "Call for Agent Pierce, Sir. Please put on your headsets."

Bullard pulled two headsets from the mounts above their heads and handed one to JP while he donned one himself. He gave a thumbs up to the pilot.

"JP?"

It was Frank Daro.

"What the hell is going on Frank?" she asked, her eyes never leaving Bullard's who she assumed was listening also.

"Is Arthur with you?" Frank asked, his voice tinny in the headset.

She stared at Bullard. "The army whisked us away before Art could join us," she said, staring into Bullard's eyes.

"And Sonny?"

"The RCMP task force have him, I assume," she said. "I suggest you get in touch with someone there and get him extradited quickly."

"Hmmm"

"What does that mean?"

"I'm not sure we want Sonny to stand any kind of trial JP."

Bullard turned his head away as if trying to award JP a little privacy, which was stupid since he still had his headset on.

"National Security, involving the President of the United States," Frank said. "As a Secret Service agent, sworn to protect the Commander in Chief, I am informing you that you must go back there and ensure Sonny never leaves Canada."

JP tried to understand the undertone of Frank's canned speech. "The Canadians don't know what they have. They'll want to extradite him, you know that."

"Which is why you have to go back there, Agent Pierce," he said.

Bullard turned back. His eyes had suddenly turned grayer, any color that might have been there before, completely gone now.

It was JP's turn to cast her glance elsewhere. She lowered her voice. "You want me to eliminate a foreign agent Frank, is that what you're saying?"

"Ultimately, you don't work for me JP," Frank said, his voice low and cold. "But we all agree here that we don't want to deal with Sonny. Things have come to light that cause us to believe we cannot risk having him talk to the wrong people."

"The wrong people being Senator Blais and his cohorts?"

"Senator Blais is still in the hospital," Frank said. "But you're getting the right idea."

"And if I get caught solving your, ah, Sonny problem?"

There was momentary silence. JP turned and saw that Bullard was staring at her, his expressionless face relaying no emotion.

"You already know the answer to that Agent Pierce," he said. Then, after a moment he added, "Leave Hart. He's a liability at the moment. We'll get him out later."

"Arthur is alone up there Frank, you know that. You're supposed to be his best friend."

"He knew what he was getting into," he said, his tone a little lighter than before. "Trust me. Handle the Sonny situation, then get back here. Hart will be fine; he'll enjoy the vacation."

"Frank, I..."

There was a crackling noise in the headset, then a soft, low hissing sound. Bullard reached forward and slipped the headset off JPs head. He then took off his own, hooked them both back to their mounts and then turned to look at JP.

They stared at each other for a few seconds and just as JP was about to break the silence, Bullard reached into the cockpit, tapped the pilot on the shoulder, then quickly slipped out the side fuselage door.

As the chopper lifted, JP watched Bullard, his suit jacket flapping in the wind from the downstream, his tie whipping over his shoulder. He stood stock still amidst the swirling noise and wind, and saluted her.

JP rolled her eyes.

Robert J. Morrow

Chapter Eighty-Four

Hart knew Sonny was hurt but it didn't look that bad.

He was obviously in pain but it didn't look too debilitating; a twisted ankle maybe or a torn tendon? There was a twinkle in his eye as he kept the gun he had obviously taken from the officer aimed at Hart. He didn't seem annoyed with himself for letting Hart catch him. No, it was more like he'd been waiting.

"I tripped," he said calmly, pointing at a protruding tree route just to his right. "Can you believe it? After all this, I trip on a fucking root." He let out a snicker and shook his head in disgust. All that training, years of slogging through the Korean jungle with heavy weights on my back, and I get snagged by that."

"Just stay still," Hart said. "They'll have called for backup and someone will be here soon."

"Ah, but that's the thing Hart. I don't plan on waiting around for the authorities," he said. "I don't have time for all that interrogation nonsense. I have to get out of here and…well, regroup, so to speak."

He pointed the gun lower, to Hart's knee. It would be a tough shot from this distance but Hart wasn't planning to see if marksmanship was another of his skills.

"You're going to help me get out of here," he said.

Hart cocked his head. "And go where?" Hart had no idea where they were, how far civilization was, other than back to where the RCMP guys were, and he wasn't sure how Sonny was going to force him to help.

Sonny pointed behind him but didn't take his eyes, or the gun, off Hart. "There are houses about a hundred yards from here. We're going to go there and steal a car."

That's your plan?"

"The plan got derailed when your partner and that dull army guy took off with the girl. Time for a new plan."

Hard didn't move. Neither did Sonny's gun.

"I realize you think that if we stalemate here long enough, help will eventually arrive," Sonny said, shifting forward and dragging himself closer. "If the Canadians take me into custody though, your friend Frank Daro will not hear what I have to say for quite a while. My diplomatic status may even avoid that confrontation altogether and get me deported home. The Canadians are very fastidious about following protocol. At the very least, it will encumber the process for a long time. Meanwhile, those to whom I answer to in my country will simply send someone else to do what I was supposed to do."

"You need the girl," Hart said.

"Actually, she would have sped things up incredibly," Sonny said. "But we no longer need her to complete our ultimate task. We know enough."

"Enough to do what? Hart asked.

"And that is the million-dollar question isn't it Arthur?' he said, shuffling even closer. Hart stood his ground. The closer he came, the better the shot Sonny would have. But it would also give Hart a chance to jump him and take away the gun. Sonny was right on one count though. Hart needed to get him out of Canada so he could be interrogated by Frank's people. To do that, he needed Sonny out of this forest. Hart would figure out the rest as they went along.

"It's kind of a twist on the tortoise and the scorpion tale but I agree. We need to team up for the time being and get you out of here," Hart said, moving forward, ignoring the gun.

Sonny's eyes scrunched in confusion, then he shrugged and a grin stretched across his face and he lowered the gun to the ground and closed his eyes briefly in acknowledgement of the pain that had no doubt been building up.

A few moments later, they stood side-by-side, Hart's arm around Sonny's waist, his around Hart's neck and shoulder. The gun was in Sonny's other hand but that arm hung loosely as he struggled to shuffle across the uneven ground without sparking more pain in his ankle. Hart held his arm with his other hand and slowly lead the way through what looked like a small animal trail in the direction Sonny had pointed.

In less than a minute, Hart noticed a gradual easing of foliage and he was able to make out the shape of a large, brick house, and then another one partially hidden between the trees. The subdivision was nearing, lit by several lampposts. The houses had all been built on a small ravine and Hart saw no break in either direction. Sonny grunted and pushed on toward the upward slope.

Loping up the hill, one hand steadying himself on the ground, the other dragging Sonny behind him, Hart gradually got them both up the rise.

As they crested the ravine, a darkened house loomed above them, a three-storey modern family home, it's manicured back yard extending to the edge of the ravine where the owners had allowed nature to take over. Standing at the edge of the lawn, Hart peered down the driveway and saw movement on the road in front of the house.

Although completely out of place, what he saw in the middle of the well-lit cul-de-sac was a familiar sight. He looked to see if Sonny had noticed but his head was slumped downward, the gun loosely in his hand. Noticeably the trigger finger was still in place.

"Wait here, I'm going to see if there's a car in the driveway we can get into," Hart said, easing Sonny to the ground at the edge of the freshly cut lawn.

Sonny was visibly relieved but kept his eyes on Hart. "You do know how to hotwire a car, right?" he asked.

Hart smiled. He wasn't going to need that skill, no matter how ancient. But before they meandered out into the open, he had to be sure that what he was looking at was a friendly. Sonny hadn't seen it. And now that he was slouched on the grass in the dark, it was out of view. Hart turned back to the house.

The last time he'd seen one of these it had left him to fend for himself.

Sitting right in the middle of the cul-de-sac, it's bubble front barely in his line of sight between the houses, was the same chopper that had whisked JP and Lena away just an hour or so ago.

Chapter Eighty-Five

JP was walking toward one of the houses, her eyes darting around taking in everything: the serene, quiet setting, the birds tweeting in trees surrounding the high-end neighborhood, and… Hart. He was crouched low against the side of one of the houses, working his way down the driveway. He was looking at the helicopter which had landed in the centre of the circle of homes, it's rotors off, the pilot standing just to the opposite side having a smoke.

She motioned with her arms and began walking toward him. The RCMP Captain and his men wouldn't be far behind her. She needed to get this done quickly and get out of this country intact and reasonably undetected.

"How the hell did you know to come straight here?" Hart asked.

JP put her hand on her hip, her other hand swinging her gun loosely. "I contacted the task force Captain on the flight back," she answered. "He told me about the accident and that his men were searching the forest from the point of the crash. I googled it and saw the housing division here and knew that's where Sonny would head; it's what I would do."

"You're alone?"

"Bullard took Lena to Washington. Frank wanted me to come back and the Army obliged."

"I figured as much," Hart said. "Thanks for coming back for me."

"Don't flatter yourself Arthur. I came for Sonny. Where is he, by the way?"

Hart groaned then turned and pointed to the way he had come. "Just behind that house. He's injured his ankle so he's waiting for me. Thinks I'm hotwiring a getaway car. He'll love that thing," he said, gesturing to the chopper which was completely out of place in the middle of suburbia.

JP smiled. "Lead the way."

"Let me go first. He's not expecting anyone else and he has a gun," Hart said. "He's going to be confused seeing you again so soon and may see you as a hostile. Let me talk to him first."

JP wasn't sure how this was all going to play out but she knew what the end result was supposed to be. And she didn't want Hart on the wrong side of things. If he got in the way, she didn't want to think about what she might have to do. She nodded and stopped halfway down the driveway. Hart crossed the yard and disappeared down the rise at the edge of the forest.

She stamped her feet a couple of times and looked at her watch. They were out of time. She strode across the lawn, both hands gripping her Glock tightly.

Chapter Eighty-Six

Sonny had shuffled to one side from where Hart had left him and was half hidden behind a small bush. Hart grinned and headed toward him, brushing away low hanging branches and small bushes.

"Minor change of plans," Hart said as he reached for his arm. But in a blurred movement, Sonny grabbed Hart's forearm, twisted and pushed, effectively forcing his body to follow the unnatural direction his arm was going and forced Hart to roll heavily into a small rut. He then let Hart's arm go and dragged his wounded leg farther into the bushes, his urgency and speed surprising.

Wondering what had caused Sonny's actions, Hart turned to see JP was still standing on the edge of the ravine, barely visible in the darkness, though the shape of a large gun pointed in his direction was clear.

"Get out of the way Arthur," she yelled down.

"What the hell are you doing?" Hart yelled back, his eyes darting between JP's rigid stance and Sonny's disappearing form. "He's injured, he can't take us both on in his condition. Come and help me bring him up."

"I don't think so Arthur," she said, her voice stark and emotionless. "Please stay where you are so I don't mistake you for Sonny."

She then began the descent, heading away from Hart, toward the bush that Sonny had slinked behind.

After rubbing his arm to get the circulation back, Hart crawled toward the bush where Sonny had gone. If he stayed low, JP wouldn't know it was him and he was fairly confident she wouldn't just shoot at anything that moved. His knee hit something hard about a foot in and Hart looked down to see the gun Sonny had been using. He must have taken it from the police officer when he ambushed the squad car. Hart didn't know much about guns but it was obvious this 9mm semi-automatic had no cartridge; there was empty space where the cartridge should be. The cop must have kept it in another pocket for security. It had been a useless weapon all along and Hart dropped it.

He had to push aside leaves and shrubs that obscured his view as he went deeper into the mini-forest and when he hit a tree stump, he decided to stick up his head to see where everyone was.

JP was about ten feet to his left, crouched, her gun leading her advance. Hart heard breathing and felt an arm slink around his neck.

"Stand up Hart," Sonny hissed. His arm across Hart's neck prevented him from getting up quickly, so he rose at the same pace Sonny did. The Korean was leaning against a tree and his other hand pressed against the arm around Hart's neck acting as a lever to increase pressure if necessary; a classic Hapkido technique. As they both slowly rose, pressing against the tree trunk behind them, Sonny squeezed his fingers slightly to ensure Hart recognized the lock he was using. If Hart tried to wiggle out of it, or attacked him with his hands or legs, Sonny's hand would automatically tighten and squash Hart's carotid artery instantly. At best, he would instantly lose any strength in his muscles. At worst, it would knock him out.

"Sonny, please," JP said, standing just a couple of feet away from us, her gun pointing in our general direction.

"You're here to kill me," Sonny said, nodding at the gun.

"That's ridiculous," Hart hissed, his voice restricted by Sonny's arm. He didn't tighten it thankfully. Hart assumed he didn't mind him talking at the moment. "We need to know what his mission is," Hart said loudly.

"They already know Hart," Sonny whispered. He raised his voice. "They've been working on it while we've been chasing around this wilderness of a country. It's why she came back." He pulled his face away from Hart's. "Isn't that right Agent Pierce?"

"They know enough to do something about it before your people have a chance to send someone else to finish what you started," JP said.

"So why not deport him," Hart croaked. "Or use his diplomatic status to get him back without any trial or media attention."

"Your friend Mr. Daro can't take that risk Hart," Sonny said. "Right again, Ms. Pierce?"

JP stepped closer, now within shooting distance "He's already escaped twice," JP said, addressing Hart but watching Sonny intently. "And why risk it? With Sonny out of the picture, Frank and General Wade have time to prepare for anyone else Kim Jong Un will send. We can put firewalls or something like that in place."

Hart squirmed. JP was guessing. Frank hadn't told her what his plans were. But he'd apparently just ordered her to eliminate Sonny. Was Hart supposed to just go along with that? Did Frank even know he was still with Sonny? Maybe he thought Sonny had escaped from the RCMP and Hart was still in custody.

"General Wade is a formidable opponent," Sonny said softly, almost musing. "He has foiled other attempts in the past. Some of his analysts are Chinese, did you know that Hart? They understand Asian ways."

Hart watched JP as she moved her gun upward, aiming at Sonny's head. Her trigger finger was firmly in place but her wrist was shaking slightly. Hart pushed backward against Sonny, relieving the pressure on his neck slightly. Sonny's attention was elsewhere and he didn't adjust to re-tighten his grip. Hart kept watching JP. She was sweating too much, her face was dark, her eyes darting between Sonny and Hart.

Then he understood. She was afraid she'd hit him.

Apparently though, not shooting wasn't an option either. Frank had obviously ordered her to kill Sonny and it looked like she was going to take the chance she might hit Hart because she may not get another opportunity.

Sonny had figured that out too. In one swift movement, he dropped his hand from Hart's neck, reached behind and below him and then pushed Hart out of the way as he whipped a loose branch in an arc toward JP's head.

JP was probably a good shot but she was distracted by the stick coming at her so her hand jolted upward slightly and her bullet embedded itself in the tree a few inches above Sonny's head. The thick branch Sonny had thrown hit the side of JPs head with a thwacking sound. She dropped the gun as her head shook from the impact, her eyes widening while her pupils rolled upward and the whites of her eyes glared into space. She seemed to fold as she dropped to the ground.

Sonny reached for the gun but Hart jumped on his back, the momentum sending both of them into another bush. Hart was still struggling to get his breathing back to normal and Hart knew he was no match for Sonny in any kind of wrestling match; he had a good twenty pounds on him. So, he rolled away from him and jumped up into a fighting stance.

Sonny did the same, which Hart found oddly comforting. Sonny was no street thug. Watching his adversary's cold, steady eyes, Hart questioned what other skills Sonny had learned since they had last met on the tournament mats in the Hong Kong gym so many years ago. Then he grinned. Sonny didn't know what Hart had been up to since their twenties either.

They circled each other as best they could on the uneven ground. Small shrubs and saplings interfered with their steps and Hart was amused to see he was handling the terrain better than Sonny. Of course, the Asian did have at least a sprained ankle, which meant he would likely try to get Hart on the ground again where he would technically have an advantage. Hart had no intention of letting that happen. Taekwondo is a stand-up game. Seasoned practitioners know that if you don't put your opponent out of commission immediately with one or two strikes, then you are in trouble. That's what he trained field agents at The Farm to understand and that's what he firmly believed. Taekwondo was known for its fast, simple, and often fatal strikes. If the fight went to the ground, you'd done something wrong. Sonny knew that as well as Hart so he wasn't worried about Sonny trying to grab him. He was more concerned about a quick, decisive strike that would put him to the ground where Sonny's Hapkido skills would give him leverage, despite the sprained ankle.

When the attack came, Hart was surprised by its veracity. Sonny covered the distance between them in an instant, his knife hand aimed at Hart's throat while his good leg snapped out in a flying side kick of sorts. But with his sprained ankle supporting the flight, he hadn't managed to get quite as much forward momentum as he probably wanted and Hart blocked it easily, stepping forward into his motion, hoping to let the knife hand slide by his neck. Instead it brushed by his ear and he heard a sharp buzz. Hart aimed an uppercut to Sonny's kidney but the Asian flew by and it grazed his hip instead.

Sonny landed on his good foot and gently placed the leg with the sprained ankle behind him, forming a low walking stance. Hart remained in his opposite stance, right leg forward, preparing for a low spinning side kick.

Taekwondo is about attacking not defending, so opponents often initiate techniques simultaneously. Hart and Sonny didn't sit back and wait for the other to throw a blow, or spin into a kick, defending and then counter attacking. They both executed blinding speed techniques at the same time. Some hit their mark, most didn't. Defence was mostly instinct with little thought. The only plan was one of attack. As a result, within half a minute or so, both men sported bruises that were slowly turning red, then purple, and sometimes black. But the flurry of motion continued. It seemed to Hart that Sonny was trying to get in a decisive blow but that he was either less effective due to his injury, or Hart was parrying better than he thought. Sonny kept pressing his hand to the side of his head from time to time making Hart wonder if one of his previous blows had stunned him more than he'd expected. Hart's finger was throbbing intensely each time he tightened his fist but he tried not to let it distract him. Sonny knew this of course, and aimed for the right side of Hart's body so his defence would have to be with that arm. Each block sent a jolt of pain up his arm and Hart could see that when he opened his palm briefly, his broken finger drooping awkwardly.

After what seemed like an hour but was likely no more than a few minutes, both men stepped backward and took a breath. They didn't speak but Hart could see Sonny's exasperation plainly. This fight was not going as the Asian had hoped. Sonny was holding his head often now and was still favouring his one leg. But one of them had to end it, and one look into Sonny's darkening eyes told Hart who the Asian thought the victor would be. Hart had never had a killer instinct. Most of his competitive bouts had gone the full three rounds and he'd either won or lost on points, not knock outs. He was a skilled fighter, not an emotional one. Even when he was with the bikers, Hart had played more of a back-up role than front artillery.

Sonny had always been the opposite, at least in the old days. He got angry quickly and that anger manifested itself into deadly attacks, or grossly misjudged mistakes. Usually it was the former which was why he had been so good in the circuit as a youngster. But he had made mistakes often enough to eventually be dropped from the South Korean team. Hart was hoping for one of those emotional mistakes now. They were both tired but Hart sensed Sonny felt this was a fight to the death. Hart didn't agree but how would he ever convince the Korean of that. He tightened his grip, wincing at the sharp pain as his hands coiled into fists. It couldn't go on much longer, he thought. Was he capable of killing Sonny? He knew Sonny would have no qualms about killing him. Not now. the Korean had to get out of here before JP came to. And they only way to do that was to put Hart out of commission. Could Hart do the same? He'd had that discussion with Frank years ago. And the answer hadn't changed. It was the main reason he'd left the employ of the CIA.

As Sonny took a forward step to put him the right distance for a spin sidekick, he also pushed his back, bad leg forward, raising his knee. It was a familiar motion, although mastered only by high-level black belts. He was going to do a 360 kick which meant Hart wouldn't know if he was aiming for his knees, his stomach, or his head until the last second. Defending his whole body simultaneously was impossible so, as usual, attacking was his best defence. As Sonny rose for the first part of his jump and spin, Hart rotated backwards, swung his head and torso toward the ground and snapped his own sidekick out and up to where he hoped the centre of Sonny's mass would be.

Hart's kick connected with Sonny's body just above his liver as the Korean began his second spin high in the air, knocking his aim completely off. A 360 kick relies completely on momentum and the body doesn't just stop in mid-air even if something gets in the way, such as Hart's kick. So Sonny continued to spin but was unable to execute the final hooking technique. Instead he was forced to land on the bad leg. Upon impact with the ground, he instantly rolled away, in an attempt to ensure the sprained ankle didn't become a broken one.

As he stood, they stared at each other. Sonny's face was contorted, partially in pain no doubt, but his frustration had clearly become anger now. He was not used to conflict taking so long.

Hart knew he had an advantage because of the wounded leg, but he also knew that, as a result of that, Sonny's next attack would be vicious, unrelenting, and intended to be final.

Dragging the wounded leg behind him, Sonny shuffled closer, hands raised, fists tightly clenched in a classic Hapkido stance. It would be a barrage of hand techniques, one after the other, with no break until Hart was either unconscious or dead.

If he could ward off the first few strikes, Hart had an idea. He circled around to the stump where Sonny had first grabbed him and looked for the dead branch the Korean had thrown at JP. She was still lying motionless a few feet away. The strike to her head had been vicious and audacious but hopefully, she was just unconscious. She'd have a serious bruise and a massive headache, but perhaps that would be all.

The branch lay a couple of feet to her side. Hart stepped closer, watching Sonny's approach, prepared to react, and hoping he would survive long enough to achieve what he had in mind.

Hands held high in a classic boxer's pose, Sonny stepped in and then swiftly kicked out and up with his front leg--the bad one--

high above Hart's head, his heel blurring as it swept upward and forward.

An axe kick, when performed against an unsuspecting opponent will land on the shoulder or side of the head with smashing downward force. But Hart knew it was a feint. If Sonny had intended it to connect, he never would have used the bad leg because the impact would shatter the weakened ankle bone. It was meant to entice Hart to raise his arms in defence, exposing his torso for an explosion of hand techniques to the chest, stomach and kidneys.

Instead, when Sonny closed in, fists pumping as in a B-rated Kung-Fu film, Hart blocked and parried, their eyes locked on each other less than one foot apart.

After exchanging several blows, Sonny stepped back ever so slightly, ready to swing out a crescent kick aimed at the side of Hart's head. Hart had been waiting for the change in tactic and moved to the opposite side, and using his front leg, swept Sonny's supporting back leg out from under him. Most of the time, this would have merely weakened the force of the crescent kick but since Sonny had been using the leg with the sprained ankle as the support leg, Hart's sweep actually dislodged his stance and he toppled sideways in Hart's direction.

Hart swooped down, grabbed the dead stick and rolled on top of Sonny as he lay exposed, face up. He brought his one arm around Sonny's neck in a similar manner the Korean had used on him moments earlier. But instead of using his other hand as a pressure lever, Hart placed the stick between his arm, Sonny's neck and his own leg. He then wrapped his leg around Sonny's waist and pulled the stunned man back over his own body and onto the ground again. This time, Sonny was face down, the stick embedded in the ground, trapped between his neck and my arm.

"Aargh!"

He tried to say more but Hart pushed Sonny's head further into the dirt and pulled back on the stick which slowly squeezed his Adam's apple. Then with his free hand, he drew back his arm and punched Sonny in the side of the head, his extended middle finger pushing into the indent by his temple. Sonny's body went limp. Hart let go, leaned back and let out a sign of exhaustion.

Hart's years with bikers and their numerous rumbles, which had often taken place in parks and campsites, had given him a chance to experiment with combining proven Taekwondo techniques with raw biker brawling. Utilizing branches, sticks, and stones during a fight was the norm for the gangs and he had combined TKD and Hapkido moves with new tricks that he had picked up from the boys. In a rumble, you never fought one guy at a time so you always needed a free hand to ward off other attackers while subduing someone, so chains, sticks, branches, etc. had always been a part of the arsenal.

"I am assuming that because that guy appears to be Asian, you must be Mr. Hart?"

Hart pulled the stick from under Sonny's jaw, quickly checking his pulse with his thumb and forefinger. He then looked up to see a man dressed in army pilot's uniform staring down at him. The 22mm he had aimed at Hart's chest didn't look very menacing but at that distance, it would do sufficient damage.

 Hart nodded.

The pilot dropped the gun to his side and let out a relieved sigh. "I'm a pilot. The only thing I've ever shot at is targets at the range. I've never even seen combat for Christ's sake. But if it was him looking up at me--" he pointed the gun barrel at Sonny--"I think I could have. I'm glad it's you I'm talking to."

"You're the chopper pilot?"

He nodded. "914th Airlift Wing of the Air Force Reserve Command, Sir." He saluted, then realizing Hart wasn't military, dropped his hand quickly. "Is he dead? And Agent Pierce?"

Hart shook his head. "Both unconscious. He'll be out for a while but we need to tie him up and get him on the chopper. Agent Pierce was hit pretty hard. No telling when she'll come to. We need to get her medical attention."

"Yes Sir," the pilot said, clearly happy that someone else was taking charge of the situation. His face clouded over. "Mr. Hart, I was told that only Agent Pierce would be flying back to the base with me. I was not told about you or a prisoner."

Hart stood up and patted the man's shoulder. "If Agent Pierce were awake, she would tell you she would take full responsibility for transporting us all back across the border. I'm afraid you'll have to trust me on that." *Pure bullshit but I'll worry about that when we get to wherever this chopper came from.*

The pilot stared at Hart briefly, then placed his pistol back in its holster. "I have grappling rope in the chopper, "he pointed at Sonny. "To tie him up. I'll see what's in the first aid kit for reviving Agent Pierce."

"Of course," Hart said, hoping that the pilot had bandages and tape but no smelling salts. Although he was concerned for any head injury sustained by Sonny's blow to JP's head, Hart didn't want her alert enough to insist the pilot do his duty and kill Sonny. Once in the air, the point would be mute.

Chapter Eighty-Seven

The pilot had radioed ahead once they were airborne and Hart settled back for the relatively short flight to the base just across the border. This was actually his first helicopter ride and he was surprised at how comfortable it was, at least once they'd straightened out and were flying more or less like an airplane. His stomach had lurched momentarily upon takeoff, as with anyone who experiences chopper flight for the first time knows, gravity, a sense of direction, and any semblance to normal fixed wing flight literally goes out the window.

Sonny was still unconscious, propped up in his seat by the door, his double shoulder seatbelt the only thing keeping him upright. JP was in the seat directly opposite, beside Hart. She too was strapped in but she was semi-conscious and mumbling to herself. Now and again, she would jerk her head from side to side but her eyes remained closed.

I'd love to know what she's dreaming about.

Hart closed his eyes, knowing he needed rest from the incredibly long day, but happy that it seemed to be all over. He must have dozed a little because he was surprised when a sudden gush of wind shocked him back to reality.

The rush of wind was coming from the open cabin door. JP was out of her seat and wrestling with Sonny's seatbelt quick release.

What the...

The pilot began screaming but couldn't be heard over the rushing wind. Hart was wearing headphones but they obviously weren't connected to any audio feed as he heard nothing. He whipped them off his head and his ears immediately popped. The wind now sounded like a tornado and though he yelled loudly to JP, he couldn't hear his own voice.

He stared in surprise as JP released Sonny from his tether and began pushing him sideways toward the door. Hart lurched forward but was stopped by his own straps. He watched in horror as Sonny's still unconscious form slipped off the edge of the seat and flopped to the floor, his one arm and shoulder drooping over the edge of the opening. Hart could see his hand flapping in the wind. Fiddling to release himself, he continued to stare as JP leaned her full weight against Sonny's lower body. Once she had his torso out of the opening, all she would have to do was lift his legs and gravity would do the rest.

JP was trying to push Sonny out of the chopper!

The pilot was struggling to keep the helicopter level. The sudden decrease in pressure was forcing him to offset his steering and the chopper began to lean to the left. Sonny's limp form bounced on an exposed strut and settled half in and half out of the doorway. JP leaned back to get a better grip on his lower body.

"What are you doing?" Hart screamed, finally free of his own harness. He reached out to grab JPs arm but the chopper dropped suddenly and he lost his grip. She turned to him, having finally noticing that he was trying to get her attention. She lashed out with her leg and caught Hart in the stomach. The kick had no power behind it but it was enough to send Hart back into his seat.

"He can't go back to the States," she mouthed, her face contorted from the whipping wind at her face. If she wasn't careful, she'd fall out the door with Sonny.

"He'll die," Hart screamed.

She gave him a deadpan stare. "I know."

Hart leaned forward and while JP was busy trying to manipulate Sonny's now unencumbered body out of the chopper, he placed his thumb at the base of her neck and pressed inward forcefully. JP tried to turn her head but the blood circulation was cut off almost instantly and her hands dropped to her sides.

Hart caught her and pulled her down and towards him until she lay on the floor of the cabin, unconscious. The chopper dropped altitude again and Sonny's body shifted a few inches further outward, the force of the wind pulling him out like a giant hand drawing him into oblivion.

Hart grabbed one of his ankles and pulled. It was like playing tug-of-war, but with Mother Nature.

The pilot turned his head and his eyes snapped open as he took in what was happening. He turned back and pushed the steering column to the left, causing the chopper to increase its sideways angle. That was enough to release gravity momentarily and Hart pulled on Sonny's ankle as hard as he could.

Sonny's head hit the transom, and a huge gash behind his ear began spewing blood. Blood spurted out the door in a long, steady stream. It was as if Mother Nature wasn't ready to give him up and the stream of blood was a tenuous thread to the outside.

Hart reached up with his other hand and seized Sonny's calf, pulling as hard as he could. As if agreeing, the blood began soaking the floor of the cabin. Sonny's body was clear of the opening.

Hart dropped the leg and lurched forward for the door handle. Leaning over both bodies, and with considerable effort, he pushed the cabin door closed. He looked up at the pilot but the man was too busy fighting to bring the chopper back to some semblance of normal flight.

Hart leaned forward and checked the pulses of both Sonny and JP, now lying side by side on the floor of the cabin. Satisfied they were breathing normally for an unconscious state, he looked up to see the pilot's wide-eyed gaze.

"What the hell was she doing?" he said.

Hart latched his harness belt and shrugged. "Obeying orders, no doubt," he said. "How much longer?"

The pilot checked the clock on his instrument panel. "About twenty-five minutes," he said.

Hart nodded. "The sooner the better," he muttered to himself, then louder, "Where's your first aid kit?"

"Behind the back seat," the pilot yelled, pointing to a compartment in the rear of the fuselage with a red cross painted on it.

As Hart grabbed for the supplies he needed to stop Sonny's superficial wound, he considered both his and JP's actions. No doubt, Frank had ordered JP to eliminate Sonny and since Hart had prevented that from happening back in Brantford, she'd become desperate when she regained consciousness and saw that they were all flying back.

Hart was aware Sonny would have to pay for his deeds. But death by smashing into the ground at a hundred miles an hour or more was not something he would wish on anyone, friend or foe.

They'd have to think of something else for Sonny, though knowing Frank it would be no less humane. JP would be angry but if Frank had indeed ordered Sonny's demise, she would be busy explaining herself and face Frank's wrath for failure. Hart wasn't concerned. After all, he didn't work for Frank.

Chapter Eighty-Eight

Upon landing they were greeted by high-ranking Army officers who picked up the still unconscious but now well trussed-up Sonny Kim, unceremoniously dumping him in the back of an enclosed Army MP wagon. It spewed asphalt as it disappeared from sight.

JP had opened her eyes a couple of more times en route in the chopper but had been too groggy to communicate. Two medics jumped aboard as soon as the skids touched asphalt and began tending to her. Within a couple of minutes, an ambulance slid to a stop beside the chopper and JP was placed on a stretcher and put inside the vehicle which followed the first one, albeit a little faster with lights flashing and sirens blaring.

"You've had quite a day Mr. Hart."

Hart turned to see General Wade, escorted by two aides on either side. He was dressed in flight jacket complete with four stars on the epaulet.

"Where are they going?" Hart asked.

General Wade put an arm on Hart's shoulder and turned him toward the main terminal building. A sign on the facia stated it was the Niagara Falls Air Reserve Station. "Agent Pierce will be well looked after at the Army Hospital off base. When she is fully recovered, she will report to Treasury in Washington for a full debriefing."

"And Sonny?"

The General smiled. "I had planned to tell my superiors and peers that the notorious spy Sonny Kim had been detained in

Canada's Kingston penitentiary for the long term. But that won't work for you, will it? Being a civilian and all."

Hart cocked his head. "He wasn't supposed to come back here was he General?"

Wade shook his head. "No he wasn't. And I'm sure through no fault of Agent Pierce's, the fact that he *is* here places us in a bit of a dilemma. His diplomatic status forces us to engage with the Koreans during his, ah… stay. It would have been much simpler to either send them his dog tags, or better yet, pass on their inquiries to Ottawa."

"You haven't told me what is going to happen to him General."

"No I haven't," the General said, smiling. "Mostly because I won't be making that decision alone. We have been tracking Mr. Kim since he first began making regular visits to California two years ago. A lot of people in the intelligence community have a vested interest in his activities."

"California, Sir?" Hart asked.

Wade shook his head as if annoyed with himself for bringing up a subject he didn't want to elaborate upon. "Doesn't matter. Not important now," he said. "For the time being he will be a guest of Military Intelligence at Fort Meade. Eventually, I would assume, he will be taken out of our jurisdiction and placed somewhere a little more, um…. obsolete."

"He'll disappear then."

"One way or another, Hart, yes, he'll disappear. But not the way you think. We're not like your friend, Mr. Daro; I mean, we're not that devious. We're military for God's sake. When people disappear on our watch, the bad ones go to Leavenworth and the good ones go to Witness Protection. Regardless, whatever happens to Mr. Kim, we will have a lot of explaining to do to the North Koreans. Thankfully, because of their ongoing shenanigans with the South Koreans, the Administration is not too concerned about overtures requesting the release of political prisoners at this point."

"I see."

"Someday, he may even be allowed to return to Korea," the General continued. "If he could be turned, of course." The General stopped and put his hand on Hart's shoulder. "Do you think that's possible, Hart?"

Before Hart could answer, the General shook his head vigorously. "No, of course he can't. We could never fully trust him anyway."

Since the General seemed happy with the answer to his own question, Hart didn't see any need to add anything.

"But since he would no longer be of any use to them in a covert capacity, I would imagine Mr. Kim would prefer to negotiate a defection of some kind."

"Perfect," Hart said, shaking his head. He'd had enough of the conspiracy crap. "General, it has been an extremely long day. May I beg a lift to Andrews Air Force Base? I can have someone drive me home from there."

"Andrews is a good choice Hart," the General said, pointing to a cream-coloured C21-A Lear jet on the other side of the tarmac. "I'll be glad to drop you off so you can get rested up. I'll send a car for you first thing in the morning. I'm sure you understand that a debrief, even for a civilian such as yourself, is necessary in this instance."

Hart sighed and nodded. He understood.

Frank wanted to see him. And General Wade was going to make sure Hart got there without any detours.

Robert J. Morrow

Chapter Eighty-Nine

"Welcome back to the home of the brave, land of the free," Frank said.

"Canada's not such a bad place," Hart said. "No igloos, lots of open space actually"

"You should have called once you'd found the girl."

Hart curled the corner of his mouth. "I was a little busy at the time."

"Hmmm," he said, finally extending his hand. Hart shook it and sat in one of the leather high backed chairs in front of Frank's massive oak desk. General Wade sat in its twin beside him. General Wade had dropped Hart at the restaurant where he'd caught a few hours sleep. Then, promptly at eight, the limo had picked him up again and whisked him out to Langley.

"Sonny isn't talking," Frank said.

Hart looked at the General. "I thought *your* people were handling his debriefing?"

"The General is the Military's liaison with the CIA," Frank said. "We're all the same people."

The General smiled and said nothing.

"Besides, he's going to talk soon," Frank said.

Hart frowned. Frank grinned. "No, you idiot, we're not torturing him," he said. "When he came to this morning, he was suffering from severe headaches."

Hart immediately thought of the back fist to the head. *No, it couldn't have caused that much damage.* Then he remembered the head banging Sonny had experienced aboard the chopper.

"We had him checked out," Frank continued. "Seems he has a growing tumour and within the past few weeks, it was edging up against his skull, causing intermittent seizures. The stress from the past day has greatly exacerbated it because he's in constant pain now."

Should I feel remorse? No, that's why he had been easier to subdue than I'd thought he would be.

"He'll be on the operating table later this afternoon," Frank said.

"He still won't talk just because you're providing medical attention," Hart said.

Frank shrugged. "Doesn't matter. He was no good to us in that condition, so we had nothing to lose. If he doesn't talk as thanks for our assistance, then we'll resort to torture." He smiled and General Wade grinned along with him. Hart rolled his eyes.

"JP is recovering, thanks for asking," Frank deadpanned, turning his chair slightly to stare out the window of his second storey office. Hart hadn't been to Langley headquarters for a couple of years, when Frank was a mere Department head. Now, as Deputy Director, the surroundings were definitely un-military issue. There were no metal desks and chairs, no obligatory picture of the President, and it was actually plush Berber carpeting underfoot. Frank's huge oak desk and the high back chairs reminded Hart of the oval office, at least from the pictures he'd seen.

"Once the doctors release her, she'll be joining us here, hopefully to shed some light on what Sonny and Lena Castillo may have discussed while the girl was his captive," the General said.

"Just in case you were wondering about her," Frank said snidely.

"JP wasn't there," Hart said. "She won't know."

"But you were, weren't you Arthur?" Frank said, turning back to him.

"I'm glad to hear JP's okay," Hart said. "You put her in a tough position."

"She's been in tough positions before," Frank said.

"By-the-way, did you ever find out who kidnapped her?" Hart asked.

"Losano is pretty confident it was his father or one of his lackeys," Frank said. "He knew Antonio didn't like having Secret Service around, especially during the South Koreans' visit. He would have been worried that their hardware deal was at risk had JP discovered a connection."

"Well, that didn't work, did it?"

Frank shrugged. JP's feelings weren't his concern. And Antonio Losano was of no further importance to the CIA, so Frank had moved on.

"Where's Lena?" Hart asked.

Frank's expression darkened and he leaned forward, placing his elbows on the table, his hands covering his face momentarily. He then looked over at General Wade whose stare was expressionless. He then looked at Hart.

"She's gone."

Hart shifted in his chair and gave Frank the best quizzical look he could muster. Frank leaned back, rested his elbows on his chair arms and formed a tent with his fingers in front of his chest.

"After her debriefing, she met with our broadband team, gave them all her notes and insights... then we had an incident."

"An incident?" Hart said.

General Wade finally spoke. "We can't detain an American citizen without probable cause," he said, turning to give Frank a cold stare.

Hart smiled. "She escaped."

Frank dropped his hands and leaned forward. "She was on the brink of successfully creating the cheapest, most effective web infrastructure in the country. BPL was always thought to be the best way to utilize existing technology to introduce new technology to the far reaches of the country, places where electricity is virtually the only government regulated commodity."

"Great political fodder," Hart said. "I can see President Emerson's address to the nation next year. All those poor folk voting for him just because he's the only one who could reach them."

General Wade shifted in his seat. "It's much more than that and you know it Hart," he said, his voice harsh.

Of course it was, Hart thought. He had been thinking of nothing but the military uses for such a broadly-based internet system since Lena and JP had first explained it to him back in Oswego. The President's directive of being able to control all communications would be considerably closer to actuality with BPL running smoothly. But Lena had gotten away from them. How? It had only been a few hours. Where would she be? And why wasn't Langley on red alert if she had escaped?

"You have a broadband team set up here now?" Hart asked after a moment of thought. "And that's why you don't need her anymore?"

"Ms. Castillo was given a loose leash to do things her way in the beginning," Frank said. "But after the press launch, when that dinosaur mobster made an idiot of himself, we knew the media wouldn't leave it alone, so we brought her technical staff here." He squirmed in his chair. "She seemed happy to continue in this protected environment."

"So the rest of the Oswego team are here?" Hart asked.

"All except the young Koreans," General Wade said. "They've been loaned out to Military Intelligence for the time being. Very clever young men and women with some very special talents. North Korea is making a stink but they can't push too hard. After all, these are the guys who hacked Sony."

"What happened to Lena, Frank?" Hart asked.

Frank twiddled his fingers and looked out the window again. "She was fine until...well, until Jay Losano walked in. Then she went hysterical. Attacked him, hitting him and yelling obscenities." He looked into Hart's eyes. "So I had her taken to an unused office to calm down while I tried to get what was going on out of Losano"

"He gave her the poison, not Sonny," Hart said.

"Be that as it may," Frank said, "we didn't know that for sure. And Losano didn't admit it initially. Meanwhile, Castillo asked the guard we'd sent with her to get her some Advil and water. He thought nothing of it. We hadn't told him to watch her, whatever. So he did."

"And she just walked out the front doors," General Wade interjected, haughtily. "Can you believe it? No one stopped her. She wasn't a prisoner. Even had an employee badge with high security clearance strapped around her neck. So she left. And no one's seen her since."

Hart pondered that for a moment. "How long ago was that?"

Frank looked up at a wall clock. "About six hours ago."

"We've got people looking," the General piped in. Hart turned to look at the old man. He knew a lot more than he was telling anyone. Hart didn't like the sound of Military Intelligence being let loose on Castillo but couldn't expect much more from the two guys who had set Lena up to create their super internet network. They wouldn't give up that easily. The General would likely have Captain Bullard forming a team to look for her since he seemed to be the General's secret troubleshooter.

"So why aren't you out there looking for her?" Hart asked Frank.

Just then, the door opened and Jay Losano stepped in. "He doesn't need to," he said, his voice confident, his blue button down shirt and white slacks perfectly ironed. "Please don't get up," he said as he strode behind the desk and stood next to Frank, leaning on the window frame.

"I hadn't intended to stand up," Frank said, glaring at him.

"I thought you'd arrested him," Hart said to Frank.

"I told you to knock first," Frank said, ignoring Hart's comment.

Losano grinned.

Frank turned back to Hart. "He told us everything and we've come to an arrangement."

"He's heading up the broadband team," Hart said. "At least till you get Lena back."

"I was about to take over anyway Hart. So we don't need Lena anymore." He strode over and sat on the edge of Frank's desk.

"My father was old school Hart," he said. "And he was not very good at subtleties. As such, the, ah… business was behind the times. The family has asked me to take over operations; legitimize what I can, but keep the boys in the manner to which they are accustomed, so to speak. And this is how I'm doing it."

"Yes, well…" General Wade stuttered. Frank waved him off and glared at Losano. "Get off my desk," he hissed. Losano smiled and stood.

Hart didn't think Losano had done much mourning over his father's demise. Not a big surprise. He was the big cheese now, though maybe Swiss more than Cheddar. He smiled to himself.

"Doesn't matter what arrangement we came to," Frank said, frowning at Hart's smiling face. "Bottom line is that the Losano family is going to finance continued research into BPL in exchange for their continued existence. Totally off government books, even slush funds. Once fully developed and handed over to the administration, they will act as supervisors and managers."

Hart laughed.

Losano's face went red.

Frank sighed.

General Wade turned away.

"So the mob is going to enforce your hold on BPL once its ready to launch nationwide?" Hart stood and slapped Losano on the shoulder. "Your father, God rest his soul, left you a hell of a legacy. You get to go legit without losing the family income. Nice."

"Can we move on," Frank said, his eyelids raised, looking at Hart. Losano's face reddened.

"What happened in Oswego, Jay?" Hart asked. "Wasn't Lena ready?"

"We couldn't take the chance," Frank answered for him. "Castillo said she wasn't sure, wanted to restrict the launch to the Eastern Grid, roll out to the whole country later", Frank said. "But we'd already set the launch date with President Emerson's advance team and released it to the press. That couldn't change."

"So that's when you came up with the smoke and mirrors plan Lena told Sonny about?" Hart asked. "Was Richard Hattis in on that? Come to think of it, did the President go along with it too?"

Frank shifted in his seat again. Losano fidgeted with his nails. The General was still staring out the window at the greenery on the other side of the complex. Losano jumped in before Frank could answer, though Hart wasn't sure he'd planned to anyway.

"Lena was confident BPL would work on the Eastern Grid which included northern New York state, parts of Ontario and Quebec and some of Eastern Pennsylvania. We could hook up directly to that grid from Oswego." Losano said. "There was a glitch that kept occurring every time we attempted to jump to adjacent grids though," he continued. "She said she couldn't get past it. I didn't believe her."

"We knew the media would be monitoring the whole nation," Frank piped in, for now avoiding my question. Emerson's involvement meant coercion in my opinion. Richard Hattis' was more a personal thing and Frank knew that.

"We couldn't risk any negative feedback. This way, we decided to remove doubt and guarantee success, using a negative as a positive, telling the press it was a special pre-show for them, limited to about 50 miles. A full launch would come later in the month along with a promise that all registered members of the press would get a private link to the system before anyone else. That way the media could announce the new service via the service itself."

"You dangled a carrot," Hart said.

"If my Father hadn't messed things up, I would have gotten past the glitch by now. Instead, the media has switched attention to Senator Blais and his cable cohorts," Losano fumed. "So we have to spend precious time proving our pure intentions."

The General finally turned back from the window. "The media now thinks there's some government chicanery going on and that the cable and phone conglomerates may have something in their claim that BPL is a grandiose way of controlling national communications."

Hart cocked his head and lifted an eyebrow to Frank. That was, of course, exactly what BPL would be, should Frank be placed in charge.

"She told Sonny there was a separate restriction code she'd developed that had to run simultaneously with ArmourNet in order for it to work," Hart said.

Losano stopped fiddling, and both he, Frank and General Wade stared at him.

"Sonny was using me to force Lena to give him that code," Hart said. "It was probably the first thing she could come up with in her panic. But the cavalry arrived before things went any further." They were all staring at him. He could smell the wood burning. "Personally, I think she was lying, just trying anything to save me."

"She...ah, she wouldn't have been able to do that without me knowing," Losano blustered. Frank turned to look at him, then back at Hart.

"You think she was buying time?" Frank asked.

"Looking back now, I think so," Hart said. "But she was excited about something. Something she wasn't telling Sonny."

"How would you know that?" General Wade asked. "You said yourself she was panicking, concerned for your safety, and no doubt her own." He scratched the side of his head, an itch that wouldn't go away.

"I've been watching her, and Jay here, for most of the summer," Hart said. "When she had breakthroughs she would come to the bar and celebrate with a glass of pinot. I got to know what that sparkle in her eyes meant. She had that same sparkle yesterday, just before Sonny began, ah... playing with my body parts."

"What kind of a breakthrough?" the General asked, his hands pressing against his knees as he leaned on them.

"Like I said, the cavalry interrupted us, and your super soldier whisked her away before I could ask," Hart said. "So I don't know. I can't even be sure it was something she hasn't already told you. I simply have no idea."

Frank looked at the General. His shoulders drooped and he shook his head slowly.

"She brought me up to speed on everything we'd been attempting in Oswego," Losano said, his arms gesturing wildly.

"She didn't leave anything out, I'm sure of it. She wouldn't take the chance that she couldn't just walk away from it all. She wanted out. She was done with all the secrets, the power struggles. She just wanted to hand it all over to us. She was never into heavy complications and political interests."

He didn't look fully convinced.

Neither did Frank.

"Are you sure she gave you everything?" Hart said, looking at Losano. He stormed around the desk and stood in front of Hart, glaring down at him.

"Why wouldn't she?" he said, hands on his hips. "She doesn't want to disappoint the President. She wanted out and I am the only one capable of completing the work. She knows I am the only one who can finish it." He brushed a hand through his hair quickly. "Why would she tell you something she hasn't told me?"

Hart turned to Frank. "At the time, she was telling Sonny, not me. She thought she was saving me from torture. I don't even know if it was the truth. She would have said anything at that point I think."

"It won't work without her," the General said, flopping back in his chair. "I knew it!"

"But I have the team working on it around the clock," Losano blurted. "It's just a few simple lines of code, that's all."

"Leave us Jay," Frank said.

"I want to hear…" Losano said.

"Now!" Frank said, slamming his hands on the desk.

Losano stepped back, the anger on Frank's face startling him. He glared at Hart, then the General as he backed toward the door.

"We'll be ready to launch soon, I assure you," he said, though his tone revealed anything but assurance.

Hart waited till the door closed behind Losano. "He was working with Sonny you know."

The General leaned forward. "How did you come up with that?" Hart noticed Frank didn't respond, just waited for me to continue.

"The South Koreans were given the contract to manufacture the consumer hardware, right?"

Frank nodded.

"And Sonny came on their shirt tails as the manufacturer's representative." He nodded again. "But a lot of South Korean manufacturers have plants in North Korea; a somewhat closely held secret anomaly, but true none the less. Samsung, Hyundai, Kia and Singun all have large North Korean factories. Messy politically, but cheaper labour, and the North gets their much-needed financial cut."

"Which is how Sonny was able to cross the DMZ so easily," General Wade said, his anger dissipating as he began to work things out in his head.

"And meet with anyone he wanted to," Frank added. "Best we could figure, he's been involved in several recent internet hacks."

"Like the one on Sony? And the Stuxnet thing?" General Wade asked.

Hart had no idea what a Stuxnet was but he was beginning to realize who those Korean kids were and why the General had hidden them somewhere underground.

"We suspected North Korea all along for much of the cyber attacks of late," Frank said. "Their Bureau 121 was credited with the Sony hack and others that haven't been made public."

"And we now think Sonny ran the team," the General added. "The team which consisted of some of the kids over at MI now."

Hart mulled that over. Made sense. Sonny was a smart guy and had always been interested in the internet back when they were younger. "And he's not saying anything?" Hart asked.

"We don't really need him to tell us about this," Frank said. "The Oswego operation is being dismantled and Losano has been Castillo's partner from the beginning, so he's the best one to finish it for us. We're pretty confident that whatever Sonny had planned wasn't going to affect the completion of BPL. In fact, he probably needed it to work in order for him to complete his task, whatever that was."

"We'll find that out eventually," the General stated. "For now, troop movements in the DPRK have subsided and things are back to normal at the DMZ. If Sonny's task had anything to do with that, it seems to have failed. Yesterday, several North Korean

Generals were arrested and we're not sure why or what's going to happen to them. The Supreme Leader likes to cull the ranks from time to time; his way of ensuring total loyalty."

"Hmmm," Frank said, clearly uninterested. "Whatever Sonny's mission was, he'll tell us sooner or later; He's not going anywhere for a while."

Frank was more concerned about BPL and its completion. Obviously counter-espionage was Wade's domain on this one, even though as Deputy Director of the CIA, Frank should have been more interested. Poor Sonny. Frank saw BPL as his ticket past the Director's chair and on to something even bigger.

"So what now?" Hart asked.

"Losano thinks he can finish the program," Frank said. "And the family business is paying for the privilege, so we'll give him the time. Meanwhile, he General will be working on Sonny to see what he can tell us. What I need you to do is help me find Ms. Castillo."

Hart stared at him. "You control one of the biggest intelligence outfits in the world Frank, what do you think I can do that you can't?"

"You knew her... know her," Frank said. "You must have some idea of where she would go."

"If it was me, I'd be heading for a beach in Sint Maarten by now, but that's likely too obvious," Hart said. "Assuming I'm willing to keep working at this Frank, what happens to her when she's found? She won't work with Losano. He tried to kill her."

Frank stared at Hart, his eyes boring into his. It was a trait he thought worked ever since he lectured Hart about leaving his sister. He thought it intimidated him. What it actually did was motivate Hart to get away from him as quickly as possible.

"She will help Losano finish BPL so that it works, even if I have to keep them in separate labs. The President has been assured he will have his fail-safe mechanism for national security situations."

"Then what?"

He kept staring, the rest of his facial muscles unwavering. "Then she can go to Sint Maarten for all I care. And hopefully she'll take her buddy with her. He's starting to drive me nuts!"

Hart gave him a thin smile. Neither Lena or Jay would be leaving the Washington area anytime soon. Not as long as they possessed the ability to create a working BPL program. They would be the target of every intelligence network in the world.

"Frank, I keep telling you I don't work for the CIA anymore, remember?"

Frank stood up and stepped to the window, one hand pulling at his chin as he stared out the window. "I hear you have a new landlord Hart."

Hart cocked his head. Where was this going?

"Apparently they feel the restaurant is not paying the going rate for a downtown Baltimore space of, what, twenty-five hundred square feet?"

Hart watched the edge of Frank's mouth curled up in a smirk.

"Weren't you telling me last month, that if it wasn't for my, ah… our benevolence here at the Company, what with all our press conferences, lunches, and staff meetings… you might have trouble making ends meet."

Hart shook his head. He may be his brother-in-law, but since that relationship had been more or less nullified due to his divorce, Frank's influence over Hart had been equally nullified. Hart had never worked for Frank, even when he had been an employee at the Farm. Frank had been one of Hart's students; a very adept one, but despite his rising star status, he still had to deal with Hart at his level when they were on the mats.

Now that Hart no longer taught there, Frank had gotten used to treating him like the failed brother-in-law he saw in his mind, as opposed to his combat skills instructor he once had tremendous respect for.

Hart had no delusions as to who his new landlord was. The CIA would never allow the building that housed the restaurant to fall into anyone else's hands since they--Frank--had invested so much money into the security and surveillance system. Being the landlord didn't really change much, except that now Frank thought he had a way to manipulate Hart again.

"Okay Frank," Hart said. "So if I don't play ball, you're going to make it difficult to pursue my dream in peace. Is that it?"

General Wade was watching them both. His hands were loosely clasped in his lap, one leg propped over the other. His suit was neatly pressed, his collar starched stiff. It looked like the same outfit he'd been wearing the night before. *Did the guy have duplicates, complete with all the badges and pins?*

"I just need you to find her Hart," Frank said, interrupting Hart's meanderings. "Nothing will change in your life if you just help me out here."

They stared at each other for what seemed like several minutes but was probably only a few seconds. For now, Hart realized he had little choice.

"I can't guarantee I'll find her Frank," he said. "I've only known her a couple of months. There is a lot to that girl that neither of us knows about or gives her credit for."

Frank smiled. General Wade shook his head and grinned.

"I know you'll do your best Hart," Frank said. "I'll see you next Sunday night."

Hart raised an eyebrow.

"Cynthia invited Catherine and I for dinner at the *Hart*." Frank said. "I hope it's not too uncomfortable for you, being it's a couples' thing and all." He sat back at his desk and shuffled papers, not looking at me. "Hey, maybe you should bring a date too. I know, why don't you bring Lena Lopez Castillo?"

Their eyes met. Hart shook his head and rolled his eyes.

Twenty minutes later Hart was talking into his phone's Google® voice app while he steered the Company car Frank had loaned him toward Ronald Reagan International. Peter White's melodic guitar slowly faded as the Bluetooth kicked in and the stereo dialed the number and Al's gruff voice answered.

"Good morning! The Artichoke Hart."

"Al, can you do without me for a couple of more days?" Hart asked. He heard what must have been Al lowering the phone. His voice bellowed over the noise of pots and utensils.

"I didn't notice you'd gone," Al said, a smirk evident in his tone.

"By the way, apparently we have a new landlord, so I need you to put together a list of things we need fixing around the place, okay?"

"Really? What makes you think this guy's gonna be better than the last low-life slumlord?" Al chided.

Hart grinned. "You can tell him what you think of low life slumlords next Sunday when he comes for dinner."

Al was silent for a moment.

"Shit! You're kidding me. Really?"

"Oh yeah," Hart said.

"Maybe we should move," Al suggested.

Hart laughed. "Frank is trying to get a leash on me for some reason and I think having a way to manipulate how tight he pulls might be an advantage."

"Too complicated for me buddy. Stay safe. See you later."

Hart hung up and Peter White's guitar filled the car again. He looked at his watch. He was pretty sure there were flights to Toronto daily from Washington. If not he'd drive up to Boston where he knew Logan to be a layover point for many Canadian flights heading up and down the coast. He would have to lose Frank's tail somewhere along the line, Wade's too most likely, but he'd listened to enough field agent conversations in the past to have picked up a few tricks in that regard.

Chapter Ninety

The drive from Pearson International in northwest Toronto to Brantford, Ontario took about ninety minutes. Highway 401 was the most travelled highway in Canada, stretching the length of Southern Ontario and loosely following the shoreline of the province's namesake lake. Across the top of Toronto by the airport, it was a sixteen lane mega-highway. Hart had heard that it was even more congested than the Pacific Highway in Los Angeles but he'd discounted the theory until now. Hundreds of cars negotiated the multiple lanes leading west from the City core to several suburban bedroom communities that made up the Greater Toronto Area. And it wasn't even rush hour.

As he headed west in his compact Kia rental, he had to manipulate the numerous mergers and exit ramps to ensure he remained on the main thoroughfare. He'd lost three tails back at Reagan, having bought a ticket to Paris, passing though security and then leaving out an employee entrance. A few hours later, he had boarded an Air Canada flight in Boston, confident the French authorities would be hearing an earful from Frank shortly.

Brantford lay just outside what was considered the group of bedroom communities that made up the GTA, but that was quickly changing. All this Hart had learned from the *In Flight* magazine that had been the only available reading material on the short flight from Boston to Toronto. And much like Los Angeles and New York, the so-called bedroom communities that surrounded Toronto were sizeable cities themselves. The one he'd just passed through, Mississauga, was named after a local native

Indian tribe, and was the fourth largest city in the country. Impressive until you realized that the entire population of Canada had the same population as the state of New York.

Surprisingly, the scenery was not as spacious and untouched as he had anticipated. According to that same article, Southern Ontario housed the majority of Canadian corporate head offices and a hefty twenty percent of the national population. Every square inch along the GTA to Niagara Falls corridor was utilized for residential or commercial enterprise. He'd seen more greenery on Interstate 91 in upstate New York than he had here.

As he traversed the complicated transition from the 401 to the 403, he began to see kilometre postings for the City of Hamilton. Brantford, he knew, was just beyond. After he followed the highway around the end of Lake Ontario and up onto the escarpment, he saw signs for Brantford. Both sides of the highway were farmland dotted with the occasional burst of identical suburban developments.

It had been the first place he'd thought of actually. As soon as he'd left Frank's office at Langley, he instinctively knew where he'd find Lena Lopez Castillo. Right about now he hoped his instincts weren't deceiving him. As interesting as the Canadian landscape was, this would be a complete waste of time and money if he'd guessed wrong.

Thirty minutes later, as he turned his rental car into the laneway of the farmhouse he'd left a couple of days ago, he knew he hadn't been wrong. The house was lit up on the first level and as he drew up to the gravel-covered front entranceway, he glimpsed the back of a green Jeep Cherokee in the shadows of the huge barn doorway behind the century home.

By the time he had parked and crawled out of the tiny vehicle, the front door of the house was wide open and the sounds of Adam Levine's high-pitched energetic voice wafted outward. Lena stood in the doorway, hands on hips, her head cocked to one side, a smile adorning her olive-coloured face.

"I do hope you came alone Arthur," she said, stepping out and giving him a very tight hug.

"I thought I might find you here," he said, pulling himself out of her embrace and pushing her gently inside. "It won't take long for the others to guess at it too, you know."

"So you haven't told anyone?" she asked, leading him into the living room where he had previously sat tied up in one of the dining room chairs. The equipment was still strewn all across the table but there seemed to be a lot more paper everywhere. As he ventured closer, he could make out scribbles of formulas and hastily-written notes on various sheets of yellow newsprint. A blank pad of the same paper was lying in front of the large monitor. It looked like Lena had been making notes, ripping off sheets from the pad and just throwing them out onto the table top, letting them land wherever they may.

Hart looked at her. Gone was the trembling, insecure girl he had last seen before JP had whisked here downstairs. Now he saw a very confident, bright-smiled woman who appeared very self-assured.

"You've figured it out haven't you?" he said, more a statement than a question.

She lowered her head slightly and fidgeted with her fingernails. But her gaze never left his. "I noticed it while we were here with Sonny Kim," she said, pointing at the table. "And he inadvertently helped me figure the rest out."

Hart wasn't sure if she meant the hardware or the unorganized papers.

She slumped down in a chair and motioned for him to sit in another one nearby.

"The previous owner of the farm--Michael Powless--stumbled across a way to get data to jump from one grid to another without the information frying," she said. "It was part of his work for Blackberry in the 1980s when they were building their exclusive network. But the company eventually killed anything relating to a power line service, putting all their eggs into the internet server network. At the time it was the right thing to do."

Hart just nodded and didn't let on that he had been informed of Powless' history. Lena continued.

"Email was the big thing at the time and having a secure network was vital to RIM being the leader in the field. Microsoft, IBM, Nokia, and Motorola were all developing similar platforms but Blackberry's mandate was to be totally secure to satisfy their clients, the biggest one being the US government."

"But he kept working on it after RIM killed the project?" Hart asked.

"Not really. Powless was trying to convince RIM that BPL would eventually provide the company with a secondary marketplace, a cheaper alternative to cable and phone line service. They could develop another phone model, one that hooked into a power line network and would be inexpensive for the average consumer."

"But they didn't buy into it?"

"They might have," she said. "But at the time, the hint of wireless technology was in the air and the company chose to focus their growth efforts there."

"But he kept trying?"

"He probably would have," she said, staring at me, her eyes boring into mine. "But he was killed that same year in a car accident. So, the company moved on and all this--"she swept the room with her arms--"was left untouched because Powless had no family, no will, and he left no instructions for anyone to continue his work."

Hart looked around, recalling that General Wade had told him about Powless' death and the mystery surrounding it.

"So what *did* you find Lena?" Hart asked.

A grin emerged, stretching from one side of her face to the other. She turned to the computer and began tapping on the keyboard. "Watch this!" she said.

To Hart it looked like she was writing a simple email, which in fact, she was. But when she turned to him, the grin still taking over her entire face, and elaborately hung her index finger over the enter button, Hart knew something more was going on.

"Hold on," she said and made a grandiose gesture of pressing her finger onto the enter button.

Hart leaned in and watched the screen, looking for... well, he didn't really know. After a few seconds, Lena squealed and leaned back, clapping her hands once, the echo of which sounded very loud in the small room.

"I give up," Hart said. "What happened?"

"I just sent an email to a friend in California," she said. "And he just opened it and--" she leaned forward looking at the screen. "And he's writing back as we speak." She looked at Hart, her eyes sparkling. "Turn off your data and check your email Arthur," she said, folding her hands in front of her chest, her mischievous grin infectious enough that Hart had to smile too.

He pulled out his cell phone went to Settings and turned off his data feed. The phone would now only use wireless if available. He pressed his email button. The roaming signal immediately popped up telling him there was no internet service in the area close enough for his phone to pick up. A message told him that to access his email he would have to revert to data service with a local provider. Hart looked up at Lena.

"I just sent that email across the power lines and it crossed from the Eastern NPCC Grid through the Midwest MRO and into the Western Interconnection of WECC. And it made it to Los Angeles in seconds without getting fried along the way. The combination of ArmourNet and Powless' transfer code ensured the message got through without interference." She jumped up and did a twist, then grabbed his hands and pulled him up for a quick hug. "And all through the power lines. I've been sending messages for the past three hours. It works almost every time!"

"So Powless had it figured out forty years ago?" Hart asked.

She frowned. "No, just the part I couldn't figure out. Powless was able to get messages from grid to grid with his code but his messages never got far because they fried after a few minutes of transmission. Even now, I lose the odd message but I don't know why. It seems to just disintegrate somewhere along the line. If he'd had my ArmourNet, I think he would have figured it all out and the result would have revolutionized internet service, far surpassing speeds and quality of phone line service and availability of cable at the time."

"So how did Sonny help you figure out what Powless couldn't?" Hart asked.

Lena motioned him over to another side table where a laptop was sitting open and running, white HTML code on a black background emblazoned on the screen.

"Sonny dropped this when you two were fighting," she said, pointing at a red USB stick protruding from the laptop's edge. "He'd already loaded it onto this computer. It's the exact opposite of Powless' code."

"I don't understand," Hart said.

She motioned for him pull up a kitchen chair and sit beside her in front of the laptop. "Sonny—or more likely the Korean kids in my lab who I think worked for him before—had developed coding that would burn every device connected to the BPL service, literally frying the electronics in any computer, server…any end user device running on the system. But he needed ArmourNet to safely deliver it to every device in the country connected to any electrical outlet once I had the service running."

"Okay, you've lost me," Hart said. "What would that do?"

"His code would travel safely to every corner of the country, cross from grid to grid, protected by ArmourNet. But once opened—like a virus—it would result in a kind of national power surge, and would fry the electronic components in whatever hardware was being used."

"So every computer connected to an electric outlet would burn up internally?" Hart said, his eyes wide. He leaned forward, grabbing Lena's hands. "And that would include all the government's defence computers, networked military communications systems… everything?"

"It would be a complete blackout," she said. "Every device connected to the network would simply stop working. Lights would go out in all major cities. Elevators would stop running, online banking would shutdown, even trains would stop. Pretty much anything computer related would just cease to function… instantly."

"Including military defence systems?"

"Of course," she said. "And I think that was his plan. With the US in a virtual national blackout, no one would see an enemy coming. We wouldn't see missiles, planes, even ships. The country would have been completely blind." She stood up abruptly and thrust her hands to her hips. "Just because he would have access to every device attached to the power grid; anything that was electronic."

Hart stared at her for a few moments. The implications were staggering. Could that really have been Sonny's plan? Hart didn't think he'd ever know. Nor would Frank, General Wade, or anyone else fully understand the potential disaster they had just thwarted. He remained in stunned silence for a minute or so, then shook his head, bringing himself back into the present.

"But how did that help you figure out how to make it work?" he asked.

She smiled and sat back down, here hands firmly on her thighs. "I simply reverse engineered Sonny's code. He needed ArmourNet to get his frying code to the end user unit. So, I wrote additional code that would prevent ArmourNet from releasing any self-destruct coding. Inadvertently that code also eliminated interference during the regenerator stage. That's what I could never completely guarantee; that data would pass through a regenerator without losing its speed, as well as leaking out into the atmosphere."

"Which is what caused interference in airline communications and ham radio operators, right?"

She nodded. "All this time, I'd been trying to figure out how to stop that from happening, but Sonny had figured out how to send code throughout the network without worrying about that: it didn't matter to him; he was trying to fry all the devices connected anyway. He didn't care if it leaked. So all I had to do was make sure my code stopped the leakage, and the interference and regenerator problem was solved."

Hart thought about that for a moment and eventually realized it was all over his head. "So now what?" he asked, watching her carefully. She must have caught something in his eyes because her excitement ramped down slightly and she slumped back in her chair.

"So now I perfect it," she said. "But not with those people."

He didn't have to ask who she was referring to.

"Jay Losano thinks he can come up with the solution without you," Hart said.

Lena's expression darkened, then after a moment, regained a calm demeanor. "Jay made a grave mistake. His partnership with the Koreans was wrong, and they made him do things I don't think he would have done without enormous pressure." She looked down at the tiny hole in her arm where Losano had injected her with the poison. She shivered but quickly regained her composure. She was in a state of euphoria and even Losano's traitorous actions wouldn't deter her excitement. "I guess I'll never know."

She stared out over the table and all the papers strewn everywhere. "But he will never come up with this." She pointed at the monitor, the mouse blinking incessantly, awaiting its next command. "I'm not sure I would have either. It's so, ah... primitive, that I would never have thought it would work." She smiled again. But it does... most of the time."

She suddenly stood again and grabbed both Hart's arms, pulling him close, her eyes darkening as she spoke. "You're not going to tell them where I am, are you?"

Hart stared into those beautiful, young, intelligent eyes and nodded his head. "I will have to, eventually."

She blinked but continued to stare into his eyes. Then after a moment, she nodded slowly. "I have a sponsor who will let me continue perfecting it," she said calmly. "And when it's ready for the marketplace, they have the ability to make it happen fast and hard. It will go international immediately."

"But you won't be here, right?" Hart asked.

She smiled coyly. "I have been given an entire warehouse, complete with equipment, a skeleton staff, and an unlimited budget. It's not here, but it's not in the US either."

She leaned in and gave Hart yet another hug, holding on for longer than was likely appropriate, but he didn't push her away.

This young entrepreneur was going to shake up the world someday and Hart was happy to know her.

"Frank won't stop looking you know," he said. "I can give you a week, max. After that, I have to tell him or he'll waterboard me."

She nodded demurely. "I understand. He is your boss, you have responsibilities to him, and the government."

"Actually, he's only my ex-brother-in-law, and I have no responsibilities to him at all," Hart said smiling. "My intent is to steer them the wrong way."

She laughed, a hearty, releasing laugh that was contagious. "I could fall in love with you Mr. Arthur Artichoke Hart," she blurted, jumping up and down like a schoolgirl.

"Yeah, well, we've already talked about that," Hart said.

Robert J. Morrow

Chapter Ninety-One

"To happy endings... and new beginnings!"

Frank lifted his glass of wine upward and those gathered around the table joined the toast. Even Hart's kids pushed their glasses up high, the grape juice sloshing around their wine glasses with abandon. Hart reached over to steady Lucy's arm as she swished her glass a little too enthusiastically.

The family was all there: Frank and his new, very young girlfriend Madelaine; both Hart's kids Lucy and Jamie; and Cynthia, beaming proudly at her brother while she reached out for the hand of... yep, Richard Hattis, standing beside her.

The happy ending referred to Frank's satisfaction that Hart had found where Lena Castillo had gone, albeit too late. But the analysts were there, under the gracious supervision of the RCMP, sifting through copious notes and scouring through ancient hard drives. Frank was convinced they'd find something that Jay Losano would find useful enough to complete the BPL project. He would then be allowed to approach the President with his idea of forming a new agency within Homeland to develop, maintain, and monitor the integration of a new, much more affordable national internet service, licensed to industry as an inexpensive alternative product that would be supplemented by various government-controlled power conglomerates. Frank's head was in the stars. Which meant Lena was safe on the ground for now.

"And I have an announcement to make," Frank continued, his glass still raised. Hart had already dropped his, so Hart raised it once again, turning to see Al do the same. Their eyes met and they both smiled at their equally knowing looks. When Frank made grandiose announcements, someone's life usually changed considerably.

"As patriarch of the family--" he nodded to Lucy, Jamie, Hart, and finally Cynthia--"it is my privilege to announce the engagement of my sister Cynthia to our good friend and colleague, Mr. Richard Hattis."

The edges of Al's mouth sagged at Hart's expression but they both quickly recovered before the kids caught it. Hart took a quick gulp of wine and gently placed the glass on the table as he pushed his chair back and stood up. Everyone was suddenly quiet as Hart stepped away from the table. He could feel Al's stare piercing his back and he watched as Frank's eyes narrowed.

Hart walked behind Frank, around to the other side of the table and took Cynthia in a loose embrace. "Congratulations Babe, you finally have someone else to appreciate your commonplace cooking."

Cynthia's face reddened and she haltingly hugged his waist, then pulled back quickly and pointed her finger at him. "I was cooking..."

"Long before it became your life's passion!" both Lucy and Jamie chimed in. Cynthia's face reddened even more. Hart gently pushed her aside and extended his hand to Hattis.

"You did good up there Hattis," he said. Hart hated to admit it but he really had been impressed. It was the closest he was going to come to a *welcome to the family* speech and they both knew it, so Hattis just took Hart's hand, smiled hesitantly and nodded his head.

By then, Lucy had run around the table and was pulling on Hattis' pant leg. He turned to look down at her, then back up at her father. He was gracious enough to not pick her up as she clearly wanted but just patted her head and pushed her toward Hart. And as most normal eight-year-olds would in such a situation, she simply transferred her innocent affection to her Daddy and Hart picked her up and held her close to his chest.

Everyone got up at that point and Al walked over with a tray of shot glasses filled with some neon coloured liquid. "To family!" he said, and set the tray down in the centre of the table. He gave Hart a quick warning glance and stepped back.

That was all the que Frank needed. He quickly handed out the glasses which effectively made everyone stand still and await a second toast.

"The future holds nothing but promise," he said. "For all of us!"

Once again glasses were raised and sips were taken. Al had given the kids what looked like Jell-O® shooters and Hart grinned. Al was all about the details.

He put Lucy down and walked over to Al who had quickly downed his shot and was ready to gather up the empties.

"Never a dull moment in this family," Al said.

Hart nodded. Jamie came over then and stood between them. Lucy had followed too and stood on the other side of Al.

"Is JP your girlfriend now Daddy?" Lucy asked.

Hart smiled. "Still just friends sweetheart. Not everyone needs to get married to be happy you know." Al nudged him hard in the kidney. Hart winced and curled the corner of his mouth. Thankfully, Lucy was satisfied with the answer and wandered off to her mother's side.

"He's doesn't know anything about fighting Dad."

Hart turned to his son, so young and innocent, so on the edge of manhood. "How so?" he asked.

"He has no idea what a flying spin hook kick is!" Jamie said. "And he suggested I take up boxing with him in September. Do I have to?"

Hart grinned at Al who crossed his arms and gave him a stern look. Hart thought about his answer carefully. "I think it might be good for you to get to know him a little better son. He can't be all bad; after all, he's marrying your Mom."

Jamie looked up at me. "But boxing Dad!"

"Okay, okay, let's see if I can talk your Mom into letting you train here once or twice a week. What do you think?" he said. Jamie's eyes lit up and he high-fived his Dad. "He can help you with math though, right?" Hart added, knowing full well he would never breach that or any other child-related subject with his ex-wife's new husband. Boundaries would have to be set. As much as he begrudgingly recognized Hattis' skills as a lead agent, that didn't mean he wanted him to take his place as lead Daddy. He had to admit though that he felt a little relief that he wouldn't be on tap for all those mundane Daddy duties, like swimming meets, ballet classes, etc.; he had his own official relief Daddy on board now.

"My ex used to tell me that the best thing she liked about divorce was that she had a built-in babysitter whenever she wanted to go away for the weekend," Al said.

"I am not about to become a weekend Daddy."

Al shook his head. "You idiot. I was talking about you, not him."

Hart turned to see Cynthia give Hattis an affectionate peck on the cheek. He grinned.

A few minutes later Hart found himself in the kitchen, putting together his Carciofini dish; a delicate Italian appetizer made with butterflied, lightly fried artichoke hearts together with a chili and aioli dipping sauce. Despite the family celebration, it was still Monday and Hart's turn to cook for the staff. Tonight, the family would be joining in. Frank had asked Al to show Hattis the security room downstairs and Hart had reluctantly relented. Cynthia and the kids were talking about upcoming birthday parties, so Hart wasn't surprised to hear Frank's voice as he pushed through the swinging kitchen doors.

"I was going to tell you earlier but Cynthia said it would be better to do it in a public setting," he said.

Hart didn't look up but nodded. She was right but he was still an idiot to listen to everything his sister said, especially when it involved his feelings.

"How's Losano doing?" he asked, partially to change the subject from family affairs, and partially out of curiosity. It had been a month since he'd left Lena in Brantford and three weeks since he'd told Frank that she had been there, thus giving her a chance to disappear completely.

"He's confident," Frank said nonchalantly. "But he's an idiot. He'll never complete it. He just doesn't have the know-how."

Hart stopped what he was doing and turned to look at him. "But you still have him on the project?"

Frank grinned. "Of course. We're raking in thousands in fees from the mob on the premise that he'll eventually solve the puzzle. I'm siphoning the money to more, umm… pressing problems at the moment so the relationship is a win/win for now."

It was Hart's turn to grin.

"What about Sonny Kim?"

Frank pulled up a stool and sat next to the counter as Hart continued chopping vegetables.

"He might not make it," Frank said. "His tumour is expanding and his pain is excruciating. We only give him painkillers when he tells us something."

After a few seconds of silence, Hart turned and cocked his head at Frank.

"The Koreans had a bold plan that saw them not only uniting their country but simultaneously attacking and conquering America."

Hart raised his eyebrows. Frank had figured it out.

"Incredible as it sounds, Wade confirms that troop movements near the Chinese border were amassing and the entire North Korean air force was fueled and poised to take off for parts unknown."

"The US." Hart stated.

"It seems that once Sonny had access to ArmourNet, he was going to send a destruct signal into the grids. Any house, building, military facility, etc., that had electrical power entering the premises would have been instantly taken offline; burned for lack of a better word."

Hart's raised an eyebrow but said nothing.

"By the time we could have power restored, the Korean Air Force would have crossed the Pacific and landed, en mass, all along the western coast, completely undetected. Another three hours and they would have made the east coast. You know they have the third largest army in the world? Not the most advanced, just the largest. They could have put hundreds of thousands of troops on American soil within hours of Sonny pulling the switch. And we wouldn't even know they had landed."

Hart stopped chopping and pulled up his own stool. "Whoa," he muttered slowly.

Frank nodded. They were silent again for a few seconds, Hart recalling a movie he'd seen called *Red Dawn* that had depicted a surprisingly similar scenario. He'd been thinking about it ever since leaving Canada. After a while, he looked up at Frank again. "And Lena Castillo?"

Frank stared back, a knowing glint in his eyes. "I got a call from Larry Whitman the other day," he said.

Hart shrugged. He had no idea who that was.

"He's one of Jeff Bozo's executive lackeys," Frank continued. "Seems Amazon has a BPL prototype nearing launch and they want a meeting with the President to discuss a joint administration/industry rollout as part of his upcoming election platform."

"Wow, that's coincidental," Hart said.

"Isn't it," Frank agreed, his eyes narrowing. "Seems all they want in exchange for giving government essentially full control of the thing is a contract to use their server farm, which by the way, is the biggest in the world at the moment."

Hart was aware that Amazon's servers were used by almost everyone needing a place to hide their cyber clouds.

And he finally knew where Lena had gone.

"The President has asked you to form a committee to do the meet and greet?" Hart said.

Frank said nothing but continued to stare. Despite an atmosphere of familiarity and comfort surrounding us, his eyes had grown cold, almost lifeless.

"I will be meeting with the Amazon technical team next week," he said, his voice low, almost menacing. "And I'm not going to be surprised, am I?"

Hart looked at him, trying to keep his expression empty, knowing his eyes gave away his secrets.

"I didn't know where she had gone Frank," he finally said. "And I didn't want to know. Lena was a very smart young lady and it seemed she was always one step ahead of us." In the dark recesses of his mind, he also knew that Lena Lopez-Castillo-- despite her altruistic intentions--also had the ability to shut the country completely down with one alteration to a piece of written computer code, should she ever choose to do so.

Frank stared at him with those eyes Hart sometimes found discomforting. He was a powerful guy after all. "She didn't keep any secrets from us Frank," Hart implored. "She really was struggling at the end, in Oswego."

"If Larry Whitman's inferences are even half true, I don't think she's struggling anymore," Frank said.

"I'm sorry Frank."

He glared at Hart, then suddenly, his eyes filled with color again and he placed his hand on Hart's shoulder.

"I get the same result in the end Hart," he said, tapping his shoulder twice. "But I've gained a new and unending source of funding from the Mob, so everyone's come out of the ordeal better than they went in. Even JP's new assignment is an improvement."

Hart cocked his head. He'd been wondering about what would happen to her.

"She probably won't tell you--" he frowned suddenly. "Actually, she can't tell you, but I'm sending her on a Mediterranean Cruise with the Ambassador to France. He's made a stand against a right-wing militant group that's growing in his country and there are concerns of assassination attempts."

"I gather he's single," Hart said.

Frank smiled. "And coincidentally, he just adores strong-willed American women. Says the French are too submissive."

Hart sighed. Hopefully JP saw it as more than another glorified whoring assignment. At least she'd get a tan.

"And what about me Frank" Hart asked. "What do I get out of all this?"

Frank pursed his lips and spun slowly, taking in the kitchen. The prep surfaces and stainless steel shelves were gleaming. It was Sunday and Al had just cleaned the place.

"Your new landlord would like you to take a leave of absence," he said, turning back to Hart. "They feel Al and the staff are more than capable of running things --especially since the lease payments have been made for the next twelve months. You won't have to worry about bills, at least for a while."

"And what do I have to do for the landlord in exchange for his amazing benevolence?" Hart asked, more curious than surprised.

"Well, after your encounter with Sonny Kim up in Canada, the landlord feels it's time you went back to training the troops again," he said.

"The landlord seems to have a lot of say in what happens around here," Hart said.

Frank dropped his head slightly and sighed. "You said you were bored Hart, and you needed funding to keep the restaurant running," He shifted his gaze and looked around the sparkling kitchen. "The landlord... I...am willing to help you in both regards, but I need you to do this for me. No one else can match your unique skill set and I think it will be of great value to the field agents currently in training. North Korea is going to be a place of interest for the US in the near future and I want them well-prepared for the type of, ah... underground resistance they may encounter. You are ideally suited to help with that situation."

Hart pondered about that for a minute or so. It was obvious now why Frank had readily agreed to building a dojang in the basement along with his secret recording studio. He'd probably planned this outcome all along. Hart tightened his fist and lightly banged the tabletop. He winced as his broken finger, now in a small cast, reminded him it hadn't fully healed yet.

What Frank had said was true though, on all counts. Hart hated to admit that he was, indeed, interested. Not because he thought he had something better to offer the trainees but because Frank was right, he had been bored. Oswego and Canada had been exciting. So a few weeks sinking himself into a solid training regimen just might be what the doctor ordered. Of course, free rent for a year was additional motivating incentive. Al would be very relieved. It was the least Hart could do for everyone, right?

"I want weekends off Frank," Hart said, grinning. He knew he needed to spend more time with his children, especially with Hattis lurking around the hearthstone.

"Of course. That's when we take the kids camping."

Hart groaned. Frank smiled, turned and headed toward the swinging doors.

"Oh, and Hart," he said turning back to look at him. "Please stop calling my sister *babe*. She really doesn't like it, you know."

Hart smiled, the grin extending from ear-to-ear. The new landlord didn't get to set *all* the rules.

The End

Key West Conched, second in the *Tales of the Artichoke Hart* series, is coming soon. To pre-order your FREE copy, please go to *robertjmorrow.com/next*

Find Artichoke Hart recipes at *robertjmorrow.com/recipes*

Notes of interest...

On July 6, 2012, President Barack Obama did sign an executive order authorizing Homeland Security to take control of the country's wired and wireless communications in instances of emergency.

Broadband over Power Lines (BPL) technology was developed in 1928 by AT&T but it's weaknesses, including power loss over distance, cost of equipment, and radio interference, ensured it was never fully accepted. In 2008, IBM and IBEC signed a $9.6 million contract to develop a BPL network throughout the eastern US after IBEC had successfully developed a working network in some southern states. However, in 2011, tornadoes in Alabama (not ice storms in New York) destroyed the BPL infrastructure and IBEC went bankrupt as a result.

Bureau 121, also known as the *DarkSeoul Gang*, is staffed by some of North Korea's most talented young computer experts and is run by the Korean military. In December 2014, they were blamed for the hack on Sony Pictures which led to the cancellation of the movie, *The Interview*. North Korea rejected the accusation.

The *King of Korea* is an architect living in California, though that is a title given him by the media. He was born in America but is reputed to be a descendent of the Chosun Dynasty, the last Korean monarchy prior to Japanese occupation in 1910. Although neither government officially recognize his status, he regularly travels to Korea acting as a figurehead during national holiday events. Should Korea ever unify, he would be the logical choice for interim leader, accepted by both sides, until an official election could be held.

A note from the author...

As an author who has chosen self-publishing as the best way to reach a broad market, on a continuous basis, it is imperative that I convince readers to take a few moments to write a review... or at the very least, rank this read from one to five.

Although this is not mandatory in order to enjoy reading books by myself or any other author, I can assure you that without your input, we authors sit in the dark, day after day, wondering if what we are creating actually has any merit.

Your few moments of gracious participation justifies months— even years—of pouring our souls into words.
We only need a few from you to make it all worth while.

If you are so inclined, please go to amazon and look up the title, then leave a star ranking... and if you are particular moved, a short review. If you send me the link to your review, I will send you a copy of my bestselling **"Sold Strategies: The Cheapest, Safest and Smartest ways to Sell Your Home!"** FREE of charge (including shipping) in the format of your choice. I will also send you a FREE copy of the next Artichoke Hart book, *Parisian Bred*, upon publication.

I, and every other author, am forever grateful for your participation.

Thank you!

Robert J. Morrow
editor@robertjmorrow.com
January 2017

PS: I answer all my emails.

Robert J. Morrow *spent four decades in advertising, marketing, journalism, publishing, and real estate before becoming a full-time writer. His bestselling non-fiction books on real estate can be found at amazon.ca/com or robertjmorrow.com.*

New York Fried *is his debut fiction novel and first in the* <u>Tales of the Artichoke Hart</u> *series. He lives with his life partner, Susan, in Southern Ontario.*

Discover Artichoke Hart recipes at **robertjmorrow.com/recipes**

Made in the USA
Middletown, DE
17 March 2017